# The Black Mage *Apprentice*

Rachel E. Carter





Clean Reads
www.cleanreads.com

THE BLACK MAGE: APPRENTICE

ISBN 978-1-62135-461-1
Cover Art Designed by CORA DESIGNS

*To The Boy Who Never Reads,*

*Too bad you are marrying an author.*
*I am sorry for all the times I ignored you to write this book.*
*Thanks for putting a ring on it anyway.*

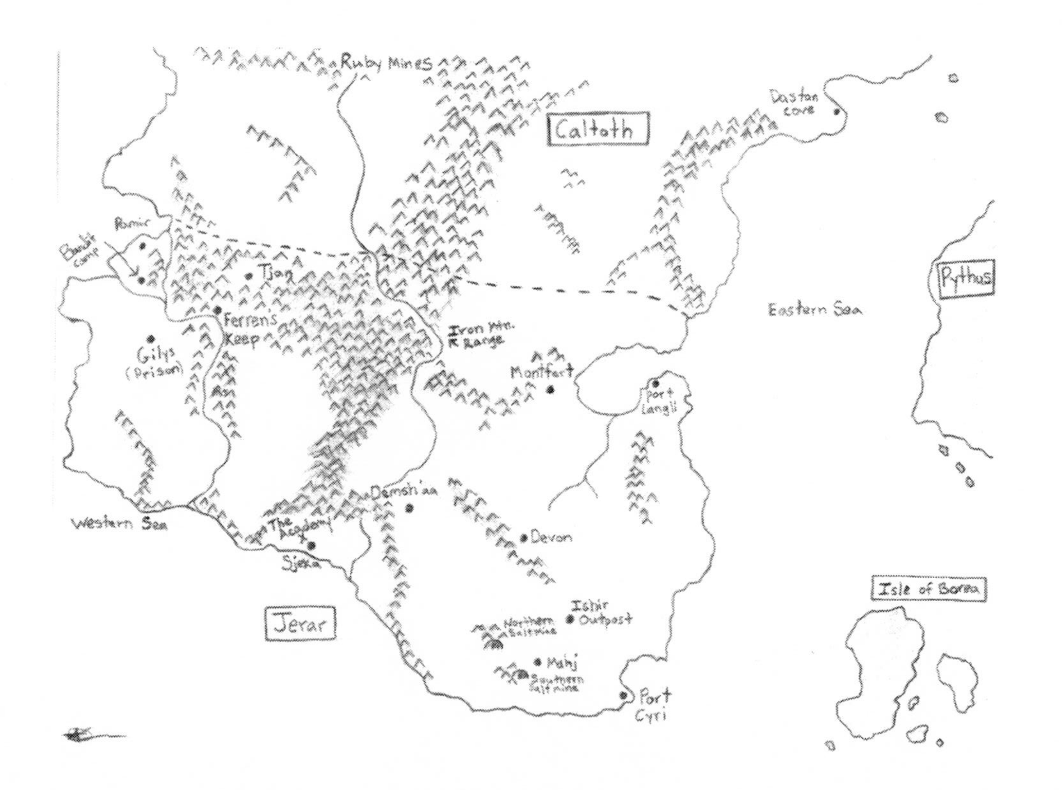
Ruby Mines
Caltoth
Dastan Cove
Pythus
Eastern Sea
Ramir
Bandit Camp
Tjaq
Ferren's Keep
Gilys (Prison)
Iron Mtn. Range
Montfort
Port Langli
Western Sea
The Academy
Sjeka
Demsh'aa
Devon
Jerar
Ishir Outpost
Northern Salt mine
Mahj
Southern Salt mine
Port Cyri
Isle of Borna

# Chapter One

I watched the two figures dance, twisting and turning as they exchanged matching blows in the stifling morning heat of desert sun. The sand shifted and clouded beneath their feet, small swells of dirt temporarily blinding my vision as the two continued to reposition their lightning-quick blows.

I studied their forms. Lissome, dangerous. I couldn't help but notice how the sweat glistened off their tanned skin, highlighting the contours of well-taut arms and shoulders. It was an observation I had partaken in many a time but had yet to grow tired of watching.

The two fighters continued their match. The taller of the two, a young man with sandy brown curls and laughing green eyes, seemed the most at ease with the procession. He countered his partner's rapid attacks with an almost lazy defense that spoke of a lifetime of training. The second young man was the opposite, trying to hide his building frustration in every blocked attempt. Garnet eyes flared underneath black bangs and my heart skipped a beat. The shorter of the two might have been less skilled in hand-to-hand combat, but it was he my gaze clung to just a second too long.

The bout carried on for several more minutes. I fanned myself with my hand, wishing desperately our faction had been assigned a cooler terrain to train in. The desert certainly hadn't been my expectation and I had not grown used to its sweltering heat. Many of the other apprentices seemed to share my opinion; there was not a full water skin to be found anywhere in our audience.

The tall boy caught the second off-guard with a swift, sweeping kick that sent his partner sprawling into the sand. The second didn't look too happy at his outcome, shooting the older boy a look of pure venom that would have sent most people to their knees. The tall boy just chuckled, offering the second his hand—which the second blatantly ignored—as the rest of the class clapped.

A man in stiff black robes stepped forward, frowning. "That will do, Ian." He turned to the young man on the ground and said in a much more friendly tone: "Darren, that was very good for a second-year, you have no reason to be disappointed."

The expression on Darren's face didn't change as he pulled himself up off the ground. His eyes stated very clearly he did not share Master Byron's opinion, and I had not the slightest doubt that the non-heir would be training in private for weeks to come as a result of today's practice. Though we couldn't be more different, it was amazing how similar the two of us were when it came to performance. The master had been praising him for weeks, but it was clear that until he was the best, Darren would not be satisfied.

"Ryiah. Lynn. You two are up."

Nerves tingling, I made my way to the front. A young woman with dark bangs and amber eyes gripped my elbow as I passed. "Good luck, Ry," Ella whispered.

Standing where the two boys had fought just moments before was a girl of Borean descent that I had sparred with many times before. Lynn gave me a reassuring smile. I tried to return the sentiment as I took my position across from my mentor. Palms sweating, I waited for the Master of Combat to announce the drill.

"And start."

Lynn was the first make a move, ducking into my circle with a low jab to the ribs. I held my guard and countered her strike with a low block of my own. She pulled back, long black ponytail flying, and I quickly placed a high kick, narrowly missing as she fell out of reach. My fingers itched to extend it with a casting and I quickly squelched the urge.

*No magic, Ryiah.*

Refocusing on the task at hand, I studied my opponent, seeking any shift in her stance that might foreshadow her next attack. Lynn's hazel eyes met mine, sparkling with a delicate innocence that matched her doll-like features. It was a lie. She might be petite but I had long ago learned the truth. The olive-skinned third-year was lethal in hand-to-hand combat and anything with a pole.

I exhaled slowly.

I had lost every single match to Lynn thus far, and while I could take some comfort in knowing she was a year ahead, I knew there were others who had already started to win some of their mentor duels. A snicker sounded in the audience, one that was reminiscent of wind chimes … sarcastic, cruel, *vexing* wind chimes. I didn't need to shift my focus to identify which second-year was behind the sound—Priscilla of Langli was impossible to miss.

Lynn gave the slightest alteration to her stance, weight shifting ever so lightly to her right heel. I jumped in with a hasty outer block while my right fist shot out at her abdomen. Lynn pulled back just in time, my hand barely grazing the thin material of her shirt.

Without hesitation I launched into a low, rounded kick and she parried it with an easy blow of her own. I fell back and instinctively angled my hips so that I was just out of reach, fists raised and ready to counter her next offense. When it did not come immediately I sprung forward, feigning a two-fisted punch while my real attack came in the form of a high kick aimed at her ribs.

My mentor was not fooled. She easily countered—stepping into the kick the second she saw my knee rise—and rammed my body with the full force of her weight. I stumbled. Lynn rushed forward kicking and punching seemingly at random. I struggled to block but I had been caught off-balance by the previous defense. A hard-packed fist collided with my stomach and another with my face.

Lynn sent a quick kick to my shin and I faltered, feeling the gravity shift from under my feet as I fell to the side. I did not have time to adjust my form before my right elbow slammed into hard-packed earth. Sand billowed up all around me as a sharp pop sounded and instantaneous pain flared up and down my arm.

I cried out as my magic's barrier broke. A swift casting came rushing from my hands before I could halt it, slamming into my opponent and sending her back-first into a nearby palm. Lynn hit the ground with a hard thud and the magic fell away, its damage done.

"Blast it, Ryiah!" Master Byron swore. His aristocratic face, normally so calm and collected, was beet red. Sweat glistened off his well-kept skin. "If you can't control your magic, you are never going to be allowed anywhere near a battlefield!"

I quickly scrambled to my feet, my face aflame. Lynn had already pulled herself up as well, and the expression in her eyes was one of pity. I thought it kind of her—I had to be the most frustrating second-year to mentor, yet she was always patient and understanding, even when my magic was knocking her into trees. Master Byron, on the other hand, was anything but.

"I'm sorry, sir, I didn't mean—"

"The Council made a mistake," the man huffed, ignoring my outburst. "You shouldn't be here. I don't know what the Black Mage was thinking, granting you an apprenticeship. You may have gotten away with that trickery in your trials but it will not fly here."

"Yes. Sir." The words were bitter on my tongue. My elbow was smarting terribly. Hot and cold pains were shooting up and down my right arm and I had less patience than usual for Master Byron's criticism. It wasn't as if I had intentionally cast. It had just happened. Other second-years lost control too—but in the two months since the apprenticeship had started the training master had taken to targeting me personally.

"What good is a girl in Combat if she is always embracing her gender's weak-minded ways? Learn to deal with your pain, Ryiah, or go back to a convent."

I opened my mouth to retort.

Ella's hand closed over my left wrist, an unspoken reminder. *Do not let him get to you.* I attempted to swallow my fury.

"Surely, Master Byron, you can't believe there is only one sex to feel pain," an amused voice spoke up. "I, myself, embrace such 'weak-minded ways' almost daily."

"Your sarcasm, Apprentice Ian, is not appreciated," the master said dryly. "I am simply making a point to Ryiah that she would be better suited elsewhere—"

"For accidentally using her magic? Sir, we have all done that—in my second year alone I—"

"Perhaps she is not the only one who should not be here," Master Byron snapped. Giving me a dismissive glance he added: "Ryiah, see to that arm—you will have to make up the rest of the exercise later."

All twenty apprentices stepped to the side to allow me to pass, although none of them met my eye as I did. I groaned inwardly. Most of them hated Master Byron as much as I did. The difference was they, unlike Ian and I, had learned to keep their tempers in check.

Holding my head high I began the short trek to the infirmary. At least there would be one bright spot to this day. Alex would be with the rest of the Restoration mages—which meant I would get to see him when I checked into their base.

I had barely seen my brother the past few weeks. Our factions had kept us busy training in opposite ends of Ishir Outpost. Any excuse to see him—even at the cost of a possibly broken arm—was preferable to the absence of my other half.

"Hey Ryiah, wait up!"

Spinning around I discovered Ian jogging to catch up with me. His hair was windblown and I couldn't help but notice how, even out of breath, the third-year was incredibly handsome. Not like the prince. But then again no one ever was.

Ian was just Ian. When the apprentices had arrived at the Academy to pick up their newest recruits, most of the older students had been wary of me. *I* was the sixteen-year-old girl who had destroyed the school's armory during the first-year trials. *I* was the sixth name to be called—an occurrence that was unusually rare in the Academy's habit of picking five students to apprentice per faction.

Ian hadn't cared. The moment the third-year had spotted me he had let out a loud whoop and set about to collecting his winnings from the rest of his friends. Apparently there had been a wager going for which of us first-years would make it; since I had been considered a long shot during the mid-winter duels Ian had been the only one to bet on me for an apprenticeship. I was surprised the boy had even remembered me from our short time during the solstice ball, but the self-proclaimed "underdog" had assured me he remembered "everyone that counted."

Since my apprenticeship started Ian had quickly become one of my closest friends, after Ella. The third-year's sarcasm matched my own, and he knew firsthand how horrible Byron could be. After all, until I arrived Ian had been the master's least favorite student.

"What are you doing?" I scolded my friend lightly. "You should be mentoring Darren."

Ian chuckled. "That self-important prodigy? He'll be fine without me..." He gave me a disarming smile. "You, my dear, are the one who needs help." He hooked my good arm with his own. "That prince has the training master worshipping the very ground he walks on. Darren could be *us* and Byron would still insist he was the next Black Mage."

"Byron's going to stick you with latrine duty," I warned, grinning despite myself.

Ian's green eyes danced wickedly. "He can *try*—but I'll just tell him it interferes with my mentoring..."

I laughed loudly. "I look forward to hearing his response."

"Anything for Byron's least favorite apprentice. It's the least I can do since you took over my torch."

"I wouldn't be so—ouch!" I ducked under a low palm's hanging branches and skimmed my bad arm against the side of its trunk.

"You okay there, warrior girl?"

"I'm fine," I said through gritted teeth. "I just want this pain to end."

"We are almost there." Ian pointed to a set of wooden doors protruding from the base of a large cliff, a quarter of a mile away.

Like most of the city's housing, the infirmary was built into the rocky face of desert crags, a seemingly endless elevation that separated the Red Desert from the northern plains of the capital city, Devon, and the rest of Jerar. I had always heard tales of a desert city carved into mountains, but I had still been speechless the first day we arrived.

"Thank the gods."

The two of us continued along the dirt path, through the doors, and into the dank, torch-lit passage of the building. The air was cooler here. There were only two guards posted at the entrance. They recognized us by our apprentice garb and let us in without hesitation. The passage split into three separate channels—I led Ian down the one to the right.

As soon as we had taken a couple of steps I heard the master of Restoration's sharp, clipped voice instructing on the proper *non-magical* treatment for scorpion stings. *Ugh.* Ian and I exchanged amused expressions and entered the Restoration apprentices' classroom.

*Normally*, one would seek out the city's main healing center to the left of the main corridor, but students were only allowed to be treated there if their injuries were grave enough...

If they weren't, we were "lessons" for the Restoration apprentices.

They had to practice on someone.

"Ry!"

Master Joan's lecture ceased the moment we entered the classroom. She shot my twin a dirty look for interrupting her talk as she confronted Ian and I with a cross expression. "What are your grievances, apprentices?"

"My right arm." I tried to avoid the curious stares from the rest of Alex's faction. I knew they wanted to be healers, but it still sent an unsettling quiver down my spine when they looked intrigued—instead of horrified—by our injuries. No one should *ever* be excited to see blood.

"And you?" She eyed Ian suspiciously.

Ian grinned sheepishly. "Too much sun?"

"Out!" The master pointed to the door.

Ian winked at me—fully expecting the master's response—and departed the room with a friendly wave. As soon as he disappeared several of the female apprentices sighed. I hid a smile. I wasn't the only one who had noticed my friend's good looks.

"Everyone—we will continue the lesson after we have finished Apprentice Ryiah's healing. Ryiah, please list your symptoms so that we can begin to consider a treatment."

I began to describe my injury—pain up and down the arm, swelling, and stiffness in the elbow. I wondered if it was broken.

"Break." My sandy-haired twin was the first to speak.

"And how do we confirm diagnosis?"

"I would project a casting to mirror bone placement—if there weren't any physical deformities or skin breakage, since those alone would confirm his suspicions without magic." That was Ronan—my brother's friend and sometimes rival, a fellow second-year that had ranked first in their trial year at the Academy.

Master Joan chose a fifth-year to perform the casting. The girl stood proudly, eyes alight with anticipation as she began her magic. I braced myself—the last time I had visited the infirmary for dehydration a painless casting had resulted in skin rash. *Nothing like trial and error to make me wary of my fellow apprentices.*

Luckily this time the girl appeared to know what she was doing. I didn't feel anything above a faint, humming vibration as my arm slowly took on a translucent outline with glowing lines shining through it. My stomach turned a little as I realized those bright orange things were my bones. There was an unnatural break in the round nook at the end of my forearm connecting to the elbow.

"Minor fracture," the girl said proudly. "Nothing we would need to realign with plating. I would recommend conservative treatment since there is no breakage and her bones do not appear to be displaced."

I swallowed, immediately grateful they would not be inserting metals into my arm.

"How would we treat with magic? And without?"

The same fifth-year replied with the proper response for both—and I was happy to hear neither detailed anything complex.

"Good. Now splint her arm as you would without magic. Byron will want her to heal naturally since it is not severe."

When the girl had finished wrapping my arm and secured it in a sling I was dismissed. As I passed Alex my twin caught my arm—under the pretense he wanted to check my bindings, but really so he could ask about Ella.

"She hasn't forgotten me, has she?"

I scowled at Alex, attempting to reposition my arm more comfortably. "Gee, thanks for asking about me."

"I'm not worried about *you*, Ry." He chuckled. "You have taken more trips to the infirmary than anyone else in your faction and I *never* hear you complain—even with that nasty Byron as your training master." Noting Master Joan's frown he quickly examined my wrist, placing two fingers to check my pulse. "Circulation is still steady," he declared loudly.

As soon as the master's back was turned Alex gave me a pleading look—one that had stolen countless hearts in our hometown of Demsh'aa. It did not work on me. "But, really," he whispered, "how is Ella? I've barely had a chance to talk to her since the apprenticeships started—"

"You see her every day at meals."

"But she's with the rest of your faction," Alex pointed out. "They expect me to sit with my own—comradeship and all that nonsense. And all you Combat apprentices have such airs."

I sighed. "Well then stop by our table after you are done with fostering your 'comradeship.' I am not going to serve as a go-between for your apologies. Tell her how you feel, or leave the poor girl alone already."

Alex released me with a groan. "You are no fun, Ry."

"Neither are you when you are hurting my best friend." I didn't feel sorry for my twin—he'd had his chance and blown it. I loved my brother—but he knew I was no fan when it came to his relationships. *Especially* his last one. Handsome, lovable Alex was a scamp when it came to the heart. It served him right that the one to break his was Ella.

"Ry." His eyes were somber.

"Yeah?"

"I miss her."

"I know."

By the time I had returned to my faction everyone had already left the training grounds and started their third session of the day: Strategies in Combat. It was the final class before our lunchtime break and my favorite since we had started our desert training.

I quickly ran up the four long flights of stairs nearest our barracks to the local regiment's council chambers. Protruding out of a rocky cliff face, the fourth floor of the great, many-pillared building contained a large hall for the outpost's Commander, highborn officials—including Baron Eli—and the local regiment of soldiers, knights and mages to gather and discuss various strategies for dealing with any and all topics of military interest. Though the Crown's Army served the capital and made official decisions in times of war, it was the duty of each city's assigned regiment to enforce Crown law and deal with local issues unless brute force was needed.

Finding Ella in the crowd I quickly made my way to the back of the hall. Ella made room on her bench and eyed my bad arm with interest. "Ouch," she whispered. "Maybe Byron will feel bad for yelling now that he knows you broke it."

"Ha." The man was incapable of remorse.

"Will you two be quiet already? I've got better things to do than listen to Ryiah complain." Priscilla, one row in front of us, shot Ella and me a nasty look.

"She wasn't complaining," Ella hissed back. "Certainly not like when you broke *your* shoulder last month!"

"I did *not*!"

"You made Darren carry you to the infirmary." The words fell from my lips before I could stop them. I immediately regretted it. *Why—why did I say that?*

Priscilla narrowed her eyes. "Oh, I see what *this* is about." She twisted her lips in a small, cruel smile. "Ryiah, I am sorry you *still* harbor *that* sentiment—but please *do* try to move on. It makes me uncomfortable to see you pining for my betrothed after all this time."

My fists clenched. "Darren and I are just friends."

"And that's all you'll ever be." She scowled. "Whatever happened back at the Aca—"

"What is this? *Have you second-years no respect for your study?* I demand an explanation at once!"

Priscilla paused as Master Byron came barreling toward the back of the room, his face livid with anger as he fixated on the three of us. His frown was particularly poignant.

"It was Apprentice Ryiah, sir!"

Ella's and my jaw dropped in blatant disbelief.

"I tried to stop her, sir, but she kept complaining about her injury and whining that Darren didn't carry her to the infirmary!"

My cheeks flamed as the non-heir—who had been immersed in a history scroll just moments before—whipped his head around to stare.

"I was doing no such thing!" I avoided Darren's gaze as I turned to face the Master of Combat. "I would *never* say that." I hoped the prince would hear my emphasis.

"And why would I believe a troublemaker over the soon-to-be wife of our noble prince Darren? Are you suggesting I should distrust the Crown's future princess?"

My mouth soured at Master Byron's obvious discrimination and I forced myself to exhale slowly. Ian had not been exaggerating the man's bias: Byron had lived as a palace mage for several years before taking over the apprenticeship training—already a classist highborn, and a sexist, he was the *last* thing we needed for our study.

"Ryiah isn't lying, sir." Ella stood and put her hand on my shoulder in a show of support.

"You aren't a source of veritable truth either, Eleanor."

"It's Ella," Ella said through clenched teeth.

The master scoffed. "That is of no consequence. I expect the two of you to assist Apprentice Ian with the cleaning of the barrack privies during your evening hours for the remainder of this week. A small price for interrupting the rest of your classmates' study. It is my hope that the extra duty will illuminate the error of your ways." He gave a loud, exasperated sniff. "Though I suspect it will not. Now, pay attention to the rest of the Commander's address or I will see to it that you *never* have free time again."

Silently fuming, I forced myself to sit tall in my seat and focus on the regiment leaders at the front of the room. Beside me Ella did the same. Now was not the time to complain. Despite the drama just moments before both of us really did want to hear what the Commander and her regiment leaders were saying. Unlike the lessons we'd had back at the Academy, these officials' information was formed entirely by first-hand experience.

Today's topic was continuing a three-week lecture on chariot combat—what the desert regiments were famous for.

Ishir Outpost was located at the northernmost boundary of the Red Desert, which encompassed the entire southern region of Jerar. The city and the rest of the desert's border were made up entirely of tall desert bluffs and steep crags with only one man-made gate allowing travel between the desert and the rest of the country. The desert's tall, rocky walls overlooked the middle plains and provided perfect vantage points for the Crown's Army in the event of a full-scale invasion on the capital, Devon. Mostly, the desert's local regiments serviced the walls as lookouts. There hadn't been a war between Jerar and its northern neighbor Caltoth in over ninety years.

Since the start of our training in Ishir I had learned that at the base of this wall were several hidden tunnels interspersed every fifty miles or so to help the central plains evacuate and give the Red Desert's regiments easy passage out. According to palace historians, no country had ever attacked Jerar's capital due to the threat just south of it.

Because of the desert tunnels and the plains' level ground, one of the first things the Crown's Army had done was order up several hundred two-manned chariots to be stored in all of the desert's northern cities—ready to be used for swift-assault should the need arise.

The chariots were intended to be the first charge with a soldier steering while either a skilled archer-knight or Combat mage led the attack. The quick speed of such a light vehicle allowed the mages and knights the ease of a distanced approach that enemies would have a hard time countering. The

Red Desert's knights and mages were known for their long-range attacks, and since Ishir Outpost was the most populace city with the largest regiment it had become one of the four territories mage apprentices and knights' squires trained in during their four-year apprenticeships.

"Soldiers of the Cavalry are exempt, of course, since they are immediately placed following their trial year in whatever region the Crown demands," the Commander noted. "It is a shame that they can't do a four-year rotation as well, but they take on much lesser roles in our service and it is not necessary for them to learn the chariots before they are placed in our city."

The imposing lady knight continued to explain the finer points of her strategy—pointing to her colleagues from time-to-time to explain what each leader would do once the chariots had left the barrier tunnels. The mounted knights would follow up with an armed assault—usually the sickle sword if they were desert natives, or the halbred if coming from the Crown's Army. Whatever horses remained were given to the soldiers—with the majority serving on foot with battle axes to break up their opponent's armor and give the knights an easier target to dismantle. The Restoration and Alchemy mages would remain in the tunnels—equipped for battle, but prepared for healing and the latter for a last minute defense.

They had left no possibility unplanned.

Though we went over various techniques for breaking up enemy lines and securing a victory, the one thing the Commander and her council never told us was exactly where those tunnels were located. We didn't know their number either, and we never would... unless we were given a position in command or participating in an actual war.

Because Jerar's capital had never been under siege, the Red Desert's tunnels had never been used. The laborers that had helped build them had died several centuries ago. The only people who knew their exact coordinates were either dead, or currently serving the commanding post in one of the desert or plain cities. The only exception was the royal family. Not even the various barons or ruling lords in the affecting cities knew.

From everything I had gathered the tunnels were Jerar's most safeguarded secret. It hadn't been said directly but I was almost certain they punished offenders with death. There were rumors that those who went looking for them never returned. And then there was the mysterious death of Ishir's past Commander who had been in the prime of his health when a sudden illness had rapidly taken his life after only three years into his reign.

*Definitely* a secret.

By the time our two hours were over I had forgotten most of my earlier problems. Priscilla, Master Byron, and my new injury were just small, annoying blips in my otherwise perfect life. Every time I walked away from Strategies in Combat I felt like I was a part of something great. No one and nothing could take that away from me.

I was an apprentice now. For Combat, the most prestigious faction of all. *I* had defeated more odds than any of the other war schools. In the School of Knighthood almost half of the first-year pages were made squires. In the Cavalry? Three-quarters of its applicants made soldier. The Academy? Less than ten percent.

I wasn't even considered lowborn anymore—as an apprentice mage I was now afforded the same status as a noble. Not even squires had that privilege. Magic was rare. And important. So I was.

And in four short years I would be a mage of Combat.

"You sure look chipper for someone with a broken arm."

Breaking free from my daze I spotted Lynn waiting with Ella's mentor, Loren, a tall dark-skinned youth with startling blue eyes that my brother loathed. It had been he who had spoken.

"Thanks for reminding me." I gave Loren a wry smile. Ella and I followed him and Lynn down the stairs to the third floor. The great building hosted four levels—the first was the privies and wash chambers, the second the squire/apprentice mage barracks (depending on whose year it was to field train—we were never in the same city together), the third was the dining commons, and the fourth for regiment meetings. It wasn't as grand as the Academy—but it was still impressive.

"Is Ian staying behind to do extra mentoring with Darren today?" Lynn joined me as I found us a seat. The room was smaller than the one we'd had at the Academy—and there were only three rows to choose from. Before there had been over a hundred of us—now there were only sixty, well, sixty-one since the exception the Colored Robes had made for me last year. Twenty apprentices from each faction—five for each year.

"I doubt it." The troublemaker was far more likely to be trying to talk his way out of the chore Byron had just assigned. I repeated what Ian had told me on our walk to the infirmary. "Wish I could see him do it," I added.

Ella picked at her plate, avoiding a curry she had deemed too spicy for her liking. "I'm surprised he would try."

"What are you talking about?" I stared at my friend.

Ella did not reply—suddenly too busy chewing to answer. Lynn, meanwhile, seemed unusually upset. My mentor hid it quickly though, masking her discomfort with a bunch of questions about my arm instead. I quickly forgot my own as the girl barraged me for answers. *Would I still be able to train with her? Did I think it would affect my castings? Was I sure Byron wouldn't let the Restoration apprentices cast a healing for it?*

"Ladies. Loren. I hope you didn't mourn for me while I was away."

Glancing up I saw that Ian had returned, looking no worse for wear than usual.

"Did you even talk to Byron?" I asked suspiciously. The third-year seemed too cheery to have just come from a chat with our training master.

Ian took the seat opposite mine as he slid in next to Loren. "Nah. I decided it was a wasted effort."

Out of the corner of my eye I noticed Ella and Loren exchange meaningful looks.

"So did anyone else notice how Commander Ama keeps avoiding divulging where those tunnels are?" I asked, finally breaking the awkward silence.

Lynn shrugged. "It doesn't matter much. I don't see Jerar going to war anytime soon." She turned to Ian. "What do you think?" she teased. "Are we ready for war?"

Ian's eyes twinkled mischievously. "Why don't we ask our very own royal since it will be his father signing those summons?" He stood up and pretended to scan the row of Combat apprentices for the non-heir who was, as usual, missing from the table. "What a shame, my charming mentee is absent. *Again.*"

Darren hadn't taken a lunch with the rest of our faction since we had started. Instead, he spent the hour drilling with Byron *personally* in the training grounds. I wasn't sure whose idea it had initially been—the man hero-worshipped the prince—but I understood Ian's irritation. No one else got exclusive training with the master; Byron was grooming Darren for success and leaving the rest of us—particularly the ones he didn't like—to rot.

I had confronted Darren about the injustice a couple weeks back and the prince had just laughed in my face. "*What did you expect, Ryiah? Not everyone is going to treat us like equals. You got lucky with the first-year masters at the Academy but you are going to have to learn to accept the injustice now—it's* always *going to be here. Especially while* I'm *around.*"

He'd made a good point—even if I hadn't liked what it meant.

Since Ian was Darren's mentor he took the prince's absence more personally than the rest of us. The third-year didn't trust Darren. I think the prince's aloof nature unsettled him. And Darren's competitive drive only made things worse.

I sympathized. More than anyone else at our table, I understood Ian's plight. I had gone through the same thing the first time I'd met the non-heir—and it had taken me ten long months to stop second-guessing Darren's actions.

Normally, the mentor-mentee relationship was a good thing. It gave two apprentices the opportunity to bond over shared trials and common goals in training. Each pairing lasted a year before the partners were switched. We would have two years leading others and two years following them. The varied approach would give us the chance to be the best and the worst, and the experience was supposed to make us better for it. Ian undoubtedly interpreted Darren's extra training as an affront instead of what it really was: a lifetime of expectation.

I think there were very few who understood why Darren acted the way he did. *I* wasn't an expert by any means—but the prince had made certain remarks last year that had led me to believe his role was more demanding than people realized. Otherwise, how else could one explain why a *prince* was more accustomed to injuries than the rest of us? Darren had never once lost control of his magic in training—and as one of the few apprentices that could pain cast that was *highly* unusual. It led me to two possible conclusions: Darren was perfect, or he had trained in far worse pain than the rest of us.

It was hard to accept the latter, but no one—not even the current Black Mage—had ever had a flawless apprenticeship. I knew firsthand how hard Darren worked. After all, his ambition was the reason we had become friends—though it had taken *many* misunderstandings to get there.

"I understand wanting to be best, I do," Ian continued. "But there is nothing wrong with a little bit of amity. Would it kill the prince to take a meal with his factionmates?" He directed the attention to me. "I mean, look at Ryiah. She is just as stubborn, but she still manages to have a conversation with the rest of us."

Ella winked at me conspiratorially. "Oh, Darren still has 'conversations' with some people."

I glared at her. She knew very well there was nothing going on between Darren and me. Maybe there had been at one point—but it was long gone. His betrothal to Priscilla of Langli, one of the wealthiest young women in the kingdom—and my personal nemesis, had made that perfectly evident.

Ian's eyes met mine. "That's right, Ry. You and Darren are actually *friends*." He pronounced the last word with mock distaste, grinning. "So how did you do it? What makes the cold-hearted princeling mortal like the rest of us?"

I fidgeted in my seat. The last thing I wanted was for the others to find out about last year's transgression. Especially Ian. I suspected my feelings for the curly-haired third-year weren't strictly platonic—and I didn't want him to think that I was, as Priscilla put it, "pining" for Darren. *Because I wasn't.*

Ella giggled. "Oh I don't think it's something you would want to attempt yourself, Ian."

"Why?" Ian raised a brow. "What did she do that I can't?" He turned to me and gave me his most disarming smile. "Ry, just tell me whatever you said to convince him to make him give up that ridiculous pretense."

"It's not an act." I kept my eyes averted as I said: "Darren just has a really hard time opening up to people he thinks are beneath him…"

Ian gave a fake gasp.

"…But I'm sure after a couple months he'll realize you *are* trying."

Ian stole a handful of grapes off my plate. "That, my dear, is the worst explanation I have ever heard." He added half-serious, "If I didn't know better I would say you were *defending* him."

"I'm not," I said quickly. Too quickly.

"Did something *happen* between the two of you?" Ian leaned across the table to look at me.

I flushed. "No."

Ella coughed loudly.

Ian withdrew, grinning. "So that Priscilla girl *was* right. You are a terrible liar, Ry."

I wished I were anywhere other than the commons. My humiliation could *not* get any worse.

"Don't worry," Ella added wickedly, "No one cares that you kissed the prince."

I was wrong.

# Chapter Two

The second half of my day didn't get much better.

I was on my way to the fourth floor to begin a lesson on desert castings when I ran into Darren.

"So I heard that you wanted me to carry you to the infirmary."

I gave the prince what I hoped was my most disdainful expression. "I don't know what you are talking about."

A corner of the non-heir's lips twitched, and I had the distinct impression he was on the brink of laughter. "Don't worry," Darren said, "I have a hard time imagining you'd let *anyone* help you."

I held my stance—praying that my friends were taking their time to catch up. "You know me well." Apparently, he hadn't made the connection to his mentor's earlier absence—but I wasn't about to tell him. Ian had joined me because he wanted to—not because I was some inept apprentice in need of rescuing.

"Even if you *had* asked, I wouldn't have carried you."

*This was the person I had spent half a year 'pining' over?* I must have been mad.

"I'm not saying it to be mean, Ryiah. You don't need to give me that look."

I continued to glare at him.

"Byron is good for you."

I put my hands on my hips. "I don't need another 'adversity builds character' speech, Darren. That man is a chauvinistic pig. Where's *your* adversity?"

Darren raised a brow. "I'm looking at it."

I gave an exasperated huff and went to go find a seat in the back of the room. I was so distracted I didn't notice when Ian slid into the bench next to me.

"Lover's quarrel?"

I glared at the third-year. Ella, Lynn, and Loren were chuckling. "I hate all of you," I told them.

None of my friends paid the threat any heed. Grumbling, I resigned myself to two hours with fools.

"You heard those Combat mages earlier. Distance is *everything*. You do not want to get close to the enemy—a mage's life is far too valuable to be wasted this early in battle! If the Crown wanted to send in someone expendable they would be using soldiers, not mages!"

Grimacing, I set to projecting my next attack. *Thank the gods the local infantry isn't with us to hear him today.*

Three hundred yards in front of me was a long wooden fence, six feet high and dotted with dangling wreaths. Normally the backside of the regiment's horse pasture, today the horses had been stabled—as per the last three weeks of practice. Now, the fence served as an imaginary enemy line—and the target? Sloppily woven wreaths that represented the weak spots in the opposing forces' defense: the armpit, the eyes, and the plate armor nearest the chest. The goal of the exercise was to hit a wreath with casted arrows—a type of long-range magic similar to the longbow exercises we had been drilling on every morning for weeks now.

If we hit a wreath but the arrow fell, or the arrow did not hit our target at all, then our casting was considered a failed attempt. Our projections needed to be just right to travel the great distance and embed themselves into a target's armor. It wasn't an easy feat.

Most of the second-years, myself included, had only had one or two successful castings since we'd begun the afternoon drill.

As the Commander had mentioned earlier, chariot attacks were Ishir's preferred method for initiating battle. Combat mages would be the first to strike—and even though we would be discharged at the same time as the knights, our castings would give us the ability to reach our targets from a much greater distance, *much faster* than non-magicked weapons. Long bows were usually limited to four hundred feet, and other ranged weapons even less—but that was *without* magic.

If a mage mastered the technique for long casting, not only would he or she be able to project arrows further than any knight, but eventually much heavier artillery as well.

It would be a great advantage.

Out of the corner of my eye I watched as Lynn cast out her arrows. No physical weapon in hand, the entire casting was formed by a projection in her mind. She barely flinched as physical shafts manifested themselves from thin air—pulling back against an invisible force and then racing into the distance, embedding themselves deep in a wreath already brimming with arrows directly across from her.

"Apprentice Ryiah it should not take this long for you to form a casting!"

Snapping out of my thoughts, I hastily cast out three conjured arrows in succession. They fell uncomfortably short of the target. As soon as the missiles hit the ground I let them dissipate, dissolving into empty air. I took a deep breath as I prepared for another casting.

"Don't let him get to you, Ry."

I shot Lynn a grateful smile and then returned to the task at hand. I had let the pain in my arm—and Master Byron—detract from my focus. This time I would not be so careless. I recounted the three-foot arrows and the long, elm bowstave we used in practice. I imagined the horrible, heaving tension from drawing eighty pounds of force against my left side. Then I let the shafts fly, soaring toward the wreath with as much strength as I could summon. The mental exercise was just as exhausting as the physical act.

Halfway into their flight I was building the next projection, concentrating on the mental image with everything I had. The ground beneath my feet trembled and I dug into it with the heels of my boots, holding my stance and casting steady as I released another assault on my target. Master Byron was undoubtedly testing us—seeing if we could hold focus in a chariot's bumpy floor.

My second and third castings met my target with success: each time at least one of the three arrows hit a wreath.

I kept going. Thirty minutes flew by before I realized it. My luck continued—at least half of my castings met with success, and the others were not far off.

After five more minutes my stomach began to turn and a nauseous feeling spread up into my lungs. I tasted something bitter and my vision flickered in and out in a familiar warning. My skin was instantly clammy, and a thick perspiration broke out across my tanned skin that had nothing to do with the stifling heat.

As soon as my legs started to shake I called off my magic and watched as the arrows disappeared mid-flight.

Then I bent low with my head between my knees and waited for the dizziness to end. After a couple minutes I began to feel better. I straightened, taking in the rest of the class.

With a small flash of pride I saw that Priscilla, Ella, a third-year named Bryce, and Ray—the dark-skinned boy I had lost to in the previous year's trials—had already quit. Lynn looked like she was about to follow suit, and Darren and Eve were little better. The older apprentices were fading equally fast… though some had been casting with more advanced artillery than arrows.

During my trial year at the Academy the Combat master had always urged us to cast until we had nothing left to give.

It had been the fastest way to build our magic's stamina—but it had always had an unpleasant aftereffect, and more often than not it left us sick, fainting, or even unconscious.

Now that we were apprentices our training had changed. After midwinter we would be actively serving with the local regiment for five months in desert patrols. All of our drills now were preparing us for actual combat. Which meant that stamina was no longer as important as survival.

Testing limits had made sense in our first year when the masters had been trying to build our magic as quickly as possible, but now the focus was strategy. We all had different levels of potential—the point in which our magic would stop developing—and after the trial year its ascension was usually much slower.

No one's power was infinite. The closer we were to our limits, the slower our magic progressed. Even then, most mages' stamina stopped building by the time adolescence was over. A couple might continue on into their early-twenties—but that was not the norm. Once a mage reached his thirties it would begin to decline even if that person was diligent in their daily practice. It was the main reason our Candidacy took place so often: we needed the strongest Council possible, even if that meant changing our Colored Robes every twenty years.

"You are preparing yourself for a true-to-life battle," Byron had declared on our first day of apprenticeship. "If you are approaching your limits you need to turn back and call off your magic. The only time that I *ever* want to see you fainting is if you are at no risk of danger, or the casting's outcome is worth your life."

In the simulation today we were preparing for chariot attacks. Casting just one more arrow on the enemy's front line—undoubtedly made up of "expendable" foot soldiers—was not worth losing consciousness and falling from a moving chariot. The casting wouldn't kill me, but it would leave me an open target to those who could. The point of the exercise was to attack and retreat—not attack-and-then-fall-out-of-your-chariot-and-be-killed-by-an-angry-mob-of-enemy-soldiers.

The rest of the class finished minutes later. As soon as they had Byron launched himself into a full-blown speech praising Darren and insulting the girls at the same time. It always ended the same way.

Women were weak. We were silly, temperamental, and emotional. We should always follow, never lead. We shouldn't try to overreach in our magic. Men would always be able to cast better. It was simply a part of their disposition as warriors; women had never intended to be seen in such jarring roles and would therefore always be "lacking" in Combat.

While the master occasionally gave Priscilla good remarks I was certain they were only for the prince's benefit. Byron didn't even pretend with the rest of us.

I wondered what Eve thought of the master's bias—but the violet-eyed second-year never spoke up, and I suspected she didn't care. I could sometimes sense Priscilla's irritation, but the highborn was smart enough to keep her temper in check. Ella was just as outspoken as Ian and I—but since the master didn't target her quite as much she tended to spend more time pitying me rather than contradicting the man directly. The older female apprentices were few in number—my year had an uncommon ratio, four girls and two boys—but they seemed to maintain the same strategy as Eve. Stay silent, and the master would ignore you. Unless you were me.

"And Ryiah. Stay focused next time. I will not let that arm be an excuse for your casting to suffer."

Today had been my best castings yet. I'd hit the target more times than most of the second-years. And only that one attempt had failed to reach the fence. I had even outperformed Ella's mentor Loren, and that other third-year, Bryce. But, as usual, the master had failed to notice anything other than my faults.

I let the anger slide off me—albeit very slowly—and started my retreat to the dining commons. Our training took place a mile from the main building that housed our barracks and the rest of the amenities. Normally I resented the long walk after a full day of practice but today I was happy to have some time to clear my head.

*My apprenticeship is more important than strangling Master Byron*. I repeated the motto over and over again. If I said it enough times it would become true, or so I hoped. Each time it was getting harder and harder not to counter the master's critique. I'd lost my temper a couple of times during that first month—and now three months into our training the tyrant was still punishing me for it.

"Oops, *so* sorry!" A horrible jolt shot across my bad arm as someone came barreling into it. Biting back a yelp I glowered at Priscilla.

"You did that on purpose!" My pain was making me see all sorts of crazy colors, and I no longer cared if the master had rules about casting during non-lessons. The girl needed to be put in her place—and if today's practice was any indication then I had a good chance of beating her.

"You can't prove it."

"Prove it?" I snarled. I hoped Master Byron was too far away to hear us. "I don't need to prove it. Why don't you challenge me directly instead of acting like the coward you are!"

"Ryiah!" Darren's hand closed around my good arm. His voice was stern. "Don't."

"Why are you stopping her?"

"Why are you stopping *me*?"

Priscilla's and my questions were instantaneous. The non-heir regarded his betrothed and me coldly. "Because if you duel Ryiah this time, you'll lose."

"She *cannot* beat me," Priscilla scoffed.

Darren kept his iron grip on my arm. "She *can*. And if you do anything else to taunt her I won't stop Ryiah from trying."

I had the pleasure of seeing the raven-haired beauty turn an unattractive shade of red. "I-I'll tell Byron she attacked me!"

"Priscilla." Darren's patience was growing thin. "If you do I will tell him the truth… We may be betrothed but Ryiah is my friend. I try to stay out of your disagreements, but if you do this I will take her side."

The girl let out a frustrated huff and stormed off. A scattered clapping rose up from the rest of the class—some of my friends even whistled. I blushed uncomfortably and Darren dropped my arm like it had scalded him.

I noticed Master Byron wasn't as far away as I thought, but it was quite obvious he had refrained from interfering since the prince got involved. He stayed silent, watching me with an irritable expression.

*I guess there are perks to his bias.*

"How's your arm?"

I jumped as I realized Darren was still standing next to me, waiting for an answer. It was the nearest we had been since that day in the Academy towers—only then I had been trying to figure out whether or not to trust him.

"I—I'm fine," I stuttered. I felt unusually light-headed. I wasn't sure if it was from Priscilla's bump or the former pressure of Darren's hand on my arm. I hoped it was the former. "Thanks," I added quickly, "for saying what you did."

"I told you we were friends, Ryiah." He was smiling.

"I know," I began, "but you two are betrothed…"

Darren's face hardened. "She'll come around," he muttered.

"Ry, what happened?" Ian, Ella, and Loren had arrived. The three of them had been too caught up in an animated conversation to take notice until Priscilla had marched past them.

"Priscilla being Priscilla—only this time she managed to clip my arm in the process." I gave a weak laugh. It still smarted terribly and I knew Byron would never let the Restoration mages touch it. For once it wasn't about me, at least. Like the rest of the masters from my first year at the Academy, Byron believed pain was something *all* apprentices needed to bear.

Ian noticed my grimace. "You need to get that seen to." He paused. "I bet we can get your brother to take a look."

I protested—but my heart was not in it. I expected Darren to make a sarcastic remark about how "pain makes a mage" but he was oddly silent.

"I don't care, Ry. I'll tell Alex not to fix it. Byron would notice anyway if he did, but Alex can at least suggest something for the pain." He gave Darren a small smile—despite what he said about the prince, I knew Ian really did want to be friends. "I can take over from here, Darren."

The non-heir studied the two of us, brows furrowed. I wondered what he was thinking.

"Of course." Darren's face had returned to a blank slate. With one last glance in my direction me he said, "Ask your brother about arnica."

Alex was peeling a mango when we found him in the commons. He seemed surprised to see all of us, especially Ella—but he recovered quickly.

"Arnica, huh?"

"Do you know what it is?" I pressed.

"Of course." His eyes met mine in mild amusement. "I'm just surprised Darren even knew to suggest it. It's not a common ingredient."

Ian turned to my twin. "Well? Can you get it?"

"I can... But I'll need help..." Alex's gaze fell to Ella standing next to us. He swallowed. "The healers keep all their supplies locked away in the main wing. I will need you to distract them while I get the salve. Now would be our best chance, while Master Joan is at dinner."

Ella did not look at my brother as she said, "Then let's go." She turned to Loren apologetically: "You don't have to come if you don't want to."

Loren shook his head, eyes dancing. "And miss the fun?"

A flash of irritation flared in my twin's eyes, but he said nothing.

The five of us began the walk to the infirmary. Ella, Ian, and Loren spent most of the time in animated conversation—my brother and I in awkward silence. Alex kept stealing jealous glances at Ella and Loren in the back of our group and I had to kick him to finally get him to quit.

"Ouch!"

"Stop glaring at Loren!" I scolded.

"I wasn't."

"You were."

My brother frowned. "Are things serious between those two?"

"They aren't courting if that's your question," I replied tersely.

"Yet," Alex grumbled. Sliding in closer to me he said in a hushed voice. "You have to get us alone, Ry. Tell Ella to go with me when I get the arnica."

"Why should I?" The last time the two had been in the same room together was when Ella had walked in on him kissing a Restoration apprentice. That had been a month ago when they'd still been courting. My friend had told me all about it afterwards, sobbing in the barracks and swearing she would never talk to my twin again. She had kept her word and I never urged her to try.

It wasn't the first time my brother had done this. In Demsh'aa there was a mile long list of the hearts he had broken in his wake. The difference was that this time my brother seemed to regret it. In fact, he had even broken down and cried after a couple of days of silence, begging me to talk to her.

"I need to explain what happened," Alex continued. "*Please Ry.*"

His blue eyes bore into mine desperately. I felt a wave of empathy and cursed my twin for his uncanny ability to elicit sympathy. No one could look into those pitiful blue eyes and say no.

"Fine." I gave my brother my most cross expression. "But if you make her cry I will *never* help you again, Alex. Ever."

Alex's face lit up so much so I cringed. "Thank you, Ry!" He reached out to hug me and I jumped out of his way. He chuckled as he realized his mistake. "Forgot about that arm," he admitted.

Ten minutes later we arrived at the infirmary. I found Ella as we entered the building, nodding to the guards as we passed. The soldiers grinned and Ian snickered.

"I think you've got admirers, ladies."

I rolled my eyes and nudged Ella forward. "I think you should go with Alex. He might need back-up and I can't go since we are going to need my injury to distract them."

Ella was immediately uncomfortable. "Does it have to be me—what about Ian? Or Loren?"

"Just talk to him." She trusted me. I hoped I would not regret asking.

Ella fixed me with a tired expression. "I am doing this for *you*, Ryiah—not him."

"Thank you."

We found the left corridor. Loren, Alex, and I immediately crowded the desk. The three of us began chattering loudly about my arm while Alex and Ella snuck past the attendants into the supply room. I kept my eyes open for any passing healers while Ian and Loren continued to talk. Five minutes passed and then they emerged, proudly concealing a small jar in Alex's fist. The two of them looked happier. I wondered if things were resolved.

Ella's eyes caught mine and she gave a timid smile. I started to return it—and then my face fell as a young woman in red mage's robes blocked their escape, fixing the two with a steely-eyed frown.

"Apprentice Alex, just what do you think you are doing? Do you have an authorization for that?" The jar and their guilty expressions hadn't escaped her notice.

The mages behind us were too busy with Ian and Loren to hear.

Alex gave the healer his most easy-going smile. "Kyra, my poor sister over there is in pain."

The mage's eyes flickered to me and her expression didn't change.

Alex sidled over to the young woman, unperturbed. He leaned in conspiratorially and stage-whispered. "Please, Kyra, you wouldn't want Ryiah to suffer, would you? Master Byron's rules are just pointless... what is the harm in a little relief?"

I watched as the healer's face waivered from resolve to doubt.

"Wow." My brother breathed loudly. "I just realized your eyes are green. I knew you were beautiful but I—I—" He pretended to stutter, flustered by her attention.

Kyra's cheeks turned pink. "Stop that." But I noticed she said it a lot more gently.

"Please, Kyra?" My brother gave his most innocent smile.

She sighed. "Fine, Alex, but just this once."

"You are as kind as you are stunning." Alex caught her hand and kissed it lightly, winking.

The Restoration mage watched him, pleased. "You should join the healers for a drink one night," she said abruptly. "We go to the Crow's Nest every Sunday—perhaps I will see you there next time?"

My twin grinned. "I wouldn't miss it."

As soon as the young woman had vanished Ella snatched the vial from Alex and turned to me, eyes flashing. "Let's get out of here, Ryiah." It didn't take much to ascertain why her mood had suddenly changed.

"Ella wait, it wasn't what you—I was helping!"

"I don't want to hear it, Alex."

"Ella, I meant what I said back there—"

"The only person you love is yourself!" Ella cut my brother off coldly. "You just can't help yourself. It's not your fault—when this girl kisses you or that girl misinterprets your gestures you are blameless. Well, I'm *not* going to wait for it to happen again. *We are done.*" She grabbed my good arm and dragged me out of the building, not waiting to see if the rest of our group followed.

I didn't protest. As soon as we were outside the infirmary I apologized profusely.

Ella shook her head.

"Don't hold yourself responsible, Ry. You aren't accountable for your twin's actions. You warned me that first day at the Academy. I... I just have this bad habit of falling for the wrong ones."

Thinking about Darren earlier—and my reaction to his hand on my wrist, I said sadly, "I think we have that in common."

After a short dinner we were once again on the practice field for our final lesson of the day. We were separated into two groups: those who could cast using pain, and those that couldn't. Ian, Darren, Eve, Lynn and I stayed behind with a small collection of older apprentices. Ella, Ray, Priscilla, Loren and the rest of the class retired to the far side of the grounds to continue the target casting from earlier.

Now more than ever, I was grateful for the arnica. I was finding it much easier to control my castings when the pain in my arm was not fighting my magic.

"No, no! *Slowly*, Ian!" Master Byron's command echoed across the cold night air. "If you keep that up you are not going to be able to control it."

"*Again.*" Darren's voice was thick with sarcasm. The two of them had been trading barbs for the past hour—mostly because Ian kept losing control of his castings. We were supposed to levitate our partners—only Ian hadn't quite mastered the correct pressure to use. Darren had been dropped and tossed backward more times than any of the others, and he appeared to be growing less and less patient.

I wasn't sure whether to laugh or cry. Ian was miserable at pain castings—and Darren was amazing, second only to two of the fifth-years that were with us.

"Mentees, you are up."

Lynn slowly withdrew the blade from her hand, letting me drift gently to the floor. To my left I heard a loud thump and Darren's subsequent curse.

"Master Bryon, I need to change partners for this exercise. This is ridiculous."

All heads turned to Ian and Darren: the former looked sheepish and the latter, furious.

"Fine. Darren, Ryiah, change mentors."

As I passed the non-heir by I glared at him for making me take Ian. The last thing I needed was to be dropped repeatedly on a bad arm. "I have a fracture."

"Good thing you have the arnica."

*Some "friend."* I sat down cross-legged in front of Ian, returning to the start position as I reached for Darren's knife. At least it was my turn.

"All right, mentees, this time in your castings I want you to focus on time. Try to hold your partner in the air for as long as you can. Once you feel comfortable, try alternating the pressure and keeping the same five feet level. Being able to maintain a stable pain casting—no matter the pressure—will help train your magic should you be caught off guard with an unexpected injury." The man paused, his ice blue eyes locking onto me. "Some of you could certainly use the practice."

Ignoring the disparaging comment, I set to work in my casting. I would gladly practice Byron's drills all night, if only so he could see me try. Not that the man would ever acknowledge I was. Trying, that is.

"If you drop me I won't hold it against you."

I tried to smile at Ian but it did little to mask the anxiety in my throat. *Concentrate Ryiah.* I gently dug the blade into my right palm, refusing to flinch as the sudden pain released my magic. Ian was instantly hovering in the air.

I let him float for a minute more before I decided to test the pressure, alternating between light spurts of pain. Ian remained level. I took turns nicking my fingers and sliced deeper into my palm, trembling as my casting fought to increase and dissipate in union with the hurt. I willed it to hold and braced myself as magic and pain continued to surge through me, struggling to break free.

My eyes watered and burned but I ignored them. Ever since the incident during my first-year trials pain had made my magic unstable. Which meant the past three months were a nightmare to train in. Every little injury opened a floodgate of pain magic—and if it was bad enough, like in the case of my fractured arm earlier, I wasn't always able to hold it back.

Ella suspected a barrier had broke—the one that usually kept my pain magic at bay. During the trials I had attempted a pain casting, spearing myself with a sword and sending an entire building crumbling in its wake. The act had been rash, and it only made sense that so much magic and a near-death experience would leave a large crack in my defense. Normally people built up to that level of casting, slowly, with incremental levels of pain—not the other way around. Master Byron had implied as much when I had first come to him with the question.

"Practice. It is the only way you are going to exert any control over your pain castings. We avoid teaching it to the first-years for a reason, apprentice. Now because of your ill-chosen act you will be battling powers much stronger than a second-year should deal with."

It was the reason the masters saved the method for apprenticeship.

"A mage is always fighting against pain castings during injury—usually they spend years working up to the magic you will be fighting now. You broke a barrier that requires a control you do not—and will not—have for many years."

I had been crestfallen and angry when I'd first heard the master's diagnosis. But Darren, in a random moment of kindness, had pointed out something I'd missed. Yes, I would be forced to battle stronger forces than everyone else who had pain magic, but I would also be competent faster as a result. "I did something similar to you two years before I joined the Academy," he'd confessed. "I still fight pain magic when I get hurt, but if you were to watch me pain cast now you would see I have a lot more control than the others." And he'd been right.

Blinking, I realized that Darren and I were the only ones still casting. The other two mentees—two fourth-years had already quit. Moment later my own palms trembled and I knew it was time to end.

I lowered Ian to the ground, releasing the pressure of the knife.

Two minutes later the non-heir followed suit.

"Well done, Darren. Ryiah that was... acceptable." The master seemed to be pulling the words from his teeth.

The mentors took over casting. I braced myself for Ian's inevitable misstep but nothing bad happened. The third-year seemed to be concentrating extra hard: I was not thrown once during his attempt.

After a couple of minutes Ian returned me to the ground, finishing before the other mentors.

I smiled at him, grateful he had managed to avoid dropping me and jostling my bad arm. "You did it, Ian!"

He winked. "It would seem I just needed the right motivation."

My heart skipped a beat. *Don't be a fool—he doesn't mean anything by it.*

Darren, still levitating nearby, snorted. Lynn lowered the prince and fixed her gaze on Ian. "Very impressive, Ian. I am so happy Master Byron's lessons are coming along."

The third-year chuckled and then glanced at her partner. "Sorry about earlier."

Darren raised a brow. "Sorry that I am not a pretty red-haired apprentice, or sorry that you were not trying?"

Ian grinned. "Might be a bit of both."

I hardly remembered the rest of our lesson. *He thought I was pretty.*

It was only much later as I was shoveling waste out of the barrack privies that it occurred to me to wonder which one I had been thinking of.

# Chapter Three

"Alright, second-years. It's the moment you have all been preparing for: today you will be participating in your first mock battle. We host one of these at the end of each initial field training. Which means that by the end of your apprenticeship you will have completed four."

Master Byron marched up and down the student line, preening in the light of his audience. "When we return to the desert after the solstice you will no longer be completing the schedule we've had you following the past few months. From January through May you will be deployed in regiment missions patrolling the Red Desert.

"Today Commander Ama and her mages will be observing your skills. They will be using this exercise to evaluate your level for future placement."

The other two masters—cold Master Joan from Restoration and Master Perry of Alchemy—took over, detailing their expectations for our simulated encounter. All sixty-one apprentices would be divided into two teams: the second—and fourth-year mentees against the third—and fifth-year mentors. It wasn't intended to be a fair match, but it would give us the opportunity to showcase what we had learned.

"Each of the teams will have a leader." Master Perry brushed back a strand of her short blonde hair and continued. "I leave it to you to elect a Combat apprentice for each. Whoever you choose will be in charge of strategy. You will have two hours to plot amongst yourselves before starting." She paused. "Please remember this is a group effort. You will not be doing yourself any favors by neglecting your teammates: if your leader is captured you will automatically lose. This person will be recognized by a black cloth they tie around their forearm."

Commander Ama joined the masters and the rest of her infirmary under the shadow of a nearby crag. We were three miles outside of the outpost, immersed in a true wasteland without a building in sight. Behind us was an endless expanse of steep cliffs, sand, and desert wildlife. Strange flowers and crooked cacti dotted the landscape.

"This is a true-to-life battle," the bald woman declared. Her voice was coarse and gruff, and the expression she wore was grim. "I expect you to treat the opposing team as a true enemy."

Ella elbowed me, snickering. "You heard her. No special treatment for Ian. He's your *enemy* now."

I shoved her back in good spirits, "I don't know what you are talking about."

"Apprentices—report to your teams now! You have two hours and a limited number of supplies to prepare for your battle."

Immediately our factions dispersed. Ella and I followed the rest of the second—and fourth-year apprentices to the shade of a large overhanging peak. Beside its face were fifteen single-horse chariots, a giant crate filled with empty flasks and common desert ingredients used in Alchemy, and thirty-one sickle swords, the most common melee weapon of the Red Desert regiments.

To our right, the third—and fifth-years clustered behind a large mesa a mile away. From the loud voices carrying through the canyon I could sense they were arguing, undoubtedly trying to decide a leader.

"Which one of you do you think it's going to be?" Ella visibly balked as Alex joined us at the edge of our group. It had been two weeks since her outburst in the infirmary, and this was the first time they had crossed paths since. My twin didn't appear to notice, however, as he was too busy staring at the others in front.

Most of the Alchemy and Restoration apprentices stood quietly to the side, patiently awaiting the outcome. It was clear they expected the Combat apprentices to make the decision. After all, we knew best what our people were like. The problem was that the role traditionally went to the best fourth-year—only Priscilla, Eve, and Ray didn't appear to agree.

"It should be Darren." Priscilla's condescending voice rang out clearly. "He's better than anyone here. He's a prince—if *anyone* knows how to lead an army it would be him, not some silly lowborn."

"Apprentices are not lowborn, you naïve little girl." The angry retort came from Jayson, a fourth-year and former lowborn. He glared at Priscilla. "It should be Tyra. Last year her advice brought our team victory in Ferren's Keep."

"Yes, but Darren has been training for a career in the Crown's Army since he was five." This time it was Eve that had spoken. "He was going to be a knight commander before he found magic—just ask him. He's had all the best tutors. We all did."

I bit my lip. Well that certainly explained how the three of them had become friends. I had always wondered how quiet Eve had fit in with Darren and Priscilla's more offsetting ways. I knew they had all lived together in court, but now it was clear they had spent many years training together too.

No wonder I'd felt so underprepared last year. The three of them had been preparing for Combat—or knighthood, at the very least—since birth.

"Fine," Jayson barked, "then let's take a vote. Everyone—not just Combat." He turned to the rest of us, hands on hips. "Well? Do you want a fourth-year who knows how to win or Master Bryon's pet, an inexperienced prince who is only in his second year?"

"I am voting for Darren," Ray said.

"Tyra," Alex and Ella both spoke up at the same time.

The rest of the apprentices quickly cast their vote and it was only after a moment of silence that I realized everyone was staring expectantly at me.

"It's fifteen to fifteen, Ry," Ella whispered.

I swallowed. My sometimes-friend, or the girl that Priscilla didn't want to lead? It was tempting to spite the cruel highborn for all the torment she had put me through last year, but doing so would be a direct slight to the boy that had helped me more times than I could count.

Darren's eyes met mine, amused. It was clear he expected me to vote for Tyra, the same as my brother and friend. And who would blame me? She was older and she *had* led her team to victory...

"Darren." I couldn't let the prince down. Even if I wanted to.

The non-heir's eyes flared in surprise and I was rewarded with a small smile that made my insides melt. *Calm down, Ryiah, you've moved on—remember?* His betrothed scowled. Apparently Priscilla had wanted me to vote against Darren. What was that about?

I didn't get a chance to consider the implication as the prince set to work outlining our first line of attack.

"Only the mentees have the chariots. We have to assume the masters want us to practice the groundwork they've been laying out in our study these past three months. The mentors, of course, will already be skilled in defense—isn't that what you practiced last year in the mountains, Tyra?"

The fourth-year studied the non-heir, dark skin glistening under the full light of the stifling desert sun. It was clear she appreciated him taking the time to seek out her advice, even if she wasn't a leader. "We learned how to hold off a siege," she affirmed, "but my team won last year concentrating our strike on a small section of their barrier where their weakest apprentices were located."

Darren nodded. "I am sure the mentors will be prepared for an attack like that this time. More than likely they'll alternate fifth—and third-years down their line instead of keeping all of their weakest in one spot, but I wonder... Last year where did they keep their Restoration and Alchemy apprentices? Were they helping the defense, or were they hidden away with the leader?"

"Hidden."

Darren smiled to nobody in particular. "Perfect." He straightened and faced the rest of our group. "That's how we'll beat them. *All* of our factions will charge—not just Combat.

"Restoration, those chariots all hold two riders. Each one of you will be paired with someone from Combat. You have two jobs: you will steer the cart and see that your partner is safe. The Combat apprentice will be busy leading the strike so if things go wrong it will be your job to turn the cart around and heal them when it is safe to do so.

"I want Alchemy to start preparing any airborne potions you can think of: liquid fire, fog, sludge, anything that can blind the enemy or help break down their defense. Make as many as you can and store those in flasks in each of your carts... Each of you will lead a second chariot strike behind the Restoration-Combat teams. Should things go wrong you will throw use those flasks to startle the enemy, and give the rest of us a chance to escape.

"Combat, you already know your role. Each one of you has practiced long castings since we arrived. I want you to use whatever long-range weapon you are most comfortable with. You are going to lead the assault and focus on the left side of the mentor's defense. Once we break it you will immediately seek out the mentor's leader together as a unit, cutting your way through with the sickle swords we've been provided."

For a moment there was absolute silence. I was incapable of doing anything but stare. Darren had plotted an entire battle in minutes. Jayson and Tyra were speechless. Even in our lessons mages were only required to think for their faction. It was the reason all the regiments had a knight as commander. A mage, traditionally, did not have the training to lead large numbers of men.

"We might actually win this," Ella murmured.

"Now, the first thing I need everyone to do is to find a partner for the chariots."

Master Byron was counting down from sixty—and we had ten seconds to start.

My twin readjusted the reigns of our chariot with a grumble. "Should have known she'd say no."

"You better stay focused," I warned. "If you are too busy staring at Ella and steer me into a mentor's javelin you will be very, *very* sorry."

"THREE."

"But Ronan—"

"TWO."

"He beat you in the first-year trials," I hissed. "If anyone can protect her it's—"

"ONE."

The chariots took off. Three rows of carts and horses took off across the sandy plain, trampling brush and dirt as we charged the leftmost enemy lines. Alex and I, along with the rest of the second year mentees, rode at the center of the formation. Fourth-years maintained our lead and the Alchemy apprentices covered the rear.

Though I didn't look I knew Darren was watching from the top of a southern butte behind us. As our leader, he needed to observe from a distance. Should something go wrong he would be safe from enemy fire. The prince could still shout commands using magic to amplify his voice, and if we needed him, he would join us.

As Darren had predicted, the mentors had prepared for a strike. Almost immediately I could identify Ian on the far right of their line, stuck between two fifth-years as they held formation. The Alchemy and Restoration mentors hid behind those of Combat. I could see their leader Caine at the very back of the defense, a black armband fluttering in the dry canyon wind.

The mentors weren't taking any chances. The mentees had been given an advantage with the chariots. Caine had known better than to tell his team to try and outrun our attack…

But he had also made a mistake by only utilizing his Combat apprentices to defend. The third—and fifth-years made up only ten against our thirty.

He was in for a surprise.

I launched into my long casting. Pulse racing, I attempted to block out everything but the sensation of drawing a bow to the back edge of my jaw. I tried to stifle the constant motion of the bumpy chariot as I locked eyes with the leftmost apprentice.

Narrowing my line of sight, I recognized the mentor as Lynn. I swallowed and picked the odd dent in her breastplate to focus on, squinting until it became clear, all else around it blurred.

Then I relaxed my casting's draw, letting the phantom strings slip past as my magicked arrow zipped across the clearing.

Two, three, four… I sent ten castings in the blink of an eye. The barrage continued all around me as Combat mentees targeted Lynn's defense.

At first our castings fell harmlessly, barely grazing the mentors' barrier. But then the portion near Lynn started to flicker, temporary lapses of a strange purple hue that looked like veins whenever a new casting collided against it.

As soon as we were three hundred feet away the Alchemy apprentices joined us, tossing out their fire flasks with a practiced finesse. I was at once grateful all factions—not just Combat—maintained such rigorous physical conditioning. If we hadn't, they would never have been able to lob such distances now.

The mentors' barrier emitted a loud, earth-shattering shriek. The left side began to crumble, a cloudy mass of gray and purple haze. It couldn't hold.

Our missiles began to land hits on the leftmost apprentices. I watched with a shudder as our new castings, including my own, began to hit their intended target: Lynn. Screams began to echo across the desert landscape.

There was a loud, panicked shout from Caine and then the mentors dropped their remaining defense and what little attacks they'd started to cast.

*What were they doing?*

"MENTEES FALL BACK!" Darren's panicked voice shook the canyon walls.

Alex jerked the reins to the side and I clutched our cart's railing as it began to swing wildly around.

Before we completed a full circle the ground beneath us crumbled and caved.

Mentees cried out in alarm as their carts tipped over and fell. Horses panicked and took off in every which direction. Riders were stranded. Mentee apprentices fought to find balance in the aftermath of the mentors' manmade quake.

"Alex, get up!" I grabbed my brother and attempted to drag him away from our splintered vehicle. When the ground broke it had capsized, and while I had managed to roll away unscathed Alex hadn't been quite so lucky.

My twin struggled to right himself, using my shoulder to stand while I guarded against potential attacks. In front of us I could see the rest of our team doing the same: Restoration was retreating to the butte while Combat mentees attempted to hold off the mentors' charge.

We were losing. The mentors had started to push forward with their own castings leading a counter assault. The mentees' first line of defense was dissolving. Fast.

In front of me Priscilla fell to the ground, surrounded by a pack of fifth-years.

"DO NOT ATTEMPT TO TAKE THE MENTORS ON! FALL BACK, FALL BACK, *FALL BACK*! ALCHEMY, TOSS THOSE FLASKS *NOW*!"

"Let's get out of here," Alex wheezed. He didn't have to say it twice. I immediately took off at a sprint—only to realize too late how slowly my brother was following. There was something wrong with his leg. He wouldn't make it out on his own. I looked across the plain to the mentors just fifty yards behind us. The others were emerging from the fire our Alchemy apprentices had chucked, slightly worse for wear, but still formidable. One of the mentors was casting javelins at a handful of fleeing mentees.

I saw him spot Alex…

My twin saw my hesitation and shook his head. "Run, Ry."

I didn't budge.

The fifth-year cast out his spear. My brother ran limping, trying to dodge its magicked course.

I didn't have time to think. I raced forward and cast out a large gust of wind, just enough to knock the mentor's weapon off course. I swung Alex's arm over my left shoulder and began to run-walk as fast as I could.

Just then Ella appeared, coughing and sputtering through the smoke. As soon as she spotted my brother's leg she joined me, pulling Alex's other arm around her shoulder.

Then we took off.

We managed to make it to the butte. I wondered at our luck until the haze cleared and I saw Darren, Eve, and Ray casting defense as our remaining mentees scrambled to safety. They were keeping the mentors at bay.

As soon as we were close enough to hear without shouting Darren pointed to a narrow trail behind him. "There's a gulch just past this rock. Keep following the stream until you find the grotto. I surveyed the whole site from the butte. If you can get to the cave you should be safe, for now. We'll be five minutes behind you—I want to make sure we get every Combat mentee we can first."

I nodded quickly and continued down the path with my brother and friend. I could hear the shrieks of pain and explosions of castings gone awry coming from the edge of the field.

There wouldn't be many of us fighting for long.

It was a half-hour later when Darren reached the grotto, half-carrying an injured Jayson as Eve and Ray shielded his approach. Four more mentees had come in after my group, and there'd been eight present when we arrived.

We were down to twenty. We'd lost eleven mentees in that first charge. Only one Combat fourth-year had made it back, gravely injured. We were not in good standing.

The prince quickly set to work preparing our next move. The first thing he did was assess our condition. There were four of us too injured to run—though the Restoration mentees we did have were attempting to fix that. We had nine left from Alchemy, five from Restoration, and only six from Combat. With the exception of Alchemy—who'd had the advantage of a rear escape—most of us were second-years. We had lost most of the older mentees in the first attack since they'd been leading the assault.

"From here on out every casting needs to count. I made a mistake ordering that foray with the chariots—Caine was too smart to fall for our tricks. We'll need to be much more careful now since we've lost one third of our team. The mentors already have such an advantage..." Darren ran a frustrated hand through his hair. "We are safe here for a bit. Eve and I cast a large boulder to block our entrance that should hold us in this narrow gulch for a while... But there are other ways in and I am sure the mentors have already started scouting the rest of the canyon for breaks in the rock."

"Are you sure they won't just try to break your boulder?" Ruth, the second-year Alchemy apprentice Ella, Alex, and I had befriended last year, spoke up. "The mentors have to know your casting won't hold forever—especially against their own magic."

"Caine is not going to sit around and wait," Jayson groaned. The fourth-year was huddled in the back of the cave, clutching his bleeding side as two second-year Restoration mentees attempted to treat it. The pained expression he wore made me squirm. "Darren is right—he's going to have at least some of his mentors scouting the gulch."

"We've got to do *something*," another fourth-year, Darla of Alchemy, said. "Before that barrier breaks and they trap us. We might have stood a chance in chariots but there is no way twenty of us can take on so many of them now. The mentors only lost one Combat mage, and she was a third-year. If we come across the mentors they will win in a matter of seconds."

"I think we should pick them off one-by-one."

Everyone's eyes flew to me. It was the first time I had spoken.

I forced myself to continue, uncomfortably aware of the attention—although this time at least it was not from Byron's insult. "You say we can't win… But you are wrong. We might be able to if we limit how many can enter the gulch at one time. It's how the northern regiment won Battle of Daggan's Peak thirty years ago." I had read all about it in the history scrolls during my first year at the Academy. I'd even cited it during my oral exam in an effort to impress the judges at the end-of-year trials.

"Ryiah is right." Ray's eyes met mine. "I read the same thing: most of the regiment's knights and mages were engaged in a patrol further north so the remaining soldiers were left to fend for themselves. They should have lost against the Caltothian knights but they ended up hiding in one of the old mining tunnels and picked off the enemy one by one since the passage only fit two men at a time."

A couple mentees nodded in agreement, but most of them still looked apprehensive.

"The gulch isn't a tunnel," a fourth-year spoke up. "It's just a very narrow valley with sandstone walls—it can still fit several mentors at once—"

"Yes, but that is only the entrance we came from—and our magic is blocking it." Darren was talking again. "If Caine sends scouts they will be forced to come around the southern side. The gulch is narrower there, and with so many dead ends it would be hard for them to know which one to take. If we can separate their scouts we should be able to pick them off more easily—as far as I know they haven't ascended the butte yet which means they won't have overhead knowledge of which route to take."

The tight pressure that had been building in my chest was starting to fall away. I *was* right. My plan could work.

*Could it?*

"How do you want us to do this, Darren?" Eve was staring at the prince's shoulder. I'd barely noticed it before but now I could see a huge gash in his linen shirt. The light fabric had burn marks and the exposed flesh underneath was a nasty shade of pink. One of the mentors must have used fire. I continued to stare at the burn, horrified.

My stomach rolled uncomfortably.

"Are you going to be sick?" Ella nudged me.

I swallowed the bile back and prayed my face wasn't as pale as it felt. "I'll manage."

Darren cleared his throat. "I want Restoration to stay here. All of you do your best to heal the injured party and anyone else we send back. There is no purpose in you risking safety now... Alchemy, I want you to guard the front entrance where Eve and I cast the boulder. It will be safer than patrolling, and all of you should have some experience with the sword in case the mentors are able to break it before we return.

Jayson will stay with you—he's too injured to help Combat but at the very least he can keep watch.

"The rest of us will pick off mentor scouts from the southern entrance. We'll stay together until we can get a better idea of whom Caine is sending… It's a long shot, but if we can eliminate at least some of the Combat mentors we might just stand a chance."

"But what about you, Darren? Shouldn't you stay behind with the healers for that burn?"

"You're our leader—if you get caught it's over!"

Darren ignored the others' questions and then sighed. "I need to go with my faction. I would make Jayson too if he could walk. We are only second-years: if we come up against a fifth-year scout I need to know that we are giving it our best effort."

I descended the steep butte carefully. I was all too conscious of how risky it was too climb loose sandstone… but if Darren had done it then so could I. Someone had to, and thanks to my reputation for scaling a cliff during Combat's orientation last year I'd been the first choice now that our leader was injured.

When I reached my last foothold I jumped, landing lightly in the shallow canyon stream below. The rest of my year was waiting for me at its bank. Their expressions ranged from apprehension to anxiety.

"How many did you see?"

"Four. They were together but it looked like they were separating at the fork. One of them was Ian. I think another was Priscilla's mentor Bryce. They were headed toward a dead end. The other two were fifth-years and they were following this stream that leads to straight to our camp… I didn't see anyone else following, but it was hard to see past that crag."

"Alright. I want Eve, Ray, and Ella to take the two headed toward us; Ryiah and I are going to go after Ian and Bryce."

Our group exchanged nervous glances. This was it.

Ray turned to Darren. "Are you sure you'll be fine—maybe someone should switch?"

"You three have the fifth-years." The non-heir stiffened. "I am sure Ryiah and I will be able to take on two third-years, injuries and all."

As soon as we had parted ways and started down the trail I spoke up. "So what is our strategy?"

Darren's eyes met mine and then he hunched over, ribs shaking with laughter.

"What is so funny?" I demanded.

"Nothing." He was fighting to keep a straight face.

I stopped walking and grabbed him by his collar, careful to avoid his shoulder.

"I'm sorry," he said grinning down at me, "I just thought the plan was obvious."

"What are you talking about?" I was instantly suspicious. Did he expect me to take on two mentors all by myself? Why would *that* be hilarious? Unless he was looking forward to watching me get beat to a bloody pulp?

"Ian. He's the best third-year—despite the fact he jokes too much and can't pain cast."

"And?"

"And I want you to distract him while I get rid of Bryce."

"You take the weak one and leave me with Ian?" I glared at him. "Are you mad? *You* are the best second-year and the only one that would stand a chance against him!"

"Yes, but I would still lose to him, Ryiah. I've used up too much magic. You would too—*if* you were fighting him. But you are not going to fight him."

"So I'm just—what? The sacrificial bait?"

"No."

"Then *what*?"

Darren's eyes twinkled mischievously. "You are going to fake an injury. I am going to cause a distraction that gets Bryce away and you are going to convince Ian to come help you."

"Help *me*? He's a mentor, Darren! He's not on our team!"

"It doesn't matter." Now he was smirking. "Ian will help you anyway. That third-year has a blind spot where you are concerned. I am willing to take our chances on him falling for your little trap. I'll ambush him while he's distracted and then you and I will both take on Bryce together."

"Ian is not going to be fool enough to fall for that!"

"Do you have a better plan?" The prince's gaze fell to my mouth. "Or are you just going to stand here and argue?"

Two spots of red appeared on my cheeks. "You are asking me to fight dirty!"

"Stop being so self-righteous," the boy drawled, "and just say you'll do it."

"You arrogant, conceited…" I was at a loss for words.

Darren's eyes met mine in amusement. "Yes?"

I glowered at him. "Fine! *Fine!* We'll do your ridiculous plan!" *Was this always how it was going to be for us?* I dropped his collar. "I don't know why it is so difficult to be friends with you."

Darren grinned. "Because it's us, Ryiah." Then he pointed to the edge of our trail where the passage became entirely paved in sandstone. A soft light reflected off the walls and into the bright blue sky above. It was just past those rocky structures that our enemy awaited. "You ready?"

I sighed. "As I'll ever be."

"Ian! *Ian!*" I whisper-shouted as loud as I dared. Bryce was just two hundred yards away, investigating a mysterious noise that had come from whatever Darren had just casted. The non-heir was slowly edging his way out of the shadows as the curious third-year passed him, searching for the source of the sound.

"Ry? Is that you?" Ian had turned and was peering into the entrance of the small cave-like formation I was hiding in. "Why are you calling me? I'm not on your t—"

"Ian, I-I'm hurt." I felt a stab of guilt as I whimpered the lines I had recited many times in my head. "I got lost—m-my team doesn't know where I am… I need to go to the infirmary and I c-can't walk." Then for good measure: "Ian, I-I think I b-broke my leg."

I was ashamed to say that I really did sound like I was crying. *Curse you, Darren,* I thought, *for making me do this!*

"Okay, Ry—I'm coming. Just stay still!" The curly-haired third-year was inside the cave in seconds, hazel-green eyes wide with concern. "Ryiah," he said, "I don't even want to think what would have happened if you'd been trapped here all day!"

My words were stuck in my throat. Shame squeezed at my chest. I couldn't remember why it was so important to win anymore. Ian looked so concerned...

I wanted the charade to end.

"Ian…" I could see Darren slowly approaching. He was close now.

"Can you stand?" Ian kneeled down to take my wrist and examine my "bad" leg.

I swallowed, hating myself. *Ian run. Ian, get out of here before it's too late!* "Ian, I'm sorry."

"Why should you be sorry?" He glanced up so that his eyes were level with mine. His humor was gone, and in its place was an emotion I couldn't place. The third-year kept his hand on my wrist, swallowing.

"Ryiah…"

There was something strange about the way he was looking at me.

"Ryiah," the third-year repeated softly, "there's something that I've—"

A thunderous wind roared across the cave and Ian was sent flying face first into the sandstone walls. He crumbled to the floor, unconscious.

"*Darren!*" I shrieked. "*Why would you do that?*"

The non-heir appeared, looking harried. "Come on, Ry, we've got to get moving."

"I can't just leave Ian here like this!"

The non-heir crooked his head to stare at me. "Ryiah, we talked about this. He'll be fine. The healers will come soon enough. We have to—"

"Well, well, if it isn't the princely leader and his assistant," a frosty voice drawled.

Darren and I almost knocked into each other in our haste to spin around. *Too late.* Caine was standing at the entrance of the cave, flanked by two fifth-years and Priscilla's mentor Bryce.

"Caine." Darren's voice was emotionless. "I should have known."

"Really, Darren, you think I'd just send in two defenseless third-years for you to pick off one at a time?"

"I had hoped you might. You never were known for your brains."

"Well I *know* you, Darren." The fifth-year smiled coldly. "I knew if I sent in two scouting parties you would send your best men after the fifth-years... But you would be too proud to stay behind when you saw a harmless pairing of third-years, even *with* that burn I gave you earlier. I figured you would go in alone but I see you had some sense to bring along this one as well... Not that it matters one bit since you both will be surrendering now."

"Ryiah." Darren's voice was low as he reached for his weapon. "Get behind me."

"Are you joking?" I whispered. "I'm fighting with you!"

A flash of blinding light lit up the cave and a thunderous roar filled my ears. Flames covered every inch of the rocky enclave from floor to ceiling. They stopped only inches from Darren and I. I gasped as I realized the cause.

Darren had thrust the curved end of his sickle sword into his open wound, blood spilling out across the stone floor as he cast out a barrier to hold the three fifth-years' casting back. He was pale and his defense was trembling.

Small spurts of smoke and ember were starting to break his casting's hold.

I barely had time to think before I grabbed Darren's hand and joined his magic with all the force I could summon.

"Don't—" Darren began, undoubtedly remembering what had happened during my first-year trials the last time I had attempted to pain cast.

*Control*, I told myself, *my pain does not control my magic— I do*. I thrust my right arm through the barrier, pushing it into to the hungry flames beyond. A thousand types of pain coursed through me, red-hot fire eating away at my flesh and my skin and my blood until my entire body was filled with a violent need to release.

Hysteria and agony rose up, fighting to take control of my casting. I fought them and clung to Darren with everything that I had. The flames seemed to pour right into my veins, an army of fire exploding all over my insides, drowning me.

My magic was a wild stallion raging within, rearing up against its prison of ember.

Shadows danced across my eyes, a red and orange waterfall of flame. My legs were quivering and the pain was too much. I felt the wave of fire taking control and the magic deep within me, threatening to explode-

Darren's hand tightened on my own. A sharp swell of coolness flooded my skin, erasing the fire and pain and returning me to myself.

We pushed back with magic. Together the two of us began to take one shaking step, and then another, until Caine and his friends realized too late what was happening.

The fifth-years and Bryce hastily released their casting, but the force Daren and I had cast was too much. The four mentors were sent sprawling into the sand. Two of them were instantly knocked unconscious, colliding against a short boulder. Caine and Bryce crawled backward on their arms in an effort to escape.

Darren dropped to his knees. Our casting fell. I found myself struggling to stand. When I tried to call on my magic there was nothing left to summon.

I grabbed Darren's blade—my own lost during the chariot attacks earlier—and dragged it toward the fifth-years' leader. My legs shook so badly I stumbled halfway across, slipping with a cry as my burned hand grated against sand.

I attempted to push myself up—but the pain was too much. I couldn't do it.

Caine began to laugh, dirt and blood spilling from his mouth.

"Surrender, Caine!"

The fifth-year stopped laughing and I blinked. Three dark figures emerged from the sandstone passage behind us. As they drew closer I recognized Ella, Eve, and Ray—all of them a bit bloodied and bruised, certainly worse than when we had parted an hour before. Ray was limping and Ella favored her arm, but the three still looked heroic under the full light of sun.

They looked even better when they cornered Caine and held three curved blades to his throat.

The fifth-year spat at them and tore off his black armband.

*We won.*

Loud whoops filled the air. I heard—rather than saw—Darren collapse behind me.

The others ran over to check on their fallen leader. Ella found me and helped me up. I barely had time to point at the cave and murmur "Ian" before my vision, too, faded to black.

# Chapter Four

"Ry, how are you feeling?"

Opening my eyes I saw that I was in the infirmary and surrounded by rows of empty cots. Beside me was Ella. I wrinkled my nose. The room smelled strongly of herbs and rubbing alcohol, and it was unusually chilly compared to the warmth of the barracks.

I sat up right away and stared down at my arm. There was only the slightest tinge of pink. Nothing else to suggest I had held it into a fire for several long seconds, and not a single muscle in my body ached. I felt as if I'd woken up from the most restful night's sleep—something I had never once experienced since I'd arrived in the desert. I took a deep breath. "How long have I been out?"

Ella looked down at me sympathetically. "Almost three full days. That burn on your hand..." She gulped. "It was terrible when the healers first brought you here." My friend gave my shoulder a reassuring squeeze. "Only you and Darren are still being treated now though—everyone else's injuries weren't as severe so they've already returned to the barracks."

"I'm surprised Byron let the mages heal us." I scanned the room, looking for the prince. I spotted Darren near the back, still sleeping and covered in blankets. One of his arms was hanging off his cot. He looked almost childlike with his black bangs falling to the side and his lips slightly parted. *He looks so innocent*, I noted wryly. Darren *never* looked innocent.

"Well, we *are* departing tomorrow for the Academy."

I had forgotten.

Ella continued: "None of the masters wanted a bunch of crippled apprentices holding up our progress to the school—it already takes ten days to reach Sjeka, as is. Besides, Loren told me they always do this after the mock battles. He actually said that we had *less* injuries than the one last year, can you believe it?"

I gaped. "Less injuries?"

"I know. My thoughts exactly." Ella grinned at me. "I'm excited for the feast tonight—the masters haven't formally congratulated the mentees yet and tonight the whole regiment will be there when the Commander gives her speech. Loren said they usually have it the second night but since you and Darren were still in the infirmary they decided to wait until the two of you were healed." She chucked. "It wouldn't be right if our two victors were unable to attend."

Memories of that battle in the sandstone gulley came flooding back. Many things stood out—Ian touching my face, Darren casting our barrier, the pain of fire, the sudden strength when I had been able to take control of my pain casting…

And Ian. Ian flying headfirst into that stone wall.

"So everyone else has recovered?" I found myself suddenly anxious. Where was Ian? Did he realize that I had tricked him?

*Did he hate me?*

"Of course they have."

I glanced at Ella and the carefree expression on her face. She had started talking about the feast tonight, going on about how excited she was for our win. I wanted to ask about Ian, but I was afraid of what she might say. Even though Ian *had* been on the opposing side, I didn't think she would approve of my tricking him. It was a rotten thing to do to a friend.

But I had wanted to win, and Darren's plan had been easy. Too easy.

If only Ian hadn't been so eager to help me, so innocent.

*If only Ian had stabbed me in the back before I had stabbed him.*

Priscilla found me later that evening, just as I was changing out of my infirmary clothes and into the outfit Ella had left behind. It would be the first dress I had worn since our naming ceremony, and the first one I could call my own. One of the perks of being an apprentice. With my new income it had been easy for Ella to talk me into buying it. Something special that an apprentice could wear to indicate her new status.

"Caine told me you and the prince spent a lot of time together in that canyon."

I spun around and found the highborn looking me up and down with distaste. "What do you want Priscilla?" I asked exasperatedly.

"You need to leave Darren alone. Whatever idealistic notions you've got running around in that head of yours, the prince will never leave me for a lowborn."

Not this again. "Priscilla—"

"My father is the wealthiest baron in the realm. Darren *needs* this marriage." She frowned. "Jerar has the greatest army in the world but if the Crown wants to keep it that way they will need my dowry. No amount of infatuation will change that."

"Just what exactly do you think happened between him and me?" I pulled the dress over my shoulders, marveling at the fluid blue shimmer. It was easily the prettiest thing I owned.

Priscilla just scowled at me. For all her words, I could still see the resentment radiating from her form. I wondered if this was really about Darren—who had never shown the slightest interest since we joined the apprenticeship—or the fact that I had done well in the mock battle while she'd been forced to surrender almost immediately.

I had come a long way since the two of us had first met. I wondered how I would feel if I was her—the beautiful girl who had once been third in our faction, now easily the worst one here. She was still an apprentice—and she still had Darren, but for once I was better than her. And it felt good.

*I'm not that pitiful little girl you bullied last year.*

"If you'll excuse me, I have somewhere to be," I told her smugly. "A feast in your betrothed's and my honor, I believe." I sauntered out of the barracks with the biggest grin on my face.

"Ry!"

The second I stepped out of the barracks my twin spun me around, laughing. "I can't believe you and Darren actually pulled it off!"

"Put me down you big oaf!" I greeted my brother chuckling. "You'll ruin my dress!"

Alex released me and held out the nook of his arm. "Do I have the pleasure of escorting a Combat champion this evening?"

"Am I your second choice?" I teased.

"No." My brother reddened. "Ella was already going with that Loren fellow."

I sighed and put my arm through his. "Then you most definitely have the pleas—" I froze mid-sentence as I noticed the couple descending the steps below us. Lynn, looking delicate and lovely, was being escorted by a certain curly-haired third-year with laughing hazel-green eyes. *Ian.*

My heart caught in my throat. I didn't realize I had stopped moving until Alex was waving his hand in my face.

"Ry?" My brother tilted his head to peer at me quizzically. "What's wrong? You look as if you've swallowed a bug."

I faked a smile. "No, I just spotted Lynn… and Ian." I tried to say it casually but I was pretty sure my voice squeaked near the end.

"Oh right." Alex nodded. "The third-years from your faction. Do you want us to go catch up to them? It's a long walk to the regiment's ceremonial hall, it'd be nice to have some company."

I started to protest but my brother was already off, dragging me in his wake.

As soon she spotted me my mentor waved and pulled on Ian's arm to wait for us. "Ryiah," she said cheerfully, "I am so happy to see you are feeling better! I wanted to let you know there are no hard feelings for what happened on the battlefield…"

I could not look at Ian.

"…You've got to do whatever is necessary to win." She giggled. "I guess I should be happy it happened to me in the beginning. Ian told me he got pounded pretty badly in those caves, can you imagine?"

My face was aflame and I felt like vomiting. I was holding onto Alex's arm to steady myself.

I forced myself to look at the curly-haired third-year who hadn't spoken a word yet. "How are you feeling, Ian?"

Indifferent green eyes met my own gray-blue ones. "Fine."

An awkward silence followed and Alex finally broke it—only to make things worse.

"Say, Ian, I don't think I've met your enchanting lady this evening? Who might she be, and is she taken?"

Ian's eyes fell away from me and he smiled at my brother. "Lynn is Ryiah's mentor. And she is taken." He reached down to take the third-year's hand in his own and brought it to his lips with a light kiss. "After suffering three years of my charm, Lynn has finally allowed me to court her."

My twin gave a dramatic sigh. "What a shame. The good ones are always taken."

A huge wave of jealousy had reared its ugly head and was raging inside my throat. Ian and Lynn? *Ian* and *Lynn*? *What about Ian and me?* I remained unable to speak for the rest of our walk to the hall, and as soon as we reached it I immediately parted ways with the third-year couple, citing some made-up excuse about finding my seat at the grand table.

I was so consumed with avoiding Ian and Lynn that I didn't even notice Darren and Priscilla standing right nearby.

"Ryiah." The second-year girl stopped me coldly in my tracks. "Ryiah's brother."

Alex gave the girl an incredulous look. "Well hello to you, too. And Darren." His lip curled. He didn't like Priscilla but he loathed the prince. The two of them had clashed last year over a misunderstanding between Darren and me.

The non-heir ignored my brother and met my eyes instead, smiling. "Hello Ryiah, are you ready to be the center of the masters' toasts tonight?"

I should have smiled back, or said something witty, but as I looked to Darren all I could see was Ian in the caves. Ian touching my face—about to say… Something. He had looked at me so tenderly. For a moment I had thought he'd been about to tell me… It didn't matter now. He hated me. I could tell from the way he looked at me.

It was Darren's fault. And it was mine for listening to him… but I wasn't in the mood to acknowledge *that*.

I didn't answer and Darren's brow furrowed. *Good*. Beside him Priscilla looked pleased by my reaction. *I didn't do that for you*, I thought sourly. The couple departed.

For just a moment Darren turned his head back around to stare at me but I avoided looking at him as I took my seat beside Alex.

"Tonight we celebrate the incredible prowess of our mentees. This is the first time in a decade that we have had the second—and fourth-year apprentices win one of our mock battles. I take this as a sign of great potential to come—and I hope all of you will keep Ishir Outpost in mind after you have taken up your mage's robes." Commander Ama looked out at the crowd, beaming.

"That said, there are two apprentices that stood out in particular for their performance. Never have two second-years been able to single-handedly accomplish what it usually takes a whole team to do... They both practiced advanced levels of pain casting with enough control to save their squad. I would like to toast Apprentice Ryiah for this huge victory, and Prince Darren even more so for his excellent command. May great things come of you both."

I held my glass up and accepted the toast bitterly. My victory had come at the cost of a friendship. I swore I would never make the same mistake twice.

"He always did like her best." The good-humored remark came from Alex to no one in particular as I shrieked, dismounting from my saddle to race across the Academy field to a thirteen-year-old boy with blonde curls and lively blue eyes.

"Derrick!"

"Ry!" My younger brother dropped the shield he had been holding and ran at me—the two of us colliding in a hard embrace. I immediately started crying: I hadn't seen him in months and before that it had been a whole year apart.

"I can't believe you're here!" Derrick wheezed. "This place is so much harder than I thought!" He snapped his finger to show me how he cast and I only cried harder. The last time I had seen him he hadn't even known he had magic.

I blinked. Was it just me, or had Derrick's hands gotten a lot larger? And what about his arms? Was he taller too? "You're huge!" I crowed. "How did you go from looking like me to Alex in a couple months?" It was no secret Alex put on muscle a lot easier than I—even if I was in Combat and trained my body a whole lot harder.

"First-year! What are you doing? You heard Master Barclae: *no talking to the apprentices!*"

Derrick cringed. "I hate Sir Piers," he muttered, only low enough for me to hear.

I wiped my tears away, laughing. "I'll find you later—meet me by the stables after your dinner?"

My young brother eagerly nodded and I left the field, giving Sir Piers a gallant wave. The commander squinted into the distance and as soon as he recognized me he grinned.

"Welcome back, *apprentice*!"

They showed us to our chambers and I couldn't stop staring. After the end-of-year trials we had departed almost immediately with the apprentices to Ishir Outpost… Now, we had two months to reside at the Academy, only instead of the overcrowded barracks we had paradise.

As an apprentice we were given all the accommodations a lowly first-year lacked. Private rooms with the softest sheets, personal fires, a maid, and even an overhanging balcony with a view of the Sjeka coastline: jagged cliffs and the white, foaming waters below. The bedposts were carved from rich cherry wood and the cold marble floor was covered in silky furs from the white snow cats of the north.

As I wandered about my chambers I found an interconnected alcove with a tub for bathing and a basin for my hands. In each drawer of a well-made cabinet were freshly pressed cloths for drying and additional blankets for cold winter nights. There was already a small shelf with several books for study and a large chaise for lounging.

"Try not to look so lowborn, Ryiah." Priscilla's cutting remark broke through my reverie.

She and one of the fourth-year girls stood in the hallway peering into my quarters and watching me with ill humor. The two of them had been nothing short of miserable the entire ten-day journey here.

"It must really bother you," I snapped, "that I am no longer lowborn."

Priscilla sniffed. "You may be an apprentice but you will never be one of us."

Ella appeared abruptly and shoved her way past the cold-hearted girl and her friend. "You ready to see our new training rooms?" she asked, ignoring the others.

I grinned and slammed my clothes quickly into the trunk at my bed. "You don't have to ask me twice!"

"We did not return to the Academy for two months to listen to you romance your factionmates, Apprentice Ian! If you can't pay attention to your studies then you clearly have too much time on your hands. I want you mucking the stables until we depart next month." Master Byron's irritated voice cut through the slow murmur of the rest of our class.

I felt a twinge of satisfaction as the curly-haired third-year returned to his table with Darren at the corner of the room. It had been hard to ignore the way Ian kept touching Lynn's hand, or the way she blushed whenever he did. The two had been carrying on a shy romance for weeks now and since she was my mentor there had been no escape. It was much worse because I kept wondering if that could have been me, and then I spent the rest of the time hating myself.

Each mentor-mentee was supposed to be plotting strategy for the Master of Combat's current problem. We were given thirty minutes each time to trade suggestions and research using the books the Academy servants had provided. Then we presented our findings to the class going around in a circle. Each time Master Byron chose a winning approach, citing a group's merits and weaknesses for desert combat.

Lynn gave me an embarrassed smile. "I'm sorry, Ryiah, I know I shouldn't be talking to him. I just can't help myself!"

The sweet apology should have made me smile, but instead it just sent stabbing pains down my spine. I felt an unnecessary irritation at my mentor and I knew it wasn't sourced by logic. "I understand," I heard myself say coldly. *Be nice!* I swallowed and forced myself to say with more warmth, "What do you think about a flash flood casting?"

"It's perfect!"

We finished the exercise and then watched as Master Byron tore apart everyone's solution but Darren's. The prince's plan wasn't always the best, but even if it wasn't you would never know from the way the master praised his "insightful thoughts." It was a group effort but it was clear the man had nothing to say about the non-heir's partner.

And, of course, the man had even less to say about the girls. Whenever one of us was up Byron would immediately look bored, and then he would spend the next twenty minutes picking away at our strategy.

"Why does he hate women so much?" I complained to Ella and Lynn later that evening. I had avoided looking over at Ian the whole meal.

"You really don't know?" Loren slid into his seat beside Ella, grinning. From the way his eyes danced I knew he had a story to tell.

"Byron grew up in one of those old families that didn't think women belonged in battle. His great grandfather was actually the Council of Magic's biggest adversary when they decided to change their ruling to let them in... Anyway, fifteen years ago Byron was one of the top contenders in the last Candidacy. He made it into the top three but when he dueled Kara, one of the best Combat mages in the Crown's Army, he lost. Marius won, of course, but Byron was so upset over losing to a woman that he left his wife... There are rumors that he still harasses the Council to this day exclude women from mage studies."

"But he trains women every day! How did he end up a master?"

"Because whether or not he's fair, he's good at what he does. The local regiments all praise the apprentices that have come from his term—male *or* female."

I made a face.

Ella managed to say exactly what I was thinking. "Well at least he's not the Black Mage. I don't think Ryiah or I would even be here right now if he had been on the Council."

A half-hour later I was depositing my tray when Darren approached me.

I started to push past but he caught my sleeve.

I stared at him. "What do you want?"

"Did I do something wrong?" Darren was studying my face. "You haven't said one word to me since that night in Ishir."

*Was* I *the one bothering* him*?* "I have nothing to say to you." I made way to leave.

"Ryiah." Darren reached down to grab my wrist. The second his hand made contact my skin tingled. My heart began to race, slamming against my chest.

I swallowed and hated myself for liking it. Like Ian, the prince was off-limits. I was tired of my traitorous heart wanting things that were taken.

Or, more importantly, people that I didn't *want* to want.

"What did I do?" Darren's words were quiet, desperate even.

I opened my mouth-

"Excuse me."

I jumped as Ian squeezed past us, avoiding my gaze as he did.

Shame squeezed at my lungs.

Darren watched me. A slow anger was spreading along his jaw. "This is about *him*?"

My silence was gone. "And why shouldn't it be?" I countered. "You made me betray him."

"If you had challenged him outright we would never had have enough magic to take on Caine afterward."

"A friend would never have done what I did."

"You are Combat, Ryiah. You can't blame yourself for using every possible advantage to get us that victory."

I glared at him. "You are right. I don't blame myself. I blame *you* for talking me into it! You really are the coldest person I've ever met!"

Fury flared in the non-heir's eyes. "When you are ready to apologize," he said tersely, "you can come find me."

Before I could take one step the prince was already gone.

# CHAPTER FIVE

The next couple of weeks flew by, though they certainly weren't without their awkward silences and angry pauses on the part of my two biggest fans. The prince and his mentor continued to ignore me during our practices. I quickly got accustomed to feeling a sense of shame whenever I was in the same room as them. It was particularly excruciating during our after dinner practice when we performed our pain castings... but somehow I managed to shut out that feeling as the days went on.

Instead of letting their cold shoulders get to me, I was more than happy to spend time with Ella. My friend and I didn't have a curfew or restrictions now that we were apprentices, so we spent a lot of time wandering the small village of Sjeka during our free time. Alex somehow managed to get himself in trouble with Master Joan, so he wasn't able to join us, but my younger brother Derrick did. He was *supposed* to obey first-year conduct, but the chance to spend time with his older sibling was too tempting to ignore. I would have been lying if I said I minded.

"I don't think I'm good enough," Derrick confessed on the last evening before solstice. "I'm afraid I'll disappoint Mother and Father." He swallowed. "And you and Alex."

"Derrick." I reached out to take my little—well, not so little anymore—brother by his shoulders. "You can't—it's not possible. We love you too much to care if you get an apprenticeship or not."

"But you and Alex—"

I shook my head. "It doesn't matter."

"My brother didn't get one," Ella added, scooting closer on our bench. We had picked one overlooking the Sjeka coast—far enough away from the Academy that no one would spot Derrick, but close enough that we wouldn't get lost in total darkness on our return to the Academy. "I still think the world of him." She snorted. "Or I would, if he didn't hound the card tables. But I still love him."

"But Combat's my dream!" Derrick moaned. "And everyone is better than me!"

I gave him a small smile. "That's only in casting."

"But that's the part that matters!" Desperation was bright in his eyes and my heart lurched. I had been in his position one year ago. It hurt me to see him look at me with the same hopelessness I had felt.

"In Ishir I trained with the regiment," I pointed out. "Every morning we spent two hours training with the soldiers and knights, not just the mages. The things those men and women were able to do—it would make anyone proud to come from the Cavalry or School of Knighthood... I know it's not what you want to hear, but you don't need magic to be strong, Derrick."

My brother fidgeted with something in his hand. The odd glint caught my eye and suddenly I laughed.

"Is that...?"

My brother couldn't help smiling. "Yeah."

Ella peered curiously over his head to see what I was staring at. In my brother's tanned palm was a simple copper ring—tarnished in spots and not particularly attractive. It had a thick band with an "R" embedded on its surface.

I had given Derrick that ring years ago. It was actually my ring, and Alex had one just like it. Our parents had given them to us on our seventh birthday. Derrick had only been four years old at the time, and he hadn't quite gotten used to the fact that Alex and I were twins. He had thought it meant that I loved Alex more, and it had upset him to no end that I should share such a shiny trinket with one brother and not the other. Derrick had cried until I'd finally caved—and so I'd given him my own ring, telling him that the two rings now belonged to "both of my *favorite* brothers." I hadn't thought much of the ring since, and I wasn't sure Alex still even had his, but after all this time Derrick had held onto mine.

I thought of Darren with his cruel older brother, Prince Blayne. Those two would never be close. On the other hand, I had a twin who knew me like the back of his hand, and a younger brother who could make me laugh or cry with the simplest gesture. *I* was the lucky one.

"This place doesn't change at all." Alex's amused voice carried into my room as he opened my chamber door without warning.

"Alex!" Ella shrieked. "Get. *Out*!" She grabbed the nearest book off my nightstand and lobbed it at my twin's head.

"What are you..." My brother flushed a very deep shade of red as he realized he had walked in on us getting ready for the solstice ball. Though we were already in our underdress, it was still inappropriate. "I'm—" The book hit his face with a loud slap and he ducked out of the room.

"He is lucky I didn't cast fire!" she muttered darkly.

I snickered. "I think he's lucky regardless."

"Oh you!" Ella punched me lightly in the arm. "You are not helping at all!"

"Well it *has* been months." I sighed. "I think it's time the two of you moved past what happened. I don't like walking on eggshells."

She gave me a look. "You are one to talk. Has Ian said a full sentence to you since the mock battle?"

I cringed. "Fine. How about we both put the past in the past tonight? You don't have to accept my brother's apology—just talk to him."

"And you'll apologize to Ian instead of moping around like a beaten lamb?"

I raised a brow. "You've been waiting to say that one, haven't you?"

She grinned. "Perhaps." The girl pointed to the back of my bodice—which was in a shameless state of disarray. "You haven't been practicing like I told you."

I looked at the ground, guiltily. Practicing courtly manners and learning how to dress like a highborn had been last on my list of things to do.

"One day I won't be able to help you," she teased. "And then what will you do?"

"Wear my mage's robes?"

"Ha."

I had told myself over and over that I would fulfill my promise to Ella. And I really had intended to keep it. But that was before I had entered the grand atrium and seen the two of them dancing. Amidst a sparkling purple glow of the Alchemy first-years' lights, Lynn looked even more a queen than Priscilla in her blood red dress. Lynn's hair was done in a simple bun with two strands falling neatly in front, and she wore a dress of sparkling green and silver trim that glowed like magic every time she spun.

Beside her Ian looked every part the nobleman, and even though I knew he had spent his childhood working for blacksmith parents, it was hard to believe he had not been raised at court. He looked so carefree and charming with his sandy blonde curls just slightly swaying as his laughing green eyes lit up the room.

I couldn't do it. Not while he looked so happy. I wouldn't ruin his evening by dredging up the past. He and Lynn deserved to enjoy their night without an obnoxious, hardheaded mentee getting in the way.

"Ryiah, come meet my friends!" Derrick came running up to me and grabbed my arm, dragging me away from the dance floor and onto one of the benches I had sat with my own group last year.

*The same place I met Ian.* I bit my lip and focused on the introduction—giving my little brother and his first-year colleagues the attention they deserved. I had only meant to stay a few minutes before finding Ella and Alex... but those first-years were so excited to have an apprentice to answer all their questions—especially one so infamous as me—that they kept me long after I had intended to leave.

Before I knew it Constable Barrius was coming around to send first-years on their way. He caught sight of me and recognition sputtered on his face. "You." I was the girl the staff would never forget, and how could they? I had destroyed an entire building.

I paled as the man's scowl deepened.

"You want to know who got stuck cleaning up that mess after your trials, girl?"

"I am—"

"Don't apologize, apprentice, the man is merely jealous he hadn't thought of it sooner."

I whirled around to find a chuckling Sir Piers. All of the Academy staff had been present for the ball, but I hadn't had the chance to catch up with any of them, least of all my favorite teacher.

"Sir Piers!" I wasn't sure whether it was appropriate to hug the older, dark-skinned commander but I found myself doing so anyway. Out of all my teachers, he had always been the nicest—despite his no-nonsense ways and loud demeanor. He alone had stood up for me against Priscilla when she had bullied me in class. The man had congratulated me after the naming ceremony too—but I'd been so busy with my newfound apprenticeship I hadn't had a chance to thank him.

The two of us exchanged amiable greetings as the constable left in a huff. Piers asked me how my training was going as an apprentice and if I liked the desert, and I asked him about his newest batch of first-years. I found I liked the trainer even more; now that I was no longer his student he opened up to me about what it really was like to teach the Academy students and his life as a former commander of the King's Regiment, the personal guard to the Crown.

Eventually we were forced to part ways—the rest of the staff and students had long since departed—and the man winked at me. "This is your last night of fun, apprentice. I suggest you grab that troublemaker friend of yours—Ella, I believe—and the two of you share a good laugh. Once you get back to that desert the hard part begins."

I thanked him and promised to do just that.

I couldn't find Ella anywhere. She wasn't in her chambers and she wasn't in any of the training rooms. The palace bell had just tolled eleven, and after ten minutes I decided to go find my twin instead. Alex was missing as well. *Well, I had told her to talk to him…*

I considered searching for Lynn and Loren, but the first would inevitably be found with Ian, and the latter… well, as friendly as he and I were, it was always around others and we had never had that much to talk about on our own.

*Fine, I'll just go to bed early!* I shut my door and collapsed on my four-poster bed—dress and all—and then proceeded to stare at the ceiling.

I wanted to sleep.

But I was too restless.

I tossed and I turned but it was no use. An hour passed by and it wasn't getting any better. Scouring my nightstand I found one of the small vials I kept packed in my bag. A sleeping draught. It wasn't the ideal solution—usually Alchemy's potions left me queasy—but I did not want to spend the next day falling off my horse on the long trek to Ishir because I hadn't gotten enough rest.

I swallowed the bitter liquid in one long gulp and then lay back down on my bed as I waited for it to take effect.

Everything became quiet, heavy, rhythmic. My eyelids fluttered shut and I was only vaguely aware that I was still wearing my dress…

The loud clatter of a fallen sconce jerked me awake.

I sat up, suddenly dizzy. Someone in the hallway outside was cursing. *Had they no respect for the sleeping?* I tried to lay back down, only to be awaken again by a second clatter as the person tried to replace the sconce and dropped it again.

I stumbled out of my room with a purpose. The chamber door spun as I swung it open and tottered out into the hallway. The Academy's illustrious blue fire torches lit up the passage enough to see door panels, but I still had to squint to see in the darkness.

"Get some decency!" I scolded the shadow. "Some of us are trying to—" I yawned. "-Sleep in peace."

"Ryiah, is that you?"

"What of it?" I grumbled. The contents of my stomach came riding up. *Oh no.* I clutched my ribs. I should have known better than to take a sleeping draught on an empty stomach.

I quickly sat down. My head was spinning. Everything was spinning. I did *not* feel good.

"Are you *sick?*" The shadow approached and I saw hazel-green eyes. It was all I needed. I burst into hysterical laughter and then immediately regretted it. *Could this night get any worse?*

"Where's Lynn?"

Ian started and then shook his head, frowning. "You should go to bed, Ryiah."

A wave of nausea hit me and I swallowed hard. I needed to say something first. "I should have fought you outright," I croaked. "I'm sorry for that day in the desert."

Ian sighed, and the next thing I knew he was sitting down next to me on the cold marble floor. There was silence for a moment—just the sound of quiet hearts beating as we leaned against the wall, shoulder-to-shoulder in shadows.

"I've been acting like a jealous fool," he said abruptly. "You have nothing to apologize for Ryiah."

"But I—"

"You did what needed to be done."

*Wait. Did he say...?* I turned to face the third-year. "Did you say jealous?"

The mentor regarded me grimly. "We are Combat mages, Ry. You wanted to win, and I understand why you did what you did." He exhaled softly. "When we were in that cave... I guess I just thought things had changed between us." He played with a button on his sleeve. "But then I realized it was just a part of your plan, and that you had let *him* talk you into it. I wasn't mad that you had done it but..."

The third-year swallowed. My eyes fell involuntarily to his well-tanned hands, so big and strong. I remembered when he had reached out to touch my face.

"I guess it just felt like you were choosing Darren over me... Which is ridiculous because I always knew you liked him best."

"I don't!"

Ian put a finger to my lips to quiet me. An explosion of warmth ran down my spine, making me lighter than the draught had ever made me feel. My sickness was instantly forgotten.

"You do, though." Ian reached down to brush a strand of hair that had fallen in front of my face. I held my breath.

"Someday, Ry, you are going to realize who Darren really is. He's a prince, and he's only going to break your heart."

"But I don't want a prince!" I protested, suddenly panicked.

"You say that but I see how you look at him."

"Well then you are a fool for not seeing how I look at *you!*"

Ian was silent. The third-year's eyes met mine and I could see the small flecks of gold that dotted his irises. He looked wistful.

"Alex, *Alex*, be quiet!" Ella's loud giggling voice carried across the dark passage.

My head jerked in the direction of my friend, and Ian abruptly stood. "Goodnight, Ryiah," he told me.

"Wait, Ian—"

He just shook his head sadly. Then the third-year disappeared into the dark hall, intent on his room.

Moments later I saw my twin and friend stumble into the light of a nearby flame, the two of them laughing with their eyes aglow. Neither of them had seen or heard me. I watched in silence as Ella attempted to pull away to enter her chamber two doors away. Alex grabbed her, chuckling, and kissed her like he had all the time in the world.

My jaw dropped and I let out an inadvertent gasp.

"What *was* that?"

"A mistake."

"No." I eyed her skeptically. "That did not look like a 'mistake.' That kiss lasted *at least* ten minutes."

Ella blushed. "Ryiah, I really wish you hadn't been there."

"It wasn't my intention." I yawned loudly. My head pounded awfully: the draught had been a terrible idea. I would be feeling sick the entire ride out and this time we would be in snow for *at least* three days before we passed into warmer climate.

Looking out at the freezing landscape I shivered and wrapped myself tighter in my furs. At least in our morning practice we'd been able to stay warm by activity; now there was nothing to keep my blood flowing as I sat astride my mare for ten hours at a time.

I *hated* being cold. I considered casting a small fire in my hand to keep warm, but I knew if Byron caught me he'd be livid. I needed to learn to deal with the elements the same as everyone else. When I was serving in a regiment someday I'd be asked to conserve my powers for battle. "Wasting magic on mundane comforts" could be the difference between victory and defeat.

The irony was that Ella hated the cold even more than me—yet she seemed blissfully ignorant, undoubtedly brought on by her happy daydreams regarding my twin.

"Why were you in that corridor anyway?"

Ella's question brought me back to focus, but I blanched at responding so close to the others. We were riding out in a two-columned formation and the icy winds made it easier for people to listen than talk. I didn't want the whole faction hearing about my strange run-in with Ian, or how I had come so close to begging him to leave Lynn… Or how he had insinuated I still had feelings for Darren. *That* would be the worst humiliation of all.

"I cast a sound barrier," Ella told me quickly, "why else do you think I would have been willing to discuss Alex?"

I glanced around our surroundings. I couldn't see anything. "Where? *How*?"

"It's something I taught myself years ago," she explained, "you can't see it because it's intended to deflect noise, not sight." She grinned. "Watch this!" The girl leaned back in her saddle and clapped loudly behind her.

*Nothing.* There wasn't a sound. But there should have been—especially when Priscilla turned around from her saddle and opened her mouth to make a crude remark to Ella for interrupting her quiet.

I made a mental note to ask Ella how to cast that barrier in the future. That skill would be very valuable—especially if it meant that private conversations would actually stay private, and that I'd be able to block out Byron and Priscilla's insult.

I took a deep breath, and then proceeded to detail the rest of the previous night—not sparing myself as I described what had been said between Ian and I. When I was finished she didn't look surprised.

"You can't blame him. He's afraid of getting hurt."

"I would never hurt him!"

Ella shook her head smiling sadly. "Ryiah, you can lie to him but not to me. You still like Darren."

I swallowed, a lump stuck to the bottom of my throat. "But I don't want to," I finally said. "And I do care for Ian. I don't fancy myself naïve, it's Ian that I want."

"But that's not enough. You need to show him." Her eyes were somber. "He might be weak enough to listen to your words, but he won't believe them until you put his fear to rest."

"But he is avoiding me!"

"Find a way, Ryiah. If you really want Ian, you will find a way."

"Is that what you told Alex?" I stared at her wonderingly.

"Yes. But like you, I'm not sure your brother will know how. It's an easy thing to want someone, it's another to love them."

# Chapter Six

"When we reach the barracks I expect each one of you to brush down your steed and put your tacks away prior to settling into your meal." Master Byron's voice rang out clearly in the frigid desert air.

I rubbed my numb hands, teeth chattering. So much for a warm desert—the plains we had passed through had been better. Who would expect the hot sands of Ishir to be so cold in January? Glancing around I saw the rest of the factions giving out small puffs of warm breath: the only source of heat for miles.

We had just passed through the Red Desert Gate and we had ten more miles before we would reach the city's outpost. The giant gate was the only manmade barrier in the entire bluff wall separating Red Desert from the rest of Jerar.

The sudden thundering of hooves drew me from my thoughts. I stared out into the darkness—searching for the source of the noise, half-wondering if we were being attacked—when I spotted one of the Ishir Regiment riders galloping toward us.

"Master Byron, Master Joan, Master Perry!" the man practically fell out of his saddle as he pulled to a sudden halt in front of us.

"What is it, soldier?" The Master of Alchemy nudged her horse forward to peer down at the breathless young man. "Is something wrong?"

"Ma'am, we've just received new orders. Commander Ama asked me to come find you right away. The Red Dune bandits have taken over the Mahj salt mines again. The local infantry couldn't hold them off—we suspect they're using magic—and our whole regiment has been ordered to help!"

Perry sighed loudly. "Well there goes any semblance of sleep."

Master Byron informed the soldier that we would join the commander and her men at once—just as soon as we exchanged our mounts for fresh ones at the nearest village. When the soldier departed the Master of Combat turned to all three factions to remind us that we were now serving as an extension of the local regiment.

"I had hoped we would have a couple of days to rest up before your first patrol—but it appears you will be starting right away."

It was a two-day journey, Byron added, but it wouldn't be too hard as we had enough supplies to last us the rest of the way there. Once we reached Mahj we would be housed with the rest of the regiment in makeshift tents since the town was already inhabited by local miners and a small handful of desert farmers. We would need to treat our orders with extreme prudence. Salt was a vital trade between Jerar and its easterly neighbors, the Borea Isles and Pythus. We could not afford to lose such a valuable resource.

"The bandits will be less skilled than an enemy knight," he concluded, "but it worries me that the locals suspect magic at play. Exercise extreme caution and make sure to obey *all* of Commander Ama's orders. This is not a mock battle. The masters and I don't want to lose any apprentices in this deployment."

❧

I dug my shovel into the dusty earth, scattering sand and rocks as I tossed its contents behind me. I wiped my brow, shivering and hot at the same time as I continued digging the women's trenches for the Ishir and Mahj regiment. It was hard, dirty work.

It didn't surprise me that while everyone else was setting up camp *I* was the one servicing the tasks no one wanted. Master Byron's dislike had no end to its unpleasant consequences. I longed to be with the other Combat apprentices taking care of the horses, cleaning the weapons, counting the inventory, prepping the cots… but instead I was stuck here. Digging trenches.

Alex had been put to work with the rest of Restoration—there were already casualties to the battle of the Mahj salt flats—and he was busy learning and using his magic to make a difference. Alchemy was busy prepping various restorative and fighting drafts to help with the efforts as well. Both factions were behind the scenes, so to speak, so their masters had let them actively participate in the local efforts.

Master Byron, on the other hand, was keeping Combat as far from battle as possible. "They have enough warriors," he'd chastised our group for complaining, "what the regiment needs is swift hands to help with their camp's upkeep since their Combat mages will be too busy to do it themselves. I am not going to lose *my* apprentices because they are too big for their britches." The locals, of course, couldn't help us because half of them had been barricaded in the mines, and the few farmers that the Mahj oasis held were busy preparing meals for the whole camp.

I groaned. The regiment mages were getting *all* of the glory while the Combat apprentices were stuck playing house. This was not the life of a warrior I had imagined. I knew it was wrong to be jealous—*especially* when I had seen the injuries of Mahj's local command—but it was impossible not to resent the others after months of preparing for battle.

"You would get a lot further if you stomped your shovel blade along the surface before digging."

I paused to look up from my labor and see Darren, holding a water skin in one hand as he leaned against a nearby palm. The non-heir had been one of the lucky ones to guard the oasis instead of performing menial tasks.

I swallowed, remembering the way our last conversation had transpired. I had managed to put it out of my mind until now, but I couldn't help remembering how Ian had said I'd been right to do what I did in that canyon. I had yelled at the prince for helping me win, and I thought I had been justified. But the only reason Ian had been upset with me was because he thought it meant I liked the prince better, not because I had been a bad friend.

Which meant Darren had been right all along. And I had been a bad friend—only not to the person I'd thought.

Following the non-heir's advice I loosened the topsoil first and was surprised how much easier it was to dig. *Right again*. Sighing, I set down the shovel and approached the fig tree Darren was residing under.

I opened my mouth to speak but Darren spoke first. "I'm sorry."

I shook my head. "No, it's me who should be apologizing."

"Ryiah." Darren's garnet eyes met mine and he smiled. It was the first time I had seen him smile without the trace of sarcasm I was so accustomed. I lost my breath. "Just let me apologize."

I started to say he didn't need to, but the way he was looking at me made the words get lost in my throat.

"I was right to tell you to trick Ian. Any Combat mage would have pressed the same advantage—"

*I should have known he wasn't going to apologize.* The tightening in my chest deflated, just a little.

"-And while I *know* I was right, I still find myself thinking I was wrong. Because of you, Ryiah." His gaze fell away and he was staring at the back of his hands. "I hurt you by hurting him, and for that I'm sorry."

My jaw dropped.

"You want to know something ironic?" Darren's lips were twisted in a grimace. "Until you, I'd never really had a friend. Not really."

"But Priscilla and the others—"

"Priscilla? Our lives are forever bound because of her parent's wealth and the fact that my father covets it. I understand her, but I don't respect her. Most of the highborns are like that." He laughed, but it was bitter. "Eve is different. Her father is the commander of the Crown's Army and we grew up to similar expectations. We aren't close, but..." Darren exhaled slowly. "But I'm close to you. Or I want to be, but I keep making a mess of things every time I'm around you. I respect *you*, Ryiah. I told you last year you were the one good thing about the Academy and I meant it. You aren't like anyone else here, or any person I've ever met. You've overcome so much and yet at the end of it you are still kind. You still *care*." He ran a fist up his jaw and through his hair. "I'm not like you. I've never cared about keeping relationships or sparing people's feelings. All I've ever cared about is power: how to get it, and how to keep it. I told you as much when we met."

"Darren," I said softly, "you don't have to explain yourself."

"But I do." His jaw clenched. "See, Ryiah, I didn't care that Ian was your friend. I knew what I was suggesting. I knew it would make things difficult for you and I'd be lying if I said there wasn't more than one motivation in mind. Even after you did it I was happy. We'd won. I'd got what I wanted."

Darren's eyes locked on mine. "I was fine right up until you stopped talking to me. All of sudden I *cared* what someone thought of me. Because we are friends. And making you miserable and angry makes me miserable and angry. I don't want to be the person to make you mad or cry, Ryiah. I want to make you laugh. I want you to make *me* laugh, because gods know you are the only one who can. So, yes, I am sorry, I am sorry because even if I was right, I was also wrong. And I'd rather lose a battle than your friendship."

"It would take more than that to lose me." It was the only thing I could think to say. I'd never seen this side of Darren before. For all the time I'd known him he had kept his feelings bottled up under a layer of sarcasm and wit. I'd never heard him speak so openly. I knew I cared for him—probably more than I would ever admit—but to hear what I meant to him—even if it wasn't what I wished—still touched me.

His eyes flared in the shadows. "Do you really mean that?"

I nodded and then bent down to adjust a bootstrap, more to busy my hands than anything else. When I finally straightened I saw Darren watching me, a strange expression on his face.

It made my blood pound loudly in my ears. I bit down on my lip, hard. My eyes were glued to his and I was hit with an overwhelming desire to close the distance between us, to reach out and take his hand in mine…

*"You still have feelings for the prince."*

*"It's Ian that I want."*

Was it? Was it really?

"Ryiah." Darren suddenly dropped my gaze, looking anywhere but my face. "If things were… If they were different—"

"Help! *Help!*" The silence was broken by screams coming from the other side of camp. Darren and I immediately broke into a run.

We caught up to the rest of our faction to find several Mahj soldiers retreating from the northern trail, large burn marks up and down their arms. And blood. Lots of blood. It was pouring down their faces, chests, legs, *everywhere.*

I immediately felt sick.

"The raiders," one of the men wheezed, "they have *magic!*"

"O-only ten of them," a woman soldier coughed. "But too much power! And t-too many!"

"Where's Master Byron?" Caine's cold voice rang out clearly. "We have to help!"

"He's with the Ishir regiment." Darren took a step forward. "They needed help recovering the southern mines."

"I-it's not the southern ones the raiders are a-attacking now!" another soldier choked. "We can't hold them off—not without mages of our own! We can't wait for reinforcements and they are destroying our mines!"

"Then we will help you." Darren spoke decisively.

"Thank you." The man collapsed to the ground.

I saddled my horse with trembling hands. I suddenly didn't feel so sure of myself. All this time I had been so eager to fight and now I didn't know why. There was nothing exciting about battle and any injuries I got now would not be so quickly attended to. Any one of us could die out there.

I tried to calm my frantic nerves as I checked the reins and tucked my sickle blade into its curved sheath, hiding a dagger in the padding of my left ankle. Thankfully I was dressed for battle. I was already wearing pale linen breeches and a riding shirt that was the norm of the desert peoples. I tightened the belt at my waist and wished vaguely desert fighters wore armor. I felt exposed with no chainmail and only a thin wooden shield to carry. Desert nomads and raiders fought by agility and wore clothing suited to their environment.

I hope that still applied in winter.

"Ryiah!" My twin came stumbling into the stables, fear written all over his face. "Tell me it's not true! Tell me you and the rest of your faction aren't going after the raiders without Byron or Commander Ama's men to protect you!"

"I have to." I mounted my mare, trying to look more confident than I felt. "Byron and the rest of them are held up at the southern mines. We just got report that the northern ones are being attacked—the ones we supposedly recovered two nights back, and they've got *mages*, Alex. One of the Mahj soldiers told us so right before he *died*!"

My brother didn't look happy. He looked angry. "Ry, you need to wait for the regiment! You don't know how many mages they have!"

"They'll kill the others!" I burst. "We have to try and help—"

"But what if they kill *you*?" Alex cried. His eyes glistened and he was white as a sheet. "Or Ella?"

I tried to be brave. "They won't." I felt guilty leaving him so distraught, but Alex was Restoration: he would have to learn to deal with this fear—especially since his sister and the girl he loved were Combat.

*I* would have to learn to leave him behind.

We had been riding for almost an hour when we finally spotted something in the distance. At first it had been hard to see anything in the darkening of night, but eventually the twinkling desert landscape began to reveal itself.

"There!" Caine pointed to a herd of slaughtered camel. There were heaped in a pile of bloody carcasses next to a pair of toppled caravans and just further west were two large mile-long pits surrounded by chunks of rock and large sprawling slabs of white. The northern salt mines.

Almost everywhere were deep fissures that continued to spread, rattling the earth as they ripped across the flat salt beds, scattering Mahj soldiers as they went.

Just in front of the mines was a blood bath. Young men and women were sprawled across ditches and sand, caked in blood and nursing their injuries.

There were still about twenty soldiers standing, attempting to avoid the quakes. They fought to press a handful of darkly clad raiders back. Away from the precious mines and their valuable resource.

They were losing.

The raiders continued to draw closer, only ten in their midst but undeniably dangerous. I could see bright flares of magic spilling from their hands as they continued to target the earth—more focused on destroying the mines than the men fighting them. Already one of the mines had collapsed.

White mists scattered the sharp desert wind. It made no sense. Why were the raiders attacking the mines? How could ten untrained individuals possess so much magic—unless they really were mages as the locals had claimed?

The raider-mages didn't bear Caltothian or Jerar mages' robes. They were dressed in loose desert garb, muted browns and blacks with hoods that fell over their eyes and scarves that left the rest of their face hidden from view. It must have been how they'd been able to sneak up on the Mahj regiment undetected. Blending into the night as the red desert sun left its sky behind.

One of the raiders spotted us. "Leave us!" His voice echoed across the expanse. Magic amplified the volume of his voice. "I give you the same choice we gave these men here. Return to your camps and we will let your people live!"

"Relinquish our mines and we will let *you* live, you filthy bandit!" Caine hollered back. He had assumed the role of command as the highest ranked fifth-year in our group. His stallion fidgeted nervously under the trembling ground, clearly wanting to go anywhere but where his rider was leading him.

"This land belongs to the Crown." Darren had brought his horse forward to join Caine at the head of our party.

"*You?*" The gruff raider looked surprised. Then he smiled wide, white teeth flashing. "Well this is *unexpected*." He laughed hoarsely and roared to his companions: "Friends, the orders have changed: kill them all! Do not let that young princeling escape!"

A thundering roll broke from above and the sky lit up. Screams filled the air as the Mahj soldiers nearest fell to the ground, writhing. Bright yellow shards of lightning tore across the air, crippling each man and woman they touched.

In an instant the remaining soldiers had fallen. Twenty quivering bodies thrashed against the sand as flesh and bone exploded, covering the air with a thick, crimson mist that reached our line up a quarter of a mile away.

"What have we done?" Ella's voice quavered. I didn't know how to answer. Fear had taken complete hold of my body. I clutched the reins, hands trembling and panic coursing through every inch of my skin. Hysterical sobs were threatening to break, mourning the last moments of my life. I was a coward.

The raiders had slaughtered twenty soldiers in a matter of seconds… And now, now they wanted to kill us.

This wasn't a battle—it was a massacre.

And I wasn't the only one who thought it. It was clear in the dread that filled Caine's expression that he hadn't prepared for this outcome. Darren had gone white as the sand. Eve's eyes were wide as saucers and Ian and Lynn looked like they were ready to faint.

I tried to speak, but fear had lodged itself too deep in my throat. We couldn't run. The raiders had horses, and they knew where we camped. They knew we had Darren.

We had to stay and fight.

"S-shield Darren," Caine finally stammered. "We need to p-protect the Crown!"

"No! We need to…" Darren's protest fell on deaf ears.

Another deafening boom and the ground below us caved and shuddered, just as a bolt of lightning shot out from our right. Instinctively the entire faction cast out. Our magic was a large purple globe that crackled and moaned.

The raiders' magic rippled against our magical barrier before finally fizzling and sliding down to the scorched earth below.

"Pain cast!" Caine gasped. "Now!"

"We can't just hold this casting forever!" Darren argued. "We will waste all of our magic!"

"We need to target the raiders one-by-one, like you did to me in the mock battle," Lynn said.

"Leave the second—and third-years here, we have ten of us. We can take them on ourselves!" That was Jayson.

"Our best chance is all of us!" Ian protested. "We have more together than them!"

"But they are as strong as mages," the quiet voice was Priscilla. Even she was afraid. "We are only apprentices."

"Whoever wants to run, *run*. I'm staying."

"No, Darren, they'll kill you!"

"I'm with the prince."

"Me too."

In the end everyone was staying. And we were all fighting.

The first thing we did was dismount—there was no advantage on moving ground and our horses would only hinder us in battle. We quickly laid out a plan of attack, Caine and Darren plotting the course. The rest of us held onto our casting… but the barrier was starting to smell like molten rock. There was a tinkling like glass whenever lightning touched the same spot twice.

It would not hold much longer.

"*Now!*"

On Darren's command we released the casting and separated into two parties: those who could pain cast, and those that couldn't.

The group that couldn't formed a running barrier, long casting arrows and javelins with as much force as they could.

The raiders easily deflected their attacks, choosing in turn to send off their own missile assault of arrow and axe. Lucky for us, weather castings like lightning were too costly for the enemy to maintain.

Meanwhile the rest of us stayed behind. Using whatever blade we had on hand we dug deep into our palms, summoning as much warm air and sand as we could. There was loose earth everywhere: plenty of debris for our casting. We thrust our castings together, allowing the joint power to fuel our magic.

Our dust vortex began to cut across the fissured plains, fast and deadly in its course. The other apprentices were ready and ducked to the side, allowing the tower of sand to pass. The raiders beyond hastily threw up a barrier and dropped their long castings, unable to see anything beyond the fast whirlwind of sand that was blinding their sight.

But then they made a mistake: the raiders cast lightning.

With the heat of the raiders' own magic the vortex's particles fused together and melted. Sand had conducted their lightning, and within seconds the whirlwind transformed into a petrified web of sandglass.

It shattered their barrier.

Searing hot glass streaked out like jagged claws from the sky, piercing the raiders closest. Cries and screams followed. Several collapsed. White dust and blood rose up in a pillowing cloud, a hazy red clotting the air.

The non-pain casters of my faction charged forward while the rest of us released our magic.

I knelt shakily, retching into the sand. Others around me were doing the same. We had reached the end of our limits. If we tried to cast again we would end up unconscious. I took a deep breath and then froze.

There was a rustle to my left.

Darren stumbled out onto the field, determined to help the rest of our faction. I watched him, wishing I could follow suit. How was he still standing?

*The prince always did have more magic than the rest of us.*

Glancing out at the battle ahead I could see the odds had shifted. Ella and Loren stood out clearly with Caine, and the three of them were leading an assault on the remaining raiders. Five apprentices, including Darren, were close behind. Only three of the raiders still stood—but they were burned so badly they were having trouble casting.

I choked back relief. We were winning. Seven dead, three injured...

One of the dead raiders rose, scorch marks trailing like dark rivulets across his face. The others didn't see him—and Darren, Darren was too busy casting to notice.

I gave a hoarse cry but he was too far away.

"*No!!!!!!!*" Caine spotted the raider and launched himself forward, shoving the non-heir to the ground. The arrow embedded itself in the boy's chest.

Caine did not scream. Eyes open, mouth shut, he toppled to the ground, soundless. And then he went limp.

Darren struggled to pull himself up and make sense of what happened. Then he spotted Caine and a strangled scream severed the air. Magic flew from his hands. The raider who had just feigned death moments before dropped, lifeless.

Then Darren fainted. I started forward but my stomach rose up, roaring complaints. Unhappily, I stayed where I was and watched as another apprentice went to help the fallen fifth-year and the prince instead. Caine was gone. There was nothing anyone of us could do.

In the distance I could hear the shouts of the Ishir Regiment. *Thank the gods.* I clutched my ribs and breathed in a gasp of relief. The reinforcements had come.

Galloping forward Master Byron and the regiment mages charged the three remaining raiders, casting heavy metal nets that encased them within seconds. They sent in groups of men to take care of the bodies, the fallen soldiers and Caine, and then, finally, for us.

The last thing I remembered was my twin's face.

Bloodshot eyes. Alex. Screaming. "*Where's Ella?*"

I pointed, and then I shut my eyes.

# Chapter Seven

"He's not eating. He hasn't eaten anything in days." The hysteria in Priscilla's voice was rising. "Please, Ronan, do something."

"I can't—he's in grief. The only thing that will help is time."

"*That's not good enough*!"

"Apprentice Priscilla, if you cannot keep your voice down I must ask you to leave." Master Joan's frosty voice cut through the air like a whip. The apprentice let out a shriek and stomped out of the infirmary tent, flies buzzing all around her as she snapped the flaps shut.

I opened my eyes, uncomfortably aware of the pungent smell of sweat and blood that was filling my nostrils. Thick, foul-smelling hides covered the tent frames. Everywhere I looked, soldiers and apprentices lay in cots. Bandages and vials were piled on tables nearest their beds. Restoration mages and apprentices dotted the room, alternating from one patient to the next as they continued to cast and treat naturally depending on their patient's symptoms.

In the cot nearest I could see Ella. Her dark skin glistened under the cracks of sunlight that were coming in through the entrance and black locks were plastered to her neck. She was already awake. As soon as she spotted me she gave a small smile. "Never thought we'd make it out alive," she croaked.

A Restoration apprentice raced forward to bring her water and then turned to offer the same to me. I drank down the cold liquid greedily and immediately the sharp headache I'd been feeling faded into a minor ache.

"Alex, your two favorite patients are awake," the girl called to my twin at the far side of the room. My brother rushed forward, a thick line of sweat staining his forehead as he attempted to wipe it away—only to smear blood and grime in its place. He looked worse than I felt. I wondered how long he'd been here treating us.

"Ryiah… Ella..." He immediately fell to the floor between us with a thud. His blue eyes were glittering.

"Calm down, handsome, they weren't going to leave you." The apprentice rolled her eyes at my brother's dramatics. "Your sister and lady love just needed some rest."

My twin didn't appear to hear. He kept staring at Ella, and there was something about the way my brother looked at her that made me feel like I was intruding.

"I—I thought I'd never see you again," he rasped.

Ella coughed weakly. "It would take a lot more than that to kill me."

"Don't say that." He reached down to take her hand. I immediately averted my gaze. "Don't ever say that. You have no idea what I went through knowing you were out there, fighting…"

"Just stop talking and kiss me, Alex."

I attempted to stand, ignoring the protests of the Restoration mages around me as I left the two of them their privacy. As soon as I had left the tent I found Eve standing outside, looking upset and staring out at the rest of the oasis in frustration.

"Eve." I walked over to the pale girl. "How is everyone?"

"Caine's dead. Ten knights and one of the Combat mages from Ishir are dead. Half the Mahj soldiers are dead. How are we supposed to be?" The girl's voice broke and I realized she was close to crying.

"Have the prisoners talked?"

"They killed themselves before the regiment could question them. Slit their necks with their own blades as soon as the nets fell."

"Do you know if they were Calothian mages?" I asked suddenly. "Did we find out who they were?"

She laughed coldly. "They were *ours*. It's why they kept their faces hidden. I even recognized two of them from the Crown's Army… They weren't bandits or raiders, Ryiah, they were *rebels*. My father's men. Men I knew. *Why would they do this?*"

"Rebels?"

She drew a shaky breath. "It's why they were so prepared. Commander Ama thinks they wanted to stop the salt trade between Jerar and the Borea Isles. She said this is the first time this has happened—and she is sending a letter to the palace in Devon to alert my father and King Lucius." Her eyes met mine, suddenly anxious. "If some of the mages are leading a revolt then we can't be sure this won't happen again. Who knows how many others they may have recruited. What if this was only the beginning?"

There hadn't been a war within Jerar or any of the neighboring continents since Jerar had signed the Great Compromise almost a century back. There were rumors that Caltoth was trying to expand its southern border, but there had never been a formal demand and the Crown was careful to avoid a war with its northern neighbor at all costs. Breaking the multi-country treaty would end any support with the other two continents and cost us dearly.

Not once had I considered a rebellion in our own kingdom. Unlike Caltoth whose taxes were excessive, the Borea Isles with its high poverty, and Pythus with its stigma against women, we lived a relatively comfortable existence. The three war schools gave our men *and* women the chance to rise from the lower trades to one of well renown. Even as merchants, my parents had never once complained about the demands of the Crown.

"Do you think the mages were employed by Caltoth?"

Eve shrugged. "It's the only explanation. Why else would they turn against the Crown? A mage lives a better life than most highborns."

I swallowed. "They wanted Darren. The second they saw him their leader ordered an attack."

"Yeah." Eve glanced back to the tent—the non-heir was no longer inside but she must have heard Priscilla too. "He's not handling it very well. He feels personally responsible for Caine's death…" She sighed. "I tried to reason with him but I don't think Darren is willing to listen to anyone right now."

The following night, on the last evening before we departed Mahj the locals put together a large funeral pyre for the fallen. Seventy-one bodies were placed on the wooden platforms, and when they lit the fire it burned heavily into the black desert skies.

Each one of us stood quietly at attendance, solemn in the face of our heavy loss. Many of the regiment leaders from Ishir and Mahj spoke highly of their men, and even Master Byron gave an earnest speech for Caine. There was something terrible about losing someone so young—and he had been so close to his ascension, only five months from earning his black robes of Combat. It had been twenty years since the Academy had lost one of their students in training. An apprenticeship was supposed to be a sheltered form of learning, yet the last battle had just proven how even that was not a certainty.

Several fourth and fifth-years retired early that evening, mourning their comrade's loss more heavily than the rest. My heart went out to them. I hadn't known Caine very well, except for that day during our mock battles, but it was clear he had been a promising student and mentor to those who had known him. More than the rest, Tyra and Jayson had seemed particularly distraught during the rite.

I glanced to Darren to see how the prince was faring. I had barely seen him around camp. Alex had told me that morning he was still refusing treatment from the infirmary mages.

The prince looked sickly—too pale, *far* too pale for someone that had spent an entire summer under a hot desert sun. There was a hollowness to his face and his clothes seemed unusually ill-fitted. His eyes were black. No longer garnet, they seemed to me two lakes of shadow, unfathomable against the red pyre of death.

Priscilla took Darren's hand, but he showed no knowledge of her presence. The prince watched the dancing orange flames and I was convinced he saw nothing else.

He looked so fragile standing there. So lost. I felt a strong urge to help him any way that I could. But *she* was there. And there was nothing I could say that hadn't already been said.

After the pyre there was a feast. Local custom dictated food and dance to honor the dead. A flask was passed around the circle. A group of the miners returned, carrying a set of pipes and a couple of local instruments.

People immediately broke out into groups, clapping and laughing as they spanned across the fire in a familiar folk dance. Most of the apprentices watched but a couple joined in. Alex wasted no time taking Ella's hand, and as I watched the two of them spin I felt a hot wave of jealousy sweep over me. I wanted to dance. I wanted to be swept up in the long desert night, sending a farewell to the fallen and embracing the living.

I looked one more time to Darren. The prince was emotionless, numb. I thought back to that night two days ago, under the shade of the palms. What had he started to say? *"If things were different."* They would never be different. Knives stabbed at my chest as I watched Priscilla embrace him, giving him a long kiss on the mouth and wrapping her arms around his neck while he stared into space. She was beautiful, rich, and he was hers. Not mine. Darren would never be mine.

I looked to the other side of the circle. Ian sat next to Lynn, listening patiently as my mentor chattered away. He was smiling—but the smile never reached his eyes. Something was missing. *Was it me?*

He wanted me. I knew it. He had almost kissed me in that canyon, and I had seen the way he looked at me that night in the Academy halls. "*If you really want Ian, you will find a way. It's an easy thing to want someone—it's another to love them.*"

Ella was right. Ian was right. I needed to make a choice now: the cold, distant prince or the laughing friend. And once I chose I needed to fight for it. I would never win the former, and maybe not even the latter... But I could try.

Picking up the hem of my trailing orange and gold-beaded skirts, I stood, brushing the dust out of my loose red hair as I walked across the sand. I stopped when I was in front of Ian, suddenly nervous and not at all myself.

"Dance with me."

Lynn stopped talking to stare at me. My mentor had confusion and outrage written across her face. I felt horrible. I should stop. She didn't deserve this.

But I had said I would fight. I was tired of wanting something I couldn't have. There was someone I could have, *maybe*, but in order to know that I would have to try. Even if that meant hurting someone else.

I remained stubbornly still, ignoring Lynn as I smiled down at Ian.

The curly-haired third-year studied me—a question in his eyes. I could see the fear, half-hidden between flecks of gold. A small grin tugged at the side of his mouth. Then the laugh lines took over and he was smiling wide, mumbling an apology to my mentor as he led me to the floor.

"I don't really know how to dance," I muttered as he placed one hand on my waist and lifted my arm with the other.

"Then why did you ask me?" His eyes caught mine and held them.

"Because I never want you to dance with anyone else."

The music started up again. A wonderful tune, full of stomping beats and carefree whirls. Ian abruptly spun me, and the two of us launched into a makeshift dance with the rest of the crowd. I was reminded of that night we met at the Academy ball—the night he had made me feel like flying.

My dress shimmered as I spun, the beads reflecting the light of the fire and creating a heady rush of glitter while I slipped in and out of his arms. I couldn't stop laughing and Ian's eyes were two embers aglow. My cheeks burned with the fervent rush of the dance and I found myself unable to stop, trapped in an endless feeling of right.

Nothing had ever felt as sure as when Ian caught me and slipped, the two of us almost falling to the ground in a dizzy rush. He barely pulled us up before we returned to the floor, the two of us unable to keep the silly grins off our faces as we spun around the campfire light.

"Are you really mine?" he whispered. His mouth was close to my ear.

"You were all I ever wanted."

He chuckled and dipped me, spinning me around once more. And again. And again until I was a twirling mess of color and gleam.

Then he caught me.

Two green eyes locked on my own and I was unable to breath.

My heart caught in my ribs, a frantic beating in my chest. I was falling, flying, safe.

It was the best night of my life.

The next couple of months passed in the blink of an eye. No sooner had we arrived in Ishir we were called back into the desert. Each time we returned to the outpost we were summoned for another patrol. Thankfully, these ones were a lot less difficult than the first.

Eventually we reached the end of our term and headed out to Devon for the yearly ascension ceremony. It was time for the fifth-year apprentices to become mages.

For Alex and I, this was the first time we would see the capitol and its infamous palace. Everyone always said it was more stunning than the Academy, but I had always found that hard to imagine. Especially after spending two months in its grand chambers as an apprentice.

But the others weren't lying.

"No. There is no way *that* can be the palace." My jaw dropped as I stared out into the distance.

"Really, Ry, you act like you've never heard anything about it."

"But it's just so *huge*—"

"I told you that.

"And *high*—"

"Again, I—"

"And *high*!"

Ella snickered. "Well now you are just repeating yourself."

Far past the rolling hills and rocky crags below was a towering structure that seemed as tall as the clouds above. The King's Road snaked across the clustered landscape, a large paved path that wove around thatched huts, tiny shops, and lumbering temples. Large hanging jacaranda dotted the landscape, beautiful blue and lilac blossoms sprouting from their branches as lush grass covered the grounds in every which direction.

As the road approached the towering palace the landscape shifted, flowering trees were quickly replaced with majestic mountain foliage and a rugged mountain backdrop. At the base of the palace walls was the town square: cobble streets and the wealthy merchant stalls sporting luxury goods and services.

The palace was enclosed by walls that were as tall as the Academy had been. They spanned thirty feet high and were made of the same dark brick material. Every so often an even taller pillar protruded from its length housing the palace sentries with unlit torches and narrow openings lined strategically across.

I couldn't see much of the palace from the road—the walls were too high to see its base—but the structure still doubled the wall's height, and some of its towers even more so. The palace was made up of gray stone and mortar, a lighter shade than its fortification, but it also housed large, stained glass windows at staggering heights that shimmered under the direct light of the sun.

The roofs were darker than the rest of the palace. They cut rounding peaks into the sky. It was so beautiful I forgot to breathe. *This* was where Darren lived? Why had he ever bothered to become a mage? I would have never left home.

"This is what all of us lowborn folk missed out on." Ian had nudged his mare closer to ride next to me. Then he reached out to take my hand in his, sending a warm tingle down my spine as he squeezed. This year was the second time he was seeing the king's palace.

The three of us followed the trailing parade of apprentices down the cobbled road, finally halting at the palace gates. The masters came forward to give our introduction to the local guard, and the soldiers opened the groaning doors to what lay just beyond.

My jaw dropped—again. Beyond the towering gate's walls was a lush garden filled with thriving flowers of every shade, well-manicured brush, cherry blossoms, and a giant, sprawling fountain that hosted a rippling tide of clear, sparkling waters.

To my right lay a long trailing path to the stables, armory, and the massive training grounds. Each structure was in meticulous condition. The guard's bright red livery stood out amongst the large stone buildings. The compound was huge. It housed the King's Regiment and all of the local guard. The Crown's Army, I knew from our lessons, was stationed just outside the city limits. Ten thousand men was much too big a number to fit within the palace walls.

I also knew from our studies that the King's Regiment's housing was in the actual palace itself. As the elite guard to the royal family, the regiment had specific chambers closest to the king and his heirs. There were only thirty knights and mages in its division, but they were usually the most powerful in the land and recruited directly from promotions in the Crown's Army and the Candidacy itself. While the Crown's Army was deployed from time to time to assist with various efforts, the King's Regiment only ever left the palace to accompany the king—or one of his sons like the band I had seen Darren passing with on my way to Sjeka almost two years ago.

To the west lay a continuation of the palace gardens—a place for the courtiers to wander during their residency. I could see highborn ladies-in-waiting strolling the grounds in extravagant dress, with hair perfectly coiffed and powders perfectly pressed and red, red lips. Young highborn men, off-duty knights, and the sons of high-ranking nobility were seen walking the grounds, placing bets and discussing mundane subjects with a practiced flourish that could only come from a lifetime of court.

"Toss me off one of the balconies if I ever talk like that," Alex muttered. We had just given our horses over to the hostler and were walking the remaining steps to the palace.

Ella gave my brother a long look. "You know I grew up here, right?"

His face burned and she laughed. "It's fine, I was never a fan of their habits either."

The four of us followed the rest of our factions in through the palace doors.

By this time I had given up expectation. The second I entered the enormous castle I was ready, and I was not disappointed. Marbled tile covered the floors in elaborate design, a mixture of red, gold, and purple swirl. The walls were dark stone, covered in gold and purple tapestries that depicted various battles and past monarchy in succession. Elaborate gold-plated pillars highlighted the corners of each room as giant stained glass windows let in a cascade of colorful lights…

Everywhere I looked corridors branched into twisting passages, stairs, and chambers in a maze of direction. There were so many twists and turns I didn't know how I would ever find my way out.

"They've got three libraries, two ballrooms, the throne room, a grand dining room for the king's family and special guests, two large halls for the nobility to take their own meals, two kitchens, four servants quarters, a privy at the end of each floor and at least two hundred chambers besides the ones reserved for royalty and the King's Regiment." Ella couldn't contain the irony in her tone as she described the palace—down to the exact count of jewels encrusted in its ceilings.

"Well they say Jerar *is* the wealthiest nation," Ian remarked casually.

"It's second." All of us jumped as Darren appeared behind us. I hadn't even realized he'd been listening. I had thought he was in the front of the group with Priscilla, Eve, and the rest of the highborns reminiscing on their shared childhood.

"Caltoth is the wealthiest," Darren expanded. "We have more land, citizens, power… but they have the ruby and emerald mines in the North."

"That many rubies, huh?" Ian grinned. "Their streets must be paved with them."

Darren's jaw clenched but he said nothing. When he finally spoke there was a stiffness to his words. "The Caltothians are actually very frugal. My father suspects that is because they are using their wealth to build a secret army." He raised a brow. "Though their ambassadors have denied this whenever they visit."

I stared at the prince. "Do you think Caltoth is using their wealth to buy off our mages as well?" I hadn't forgotten the rebel attacks in Mahj.

"I wouldn't be surprised." The prince gave a curt nod to the rest of my group, letting his eyes fall on me last. "If you'll excuse me, I have some affairs to attend to now that I am home."

Darren retreated with a quick explanation to the masters. The rest of us followed the palace servants to the chambers we would be residing in for the next week before the ascension. While the fifth-years' affair would only last one day, we had the six days prior to enjoy ourselves. It was the only respite we would receive each year until our own ascension. As soon as the ceremony was over we would be returning to the Academy with most of the king's court to watch the first-year trials and pick up our newest batch of apprentices.

"Do you want to take a tour of the city after you've unpacked?"

I smiled up at Ian—he had walked me to my new chambers instead of following the rest of the young men to the men's one hallway over.

"I would love to."

"Then I would love to take you." He started to pull me close, but the two of us broke apart when the sound of angry footsteps sounded behind us.

"Apprentice Ian," the Master of Restoration snapped, "you know the Code of Conduct! Do *not* make me report the two of you to Master Byron."

"I'm sorry, Master Joan." Ian gave her his most disarming smile. "I was only assuring Apprentice Ryiah safe passage."

She narrowed her eyes. "You are lucky I detest your master as much as I do—if I didn't you would already be reported for your flagrant sass."

"Yes, ma'am." Ian was grinning. It was no secret Master Joan hated Master Byron for his sexist ways. She would sooner swallow poison than report us. The man complained loudly to anyone who would listen that she and Perry were an "abomination" as female mages.

"See to it that we don't have this conversation again."

"Yes, ma'am."

"Apprentice Ryiah." The woman turned her focus to me. "Since you and that boy are in no apparent hurry, I will need your assistance returning those books to the palace library."

She pointed to a mountain of crates beside her door. "I'd have the servants take them, but we wouldn't want you Combat apprentices to lose that muscle you worked so hard building would we?"

I nodded meekly. *So much for that tour of the city.*

Seven days came and went before I even knew they had passed. In no time at all the robe ceremony for the fifth-years ascensions had passed and I found myself in a crowded ballroom filled with hundreds of simpering courtiers and regiment mages who had come to celebrate the fourteen new apprentices to join their ranks.

"I can't wait until it's us." Ella stood next to me against the large tapestried wall, gazing in earnest at the four new Combat mages wearing their black mage's robes proudly. Their faces were flush with excitement and they were currently in talks with the regiment commanders of some of Jerar's most prominent townships. Whenever an apprentice became a mage they were offered positions in accordance with their rank during the ascension ceremonies.

Unfortunately that rank was decided by Master Byron. Whose bias had led to fourteen straight years of women apprentices ranking last.

But I was not going to think about that now. I had three years to change his mind.

Taking a long swallow of a chilled juice that one of the servants had offered me I focused on the rest of the ballroom crowd. While most of the others were regulars at court whose only interest lie in what their highborn friends were wearing, there was still a large number of mages in attendance—including the Colored Robes who had come to officiate the ascension and offer congratulations to their faction's newest members.

The Black Mage was wearing his signature robe. The silken black layers were etched in an intricate gold design with small red and yellow gemstones dotting its fallen hood. He looked uncomfortable in such lavish dress—probably because mages only wore their robes during public occasions, choosing to spend the rest of their time in more comfortable garb for battle. I could see the two gold earrings in his left ear, dangling under the bright lights of the hall.

I longed to approach him. The dark skinned man with the piercing green eyes had gone against tradition and vouched for me to become the sixth apprentice of my year. That alone would have been enough to make me worship the man, but he was also the best Combat mage in the realm. The man had won the Candidacy fifteen years ago and before that he had served as one of the leading mages in the Crown's Army.

"He won't bite, you know."

I blushed. "You caught me."

Ian grinned and grabbed my arm, dragging me forward to the most important, most powerful mage of Jerar. "Hey, Marius, I think you have an admirer."

I turned the shade of the tapestry behind me as the Black Mage swung around, white teeth flashing. "Is that Master Byron's least favorite apprentice I hear calling my name?" The man's tone implied a longstanding joke.

"Not anymore." Ian nudged me forward, chuckling. "Ryiah has taken over the job for me."

Recognition flashed across the Black Mage's features and he smiled. "Ah, Ryiah, well it is only fitting. That cranky old frog *would* hate the first-year I personally nominated." He held out his hand and I shook it, palms sweaty and unable to breathe.

After a couple minutes of listening to easy banter between the curly-haired third-year and Marius, I finally found the courage to speak. "I am so grateful you vouched for my apprenticeship." I took a deep breath and continued quickly before I lost my nerve. "And I hope I do not disappoint you."

The man raised an amused brow. "My dear, you can not disappoint me—why the prince was just telling me earlier you and he led the mentees to victory for the first time in a mock battle in over a decade." His eyes danced. "Two second-years... why, I might be in the presence of my successor now. What do you think, Ryiah? Are you going to be taking part in the next Candidacy?"

Was I dreaming? This *had* to be a dream. Because in what life would the most powerful mage of the realm be suggesting I was a contender for *the* robe. Not the traditional plain black robe of my faction—but the special robe, the only one etched in gold and encrusted with gems. The one passed down over seventy years among the Candidacy's winning mages. The Colored Robe. The robe that made a mage the *Black Mage*.

"Well now you've done it." Ian grinned at Marius. "She won't be able to talk all night."

The Black Mage was being called away by the other two Council members. He sighed wearily. "Politics again... I apologize to you both but I must return to my Council." His eyes crinkled as they fell on me. "I hope this isn't the last time we talk, dear Ryiah. I look forward to hearing your accomplishments as the years progress... perhaps my status will seem a little less daunting then." Then the man gave a final nod to the both of us and disappeared into the crowd.

"I have never seen you speechless." Ian was watching me with wonder.

I made a face and shoved him gently. "You've never put me in front of my idol before, either."

Ian caught my arm and his hand lingered on it just a moment too long. "Meet me in the library." There was a hunger in his eyes that sent a stampede of sparks stammering across my chest. "No one will be in that drafty old place—not with the feast going on all night out here."

I had to remind myself to breathe, and when I finally did, butterflies were flooding my spine, from the top of my neck to the tip of my toes. It was the feeling I had every time Ian touched me—every time he whispered that he want to see me alone. We hadn't had many opportunities in our constant deployment—but here at the palace...

"I-I'll leave in a minute," I stuttered. "There's just something I have to do first."

"Don't take too long."

The words brought another rush of heat and I flushed. "I won't."

As soon as Ian had left the room my memory returned and I inspected the room, searching for the one person I needed to speak with. I spotted him through the great doors that led through to the grand balcony. While many of the palace chambers hosted small patios of their own, only the main ballroom had views as stunning as the one below. It faced north—directly into the dense mountains below which reminded me of home in its green majesty.

Beside him was *her*. Wearing a splendid dress of lavender and yellow lace she looked like she belonged here: the future princess of Jerar. Priscilla's brown hair was done up in the latest fashion, small tendrils escaping an elaborate twist, held high by rusted gold clips.

I watched the two of them for a moment—the dark-haired non-heir and his betrothed. Neither looked happy, and from the way Priscilla's lips kept moving I suspected they were arguing. I watched as the girl thrust her drink glass into his hands and stormed off. Darren watched her go with a weary expression.

I hesitated. This probably wasn't the best time to approach him. The non-heir had been acting strange all week... but after hearing what the Black Mage had said earlier I felt a responsibility to seek him out.

Praying that the prince wasn't in a foul mood—as he'd appeared to be every day this week—I approached him on the crowded dais. "Darren?"

The young man spun around, shoulders rigid.

"I'm sorry, I didn't mean to startle you..."

Instead of looking to me the prince scanned the crowd behind us. After a moment the tension left his shoulders and his eyes met mine, seemingly relieved.

"I talked to the Black—I talked to Marius. He said you gave me most of the credit for that mock battle in Ishir." I swallowed. "You didn't have to, it was mostly you…"

"I don't give credit unless it's due." Darren's lips held the faintest trace of a smile. "You already know this."

My cheeks burned and I forced myself to continue. "It means a lot—to have him think so highly of me. He's the best mage there is."

"Ryiah." Darren's eyes seemed to gleam in the setting sun. "You have such a low opinion of yourself, but you have no idea what the rest of us think of you already."

"But Master Byron—"

The prince's eyes flashed. "The man is an idiot."

"But he's a master!"

"You can be a great man and still be a fool. Many of our country's leaders can attest to that. Were they still living."

"That's your great grand-parents you are alluding to." I couldn't keep the grin from my face.

Darren sighed. "Unfortunately yes. And they are not alone. People make mistakes all the time—some of us just are in more of a position to leave an impact when we do."

"Have you talked to your father and brother about what happened in Mahj?"

The prince gripped the railing tightly and I could see the white knuckles beneath.

"I'm sorry," I began, "I shouldn't have—"

"They want me to leave the apprenticeship." His words were quiet, angry. "They said it is too much of a risk for me to continue."

"You can't leave!"

"I told them I'm not." He hesitated and then looked to me, suddenly unsure. "You don't think I'm making a mistake? That maybe I shouldn't? Because of Caine?"

"Caine died protecting someone worth saving!" I burst. "Of course you should stay! People want to see their prince fighting with them!"

"But maybe I just put us at more risk."

"Those rebels would have fought us whether you were there or not." I reached down to grab his wrist, ignoring the telltale spark that shot through me as I did, adding earnestly: "You are one of the best apprentices we have! We *need* you to fight with us—not hide out in some palace like a sheltered pr—" I cut myself off, uncomfortably aware of how close I had come to insulting the Crown. It was treason to even say what I'd already started.

But Darren didn't look angry. He looked relieved, pleased even—like I had affirmed what he already believed. "Especially if war is in our future."

I froze. I wasn't sure I had heard him correctly. "Did you just say—"

"Nothing is certain." The prince's eyes fell to my hand on his arm and I blushed, hastily releasing him. "Don't tell anyone, Ryiah. My father and brother are reluctant to say so, but after the news from Mahj there have been several meetings between the Council and the Crown's advisors. They suspect Caltoth played a part."

"I won't."

"Thank you. I probably shouldn't have said anything." His eyes caught mine and he grinned crookedly. "It's just so easy to say things when you are wearing that dress."

I started to nod and then froze as I realized the last part of his remark. "I…" The blood had rushed to my face and I was suddenly very, *very* aware of how close we were standing. My traitorous body was reacting very happily to the proximity.

"What happened to that one you were wearing that night in Mahj?"

"T-that?" I was a stammering fool. "It's h-hardly appropriate for the palace."

"That's a shame." Darren's garnet eyes refused to leave my face and I thought I would burst into flame. "I never got to tell you then—but you looked really nice that night, Ryiah."

Ian. *Ian*. Where was Ian? What was wrong with me?

"I know I shouldn't be saying things like that." The prince made a frustrated noise. "But I am tired of—"

"Darren! There you are! Have you any idea how mad Father is? He just spoke to Priscilla—she said that you are staying!"

Irritation flared in Darren's eyes as he turned to regard his older sibling coolly. "Father cannot make me withdraw my apprenticeship. I'm not you. I have no responsibility to remain at the palace!"

"Save it for Father!" Prince Blayne snapped. Ice blue eyes narrowed on me. "You, lowborn, don't you have somewhere else better to be?"

"I was just—"

Darren took a step forward. "Don't talk to Ryiah like that, brother."

"Don't tell *me* what to do, Darren."

The two glared at one another and I immediately mumbled a hasty excuse and made way to leave.

I was halfway to the library and then I doubled back, realizing I had taken the wrong passage. When I turned the corner I found myself face-to-face with the heir to the throne. Prince Blayne was dressed stiffly in a blood red shift and dark brown trousers. He still had the short brown hair I had seen him with during the first-year trials, and he was wearing a gold chain bearing the signature black hematite of the Crown gem around his neck. Darren had a similar one but I hardly saw him wear it—unlike his older brother who seemed to dress in a constant state of prestige.

"Ryiah, is it?" Blayne said my name slowly, distastefully.

I recoiled. "Stay away from me." I hadn't forgotten what the crown prince had tried to do to Ella. He might be the heir to the throne, but I carried no respect for someone who tried to assault my friend.

Blayne saw the fear and determination in my eyes and he laughed coldly. "Oh, so Ella told you about us, did she? That girl never did know when to shut her mouth." White teeth flashed like a predator. "Not that I didn't try."

I felt a chill run through me and I was at once grateful that Alex and Ella had foregone the ball that evening in favor of a tour of the markets instead. My friend had been afraid of running into Blayne after the ceremony, and it appeared she was right to feel so.

"What do you want?" I was determined to part ways as quickly as possible.

"Ryiah, Ryiah, that is no way to treat a prince."

I said nothing.

"Well, I'll make this short. End your friendship with my brother. Do not get between him and Priscilla."

"I'm not—"

"Don't lie to me," he snarled. "I knew exactly who you were when I came between the two of you back there. And don't think for a moment that I don't know exactly what you are doing… Let me *assure* you, it will not end well if you continue to try."

"I'm not 'trying' anything!"

"And see to it you don't." He watched me closely. "Priscilla of Langli is worth a quarter of this country's treasury in gold. We need her dowry should we go to war with Caltoth."

I attempted to feign shock.

"Don't look so surprised, Ryiah. I already know my fool brother told you. The servants hear everything."

"Well then why are you telling me? I'm just an 'insignificant lowborn?'" I was growing more and more wary.

"I am letting you know that if you and your precious friends want to live to a nice ripe age you will leave my brother alone."

"Are you threatening me?"

"I am simply reminding you there are consequences to your actions. Darren knows them." He sneered. "But lately he has been suffering an unfortunate state of forgetfulness. I thought it was my duty to find you and remind you of the same—since the two of you are so..." He paused. "*Close.*"

"Darren is my friend. Our friendship isn't going to start a war." I folded my arms defensively. "If you are so concerned about him and Priscilla why don't you just marry her yourself?"

"Because I am in talks with a Borea Isle princess, you insipid girl!"

His hand came down before I'd even realized he'd raised it. There was a loud clap and then my cheek was on fire, my face jerked rudely to the left as the crown prince withdrew his arm.

My insides burned red, hot anger threatening to consume. "Hit me again," I gasped, "and I will forget you are a prince!"

He slapped me again—only this time I was ready. I immediately sent out my casting: a full rush of force that sent Blayne colliding against the wall behind him.

"You dare to attack your future king!" Blayne screeched. "Guards, seize her!"

Four of the king's personal regiment turned the corner and grabbed me, muffling my cries as they held me down. Two of them were wearing mages' robes.

A rush of fear swept through me as I remembered Ella.

"Let's see how brave you are now!" the prince snarled.

I attempted to cast myself free and one of the mages slammed me against the cold marble floor. I bit the man's hand and screamed as loudly as I could.

There was a shuffle of footsteps from down the hall, and then the mage who I had bitten went flying into the wall in front of me.

"*Let her go!*"

"Get out of here lowborn, or I will imprison you for interfering with a prince!"

"You can't do thi—"

There was the sound of a scuffle and then I heard someone slam down on the ground beside me. Twisting in my captors grip I saw Ian facedown beside me—there was a large welt on his forehead. Three additional knights and the mage from before were holding him down.

"Blayne! What in the name of the gods is going on in here?" Darren's irritated voice came from around the corner. It suddenly cracked as he registered the scene before him. Ian and I held down and restrained by seven of the King's Regiment while his brother stood idly by, brushing blood off his knuckles.

"Ryiah?" Darren faltered. His eyes were livid as he turned on Blayne. "What is the meaning of this? Let them go at once!"

"Stay out of this, brother. That red-headed one tried to attack me and the boy was no better—"

"I don't care what she did!" Darren yelled. "Let her go! Let both of them go *now*!"

"This is none of your concern."

"LET THEM GO NOW OR I SWEAR BY THE GODS—"

Blayne made a face and with the wave of his hand the guards were called off. "I was doing you a favor, Darren. They should be imprisoned for defying me."

"You think the Council will see it that way if you imprison two of their future mages over a petty disagreement?"

"The Council does not control me."

The two continued their heated argument as Ian and I attempted to stand. The marble below me was slick with blood—from Ian or me, I wasn't too sure. I pulled myself to my knees and started to slide. Ian reached out and caught me.

"Thanks," I whispered, staring up at his split lip and the bruise that was already forming across his right eye.

The third-year brushed back a strand of my hair that was stuck to some blood on my face. His green eyes were filled with concern as he gently lifted my chin, checking for injury.

"Well, brother dear, it appears I was wrong after all." Blayne's cold voice cut through the air like a knife. I immediately jumped and Ian steadied me.

"Look at them."

Darren's eyes shot to Ian and I. He froze as he took in Ian's arms around my waist, but his expression quickly shifted to indifference as he faced his brother again. "I am done with your mind games, Blayne. Let them be."

The crown prince just laughed loudly. He continued to cackle as he strolled out of the hall, a malicious smile on his lips.

For a moment there was only silence. Then:

"Thanks for stopping your brother, Darren," Ian told the non-heir gravely. "All this time I spent wondering what kind of man you were… I feel silly for questioning you now."

"There is no need to thank me." Darren's tone was oddly vacant. My head shot up and I stared at the prince. His eyes were fathomless. For a moment I was sure I saw pain, but it was gone so fast I was sure I'd imagined it.

Ian released me and held his hand out to Darren. "I meant what I said: I am truly grateful. I don't know what I would have done if Blayne had hurt Ryiah here."

Darren's gaze never waivered from my face. "Anything I can do to help."

# CHAPTER EIGHT

"Does anyone have a problem with their role in the strategy I just outlined?"

I glanced around the field to see if anyone did, but, as I suspected, not one person—even Jayson or Tyra, minded. Darren had proven himself last year in Ishir. There had been no other nominations for a leader in the day's mock battle.

"Good. Now... we have one hour left. That should be enough time for everyone to get to their appropriate station along the bluff outlooks. You already have your teams. I expect you to gather as much loose boulder as possible during your off time until one of the others gives the signal fire. When they do, leave your station immediately and come to their aid at once. We will need all the manpower and castings we have to sink the mentee's barge... I don't expect us to lose—we have the advantage, we are mentors after all—but..." The prince's eyes rested on mine, for just a moment, before flitting to the rest of our circle. "But I don't want us to be taken for fools either."

"Is it just me or does the prince seem extra irritable this morning?" My twin followed me off the docks with a shy fifth-year Alchemy apprentice named Barrett trailing silently behind. The three of us were partners for today's mock battle.

"I wouldn't know." Darren and I had barely spoken in months, and every time we had he'd been unusually curt.

"I thought you two were friends."

"We… I think his brother said something to him."

"Blayne?" My brother's tone was full of unadulterated hatred. Ella had finally disclosed to him why she had left court with her parents so many years before. "Why would he involve himself in something that regards you?"

*Because he thinks I'm a threat.* But I didn't say that aloud. "Because a prince shouldn't associate with lowborns like me."

"Well Darren is obviously not worth your time if he believes that."

I was of the same mind. Though it had still taken me some time to accept Darren's newfound coldness. Our first week in Port Langli I had tried to talk to him about that night in the palace.

*"What did Blayne say to you? Why are you acting this way?"*

*Darren regarded me coolly. "What way?"*

*"You've barely spoken to me since we arrived. You seem irritated anytime I try to approach you. Even now, Darren, you won't look at me!"*

*"Did it ever occur to you that I am simply tired of your incessant chatter?"*

*I put my hands on my hips. "You are lying! Why are you lying, Darren?"*

*"So what if I am?" he snapped. "I don't need to explain myself to a lowborn like you!"*

And that had been the end of the conversation. Darren hadn't apologized, and I had refused to ignore his callous remark. I knew there was more he wasn't telling me—but until he was ready I wasn't going to go out of my way to be insulted.

"This is it?" We had reached our assigned lookout, almost two full miles out from the township center.

"It's the last tower west." I pointed to low granite steps that led to a small platform along the port's natural bluff wall.

As the most prominent trading post in Jerar the Crown had made sure Port Langli was well fortified against pirates. Luckily that had been a relatively easy feat: the port was a mile-wide cove surrounded by steep bluffs on either side. It hadn't taken much to build a couple of watchtowers along its rim, each armed with a heavy three-man catapult in case it was needed. Any ship approaching would be spotted before it could enter the bay.

Which was exactly what Darren was relying on for today's battle.

"I can barely see the cove!" Barrett complained. "Why did the prince post us here? The mentees would never sail this far out! The western bluffs are much too steep to climb and there's no beach for them to moor!"

"We'll be the last to see action," Alex agreed.

I didn't reply. I had a feeling Darren had stationed us as far away as possible so he wouldn't have to run into me. The non-heir, Eve, Jayson, and Tyra were all positioned in the towers along the eastern bluff where there were more approachable shores for a warship to breach our harbor. Priscilla and Ray had posts in the port itself along the front of the beach in case the mentees tried to enter directly... Ella, two other fourth-years, and I were stuck on the western bluff: the side hindered by steep cliff walls and a foreboding surf.

My partners weren't happy—and they weren't even a part of Combat. *Thanks Darren*, I thought sourly, *your message is loud and clear*.

"Well, we will make sure to run fast if someone lights their tower's beacon fire," was all I could say. It was cold and windy in our station. The mid-August air was unusually chilly and it had made the bluffs a terrible place to be, especially with the icy chainmail brushing against our skin. No amount of over-layers could shield us from that.

"I'll take the first watch," Barrett offered. He didn't look very eager to gather the local rock for our catapult. I couldn't blame him for wanting to avoid the task. I wasn't exactly looking forward to spending the whole day gathering ammunition until the mentees decided to make their move.

"Can't you just cast the rocks here?" Alex grumbled.

"If the mentees take the war barge Darren thinks they are using, we'll need to cast as much magic as possible to sink it," I replied. "My magic will be needed to make the rocks fly further. I can't waste it on something we can gather locally."

My twin made a face. "I bet his highness is making his partners do all the work."

I wasn't sure that was true but I was in no mood to defend the prince. I elbowed my brother instead. "Come here and help me with this rock, Alex. You wouldn't want to do less than your ladylove. I'll be sure to tell Ella if you spend the whole time complaining while I do all the labor."

My brother's eyes twinkled at the mention of her name. "She really is wonderful, isn't she?"

I rolled my eyes, but secretly I was pleased. Since Ella had given him a second chance last winter Alex had kept to his word. He hadn't so much as looked at another apprentice, and he had kept his flirtatious charm for her and her alone. The two were happy. I could see it in Ella's eyes: she loved my brother, and he her—even more, if it was possible.

It was the way Ian had started to look at me.

*It wasn't the way I looked at him.*

"You and Ian are a great couple." Alex was studying my face. "It's what you want, isn't it?"

"Yes." I took a shaky breath and reminded myself that wanting anyone else was a farce. I just needed more time. "Yes, it is."

Several hours had passed and I was forced to remove my chainmail, no longer cold but pouring with sweat and heat from an endless cycle of carrying large rocks from one side of the bluff to our post. *This is useless*, I grumbled, *the rocks are only good if the mentees actually attack our post… If they attack*

*someone else's we are going to have to leave them behind! And that will be four hours of wasted effort.*

What was Darren thinking?

A slow fog had started to roll into the cove. I could barely make out the houses lining its shore, let alone the waters below us.

I called to my brother. "Can you see anything?" Alex was currently stationed as guard while Barrett and I collected the rock. At first I hadn't thought anything of the damp air, but now I was starting to feel drowsy...

I was beginning to suspect the Combat mentees had cast their first weather assault laced with some sort of sleeping draft that the Alchemy apprentices might have brewed up.

My brother yawned. "No there isn't any—wait! Ryiah, Barrett, one of the others just lit their signal!"

I dropped what I was holding and rushed over to the cliff's ledge. Just as Alex had said, there was a blaze of orange and red in one of the eastern towers. It was harder to see in the fog but it was definitely a fire.

"They must have spotted the mentees' warship!"

The three of us took off for the beacon, sprinting down the winding trail as fast as our legs could carry us. We had almost five miles before we would reach the fire's location. Most of the others would already be done casting by the time we arrived.

About twenty minutes into our run I saw Ella, waving frantically for us to stop. She was one station away from the beach and two more from the fire's lookout.

"We have to keep going!" Barrett panted. "We'll have to leave her behind!"

"You go right on ahead," Alex told the two of us, "I'm going to see what she needs—"

"Ryiah!" Ella shouted. "I need Ryiah!"

"Go!" I told my twin. I didn't want to think about what Darren would do if he found out I was defying orders, but I told myself it would only take a minute to find out what was wrong. Had Ella seen the fire? She must have, or at least guessed it when she saw us.

I caught up to my friend. "Ella, what's wrong? We saw the beacon down by the beach!"

Her eyes were wide. "I saw it too but then I saw something else. My partners wouldn't listen but it doesn't matter, I need someone from Combat…" She grabbed my arm and pulled me to her tower's lookout, pointing to something below in the waters. It was too hard to discern with the fog, just a cluster of darkness in the shadow below.

"I think the mentees are using a longboat," she whispered. "It's fast. It's small. It could easily approach the shore without anyone realizing!"

"But the others lit the signal fire," I protested. "Why would they light it…?" I stared down at the eastern waters. I could see a large barge approaching the shores. "See, Ella, there's the mentees' warship."

"It could be a trap."

"Ella, that's just a shadow—we have to—"

"Why would this fog be laced with a casting for sleep?" She threw her hands up in the air. "Why is it only extending as far as this side of the coast? Why would the mentees try to shield the shore from sight?"

She had a point—and she'd assumed the same as I about the casting. The fog was tainted.

"What should we do? Should we light another fire? It would only confuse everyone. No one is going to come here when there is a barge on the other side of the bluffs."

Ella studied the ledge. "We do this on our own, Ryiah. I don't want Darren blaming us if we are wrong and there really are mentees on that barge."

"So how do we get down there to the longboat?"

"Do you remember Priscilla and your mentee Merrick bragging about all the secret caverns along the coast?"

How could I forget? Priscilla and her vile cousin Merrick, who had just joined the apprentice ranks this summer, had done nothing but praise their family's township since they arrived. Port Langli, or as I liked to call it, Port of the Langli Cousins: each more loathsome than the last.

"Well, I am pretty sure I spotted a vertical opening to one of those sea caves while I was gathering rock for the catapult," she said. "It doesn't look like you can climb down… but it was an opening and the bottom was filled with water. We could jump in, find the exit, and then surprise the mentees from behind while they are attempting to scale the beach."

"But what if there is no exit? What if the tide changes?" I didn't know much about the sea but one hole in the rock wasn't enough to guarantee another, and if we became trapped…

"We can always cast our way free. You haven't used any of your magic yet, right?"

"Well, no…" I still wasn't sure.

"Then we should be able to cast enough force to break the cave walls. No, you can, Ry. If you and Darren could hold off Caine in that mock battle last year then you can do this. We probably won't even *have* to."

I made a face. "You are lucky we are friends."

"You will help me then?"

"I will. But you had better be right. Darren will have our heads if we are wrong."

*This is nothing. You've climbed cliffs five times the scale of this drop…* I swallowed. That didn't mean I wasn't scared. Climbing I could control; falling was luck.

Ella leaped into the dark waters below, and I heard the telltale splash as she landed inside the sea cave. "Ry," she called from the water, "come on, it's fun!"

I struggled to see her, peering down into over a hundred feet of shadow. Fun was the last thing it looked. I made a silent prayer to the gods: *Please, don't let this be a mistake.* Then I took the plunge, jumping into the dark hollow with my tunic flapping along the black cavern sky.

I hit the waters with a loud splash and then I was submerged into the icy pool. I emerged for air with a loud gasp, sputtering out water that had somehow found its way into my nose. "It's so cold." Teeth chattering, I swam after Ella, following the smooth, sloping ceiling with our hands as we searched for an exit in its tunnel-like passage.

The walls of the cave were stained blue and green algae dotted its ceiling. It was beautiful in a lonely, cold sort of way. My entire body was quivering by the time we had swam five minutes.

We continued our quiet trek to what we hoped was the sea's entrance.

Finally, after almost fifteen more minutes of searching in numb semi-darkness, we reached the end of the tunnel only to find it covered in the same dark limestone wall as the rest of the cavern.

There was no exit.

"It must be underwater." Ella bit her lip. The current tide meant we were fifteen feet from the bottom of the cave. "I think I can see some light below—that has to be the way the water is getting in. I'm going to dive down and check."

"Be careful," I warned.

My friend smiled, shivering as she did, and then she was gone. I waited nervously for her to return, hoping that our efforts wouldn't leave us trapped in a dark ocean cave.

Five minutes later Ella emerged, wheezing water as she did.

"The entrance is right below us. You'll need to be careful, though. Coral lines the rim and it's definitely sharp."

"Did you see the mentees? Did you spot their boat?"

She grinned broadly. "They are just west of us. I saw Ian and your mentee Merrick on the nearby rocks arguing over the best way to climb the bluffs. It's too dangerous, apparently. They are stuck and the rest of their group doesn't seem too happy. There's two second-years keeping guard of their boat right next to the cave's entrance but they couldn't see me. The cavern is hidden in a high outcropping of rock—they'd have to know exactly where to look to find it."

"Do you think it will be easy to pick them off?"

She hesitated. "I'm not sure... Do you think Ian would...?"

I laughed sharply. "He would never fall for that trick twice."

"Well, then we both cast loud distractions in opposite directions to scatter their group. When a couple of them go to investigate we take on whoever is left. Hopefully the element of surprise will even the odds."

It was a good a plan as any. Taking a deep breath I followed Ella into the dark waters, squinting with salt-burned eyes until I spotted a small crevice of light coming from below. Avoiding the beautiful but deadly reef I propelled my body through the entrance and into a bright, shallow pool on its other side.

I surfaced. A second later Ella popped up beside me. Slowly, we raised ourselves onto the slick rocky shore surrounding the cave.

The two of us crouched low and tiptoe-climbed along the rocks until we were ten feet away from where Ian and my mentee stood arguing. The rest of their group—except for the two mentees guarding the boat—were standing close by, waiting impatiently for the others to make a decision.

"I know it's somewhere around here. Priscilla and I used to play in it when we were kids!" Merrick was saying.

"We've combed this shore for an hour," Ian challenged. "We need to stop wasting time and find a new way up. The mentors are going to realize that barge is empty any minute and then they will be looking for us! We will lose any advantage we had in surprising them if we continue to look for your precious cave!"

"Fine! Go ahead and be leader—even though *I* am the one that grew up here!" Merrick tore off his black armband and tossed it at Ian.

The fourth-year bent low to pick it up, brushing the sand off his new prize with a self-satisfied smirk.

*That's the boy that I'm courting.* I couldn't help grinning. Ian looked good with the armband. Even on enemy lines. Forbidden and dangerous—especially after he stood up to Priscilla's bratty cousin.

Ella elbowed me. "Enough drooling, we've got to cause a distraction!"

A series of hushed whispers took over as my friend and I sent two castings at opposite ends of the beach. There was a loud boom and then sand went flying where I had cast mine. Ella's magic split a boulder in two.

"What was that?"

"*They've found us!*"

"We've got to get to the boat—"

"No." Ian's voice rang out clearly. "We aren't going back to the boat. Not yet. I want two five-man parties scouting the beach. We don't know that it's them. There is no way the mentors could have already made it back this quickly. You saw them in the looking glass on the eastern bluffs, did you not? That's three miles from where we are now."

Just as Ella had predicted Ian split up his team, leaving only ten behind. The rest of the mentees left in search parties to scout the remains of the beach. Merrick and Ian were the only two Combat apprentices who had stayed.

"This is too good to be true," Ella breathed. "All we have to do is capture Ian and we end the battle right now. He's practically unguarded."

"Yes, but we have to make it past the others first."

"No, not if we do another casting close by—he'll be forced to send Merrick and some of the others to investigate."

"No, he won't," I said. "He'll never leave himself that exposed. He would wait for one of the other scouting parties to return."

"Fine. Then I'll reveal myself."

"Ella, no!" I whispered. "They'll catch you!"

"Yes, but you know Merrick won't be able to restrain himself from going after me. That second-year is as vain as his cousin. He'll want to claim first capture… And while he's chasing me it'll leave Ian unguarded. That's the best odds you could have!"

I thought it over. She was right, of course. This was our one chance to capture Ian while the other Combat mentees were away. And if Ian saw that it was me again… well he might just be too surprised to make the first move. "Okay, let's do it."

Ella took off, climbing along the crags until she was two hundred yards away. Then I watched as she threw a large casting in the direction of Ian's party.

Two Restoration apprentices collapsed.

Merrick immediately took off before Ian could stop him, and I swiftly made my approach.

Summoning a broadsword I leapt out from the rocky shadows to surprise the fourth-year. Something about my approach must have warned him, however, because Ian spun around with a heavy blade in hand, ready for battle. As soon as he saw me his green eyes widened but it did not cause him to falter.

The two of us immediately engaged—the loud clang of swords colliding as my casting met his. The rest of the Restoration and Alchemy mentees nearby rushed to help their leader, but Ian waved them off with his free hand. "This is between me and Ryiah," he told them.

"How kind of you," I gasped. I blocked the mentee's swing and cringed under the weight of his blow. There was a reason Darren had struggled so much in non-magic combat against his old mentor: Ian was the son of two blacksmiths. His experience was on full display in our duel.

"Where's your fearless leader?" Ian asked. He swung hard to my right.

I fell back just in time, panting. "What?"

"Where's Darren?"

I didn't want to reveal it was just Ella and me. "No one fell for your empty warship," I lied, "they are all waiting inside the cave."

"Interesting." Ian's eyes danced as we continued to trade blows. "Darren was never one to shirk from battle before." There was suspicion in his gaze.

"He thought I'd be the best one to catch you off guard."

"I see." Ian grinned and came at me with a low crescent sweep. I blocked with a wince as part of his blade grazed my thigh. "Still relying on my weakness for the girl with red hair." He gave me a disarming smile, one that made me falter just the barest second.

It was a second too late. I heard the whistle of metal and then something heavy and sharp crashed into the back of my shoulder—biting deep, *deep* into the flesh within. I screamed, falling against the limestone ground.

Merrick's head bobbed up above me.

"Byron should have given me a better mentor," the second-year drawled. "That was hardly a challenge."

I cursed as the boy dislodged the throwing axe and held it to my neck.

"You surrender?"

"Yes." I spat at his feet, glaring up at the bragging second-year with his white blonde locks and his cruel violet eyes that were so much like Priscilla's it was startling. I could not fight back: in a real battle I would have already been slain.

I had lost.

I huddled on the ground. My whole back felt like fire—excruciating, searing hot fire. Blood was seeping into my tunic and my body was alternating between tremors and shakes.

"If Ryiah made it down here the cave must be somewhere nearby," my mentee continued. He glanced at his leader. "The rules let us torture her for information, Ian. The regiment and our masters can't interfere while we do it."

Ian knelt down to where I was, shivering and cursing with pain. "Ryiah," he said quietly, "please don't make me let him. Just tell us where the cave is."

I stayed silent. Giving up the location would cost my team a victory. If the mentees found the caves they would no longer be trapped at the cliff's base. They'd be able to sneak up on Darren and the rest of the mentors while they were still trying to sink the barge.

"Ryiah, please."

I did not look at Ian. *Be brave*, I told myself, *whatever Merrick does—the healers will step in as soon as I am unconscious. A real Combat mage would never succumb to torture.*

And I really thought I would stay strong. But then Merrick swung his axe back into my shoulder—Ian turned his head away—again and again and I screamed until my voice was lost. The second-year raised it a fourth time. "E-east..."

*Why couldn't I just lose consciousness?*

Merrick pressed down with his blade.

I cried as he dug the axe deeper. "R-right at t-the b-base, in a p-pool." I crumbled into a sob, cradling my side back and forth and fighting back tears.

Ian knelt to touch my face, gently, and then the darkness took hold.

"Two years. That's two years in a row our mentees have beaten incredible odds." Master Byron's voice was full of unabashed shock as he addressed the crowd of apprentices and Port Langli's regiment. He stood clutching a goblet of wine in his place at the center table of the port's ceremonial hall. "Who would have expected this?"

"A toast to the victorious mentees and their leader Ian. And a special mention to Apprentice Merrick for helping come up with the strategy that contributed to their victory." Commander Chen had taken over for the Master of Combat and continued to cite the merits of yesterday's mock battle.

I felt sick to my stomach. Every single one of the mentors was glaring at me with the exception of Ella, since they were mad at her too, and Alex, because he was my brother. I hadn't spoken with anyone since I had been released from the infirmary an hour before the feast. I knew all of them were waiting to tell me what they thought of my folly.

After I'd fainted Ian and Merrick had led their team to the cavern in the bluffs. From what I had heard the mentees cast a climbing rope to reach the top of the cavern's opening and then surprised the rest of my team while the mentors were busy casting at an empty barge.

It hadn't even been a fair fight. Most of the mentors had used up all of their magic by the time the mentees arrived. Darren had been forced to surrender within minutes of their approach.

As soon as the commander's speech ended I made a beeline for the door. I didn't want to run into anyone on my way to the barracks.

"Oh no you don't!" Priscilla grabbed my bad shoulder—the one that had only just finished healing but still felt incredibly sensitive. I cried out as she whirled me around to face the angry mob.

Ella was cornered as well.

I looked to the head table. The regiment was too busy in conversation to notice. Master Byron could see… but it didn't take much to understand he would never intercede on my behalf.

"How could you let that band of weaklings beat us?" Tyra demanded.

Eve studied my face. "Merrick told me it was you who told him where that cave was."

"I—"

"Why didn't you try to get help?"

"What happened?"

"We—we didn't want to confuse everyone with another fire—"

"So you decided to play hero." Darren had shoved his way to the front of the crowd. "You decided to ignore *everything* I said and go off on your own!"

I folded my arms, trying to ignore the pain in my shoulder where Priscilla's hard nails had been. "I may have made a mistake but it wasn't *my* strategy that cost the team our victory. You shouldn't have ordered everyone to leave their posts—you left us all open to attack!"

"You were the one who gave up the cave!" Darren yelled. "You told them exactly where it was—without it the mentees *never* would have made it up those bluffs. Priscilla assured me the west cliffs were impossible to scale and that her fool cousin wouldn't remember the cavern's location!"

"You really expected me to ignore enemy ships?" I cried. "Ella saw their longboat! I wasn't just going to run off and ignore them. Maybe if you had bothered to tell the rest of us what Priscilla had said..."

Darren's jaw set. "You don't question your leader's judgment! If you had just listened to me like you were supposed to..." His eyes burned black. "But even if you hadn't—what kind of Combat mage are you to give up the rest of your team like that?"

Tears filled my eyes. "I tried, Darren, I—"

"*You obviously didn't try hard enough!*"

"What kind of friend are you?" Ian had been busy with Commander Chen but now he'd returned. He pushed past me to glare at the prince.

"This is none of your concern, *Ian*," Darren snarled.

"It is when you are making the girl I love cry." Ian lowered his voice. "I thought I respected you, Darren, for what you did back at the palace... Do you even know what Ryiah went through out there? Did you even stop to ask? Or did you just assume she traded the information for an easy surrender?"

He took another step so that he was in Darren's face, forcing the prince to take an uncomfortable step back. "She was tortured, Darren. I let..." He swallowed. "I let Merrick strike her with an axe four times before she finally gave up the information! The healers spent three days attending to her—or did you fail to notice she was in the infirmary? She's not a coward—and you are certainly not the friend you claim to be if you punish her for what any Combat apprentice would have succumbed to." His voice thundered across the hall as he asked his next question: "Or do we need to see how long *you* would last under an axe?"

I didn't wait to hear what Darren had to say. I didn't wait for Ian to come find me. I left the room not caring that the others could see me crying. I heard Ella call after me, and Alex shortly after. But I kept running. Past the barracks, past the village and its busy merchant-laden streets, I kept running until I was sure they had given up following me.

I continued on four miles up the winding hillside trail until I was back at the lookout Alex and I had been stationed during the mock battle. There was two guards actively serving as sentries inside but I chose to ignore them as I sat down a couple feet away, dangling my feet over the edge of the high cliff.

Then I cried. I let the angry tears waste away until there was nothing left but a crippled set of lungs—too hoarse and too dry to do anything but breathe in and out the night sea air.

# Chapter Nine

It was our third night camped out on the King's Road on our way back to the Academy. I was supposed to be sleeping but instead I was wide-awake listening to two hushed voices outside of Ella's and my tent. At first I hadn't minded. Ella and Alex deserved their privacy… But then the conversation had turned to me.

"She has barely talked to anyone in days."

"Didn't the prince apologize? I thought Ian said that he was right there when Darren found Ryiah and apologized in front of your entire faction the next morning?"

"He did. But she's still upset."

"What does she still have to be upset about?" was my brother's incredulous response. "Darren made a mistake. Honestly, most princes never even admit that much."

Ella was quiet. Then, "I think Darren hurt her more than she is letting on to the rest of us."

"But *why*?"

"Do you remember our first year during the hazing? How upset she was?"

"So?"

"Well, I've never told you this but Darren kissed her shortly before—"

"He did WHAT?"

"Sshhhhhh. You don't want to wake her!"

"But she—he—I'll kill him!"

"Alex," my friend said sternly. "You will do no such thing."

"Does Ian know?"

"He does. It's why he took so long to court your sister—but I'm afraid he might not have waited long enough."

"Why?"

"I think she might be in love with Darren."

There was a strangled yelp on my brother's part, and then Ella continued quietly. "It would explain why she hasn't been acting like herself. If she didn't care for him I believe she would have already forgave him for what happened at the feast..."

I couldn't take it anymore. I hauled the tent flap open and glowered at the two who had nothing better to do than gossip. "I am *not* in love with Darren!" I told them angrily. "And I will prove it!"

Before they could stop me I had crossed the divide to the boy's camp and started ripping open tent flaps. "Where's Darren?" I whisper-shouted.

"Ryiah?" Ray croaked. He was in the third tent I had awoken in my rampage. "What is happening...?"

"Where's Darren?" I repeated. My voice was deceptively calm.

"H-he's two tents down." The third-year yawned.

I released Ray's flap and marched right over to the prince's, not caring that I had woken up half the camp in the process. When I finally reached it I yanked the fold across and snapped, "Darren, wake up!"

I had the pleasure of seeing the dark-haired prince jump out of his roll, clutching a dagger against his chest. He was half-dressed—in loose-fitted breeches and no shirt, so that my eyes were unable to escape the rapid heaving of his well-toned chest. A strange chill ran through me and I squelched it immediately, reaching in to grab the prince's arm and drag him out of his bed.

Half the camp was standing or peering out of their tents by the time I had pulled him into the center of the meadow to face them.

"What are you doing?" Darren hissed.

"Is everyone awake?" I shouted to my audience, ignoring him.

A series of curses answered me. The non-heir looked down at me in shock. His eyes said it all: *What is this crazy girl doing?*

"Good, I—"

"Apprentice Ryiah!" Master Byron roared, emerging from his tent, furious. "Go to bed at once!"

"I just need to say one thing first, everyone needs to hear this."

"NOW! Or I will have you dismissed from this apprenticeship for disobeying the Code of Conduct!"

I looked to Darren. "Tell him to let me talk, if you really meant that you were sorry before."

The non-heir's eyes flared in surprise—well, more so than before. The corner of his lip twitched while he kept his eyes locked on me. "Let her talk, Byron. This should only take a minute. I think."

The master grumbled angrily in reply. His bias could always be counted on.

"I forgive you." I cleared my throat so the whole camp could hear. "Darren, did you hear me? I. Forgive. *You.*"

"I heard you the first time, Ryiah." The prince was watching me with a strange expression. His eyes were locked on mine and I forced myself to look away.

"Darren acknowledges that I forgive him!" I cried. Spotting Ella and Alex—who both looked mortified—in the back of the crowd I pointed to them. "I. Forgave. *Him.*"

At just that moment Ian grabbed me from behind, covering my mouth with his hand to keep me from embarrassing myself any further. I let go of Darren's arm. "What is this about, Ry?" the fourth-year whispered in my ear. "Byron is not going to let you continue shouting at the camp all night."

I relaxed in his grip, satisfied from the look on my best friend and brother's horrified faces that I had done my duty. They would never, *ever* say that I was holding a grudge. Then, when Ian's hand relaxed I spun around so that I was in his arms, surrounded by the whole camp audience.

"And I love *you*, Ian of Ferren's Keep!" I threw my arms around his neck, not caring who watched as I kissed him soundly on the lips.

A low moan came from Ian's throat and he pulled back to look at me, wonderingly. "You can't do this here, Ryiah," he murmured, warm breathe on my cheek. "I know I like to cause trouble with Byron but this might be too…"

I continued to kiss him, ignoring his protest as I melted into his arms. This was *right*. This was where I belonged. I *did* love the blacksmith's son. I *didn't* love the prince. "I don't care."

Ian fell backward in shock—and he would have hit the ground had Darren—who had been standing awkwardly by during the whole event—not caught the fourth-year's arm just in time. I was not so lucky. I landed on the ground.

"APPRENTICE RYIAH. IF YOU DO NOT RETURN TO YOUR QUARTERS THIS INSTANT I WILL HAVE YOU REMOVED—MY RESPECT FOR THE PRINCE'S WISHES ASIDE!"

I scrambled up from the grass and gave a mock bow to my audience. "Thank you all for your time!" Then I raced out of the camp before anyone could notice how flushed my face was. Especially the prince.

"What *was* that?" Ella cornered me as soon as I had entered the tent.

"Oh, that?" I feigned innocence. "Well, I wanted to let you know that I've 'moved on.'"

"Ryiah, I didn't mean to upset you. Alex and I were only talking."

I held up my hand to quiet her. "I don't want to discuss it. I forgave Darren. I told Ian my feelings. I feel better now that I have released everything I've been keeping to myself."

"Is that really what you've been keeping to yourself?" Her tone held suspicion.

It wasn't. "It is." I held my friend's amber eyes until she finally sighed.

"If you ever change your mind about your 'feelings,'" she said softly, "you know you can always talk to me."

I did not miss her implication. But instead of answering I burrowed under my covers, determined to block out the evening's events from my mind.

*Dear Ryiah (and Alex too, sorry brother, you always knew I liked her best!),*

*I hope you are both enjoying the second year of your apprenticeship—I have heard Port Langli has the best mead—if you get time to drink that is, ha! My trial year in the Cavalry is going well. Sir Piers gave my recommendation to the head soldiers who lead it so I think I am one of the favorites… a nice change of pace from my time at the Academy.*

*Ryiah, you were right to encourage me. There is no shame here, the other applicants may not have magic or the skill of a full-fledged knight but they are still honorable and hard working. There's another boy here named Jacob—he comes from Ferren's Keep, where I think you two will train, eventually, and he has been a great friend to confide in. He knows all about life as a soldier—his dad is serving in his local regiment and he says it's always full of action since they are so far north! I know I shouldn't hope for battle—but I do think it would be exciting to fight rogue Caltothians one day.*

*Jacob told me the first station we are placed at after our trial year is a city on the northern border so I think I might actually get my wish! There's no apprenticeship after we graduate—they just place us and have the local soldiers train us as we serve... which means I might actually be stationed where you will be training in a year or two!*

*...I need to get back to study now but please write back. I miss you, Ryiah (and you, too, Alex) so it would be nice to hear from you.*

*Warmly,*
*Your favorite brother, Derrick*

Alex chuckled as he finished reading the letter and offered it back to me. I shook my head. I had already read it three times. "I wonder what he would think of that stunt you pulled during our trip back to the Academy!"

I shoved him. "You wouldn't dare!"

"Oh, but I would. You know Derrick would find it hilarious." Alex cleared his throat loudly and several apprentices looked over at him over the noon meal. "'I. Forgive. *You.*'" he declared in a high falsetto.

Several people snickered into their stew.

I put my hands on my head and Ian wrapped an arm around my shoulder.

"Let Ryiah be, Alex, I think we've all teased her enough—it's been over two months." Then he grinned. "After all... We. Forgive. *You.*"

I lurched to my feet.

"Oh, Ryiah, we were only playing," the fourth-year began.

I raised a brow. "You tease me for the night I declare my love, yet I seem to remember you being rather enthusiastic when I was kissing you."

Ian's eyes twinkled mischievously. "That was a good night." He snorted. "Until Darren had to catch me in his arms."

I cringed. I had forgotten that last part.

Ever since that night I had avoided the prince at all costs. When our paths did accidentally cross in practice or passing I had made a point to show it was not anger but humiliation that kept me distant. I thought I'd played the part very well. No one was accusing me of being in love with Darren now.

"Ryiah!" Ella had arrived late to lunch and she was frowning. "You promised you would let me help you get ready for the solstice tonight—why are you still eating?"

*That was today?* I stared at her, horrified. I could not believe we had been at the Academy for almost three months.

"Come you." She grabbed my arm, dragging me away from the table to begin our elaborate dress. "You'll have plenty of time to flirt with Ian tonight."

Ella and I descended down the ballroom stair and I felt like royalty. "You want to look beautiful for the boy who loves you," was her justification for the dress that had cost me three month's apprentice wages. "You can always wear it when you are at court as a visiting mage. You'll need something fancy that goes with your new status." I shouldn't have listened. But the second we had entered the dressmaker's shop in Langli I had forgotten any protests I had.

Now I was entering the Academy ballroom in a sweeping dress fit for a princess with my hair done in long, soft curls—quite the opposite of current fashion but undeniably stunning in the mirror once I had seen Ella's creation. I didn't have any costly gems to adorn it like Priscilla and some of the other highborn girls, but I didn't need them—my scarlet red hair was enough of an accessory.

My dress was a striking maroon, a giant silk skirt with gold tissue-thin gauze beneath that sparkled whenever the light caught its movement. There were small gold-embroidered blossoms at the corset that flowered out into a deep, swooping neckline. It was a dress that up until my apprenticeship I had only dreamed of owning.

A sneering voice caught me as I reached the end of the stair. "Are you really wearing the dreadful thing without sleeves?"

I blushed. The dressmaker hadn't had quite enough time to finish the dress in the port, and after seeing the silhouette without I had decided to leave it unfinished. "I like it this way."

"You shouldn't. Only lowborn wenches expose their arms."

Ella stepped in to defend me against Priscilla. "We expose our arms every day in practice. Why should it matter while she's wearing a dress?"

"It's an insult to all highborns."

Ella rolled her eyes and then noticed Darren standing next to his betrothed. He had remained oddly quiet throughout the entire conversation. "Darren, you're a prince, is Ryiah's new fashion offending you?"

His eyes met mine and I thought I would die from the wait. He didn't say anything and I only grew more uncomfortable.

Ella sighed. "Well, it doesn't matter what either of you think. The court was wearing dead birds in their hair five years ago so clearly fashion is *very* subjective." She hooked her arm in mine, steering me away from the awkward silence.

When we met up with our escorts the boys' jaws dropped and when they finally seemed capable of talk they rushed off to bring us our drinks for the evening.

"Now that is how you greet a lady," Ella remarked, approvingly. Alex couldn't seem to look at her without blushing, and Ian kept staring until I thought I would crawl out of my skin.

Finally Ian overcame his shock and pulled me to the side, grinning wickedly down at me. "Do you remember how we met, Ryiah?"

I blushed. "Of course, you were so charming. You told me everything I wanted to hear."

"And then I kissed your hand for luck."

"And I said you'd probably done that to all the young ladies."

"And I told you it didn't make my gesture any less sincere."

I smiled up at him. "You always were a charmer. I can't believe I fell for you."

Ian glanced around the room to make sure the masters were occupied. Then he swiftly lifted my chin and kissed me—ignoring the shocked gasps around us as he pulled me into a long, ardent embrace. When he was done he released me with a chuckle. "Should have tried that when I met you."

I elbowed him, still a bit dizzy from the kiss. "I would have slapped you."

"It would have been worth it." Ian took me by the hand. "Are you ready to dance, my lady? And you can't use the same excuse you used when we met—I know Ella has been secretly teaching you the steps."

I giggled. "Then I guess I have no choice."

After many fast-paced dances with Ian the two of us returned to the benches where he brought back some refreshment. Alex and Ella joined us shortly after. I had just reached for my second glass when a shadow darkened the hand I was using to pour.

"Have you retired for the evening?"

My hand jerked and part of my juice spilled onto the floor—narrowly avoiding the hem of my dress. I looked up to find Darren watching me.

"Darren," Ian greeted the prince enthusiastically. The two of them were back to friendly terms after my public acceptance of his apology in camp. "Care to join us?"

Darren gave Ian a small smile. "No, I'm afraid I came here with a different purpose in mind."

"What a shame." Alex didn't look disappointed at all. "Well, then if you don't want to spend time with us maybe you can ask my sister to dance since—" He paused dramatically. "-She. Forgives. *You.*" My twin burst into hysterical hoots.

I felt my face go up in flames as I glared at my brother—and Ian, who was no better, shaking and trying very hard not to laugh at my brother's joke.

"Your brother does make a good point."

My eyes shot to Darren whose eyes hadn't left my face. "Would you like to dance, Ryiah?"

"I." I froze, looking to Ian and Alex who were too busy laughing, and then Ella, who was too busy trying to get the stain out of her skirts from when Alex had knocked over his juice.

I swallowed. I wanted very much to say no…

But there was another part of me that wanted to say yes. It knew better, of course, but it was screaming too loudly to care. *Yes, yes, yes.* It was an idiotic, foolish notion—but it wouldn't go away.

*You are going to regret this,* the sane part of me warned.

I stood and let Darren lead, my hand in the nook of his arm as he led me to the center of the ballroom floor. People automatically parted in the wake of the prince and granted us extra space as was the custom for royalty. I was unaware of all the faces staring; my eyes were glued to the prince as he put one arm on my waist and reached up to put my hand on his shoulder.

"What dance is this?" I mumbled. The music hadn't started but I knew instinctively that Ella hadn't taught me the steps to the one he was about to begin.

"Don't worry," he said quietly, "I won't mind if you step on my feet."

All at once the music began and I didn't bother to wonder at how the musicians had timed their play to begin exactly when he moved my arm. I didn't stop to think about how everyone else was quiet, how the room seemed to sparkle and glow in a heady gold light as he led me forward and back. All I was aware of was his palm on the small of my back and the way my skin burned hot beneath the dress as we moved.

Darren's second hand held mine in the air, and as we continued to travel across the floor it seemed so perfect, so easy for him to lead me through the series of fast and slow steps. And it felt right. It felt impossibly, ridiculously *right*.

The corner of his lip twitched. "I hope you didn't mind my asking you."

"Why would I mind?" I was distracted by his mouth.

*Stop staring, Ryiah.*

"You've been avoiding me."

I stumbled and tripped—but Darren caught me and turned it into a low, swooping dip. "I take back what I said to you about that dress in Mahj." He paused. "You should never take this one off."

I forced myself to swallow. "T-that's not very practical."

Darren brought me higher and held me upright, not moving, as he said, "There is nothing practical about the way you look tonight, Ryiah."

*You are with Ian.* I kept my eyes on the ground. *Ian. Ian...*

"Why are you saying this?" I had no memory of the dance. I let Darren spin and twirl me around the room lost in the beat of my thundering pulse.

The prince stiffened. "Because I am a fool... And you look beautiful. And I—" Darren made himself look at me. My heart stopped. "I just thought you should know."

*Not Darren,* I told myself repeatedly, desperately. *Anyone but Darren.*

"In Devon." I couldn't stop myself. "What did your brother say to you?"

The prince's jaw set. "Don't ask me something you don't really want the answer to." He dipped me again and when he pulled me to him his face was guarded. "Thank you for dancing with me, Ryiah. Even if you didn't want to."

Darren released me and I caught the scent wafting from his shirt—a mixture of pine and cloves that smelled so much like my home in Demsh'aa it brought tears to my eyes. But it wasn't just his smell, as soon as he released me I felt cold and numb and… empty.

I watched Darren walk away, cutting through the crowd to Priscilla who stood at its edge, glaring pointedly. I continued to stare, oblivious, until Ian found me.

"Are you feeling alright?" the fourth-year asked, anxiously. "You look flushed, Ryiah. Perhaps it's too hot in here…"

But what I was feeling had nothing to do with the room. The temperature could not make me feel like I was suffocating—like something was dying, like something was shattering, breaking into a million tiny pieces as Priscilla took the non-heir's hand in hers.

Ian pressed his palm to my forehead. "You should lie down. Would you like me to walk you to your chambers?"

"No." Did I really feel this empty all the time? Or was it just that Darren had made me feel whole? What was it that I had felt when he held me? Safe. Whole. Happy. But right now I couldn't remember any of those things with Ian.

*What was wrong with me?*

I swallowed, a hard lump lodged in the base of my throat. "You should stay and enjoy the rest of the evening with Alex and Ella."

"Are you sure?" A flash of confusion dashed across the boy's features but it was gone before I could place it. "Goodnight, Ryiah."

"Goodnight, Ian." I walked up the atrium steps in a haze, hardly conscious of Sjeka's beautiful sea as I passed the looming window to the second spiraling stair of the apprentice quarters.

As I continued the walk down the long, dark passage I forced myself to replay the dance in my head. *It's an illusion. It's not real. What I feel is not real.*

But it had felt real. And I had felt it before. But it wasn't fair, it wasn't right, it wasn't-

"Ryiah!"

I spun around—and my heart leaped out of my chest. Darren. He was running through the hall, toward me, seemingly uncaring as he knocked over an unlit sconce to the floor. I opened my mouth to tell him to leave or stay or go or any of those things but before I could get a word out he grabbed me and shoved me against the wall.

Then

He

Kissed

Me.

Wildly, possessively, with a hunger that stole the will from my limbs. He kept me up against the wall, kissing me like he couldn't fight any longer. Like he was me, fighting himself and losing to a fervor that would burn him alive.

A loud gasp escaped my lips and he deepened the assault. His hands slid into my hair and I felt myself crumble, sparks shooting across my scalp and my skin and my heart until I could hear nothing but the hammering of our pulse.

"I shouldn't have danced with you." His voice was hoarse, ragged. He looked at me and his eyes were two black stars, pulling me in and drowning me. "I knew I shouldn't and I asked you anyway."

My lips parted before I even realized what was happening.

And then: *What was I doing?*

"No." I shoved the non-heir away. *How could I? What was I thinking?* A wave of shame rolled through me. "*Darren, this is wrong!*"

"You can't fight this Ryiah." Darren's eyes met mine and held them. "Any more than I can." The third part was so quiet I almost missed it. "And believe me. I've tried."

I took a step back and realized he was still pinning me to the wall.

"Let me go."

"Is that what you really want?" His eyes were unreadable.

*No.* "Yes," was what I heard myself say.

Darren leaned in close, his mouth brushing my ear. "You are a terrible liar." Then he kissed me again. Slowly. Once. Twice. Soft moth's wing kisses that made my knees buckle and collapse right out from under me.

And then I was home.

Everything smelled of pine and cloves and *him.* There was a steady burn rising in me that I couldn't ignore. My whole body was in flames. I was losing myself in what it felt like to be near him. This was what I had wanted. This was what I was missing. This was what I needed.

"Ryiah." The word was barely a whisper. "Ryiah, I have wanted to do this for so long."

*You aren't the only one.* Before I could stop myself I had pulled him back to me. My lips hovered above his for just a second before I lost control. And then I kissed him. I kissed him in a way I had never kissed Ian: hungry, hot, angry, desperate, confused, in love, in madness. I kissed him with everything I had. Everything I hadn't wanted to let myself feel-

A loud clash came from the hall behind us as someone sneezed loudly. Darren and I broke apart and I saw the telltale flash of Lynn's straight black ponytail. I could see the sconce she had accidentally kicked in her soft-footed approach.

It took me a moment to figure out what had upset her. And then I remembered.

*Ian.*

The moment was shattered in less than a second.

"Ryiah, look at me."

*Ian.*

Darren touched my face and I turned away, hating myself for what I had just done to the boy I claimed to love. And the one I didn't want to love.

"Don't do this."

"This was a mistake," I heard myself say. "I'm not—you aren't yourself—we—"

"Ryiah." Darren's eyes burned crimson. "I'm not sorry."

*I'm not sorry.* Darren's words continued to echo across my thoughts as I raced down the corridor halls. Panic invaded everything I had worked so hard to build. I had to find Ian before Lynn got to him. I had to tell him that it didn't-

"Ryiah!" Ella and Alex found me as I stumbled down the stairwell. "What happened? Lynn just told Ian she needed to talk to him and when he declined she said…" Ella's hazel eyes took in the rest of my appearance: the tussled hair, the smeared rogue, the frayed ends on the back of my dress when Darren had shoved me against the wall.

"Ry." My twin's eyes were huge. "How could you?"

I spotted Ian stumbling out of the ballroom, Lynn running after him talking rapidly. The blood froze in my veins when he saw me. Pain flared in his eyes.

He immediately turned heel and headed in the opposite direction.

I ran after him, not caring that everyone in the atrium saw me as I dashed across the room in panic.

"Ian—wait! *Please!*"

The fourth-year turned, green eyes flashing. "Don't follow me, Ryiah."

"Ian, Ian I'm *sorry!*" I couldn't speak. Tears were pouring down my face and I couldn't stop them as I stood shaking in the hall, begging him to stay.

Ian hesitated, and something slipped across his eyes as he looked back at me. "Who is it, Ryiah? Is it me? Or *him?*"

My breathing hitched and it felt impossible to speak. I knew which one I should say, but the last ten minutes could not be erased. No matter how much I wished they could. "I," I faltered. "I don't know."

"I hope you figure it out soon, Ryiah." He swallowed painfully. "Because my heart is breaking until you do."

I watched him go, hating myself.

"Ryiah."

Darren was watching me from the shadows.

"You did this!" I turned on him. "You *always* do this. You swoop in and ruin my life and then you run away leaving me to pick up the pieces! Haven't you done enough?"

His eyes stayed on my face. "Ryiah. I'm not running away. I'm in lo—"

"Don't!" I clapped my hand over his mouth, suddenly afraid. "Don't you dare say it!"

Darren stared down at me, two flames dancing across my vision. My hand trembled.

"You had your chance," I continued bitterly. "There was no one else and you chose *her*. Not me. *Priscilla*, Darren! You are *still* with her."

"Ryiah, it's not that simple!"

"But it should be!" I cried desperately. "It is with Ian!"

"Are you really in love with him?" Darren asked quietly.

My eyes stung and I forced myself to walk away. I was too afraid of what I might do if I stayed with the non-heir a moment longer.

"You don't love him." Darren's voice chased after me. Haunting me. "If you did, you wouldn't have kissed me back. Not like you did."

I didn't reply. I was too busy running away.

# Chapter Ten

I liked misery. It was the only possible explanation for why after four weeks of awkward silence and long pauses there was still no answer to Ian's question. It was wrong to draw out my decision ...but it seemed like every time Ian's name came to my lips I would remember Darren and a little part of me would shatter.

*Why are you stalling, Ryiah?* It was ridiculous. Darren was with Priscilla. He was a prince. There was no hope in saying yes to the boy with the garnet eyes who left me reckless and confused at every turn. There was no future with him. None. Darren had duty. To the Crown. Gods only knew Priscilla and Blayne had spent enough time reminding me of that.

And I was not—would never be—a mistress.

"Concentrate, apprentices, if I have to say it one more time I am going to have all of you take turns serving as your partner's mark for this exercise."

*No matter how well he can kiss.*

A surge of heat sprung from my hands and I sent my casting crashing into sky beyond. The bolt shimmered in the air, a brilliant flash of gold, and then it was gone. My jaw dropped. *Lightning.* I had just cast lightning.

"Ry," Eve said to my left, impressed. "How did you do that?"

Several others had turned to stare as well and I felt myself blushing under the attention. The younger apprentices had been trying for weeks to successfully cast the most infamous of all weather magic... I had been the first one of my year to successfully manage it.

"I—I don't know," I stammered. I tried again, holding my breath and summoning the same projection as before. Nothing.

"Weather castings feed off emotions," Master Byron noted dryly, "they are a charge to heighten one's magic. Whatever Ryiah was thinking about before her casting clearly had the intensity she needed. Lightning requires focus, but it channels emotions with it... Apprentice, perhaps you would like to share what you were thinking of before?" His words had a bitter edge and I could tell he was disappointed his favorite, the prince, hadn't been the first one to cast the magic.

"I..." *Darren's lips on mine, a dark hallway with just the two of us.* No, there was no way I was going to tell the class about that. "I don't remember."

"I highly doubt that, Ryiah. The charge to produce lightning requires a very intense emotion—one that would not be forgotten so easily." Byron was frowning and by this time I could see Darren and Ian further down the line looking at me with interest—and suspicion.

Why? Why did I always have bad timing? *Why couldn't I be good at the one thing that demanded focus—not fevered daydreams in the middle of class?* Embarrassment crept up the back of my neck and I willed myself to pretend I was anywhere else, somewhere quiet and alone where the Master of Combat couldn't draw attention to my secret fantasies.

"Perhaps it's something Ryiah would prefer to keep private." My gaze shot to Darren as he added, "Something she'd rather *not* describe..."

My whole face was aflame. When I finally looked I could see Ian scowling at the non-heir who had turned back to the sky with a not-so-innocent expression.

A second later there was a bright flash of yellow and a stark white display as lightning crashed in the air above. Only this time it hadn't come from me.

"Well done, Darren!" Master Byron was full of praise for the prince. "What did you use to cast it?"

Darren's eyes found mine. "Something I don't regret."

There was a tightening, something pulling at my lungs. I made myself look away.

"D-don't regret?" Byron was lost, unsure how to respond to Darren's vague answer. The rest of the class, all of whom had been in the ballroom during my fight with Ian, had a pretty good idea. Priscilla was glaring daggers at me. I didn't have the slightest doubt that if she tried to cast her lightning from her emotions now, she would be successful. That seemed the last thing on the girl's mind, however, as she stormed out of practice—not caring that we hadn't been formally dismissed.

The Master of Combat didn't seem to notice. He was too busy studying the prince and me. A sour expression formed on his thin lips. The second Byron released our faction I took off, not wanting to be there when the man aptly deduced why Darren and I had been the only ones to successfully cast in the day's lesson.

I had just readied myself for the evening meal when I heard a loud crash beyond the barrack walls.

Ella rushed out of the adjoining bathhouse to find me. "What was that?" she breathed. "It sounded like it came from outside...?"

As the two of us stared at one another there was a loud curse and a subsequent thud. We raced out the barrack doors to find Ian and Darren grappling on the ground just a couple paces away from the wooden building. The non-heir had a bloodied nose and Ian didn't look much better, half his tunic was ripped in two and there was a large welt on his shoulder where he had fallen against something hard.

I dove in and grabbed Darren's arm just as Ella went to catch Ian. "Stop it!" I shrieked. The non-heir immediately stopped struggling but Ella had to drag Ian back hard in order to get him to cease fighting.

"You stay away from her!" the fourth-year snarled. "You should be lucky I haven't challenged you to a duel for accosting her at the solstice!"

"Why don't you do it then," Darren retorted, "I have grown restless cooped up in this port for weeks." I could feel him loosening deceptively in my grip, readying for another brawl.

"Enough!" I jerked the prince back, throwing his balance off as he fell against the barrack wall. "This is enough!" My whole face flushed. "I'm sorry I've been avoiding you two—I really am! But this has to stop!"

Darren's eyes met mine and he said the next words slowly. "It will stop when you make a decision."

I didn't reply. I turned heel and headed for the commons. The only way I was ever going to make the right decision was if I stayed as far away from the non-heir as possible.

"You can't avoid them forever, Ry." Ella had caught up with me, panting from the run and looking slightly annoyed. "You have to make a decision soon. It isn't fair what you are doing to either of them."

"I know." My stomach was a mess of knots and I could feel shame imprinting itself across my face. We'd been having the same conversation for days. "I'm just afraid of making the wrong one."

"You aren't afraid of making the wrong one, Ry, it's the fact that you *want* to make the wrong one." She sighed. "I know you have liked the prince for a long time—but becoming Darren's mistress? That's beneath you. People would look down on you, Ry! He's still betrothed to Priscilla! You'd lose any prestige you might earn as a mage and you'd have to live with the fact that your children would never be—"

"Enough!" I turned on her, suddenly furious. She wasn't telling me anything I hadn't already considered. I knew I was a horrible person for putting poor, sweet Ian through this mess. I knew Darren couldn't afford me the happiness I deserved. I knew better. I did.

But I was tired of having everyone else point it out to me.

"If I want your advice I'll ask for it!"

"Ry." Ella's tone was alarmed. "What has gotten into you?"

"If you can't accept the way I am handling this then go find someone else to complain to!" I didn't know where the words were coming from. I didn't know why I was being so cruel. I didn't know why I continued to draw out the problem when the answer was right in front of me.

"Ry, that's not what I—"

"Really, because that's all you have done since we got here!"

"It's been a month." Ella put her hands on her hips defensively. "You aren't choosing, Ry. Admit it, you are stalling."

Hysteria began to bubble to the surface—unwanted and full of disdain. "You know what? Enjoy your dinner—because I have suddenly lost my appetite!"

"Ryiah, you need to calm down!" Ella reached out to grab my arm and I pulled away, livid.

"No, what I need is for my friend to leave me alone!" Without waiting for a response I immediately turned back toward the barracks and stomped away, shoving past both of the boys in question as I did.

*I have to get out of this place,* I decided, *even if Byron sticks me with scut work. I will volunteer on the first deployment out of here.*

I might not be able to run away from my problems, but I could certainly try.

It turned out that I would get my wish. The next morning at breakfast Master Byron announced that he had a surprise for us. A wonderful, rare, *important* one.

"Port Langli is not like the other cities we train in. Here most of a mage's time is spent on patrols. The threat is not so much war as the prospect of pirates and local thieves. Langli is the wealthiest port in Jerar, our main trading post, our most prosperous harbor. I know you have all grown restless because it's not the fast action you desire. But that is the way of it.

"Lucky for you Commander Chen has recently received orders from the Crown itself. Our local regiment is to deploy five of its own tomorrow on a special assignment that will take them out of the city. The commander has graciously offered up one spot on his ship for a Combat apprentice.

"There is a great probability this will be the only opportunity to serve in a Langli deployment. Missions like this are far and few between. Most of the regiment mages never even get an opportunity at sea. As such, I will be taking a break from your traditional schedule to host a tourney of sorts..."

I drew a sharp intake of breath and heard the excited whispers around the room. A tourney. A mission. *Deployment.* All but the second-years who had missed our time in Red Desert were restless, eager to do something besides the nightly rotations as sentries. Our time assisting the local regiment had been too quiet, too peaceful. The opposite of what a Combat apprentice trained for.

"I thought long and hard about what type of competition we should have. I considered weather casting which is such a relevant skill to have at sea..." The man paused as his eyes fell on me. "But then I thought better of it."

I scowled. *Of course.* The last thing Byron would want was a tourney centered around a skill I actually was good at.

"I asked myself what might be a vital skill to host. What type of casting do I want to reward...?" The master was taking his time, basking in the light of our anticipation. "Then it occurred to me. Non-magic combat. Time after time I have had you train without magic. Because not only does the experience aid in your casting, it also serves you when your magic runs dry. Because no one's power is infinite and at some point you will have to fight without it."

Master Byron watched our reaction to his news. There was a scattered murmur of confusion, dissent, and then curiosity.

Though we spent each morning drilling with weapons and hand-to-hand combat, none of us had bothered to pay our status much heed. I knew my standing in casting: I was better than Priscilla, better than Ray, maybe even better than Ella. But non-magic fighting? I had never bothered to rank myself.

And I was certain I wasn't the only one.

"What type of non-magic combat?" That was one of the second-years.

Byron frowned at the boy. "You will find out when you arrive. You have ten minutes to finish your meal and then I expect all of you in the training yards. Don't worry about which weapon to bring. I will have the servants bring it for you."

I was one of the first to arrive. After the master's announcement I hadn't been able to concentrate on the food in front of me. That, and things were still awkward with Ella. She hadn't spoken to me once since my outburst the night before and, though I should have, I hadn't offered up an apology. Alex hadn't known what to do, alternating between talk with the girl he adored and his mule-headed sister. It had grown to be an extremely uncomfortable breakfast.

Leaning against the edge of the rail I wondered what the contest would be. Hand-to-hand combat, sickle sword, long sword, longbow, crossbow, axe, knife, javelin, throwing daggers, staff, or something new? It would have to be something we had already learned, surely. And since the prince was Byron's favorite it would undoubtedly be something Darren was good at.

But he was good at everything.

I hoped it was anything but hand-to-hand combat. No matter how hard I trained my arms remained stubbornly slim, and there were many boys whose arm bore muscle twice the size of my own. If we were forced into a weighted match I would lose to the heavier opponent. At least with a weapon I could keep a distance. I was fast, quick.

*Please,* I thought, *let it be something I am good at.*

"I hope it's not the crossbow," I heard Ray mutter to my left.

"I hope it *is* the crossbow," a second-year said. "Or the knife."

I wanted the knife too. But I knew better than to hope for it. Byron knew I was good with it. If I knew Byron he would pick the axe. It was Darren's favorite.

It was also, coincidentally, one of my least.

"Don't look so sure of yourself, Ryiah," Priscilla drawled. "You know it's going to be a fifth-year, not one of us."

"Maybe not." Darren stepped in between us. "I happen to be quite good for my age." He looked sideways at me. "Better even."

There was a flutter in the pit of my stomach. *Stop staring!* I admonished myself. Now was not the time to be distracted. I drew a deep breath and I saw the corner of Darren's lip twitch in a sly smile. He knew *exactly* what he was doing.

"Is everyone here?" Commander Chen glanced around and then back to our training master. When Byron nodded he continued. "Good. Now Byron has been kind enough to let me pick today's weapon of choice. Since this city's most common issue is thieves I thought it best to stick with what my regiment knows best: a street fight with knives."

*Yes.* I wanted to kiss the bald man. *Thank you! Thank you for giving me a chance!*

A couple of the heavier apprentices groaned.

"Each one of you will be paired with another student at random. That person may or may not be your year. You will only have one match and your master and I will judge you according to your performance." He cleared his throat. "After all the matches have concluded you will be dismissed. Byron and I will take four hours to rank you and post the results at dinner."

*What if my opponent is a fifth-year?* Suddenly the odds didn't look so good anymore.

I needn't have worried.

They were worse.

"Darren and Ryiah."

I stood frozen in place. I couldn't move if I wanted to.

The master frowned and called out louder. "Darren and Ryiah. It is your turn for a match."

*I'm going to lose.* I had never drilled with Darren, ever.... except in the armory during my first year at the Academy, and that time I had lost. And he hadn't even been *trying* then.

*I'm going to lose.* I should have hoped for a fifth-year.

Swallowing my pride I followed the prince to a rack of blades beside the commander and Byron. I picked up a couple of different knives, weighing them in my hands, testing their grip.

I chose a medium-sized one of quality steel. I wrapped my fingers around the base of the handle so that my thumb overlapped my forefinger. The blade angled up with my wrist, locked and ready to strike. I was ready.

I stood with my feet a shoulder width apart, comfortable and diagonal to my garnet-eyed opponent.

The knowing grin on Darren's face was obnoxiously self-assured. I could hear Priscilla cheering him on loudly to my right. *You should have known Byron would never let you win.*

It was hard to imagine a month ago I'd been kissing the prince and now I was contemplating the easiest way to strike him down. Before he struck me.

*Let Darren go first,* I decided. *Wait for him to make the first move and then disarm him. Don't engage—disarm. Do not take him on without disarming him first!*

"Why so quiet, Ryiah?" Darren interrupted my thoughts as I matched him, circling so that we continued to stand across from one another leaving no side exposed. "I should think you'd be pleased Byron thought us equal opponents." He was smiling and waiting for me to take the bait. He knew just as I did our pairing was not, as the commander had insisted, random.

I stayed silent and continued to study the prince's features, not willing to waste precious energy in banter.

"Gut her like a fish, your highness!" Merrick screeched.

I bit down on my lip, hard. It was all I could do not to throw my weapon at my mentee's face.

Darren took the momentary distraction to lunge—striking in like a serpent, quick and precise.

I jumped back just in time. I shoved my knife into its sheath and then lunged forward, snatching the prince's right wrist with my right hand. I threw it back behind him while I used my left hand to gouge his eyes.

Darren swore and swung wildly with his left. I quickly pulled his blade arm and myself behind him. At the same time I grabbed his jaw with my left hand, pulling it left as I attempted to force him to the ground.

Darren wasn't going to lose easily. I could feel it in the way he pushed back. His legs dug into the dirt, fighting my weight. My arm was starting to hurt. The move hadn't worked as easily on him as it did on Merrick during our drills. I kicked off with my weight, letting my feet bear down on his arm as I tried to break the non-heir's defensive stance.

But I couldn't break it.

All at once the hand gripping his arm began to shake.

Darren was fighting like mad to break free and the pressure became too much. I lurched back, barely avoiding the swipe of his knife as I once again drew my own.

"Now it's my turn," Darren told me. His eyes danced as he slashed once left and up and then across to my right in an effort to startle me. I used my blade hand to draw each attack away from my body—but my speed was lessening as he continued to slash in a seemingly random pattern of assault.

I was so focused on blocking that I missed the quick movement when he switched blade hands.

A sharp, biting pain found its way across my stomach. A long line of blood trailed my waist. I tried not to gasp as I fell back, stumbling to avoid his next attack.

Darren pressed forward, continuing his gain.

He used my pain to his advantage and swung down on my blade arm. I cried out, dropping my knife.

The prince brought up his weapon to my throat and held it there.

"Surrender yet, Ryiah?" His hot breath tingled against my ear and I was unhappy to notice how pleasant it felt in the midst of defeat. His eyes were dancing.

I groaned reluctantly and Darren spun the knife back in his hand, watching me with humor. "You put up a better fight than I expected."

*But not good enough.*

The two of us returned to our seats. Commander Chen nodded approvingly and then sent me to a regiment healer as the next pairing began.

I glanced at the master. Byron was smirking.

When we were finally dismissed I was the first to go. I spent the next four hours watching the tide rise and fall from the harbor, studying the way the frothy waves sprayed across the pier.

Ella found me after awhile and sat down beside me, leaning her head against my shoulder with a sigh.

Guilt reared its ugly head. "I am sorry I am such a bad friend," I told her.

I felt rather than saw Ella smile. "I shouldn't pretend to understand, Ry." She paused. "I know you. If you are struggling this much with the decision it's because Darren means more to you than your brother and I realized."

"I don't want to choose him. I know a future with him would never be what I want it to be." I felt a sudden urge to explain. I tried to shove it down and bury it but I couldn't. I had been silent for too long. I needed to tell someone. To acknowledge the truth that I was fighting so hard to deny. "When he kissed me, Ella, none of that mattered. I wish I could say it did… but I've never felt anything like that with Ian. Or anyone else..." I swallowed, my mouth suddenly dry. "I know the answer is simple but a part of me won't let Darren go."

"Is that why you were trying so hard today to win the tourney? To run away from them both?" Her eyes were two pools of sparkling amber.

"Yes," I admitted. "But it didn't do me any good." I laughed weakly. "Maybe I will get lucky. They both won their matches. Maybe one of them will rank first and I can pick the one that stays behind."

Eventually, the evening bell rang and the two of us picked ourselves up off the ground. We made our way to the dining commons that were already packed with eager apprentices fighting over a list that was pinned to the door. Even the others from Restoration and Alchemy were interested.

Everyone wanted to see who had placed first in today's competition.

"Ry." My twin found me, making his way to the back of the crowd. His eyes were wide.

My stomach fell. Did I place last? Maybe Master Byron would use the contest as another way to humiliate me. Rank me even lower than the second-years.

"What did she get? Wait, what did I get?" Ella pressed on eagerly, unaware of my reaction.

"You were tenth, Ella… Ry, you were—"

My brother was interrupted by an angry shriek at the front of the room. "The lowborn placed second? This *has* to be a mistake!"

The "lowborn?" There were only seven of us in Combat, but only one that Priscilla would ever call to her face.

Darren arrived just as my brother and friend caught me falling limp with shock. I hadn't won. BUT. I. HAD.

RANKED. SECOND. "Congratulations, Ryiah," he said smoothly, "You must have impressed the commander. You lost to me, of course." He grinned, white teeth flashing. "But there's even better news—"

"W-what?" I was still too startled to take in his words.

"Ryiah. I'm so proud of you!" Ian rushed forward to embrace me and then stepped back awkwardly. "Sorry," he said quickly, his face reddening. "I keep forgetting you need time to make your decision..."

"She won't have much of it."

Ian's eyes shot to the prince and I found my own doing the same. "What are you talking about?" His eyes narrowed.

The non-heir gave an innocent wave of his hand. "One of the Combat mages dropped out from the mission so Commander Chen decided to have a second apprentice participate as well."

"And who would that be?" Ian's arms were folded and his eyes flared angrily. "Ryiah?"

Darren's smile didn't waiver.

"You rigged this!" Ian spat.

Darren raised a brow incredulously. "And how would I do that? How was I to know that Ryiah would perform so well?"

No one said anything. But I knew what they were thinking. They were just too nice to say it aloud. I hadn't really ranked second. Darren must have told Byron to do it and then talked one of the regiment mages into withdrawing.

The non-heir gave an exasperated sigh. "I didn't do anything."

"But I bet Byron would," I said quietly. "I bet he would if you suggested it."

The prince's eyes met mine, amused. "That is probably true," he conceded. Then, feigning a yawn he stepped away from our group in the direction of the barracks. "Well, I must get to packing, as fun as our little conversation has been." His eyes fell to me and the corner of his lip twitched. "Perhaps you should too, Ryiah... What was it I heard Commander Chen say? Oh yes, we should expect to be deployed for a month." Before any one of us could realize what he had said the prince was gone.

"A month?" Alex repeated, dumbfounded. "A whole month?"

Ella turned to me, eyes worried. "That's a long time, Ry."

But I wasn't paying any attention. I was watching Ian who had ripped the paper he was clutching into a hundred tiny pieces with his fists balled white around them. His eyes were red but he said nothing. A moment later he turned and started toward the docks.

My eyes followed him guiltily and Ella sighed. "Poor Ian."

"You need to talk to him." Alex locked eyes with me. "You can't leave him like this."

I stayed where I was, unwilling or unable to move, I wasn't sure. "I—I can't."

"Ry," my twin said matter-of-factly, "you cannot leave Ian to spend a month wondering if you return his sentiment while you are at sea with Darren." He threw his hands up quickly in defense of my frown. "I know, I know—you want more time… But you need to make that decision *now*. Do not make him sit at home wondering if you are falling in love with someone else. You've already hurt Ian enough: tell the lad yes, or tell him no—but do it *now*. You owe Ian that courtesy... Even if you don't think you are ready."

Ella pulled my brother aside. "Alex, it's not that simple for her."

I placed a hand on my friend's wrist. "No, it's fine, Ella. He's right. You both are. I thought I could run away…" I took a deep breath. "But if Darren's traveling with me then Alex is right. I have to choose."

"Who…?" Ella made herself stop before she could finish the question.

My lungs were breaking, but I willed myself to ignore it.

My brother pulled me in for a tight hug. "I know you'll do the right thing," he whispered. Then he brightened. "Just think, a month at sea on a secret mission. Imagine all the stories you'll be able to tell us when you return, Ry."

I willed myself to smile and failed.

"Do you want me to walk with you to the docks?" Ella offered hesitantly.

I shook my head, straight red locks falling across my eyes. For what I was about to do next, I needed to be alone.

"Ian."

The curly haired fourth-year whirled around, hazel-green eyes meeting mine in frustration. He had been standing next to the docks, staring out at the ships with his hands shoved in his pockets.

"It isn't fair—you going away with him," the fourth-year declared bitterly. "I know why you haven't made a decision, Ry. I'd be a fool not to see it." His eyes burned. "And now you'll be spending every day with Darren while he convinces you to choose him instead."

"Ian." My chest tightened and the words that were so close died on my lips.

"He's a prince," the fourth-year persisted, "and he's a better apprentice than me. How am I supposed to compete with *that*? You fell for him first and, I know, I knew that when I started courting you… but I kept telling myself that it didn't matter, that I would make you forget. But you never did… And, yes, I know you don't want me to say these things now…" He ran a hand through his hair in frustration. "But, Ry, if you go away with him I know you won't be mine when you return."

I couldn't speak; my lips were like ice and my tongue was suddenly too heavy to lift.

Ian took a step closer, bridging the gap of space between us. He took my hand in his and gently tilted my chin upward so that I was forced to meet his sober gaze.

*He's the right one.* My whole body trembled.

"Choose me, Ryiah," he said softly. "I know it's not fair—"

*You know there's only one name you can say.*

"-But I am asking you to anyway."

*The other has never—will never—be yours.*

I looked into Ian's hesitant green eyes and saw only dancing flame and dark smoldering garnet.

I choked. "I choose you." Sharp, stabbing pains erupted inside my chest and I made myself smile. *You love Ian,* I screamed silently, *your heart is* not *breaking—you do* not *love the prince.*

The fourth-year froze and his grip on me tightened. "Did—" He cleared his throat awkwardly. "Ryiah, did you just—"

*You are only mourning the loss of desire.*

"I said I choose you, you simpleton." Then, before I could lose my nerve, I pulled him to me and kissed him swiftly on the mouth. Ian responded by gathering me even closer and then, laughing, picked me up—shunning my protests—and spun me around the shore. Several fishermen hooted loudly and when Ian finally set me down, grinning, my cheeks were flaming red from the catcalls of our audience nearby.

"I should kill you for that," I told him weakly. But I was smiling.

Ian grinned. "You can do whatever you like, Ryiah, but it won't stop me from doing it again." He lunged for me.

Shrieking and laughing, I darted away only to have him catch up to me a moment later in front of the nearby stalls.

"I love you, Ryiah of Demsh'aa," he said solemnly. And then he kissed me again.

Neither of us noticed the tear slip down my face.

# CHAPTER ELEVEN

"Ian," I chided, "you have to let me finish packing! Byron will have a fit if I am late."

The fourth-year chuckled. "Maybe the grouch will let someone else go in your place." He bent down to kiss me again.

"Ian!" I shoved him away playfully. "You know this is important."

Ian gave a dramatic sigh and released me to my duties. "Fine. But if Darren makes one attempt…"

"He won't," I said quickly. My heart stopped and I prayed that Ian wouldn't notice the way my hands had suddenly stilled. Darren had been absent the remainder of last evening. I hadn't been able to pull him aside and tell him my decision.

I finished loading the last of my clean tunics into my pack and hauled the leather straps onto my shoulder. Ian wasn't allowed in the girl's barracks—even with the door open and Ella nearby– but the rest of our faction was eating and this was the only opportunity we would get to say goodbye.

"Alright you two," Ella interrupted. "The morning bell is going to toll in exactly fifteen minutes. Ry, if you don't start heading down to the docks now you are going to be late and then you'll never be offered a position with the Port Langli regiment after you get your mage's robes." She grinned wickedly. "And you know how that would disappoint Priscilla."

I started to snicker only to consider it in afterthought. Ella was right. The last thing I wanted was to give the commander a bad impression. Even if I had no desire to serve in Langli I did not want to burn any bridges. Especially since Byron would undoubtedly be ranking his least favorite apprentice last in the ascension ceremony three years from now. I gave Ian one last kiss and then sprinted out the door to meet the rest of the crew at the docks.

When I arrived, a little flush from my run, I saw that everyone was loading the last of the luggage onto the ship. Darren stood near the back, helping a large man with black braids carry a particularly large crate onto the vessel. He looked up when I arrived, but as soon as his eyes met mine he looked away immediately—but not before I caught a flash of something cold. My heart stopped and my throat became sand, coarse and dry and in desperate need of something I didn't have. *He knows.*

"Are you the other one?" A loud voice broke my reverie. I turned to see a woman in her early thirties watching me expectantly. Her skin was well weathered and her brown hair fell to her ears, cut in a similar fashion to most men in the regiments. Her eyes were a vivid green, much brighter than Ian's, and she had toned arms I envied. The best yet I had seen on a female mage.

Arms, that no matter how I tried, I would never be able to replicate.

"Y-yes," I stammered. I held out my hand. "I'm Ryiah."

"Well, Ryiah, I'm Andy."

"Andy?" I repeated, unsure if I had heard her correctly.

"My parents had the audacity to name me Cassandra but you will never, *ever* address me as such unless you want to be made to walk the plank." She grinned in good humor and the laugh lines under her eyes deepened. "So Ryiah, you must be feeling pretty special—you and that prince are only third-years and yet the two of you were the ones to win your master and Chen's competition."

I blush. "Well, I'm not sure if that's an accurate representation—"

She cut me off with a hard slap to the back. One that made me wince and cough at the same time. "Come now, no one with modesty ends up in Combat. Take the praise and embrace it!" She pointed to the bag on my shoulder. "You'd do best to give that to Cethan—he's loading the rest of the supplies with your prince friend right now. As soon as the two of you are done come find me and I can introduce the both of you to our leader, Mira."

I squinted at her through the morning sun. "Isn't Commander Chen leading the assignment?"

The tall woman snorted. "Him? No—this trip is for Combat mages only. Well except for Flint—he is... well, I'm not sure exactly, but I do know he is Caltothian and the king sent him specifically for this mission."

"Andy, stop chatting with the apprentice and get back to work. I won't have us depart late again because of your relentless need for gossip! Apprentice, I expect you to help the others load!"

Andy winked at me. "The dragon lady is calling. Best do what she says!" She sauntered off to the front of the ship's hull with a cheerful yet sarcastic response to her leader.

Awkwardly I set down my pack and went to help Darren and the large man, Cethan, with the rest of the supplies.

"Hello," I greeted the mage shyly. "I'm Ryiah."

The sullen-faced man looked up, irritated, and then gave me a list. "You can start with those crates there. Make sure each has the items I asked for—if we run low on supplies during the trip we will cut your rations before anyone else, so keep a keen eye lookout for anything missing."

I set to work counting in silence, trying not to jostle Darren as we took turns pulling the crates open side-by-side.

It was extremely awkward.

The only time the non-heir acknowledged my presence was when my elbow accidentally grazed his arm and he snapped, "Watch it!" He said it with so much underlying anger that Cethan shot the prince a wary look.

"S-sorry," I mumbled. *For everything*. He must have heard the strange pitch in my voice because the non-heir finally looked at me.

"You have nothing to apologize for." His tone said differently. Then, in his most polite, un-Darren-like voice, he added, "Can you pass that crate to your left? I think I miscounted the fish."

One week and five days of cold sweats, nausea, and vomiting. For some, seasickness ends after the first couple of days; for me, I discovered, it lasts the entire trip.

The lead mage, Mira, noticed right away. One of the first things she told me was that the commander and Byron had made a mistake sending her someone "so useless at sea."

She had continued to make similar comments for the rest of the trip.

On our last night before we reached Dastan Cove I spent most of the evening clutching the side rails, trying to rid the sensation of waves from flooding my stomach. My skin was pale and clammy. I prayed that the sensation would go away as soon as we took to shore. The night air was cold and biting and constant blasts sent me quivering from head-to-toe. I was determined to prove my worth once we hit land.

I was sick of the sea. But most importantly I was sick of being sick. I hated feeling useless and having the rest of the crew eye me with distaste, like they couldn't believe I was the one who had ranked second. They didn't question Darren's presence. *He* had been a great help casting wind to speed our travel. *He* took turns navigating and preparing the meals. *I* spent the entire time clutching the railing.

I couldn't even keep the meals down.

I swallowed hard, and cursed myself for never considering seasickness a possibility when I had signed up for a month-long deployment.

"Ryiah, Mira needs you to come back to the meeting."

I glanced up to see Darren watching me with an inscrutable expression.

I sighed and released the rail, trying my hardest to look anywhere but his face. Things had been cold, awkward, and distant between us. Almost exactly how they had been when we first arrived in Port Langli eight months back. Of course now I knew the real reason why.

"Alright, I'm coming." At that very moment I was forced to clutch my stomach and heave into the ocean below.

"She said that you should bring a bucket."

I faltered and my eyes fell to his retreating form in anger and self-pity. He had said it so carelessly, like I was nothing, like I was *no one.* It shouldn't hurt me. Nothing about Darren should hurt me. I shouldn't allow myself to feel jealous of this wall he had built up between us… but rational thinking had never played its course wisely where the non-heir was concerned.

I grabbed a pail and tried to remind myself I had no business wishing Darren would pine for me. I joined the rest of the crew below deck and tried not to let my expression waiver as five sets of eyes fell on my pale, clammy face and the bucket in hand.

"So glad you could finally join us, apprentice." Our leader's voice sounded anything but.

I took a seat silently by Andy who had the ghost of a smile on her lips.

With the exception of Andy I felt as though I was surrounded by a crew of silent, angry statues. Mira, Andy had told me, was the sister of the Black Mage, Marius. But that was where the similarities ended. The brother and sister were as different as night and day. According to Andy this was because Mira was determined to distance herself from her older sibling as much as possible. Andy said she suspected it was because Mira resented his status: "*We Combat mages are a competitive bunch, so it's natural if we aren't the best jealousy occurs—especially in families like theirs.*"

"As I was just saying, apprentice, there can be no mistakes in tomorrow's mission. You and the prince will have somewhat a minor role, but it is nonetheless vital that you two stick to your assignment and do not allow emotion—or pity—to sway your actions." Our leader was alluding to last night's revelation that our prestigious mission was, in fact, a kidnapping.

For the past week and a half we had been memorizing a detailed map of Caltoth's northeastern coast, learning the expected route we would take to arrive in Dastan Cove unnoticed. We had sailed just north of it, approximately a two-day's trek from the seafaring harbor. Flint, our mysterious traveling companion, knew the territory well. From what I had gathered he had served as a sentry there before coming to Jerar. He was to be our guide. The three mages would do most of the "blood work" while Darren and I acted as scouts.

At first I had been uncomfortable. I had been prepared for battle, spying on the enemy, stealing an important document or two. Never had I ever contemplated taking a young woman, not much older than me, hostage. She wasn't a mage, not even a fighter, merely the young wife of the baron in charge of the city... Mira and Flint wouldn't even tell us why the girl was important, only that they were under Crown orders to "acquire her."

But then Mira had mentioned the word "rebels" and I had stopped worrying about the girl's life. That attack in the Red Desert's salt mines would stay with me forever, and I had only to register the haunted look in Darren's eyes to understand how important our mission really was. Jerar couldn't afford a war. If whatever this girl knew would help save innocent lives, it was well worth it.

It took me all of the first and second day stumbling across the cold, pine-infested mountainside to get some semblance of normalcy to my gait. Darren kept shooting me impatient glances. I was slowing our progress down and we were supposed to be the scouting party.

Eventually, we made it out of the dense trees and up a cold, frost-covered peak that Flint had told us would provide easy vantage for spotting sentries. "They will not have a full guard this far north—but you still need to be vigilant. They might have changed their routine in the year since I left. They think I'm dead, but Caltothians are overly-cautious in everything."

Trying not to wheeze too heavily, I joined Darren in his shadowed alcove and scanned the land below, willing the feeling of unsteady ground to pass. Never again would I volunteer to board a ship. All my life I had lived relatively sickness-free. The gods were clearly enjoying a good joke now that I had spent almost two weeks living out the worst humiliation—and symptoms—of my life.

"Take this." Darren held out his water skin, his eyes locked on the city below us.

I took a swig and choked on its contents. I had been expecting water—not the sweet taste of peppermint.

"It's for the nausea."

I took another swallow, and then another, letting the cold brew settle into my stomach. It brought back memories of my childhood. My parents had always given us mint tea for an after-dinner treat during the cold winter nights. I was well aware of its benefits, but I was surprised the prince had cared enough to offer it. I had almost drunk the entire contents before I realized I should save some for Darren.

"Thanks." I handed it back to him.

The prince waved the skin away. "That one was for you."

I almost dropped it. "Me?"

"I found the mint at the edge of the marsh we made camp at last night. I thought it might help."

I didn't know what to say. After two weeks of silence and short, clipped sentences this was the most Darren had spoken to me. We had never discussed my decision, and now out here, alone, away from the others—and especially after his gift—I felt a need to say something.

"Darren—"

"Don't." His words were tired, and for the first time I thought I detected some bitterness. "You made the right decision, Ryiah. Let's just leave it at that."

*But I didn't want to.* I bit my tongue and tried to focus on the brightly lit port just past the rocky shores below us. In Caltoth even its coastline was a much colder, much different kind of port than the one we had come from.

The city's harbor was twice the size of Langli. I could immediately understand why Darren had called it the wealthiest nation. Most of the buildings in Jerar consisted of timber frames with moderately thatched roofs; below, all I saw was brick: house after house and shop after shop of brick, sturdy walls and heavy curtained windows (a luxury that only a king's palace or lord's castle could usually afford), wide cobblestone paths marking every direction of street, and torches at every corner housed by giant stone pillars.

And, of course, the entire harbor was guarded by as many soldiers as the entire citizenship of Langli.

I drew a sharp intake of breath and Darren noticed. "It's a very important post," he explained. "This is the harbor they ship all of their exports, including the rubies, from. My father said one third of Caltoth's militia guards it—and most of them *aren't* visible. The ones we see are the ones they want us to see."

Flint had of course told us the same thing, but I had forgotten until now—looking down at what could easily rival the capital back in Jerar.

"How many?"

"How many what?"

"Sentries, Ryiah." Darren gave me a sideways look. "Stop staring and get to work. Mira will cut our throats if we give her the wrong numbers."

I made a face. "Not yours."

"Well I still don't want to spend all night freezing while you gawk."

I almost smiled. For a moment it felt like things were back to the way they used to be between us, before that night at the ball. Before the awkwardness at the last ascension. A friendship that was slightly insulting, but with enough undisguised humor to let me know it was in jest.

After twenty minutes of counting, and then another hour of matching up Flint's landmarks to their actual positions, the two of us confirmed that the guards' formation hadn't changed. We hurried as quickly and quietly as we could back to camp.

Andy looked happy to see us but everyone else looked cold and impatient.

"Well?" Mira demanded. The mage's yellow eyes glinted like a cat's in the tiny orange light she was casting. Real fires were out of the question. We couldn't leave any trace of our presence for a patrol to find.

Darren smiled grimly. Shadows danced along the strong line of his jaw. "Everything is as Flint said."

"Good. Then we set out at first light."

I straightened the maid's dress and brushed my sweating palms against its clean underskirt, reciting Mira's instructions one final time. Even though I had just eaten, my stomach was twisting and turning and my hands wouldn't stop shaking. The sun was about to set. It was time to go.

If I failed in any part of my assignment, the mission would fail.

I was sure Mira would have given my task to someone else if she could have—but the task was best given to a woman who could act the part of a lady's maid. Mira was too famous as the sister of Jerar's Black Mage. Andy, far too imposing in size. I was their best bet.

I stepped out into the packed village square and made my way to Baron Cyr's castle, which shone like a gray beacon amongst the red sky above. There were two guards who watched my progress as I drew close. I handed the one nearest my forged papers and then entered the great doors of the baron's hall with a deep breath and a steady walk.

*"Two flights of stairs to your left after you pass a long corridor upon entry. Take the stairs and make three rights to the lady's chambers, which will be the first room you come across. Make sure you carry something so the others don't find your presence suspicious. The lady will be taking her dinner on the southern balcony since the baron is still away. She always does this whenever he travels so she can be the first to spot his ship upon its return. While she and her ladies-in-waiting are there, you must enter her chambers and locate a tapestry of the baron's keep."*

Trying to appear hurried—as if I had already been assigned some household chore instead of wandering—I scurried past various servants to the second floor and located Lady Sybil's room. I was carrying a vase of flowers I had grabbed upon entry. I quickly deposited them on her dresser.

I scanned the walls for a tapestry. I found it at the corner of the lady's bedpost and then felt underneath for a hidden latch. I twisted and a door swung back, leading into a dark passage that Flint had said would lead to a relatively unguarded cellar in the back of the castle.

*"The only people that know about this tunnel are the guards and the baron's family. The door can only be unlocked from the inside so they usually don't bother with an extensive patrol at its entrance... Ryiah, once you unlock this door you need to use something to jam it. Try a piece of cloth or something similar to keep the latch from catching. Do not cast. You can't expel any of your magic or have anyone notice you are not who you seem to be."*

I left the room after I had successfully jammed the door with a bit of leftover candle wax from the lady's nightstand.

To the untrained eye it would be easy to miss the slight line in the otherwise untouched wall and its secret door behind. It was what we were counting on.

I found my way to the balcony and then pushed my way past two guards, the ladies-in-waiting and their mistress. I feigned interest in lighting a torch overlooking the edge of the railing. It wasn't dark yet and to anyone else it would appear I was preparing for night to fall.

In truth I was lighting the signal fire to the others below.

"Miss, miss, what are you doing? The lady does not light that unless her husband is returning!" A lady-in-waiting quickly doused the flame I had just cultivated.

Panic reached out and gripped my throat like an invisible hand. The fire had only lasted for a minute. What if the others missed it? Flint had never told us that the torch was ceremonial. Mira was counting on me. They all were.

"Surely the lady does not wish to eat in the dark?" I asked with a simpering smile, trying not to grate my teeth.

The maid gave me an odd look. "She won't—her meal is almost done. She and the little lady Tamora are always done before dark."

"L-lady Tamora?" And then I saw the small child at the lady's right—a fistful of black curls like the mother, with wide, innocent blue eyes. She could not be more than five years of age.

My stomach clenched. Lady Sybil had a daughter.

"What did you say your name was?" The maid's stare had changed from annoyance to suspicion.

I swallowed as I realized too late my mistake. Even a new maid would know if her lady had children.

A series of shouts and the clamor of a sudden panic below stole the maid's attention away. She and the others rushed to the railing to see what had caused the commotion below. I pretended to do the same while silently thanking the gods that Darren had noticed my signal.

Below, on the southern edge of the city's farmland was a huge, hungry fire eating away at the local crop field and its adjoining pasture with frightening speed. The prince had done well in such a short amount of time.

Men and women were running with buckets of water, guards were searching the crowds, and there, dressed in a heavy peasant's costume, was the non-heir. Slinking along the shadows as the city erupted in chaos.

"Your ladyship—you and the child must get back to your rooms immediately!" The maid who had questioned me was busy dragging the baroness to her feet while the guards secured the railing behind us.

*"They will be fearful of an attack. Their first move will be to get the lady to safety. You must find a way to remain in her presence at all costs."*

Most of the ladies-in-waiting had already run to their quarters, but two guards stood waiting for the baroness and her child. I would never be able to join them unnoticed. Not with the suspicious maid watching my every move.

I needed to do something.

Pretending to busy myself with the lady's belongings, I cast out my magic. At once the maid's mouth and nose were covered in a thick rag, sealing her airways.

Thirty seconds. That was all I needed.

The maid let out a muffled cry, clawing at the object on her face. The guards and lady started to turn—I coughed loudly, bringing their attention back around to me. The child was too busy clutching her mother's skirts to notice.

*Sixteen. Seventeen.*

The maid stomped her feet loudly and I pretended to fall to cover the sound.

*Twenty-two. Twenty-three.*

"Miss, are you okay?"

I stared up at the guards and shook my head, pretending to be frazzled.

One of the guards smiled. "No need to worry miss, we are very apt at sensing danger."

*Are you now?* I let the casting disappear and then scrambled to my feet as the maid fell to the floor, unconscious.

"Please, sirs," I cried, "the maid has fainted. She needs a healer!"

The two men glanced at one another and I made myself shrill. "You must take her! I can escort Lady Sybil to her chambers!" The maid was young and pretty. I hoped one of them had a soft spot for the girl, enough to leave their baroness' side.

"It's okay, Red, you can take Mila—Tamora and I will be fine." Lady Sybil's voice was calm and authoritative. I felt a wave of guilt. Her sympathy for her servants would ultimately lead to her demise.

At his lady's command, the guard with short, straw-colored hair rushed forward to take the unconscious girl from my arms and hurry down the corridor. The other guard remained and followed Lady Sybil and I down the winding hall to her chambers.

Just as I began to enter the lady turned to me and shook her head ever so slightly. "I would like to be alone with my child. That is all." Her keen blue eyes watched me, and for a moment I thought I saw a flicker of suspicion. Then she shut the door, leaving me and the other guard outside her chamber.

"You'd best hide in the servants' quarters, miss," the big man addressed me. His eyes held the same doubt as his lady and my insides squirmed uncomfortably. "There is nothing more you can do here."

I hastened a glance to my left and right—a quick study to make sure no one else was watching. The man drew his blade and I threw my power at him, letting the man hit the wall with a loud thud and then crumble to the floor. I'd had a feeling the casting I had used on the maid wouldn't have stopped a choking man from attempting to cut me in half.

I quickly knelt and grabbed the large ring of keys hanging from the guard's pocket. I thrust the key I had seen him use just moments before into the door lock, clutching the guard's sword in my other hand as I prepared for the lady's defense. There was no way she could have missed the commotion.

I needn't have bothered. The others were already there—weapons in hand—as the lady cowered and begged them not to harm her child.

"I'll come with you willingly," she was saying, "just don't hurt Tamora."

Mira was standing in front of the lady while Cethan bound the baroness and placed a gag in her protesting mouth. The lady was still fighting her restraints. I realized why when I saw Andy was holding Tamora by the wrist uncomfortably.

"What do we do with the girl?" the mage asked our leader. "Flint never told us there would be a child."

Mira shifted her cold yellow gaze to me. "Silence the child, Ryiah. We'll take her with us. Andy, I need you to help me cover the front until we meet Darren and Flint outside."

I hesitated as Andy dragged the child over.

"Are you sure we need to bring the girl?" I swallowed over Tamora's cries. I couldn't imagine hurting such a small, innocent child. "Surely we don't—"

"Are you questioning me, apprentice?"

I clutched the small girl by her shoulders—they were frail and tiny, like a bird's. Her body trembled violently against my hands. I couldn't bring myself to move.

A sharp, whistling noise—like a whip lashing out into the air before us—and the child fell to the ground. I gasped and looked to Mira in horror. The leader had just cast the child unconscious. Tamora now had a small trickle of blood flowing from the left side of her head.

I immediately picked the girl up in my arms, silently loathing the woman who could be so heartless. "You didn't need to do that." I couldn't stop myself.

"You did well getting us in, apprentice," Mira replied sharply, "but if you ever jeopardize a mission again I will personally ensure you are thrown out of your apprenticeship for insubordination."

And I thought Byron was as bad as it got.

Darren and Flint were waiting for us at the end of the tunnel. They were keeping an eye out to make sure our route was safe. The second the prince saw the limp child I was carrying Darren's mouth formed a small, hard line. Flint looked surprised but unperturbed.

Mira gave orders for Darren to take over at the front. Cethan and I would stay at the middle of the pack with our hostages. Flint, Mira, and Andy would guard the back.

We took off at a run.

And we ran. Every second, every breath seemed to go on for hours as we made our retreat through an endless sea of green and brown and white. Every once in awhile Flint would shout out a landmark or a direction we missed, but for the most part the only sound was the heavy panting of breath and the crunch of pine needles beneath our boots.

Minutes into our escape Tamora awoke—but before she could cry Andy slipped something into my hand. "We were supposed to give it to the mother if she was difficult," she whisper-panted, "but I have a mind she'll play nice so long as you don't let Mira touch that child again."

I shot the mage a small smile and then held the vial to the child's lips. "*Please?*"

Tamora met my eyes, not quite understanding but seeming to trust the pleading tone of my voice. The girl swallowed the potion and then fell to sleep in my arms immediately.

*Thank the gods for Alchemy.*

Returning focus to the rocky trail in front of me, I sped up to catch up with Cethan. The man was lumbering through the forest like it was nothing, even though the lady he was carrying was easily five times the weight of her child.

"You can't be mortal," I wheezed.

The corner of the mage's lip twitched—but that was it. Cethan was too in control of his emotions to chuckle or laugh. I took it in stride anyway. He didn't smile for anything.

After three hours of running, climbing, and small bursts of hiding we reached the camp we had left behind the night before. All of our stuff was still hidden deep under brush and the others quickly set to work locating our sleeping rolls and the rest of the supplies, including a much more comfortable change of clothes (it hadn't been easy running in a full skirt but thankfully I'd had on my most comfortable boots beneath).

Cethan and Andy took charge of our hostages. Lady Sybil refused to speak except to ask for her daughter. Her eyes were red—undoubtedly from crying—and she had dark welts across her cheeks from where the gag had been placed too tight. I could see that her wrists had been rubbed raw from constant jostling during the escape, and yet despite her obvious suffering the woman remained strong. Her keen blue eyes unfazed.

Flint set out our supper: cold jerky and two fresh loaves he'd managed to steal during the hour he'd been patrolling the tunnel's exit. Everyone exhaled loudly at the scent of fresh bread. At sea we'd been living on almost nothing but overly salted meats, barely preserved vegetables, and *very* stale baker's rolls that Andy had referred to as "rocks."

I watched Lady Sybil cradle her sleeping child—Andy had explained to the baroness that Tamora would be out for two days with the dose we had given her—and swallowed hard. The lady refused to eat. It was hard to imagine a woman like that—one that was brushing the strands of hair out of her daughter's eyes and adjusting the pale silk ribbon on the waist of her dress—was responsible for the rebel attacks in the desert. What was so important about this woman? She was only a baroness with no relation to the monarchy in Caltoth. She wasn't even a mage.

Darren took a seat on the other edge of the log Andy and I were sitting on. In his hands he was rotating a bit of his bread over and over again, watching Lady Sybil with an unreadable expression. I didn't say anything but I knew instinctively he was wondering the same thing I was. I knew he carried the weight of Caine's death on his shoulders, and I could see him trying to figure out the baroness's role in all of this. We weren't allowed to question the prisoner—Mira had made that very clear on our first day out at sea—but that didn't stop us from wondering.

Somehow my hand found a way to his, almost unconsciously. Darren looked up, startled, and I gave it a small squeeze. We had succeeded so far in our mission. Soon, eventually, this woman put an end to his guilt. We had accomplished a very important thing for our country… even if we didn't know what is was yet.

The prince cracked the barest of a smile and then his eyes fell to our interlocked fingers. My heartbeat stilled. I knew I had overstepped my bounds—that I should let go before it became more than a friendly reassurance—but then I saw his expression: not anger, not longing—grief, the same look he had worn during the funeral pyres in Red Desert.

Darren wasn't thinking about me. He was thinking about all the lives we had lost in the rebel attacks.

"It wasn't your fault," I whispered.

The non-heir didn't say anything. The only indication he had heard me was the tightening of his hand.

Just tonight, I decided, I would let it remain.

We had been traveling all day with relatively no rest. Our pace was slower than the day before, but not by much. Mira was convinced the Caltothians would be flooding the forest at any moment.

We had just settled into to a quick break to finish off the remains of our water when the low crunch of leaves alerted me of approaching enemies.

*"Cast now!"*

My warning came just in time—the rest of the group threw out a barrier. Arrows began to rain down from above, hitting the magicked barrier and then falling harmlessly to its side.

Someone groaned to my right and I saw Andy had not been so lucky. One of the enemy's missiles had got to her before the casting. I started forward to help but Cethan grabbed my arm and pointed to Tamora, grunting. Our first responsibility was to the mission, not a comrade. Still, I hesitated a moment longer until I saw Darren approach Andy.

Mira shouted for us to run—that she, Darren, and Andy would hold the Caltothians off as long as they could. When it was safe they would follow—*if* they could. *"Remain with the ship as long as you can,"* she shouted, *"but if the enemy arrives you must leave us behind. The fate of Jerar depends on this mission!"*

So I ran.

The sun was already setting. Bright shards of light were shooting through the trees and blinding me as I followed Cethan and Flint along the trail. I could hear the shouts, the pounding of footsteps, the whistle of things cutting across the air, but I ignored it all and focused only on the girl in my arms and Flint's breathless direction.

We must have run for an hour before the sounds of fighting finally subsided from hearing. It made me anxious, scared for the others. *How was Andy faring with her injured arm? Where was Darren? What would happen if our leader, Mira, was dead?*

Cethan, Flint, and I slowed down our progress to double check the landmarks nearest.

There was a snap in the brush behind us and I swung around ready to cast-

It was only a deer.

Cethan grabbed my arm and we continued our trek, more careful not to leave a trace now that we were close to the ship. Flint followed behind, scattering needles and dirt over our path so that it wouldn't be quite so obvious which direction we had taken.

Finally, after forty more minutes of cautious hiking we located our ship. I handed Tamora over to Flint and he and Cethan loaded the small paddleboat with the two hostages and our supplies and then paddled out to our ship anchored deep in the waters a quarter mile beyond the shore. I stood guard at the beach, scanning the tree line beyond it for any sign of an enemy—or the others—approaching.

After the first half hour of waiting Cethan returned. Flint had chosen to remain on the ship with our prisoners but Cethan, like me, was concerned for the others. I knew he and Andy were close and had served many missions together, and while he didn't say it, I was pretty sure he cared for our harsh leader as well.

"You can search the woods, if you like," the man told me quietly after the first hour had passed. It was too dark to see anything past the rocky beach now. Both of us were growing anxious as the minutes wore on, and when I glanced up at the large man I detected fear in his gaze. Mira would have wanted us both to guard the ship but it was evident the man's thoughts mirrored my own. He cleared his throat, "I'll stay here in case anyone…"

A small glow of dim orange light cut its way along the shadows and I saw two dim figures limp slowly onto the open beach. Cethan and I watched warily, ready to cast at a moment's notice. My heart was choking my lungs, the pound of blood so heavy and frequent I couldn't hear anything over my racing pulse. *Please*, I begged, *please be the others.*

As the figures drew closer, Andy and Mira's faces materialized in the darkness.

Cethan let out a long, ragged breath. The big man ran forward to help Mira, while I went to Andy and half-carried her to the paddleboat Cethan had left in the sand. The green-eyed mage was barely holding on—her knees seemed to give out the moment I set her down. Her face was streaked with sweat and dried blood.

A moment later Cethan placed Mira down beside her. Then the two of us glanced back to the tree line. *Where was Darren?*

"Did the prince make it back before us?" Andy croaked.

My heartbeat froze and my hands dropped the oars I'd been about to hand to Cethan.

Andy swore as she realized my reaction.

"I'm going to find him."

Mira's stern gaze met my own defiant one. "We will wait for him, apprentice. You must remain on the beach. The prince knows where to find us and I need you here to serve as a look out, not a hero."

"What if Darren's lost?" I blurted out angrily. "What if he's injured and can't make it back on his own?"

The woman glowered. "Believe me when I say it would be a tragedy I'd take to heart. But it is unwise to—"

"He's a prince! I thought you served the Crown!"

"He's not the heir," Mira cut me off shortly, "therefore, Darren is expendable in certain situations. The mission we serve right now is one of those."

"But—" *What kind of mission is more important than a prince's life?*

"I am done arguing. We will wait for him here, for as long as we can." Mira had already turned her back, ordering Cethan to take them to the ship.

"I'll stand watch with Ryiah." Andy stepped off the boat, groaning.

Mira glared at the mage. "Don't for a second think that I don't—"

Andy put a firm hand on my shoulder trying not to wince. "I'll make sure Ryiah remains here, Mira, I know my duty."

The leader kept her eyes on the two of us for a moment longer and then indicated for Cethan to continue paddling.

As soon as they were out of hearing the mage spun me to face her. "Lightning," she said, "if you see it, whatever you are doing, get back to the beach. I will try to hold off the enemy as long as I can—but if it gets too much Mira will make us leave without you."

"What are you—"

"Go, Ryiah. Go find Darren."

My feet were already zipping across the sand before the words finally registered in my mind.

I tore across the dark forest. Long, black branches reached out like fingers to scrape across my skin. I cast out small balls of light, launching them in every which direction, trying to find any sign of the prince or where he had gone. The cold air whipped across my lungs like a knife. My frantic breathing was coming out in quick, sharp gasps.

Darren could be anywhere. The others had said they'd been forced to separate two hours ago. Andy wasn't sure if he had gone deeper into the woods, or east toward the beach. One thing was certain: he wouldn't have gone south unless he'd been captured.

I retraced my trail, following familiar landmarks and calling out as loudly as I dared.

As the minutes ticked by and there was still no sign of Darren my searching became frantic. My quiet shouts gave way to desperate shrieks. I no longer cared if the enemy soldiers spotted me.

I cast out large clouds of light, letting everything illuminate as if the entire forest had been struck by the sun. I knew Mira would be furious if she found out I was casting giant beacons of magic and screaming on the top of my lungs, but I was too far from the shore for my leader to stop me.

Rational thinking had given way to panic and there was nothing holding me back.

"DARREN!" I screamed. "*DARREN!*"

It had been an hour and a half since I started. My castings had begun to falter, and while I knew it was reckless to use up all of my magic, I couldn't bring myself to stop.

I made it back to where the soldiers had first spotted us. A handful of bloodied bodies littered the clearing in front of me. This was where Mira, Andy, and Darren had first held off the enemy…

All of the bodies bore Caltothian insignia. None of them had dark brown hair. I exhaled slowly. The non-heir was safe, for now.

He must have taken a different path. Or maybe he was lost. Or perhaps he had already made it back to the beach and was wondering where I was. I hadn't seen any signs of lightning yet. Andy was still waiting for me.

I had run the whole trail back, thinking I would find Darren somewhere waiting—possibly too injured to continue the way to the ship without my assistance. Now, I took my time, carefully examining each and every bit of ground in hopes of a trampled branch, bent grass, a footprint in the leftover winter frost, anything that would point to Darren or where he had gone.

At one point I thought I saw something—a bit of dried blood smeared against a rock, as if someone had been using it to prop himself up—but no matter where I turned the clearing was empty.

*He's probably already on the ship*, I told myself quickly, *you must have missed him on your way in.* I continued to prowl the forest back, shouting and casting in every which direction.

It started to rain. After a couple minutes my clothes were soaked through.

"D-ar-ren," I tried again. My teeth were chattering and it was hard to speak. I tried to wipe away the raindrops that were blurring my vision but they were falling in sheets. I could barely see two feet in front of me. "Darr—"

I broke off, crying out as a searing pain tore in and out of my left side. I barely had a second to register the pooling blood above my hips before a loud swooshing noise came at my face and I was sent staggering to my knees.

With all the magic I could muster I cast out from all sides—hoping to hit my attacker before he landed another hit.

I didn't have any time to prepare. I threw forward the first projection I could think of: fire.

But it was a mistake. The flames were quickly doused by rain. I cursed myself for wasting so much magic on the wrong casting. I hadn't been thinking. A Caltothian soldier behind me kicked my chest and I fell flat into the mud, barely rolling out of the way in time to avoid a heavy boot from crushing my neck.

"I found one!" the enemy shouted.

I heard two sets of loud boots slapping against the wet ground. I tried casting again, but my magic was gone. I had spent four hours expending my force in my desperation to locate the prince. The fire had cost me my last bit of magic. I was weaponless except for a small blade tucked into my boot, but I couldn't reach it from my current position.

The footsteps were right beside me and I shoved my hands deep, deep into my open wound, screaming. I forced the pain to bend to my will, calling out the branch of magic that belonged to me and me alone.

And then I pain cast everything I had.

I woke up to a sea of silver falling from the sky. It was beautiful. One of the stars brushed my face, and then another, and I was surprised to feel a calm, cooling sensation as they caressed my skin, dancing across my brow, my nose, and finally the curve of my jaw.

Finally. *Peace.*

I blinked and realized with a start that the silvery stars were actually glittering flakes of snow, and that I was definitely not enjoying a peaceful death. Every inch of me throbbed like it had been slammed against a wall—repeatedly. My head spun and every time I tried to move my vision seemed to fade away, leaving me with a black haze and small clusters of shadow I could only assume were some of the forest pines a little further away.

My whole stomach felt like it was on fire—especially just above my waist where one of the soldiers had managed to stab me with his knife. *Of course*, I acknowledged, *I made it much worse with my pain casting.*

The casting. The Caltothians. Had the soldiers presumed me dead? Had my magic worked? If it hadn't, where were they now? How much time had passed? Biting back a cry of pain in case any were still nearby, I forced myself to sit up and see through the dizzying fog to my surroundings.

Two men and one woman in Caltothian armor were splayed out below a large boulder to my right. I immediately felt sick. The granite behind them was stained red and their bodies were crumbled at odd angles. There was no movement in their chests, the breath stolen from their lungs. Blood covered the grass beneath them.

Three. I had just made my first, second, and third kill. Before I had even obtained my mage's robes. I bent over and vomited into the grass. There was no pride, no justice, just the appalling sense that I had lost my innocence. That I was a monster.

It didn't matter that they would have killed me first. Seeing the three lifeless soldiers—still so young and strong and now stained forever against a rock, never to take another breath– left me with a nausea so fierce I could barely breathe without cowering against the ground in a pale, clammy sweat. I had known I would kill in Combat, but I had always pictured the glory. Now my opponents were here, and they were real, and all I saw was blood.

And then I saw Darren. A strangled cry escaped my lips and I dove forward to the fourth person I had missed at the edge of the rock's base, hidden by one of the men whose armor had initially blocked my view.

I knelt beside the prince, listening desperately for a heartbeat—but I could hear nothing over the hysterical screaming in my head.

*You killed him! You killed him, you killed him, you killed him!*

I felt frantically for a pulse but it was the same. My hands were quivering too badly to tell. I saw the blood pooling underneath his hair but I refused to acknowledge it.

*He'll wake up, you'll see, he's only unconscious!* I tried shaking his arms, I tried yelling, I tried pleading with the gods.

But nothing happened.

Slowly, uncontrollable tremors took control of my limbs and I began to tremble uncontrollably. *He's dead.* I was crying and screaming. My sobs were so loud they drowned out the beating in my heart.

*Darren is dead.* My ribs were cracking apart, crumbling into a million burning shards. White ice plunged into my chest. Invisible hands were choking my lungs until I could no longer breath.

*You made the right decision, Ryiah. Let's just leave it at that.* His words brought a flood of memories and my tears turned into a flood. An avalanche of emotion and self-hatred came rushing out and reminding me that the fallen prince was more than a friend, more than the wrong decision I had pretended he was.

I saw Darren the first time I met him. In the mountain overpass as cold garnet eyes met mine in haughty condescension. If someone had told me back then that he would be the one to break my heart, I would have laughed in their face. But now my heart was broken, shattered, crumbling into pieces that would never, *ever* heal.

In the midst of my tears I saw a stark flash of lightning high above the trees. Andy's warning. They hadn't left, but they would be leaving soon. Could I make it in time? Now, if I ran, would I make it?

*But it doesn't matter. It doesn't matter one bit because I am not going anywhere.* I could never go back to Andy, my faction, my family and friends knowing I was responsible for killing *him.* My body shook harder and I realized Darren had been wrong—I hadn't been in danger of making the wrong decision, he had: me, the girl who would take his life.

I suddenly couldn't bear to be near him. I was dirty, tainted. The prince deserved better than a sobbing murderer at his feet. I forced myself to wipe away the tears, not caring that I had just smeared blood and dirt across my face in the process. I stood with my back to the prince and scanned the clearing for any sort of winter flower that I might be able to set beside him: I couldn't recreate a funeral pyre, but I could give his body one last thing of beauty before the Shadow God came for his soul.

But then I remembered. We were too far north, still in the months of winter, and there had never been a hint of blossoms anywhere along the trails we had taken. I couldn't even give Darren something beautiful, something to take with him now that he was gone.

My tears became hysterical and my legs gave out. I kneeled in the mud, sobbing. *What had I done?*

Something brushed my shoulder—but I barely felt it, the rain was drowning out everything as I fell away…

*Ryiah.*

The rain still had his voice. It hurt how real it sounded, catching the slight lilt to his tone—a hint of music edged in humor and bitterness, a mixture of darkness and light.

I told myself I didn't deserve to hear it.

*Ryiah.*

This time it was louder and for a moment, for a moment I believed.

"Ryiah." A rough hand gripped my shoulder and jerked me around. And then, suddenly, I was face to face with Darren.

The prince was sitting across from me, cradling the back of his head, the strangest expression on his face.

"I—I thought you were…"

Darren winced, keeping a hand on my shoulder as he studied my face. "You don't give me much credit," he said hoarsely, "if you thought one of your castings would kill me." He had meant it as a joke, a play on the vanity he always wore around the rest of our faction—but it only made me cry harder.

"Hey. Hey!" Darren shook me. "I was kidding, Ryiah!"

"How…?" I couldn't finish.

"I was on my way back when I heard you calling but by the time I got there the Caltothians had found you…" He swallowed. "I was about to jump in when you pain cast… If I hadn't cast my shield—well, let's just say your pain casting has gotten a bit stronger since the first-year trials."

I couldn't look at him. I was too afraid if I did I would see I was alone—that this scene was all just a figment of my imagination, a way of coping with my loss. What he said made sense, but it was just too simple, too easy.

"Ryiah. Look at me."

I kept my eyes fixed to the hem of his sleeve, but then Darren lifted my chin so that I was forced to meet his eyes. Silent tears slipped down my face.

My breath hitched.

*He's here. He's alive.*

It should have made the tears stop—but they only seemed to come down harder.

"Why are you still crying, Ryiah?" his words were almost a whisper.

I just shook my head, not trusting myself to speak.

"Ryiah." He was looking at me strangely. "Are you in love with me?"

*Was I? Was that it? Was that why I had been unable to make a decision for weeks—and, even after I had, I'd still been miserable inside? Was that why I had resigned myself to the enemy instead of going back to the ship? Was that why I couldn't stop crying?*

And then: *don't you dare tell him! You know it will be a mistake if you do!*

"Yes." My voice cracked. I hated myself for saying the word aloud.

I heard myself add softly: "But I don't want to be."

"Why don't—" His eyes met mine and Darren swore. "I should've known. I should have but I was too proud to accept it." He laughed shortly, "By the gods, it doesn't surprise me that the girl I love is too proud to be a mistress." His eyes became serious. "We are the same, you and I. Both of us are too mule-headed, too stubborn, too proud—"

I looked away, unable to hold his gaze.

"-And I am just too in love with you to care anymore." Darren's hand found my trembling one and he said abruptly, "I'll end it, Ryiah. I will call off the betrothal."

I looked up. Shock—and hope—tore across my heart in rapid succession. Then: "But what about your duty?"

"I don't care!" His face was inches from mine and I could see the anger building in his eyes. "I am tired of following their rules. I deserve one good thing. One good thing for always doing what they want, being who they want me to be—I..." Darren's grip on my hand tightened. "I want *you*, Ryiah. Just say the words and I'll do it. I'll find a way to convince my father."

I could barely breathe. Every inch of me was singing and crying out. The words were fighting to rise and I was hard pressed to stop them. I *didn't* want to stop them.

*He doesn't know what he is saying. Both of you are drunk on emotion. He isn't being rational, you aren't thinking clearly. Who's to say the king will even let him call off the engagement?* And most importantly: *Could it be this easy?*

I realized I didn't care.

"I choose you."

"You have to mean it."

I glanced up, startled. "I do!"

Darren had started to smile. "Prove it." His gaze dropped to my mouth.

All at once I was aware of how close we were sitting. My poor beating heart almost ripped itself right out of my chest. I had said yes. I had chosen him. And Darren was looking at me. He was looking at me and, and...

This time it wasn't a dream.

The sky lit up and I froze.

*Lightning.*

The ship!

"Get up!" I pulled Darren off the ground and pointed to the trees just beyond us.

"Ryiah, what are you—"

"They are leaving!" My whole face was flushed. "Andy cast lightning! We have to get to shore—they might have already—"

Darren started to run, clutching my hand in his as he made his way through the forest. I followed, hardly conscious of the pain in my side. We were two shadows in the night, racing across the darkness, our hearts beating as one.

The wound in my stomach, the dizziness, none of the aches from earlier had really subsided—but somehow the warmth of Darren's fingers in mine gave me strength to continue. I couldn't remember how close we were to shore. I didn't let myself think about what would happen if the others were gone. I just kept running, running knowing that even if they were, I had won:

Darren was alive.

If the gods had chosen to grant one wish, I was happy it was mine.

# Chapter Twelve

"Andy. Cethan. Ryiah. The three of you almost destroyed an entire mission with your reckless conduct. Never have I been so disappointed by the amount of insubordination in all my years of service. I have no choice but to recommend the three of you for disrobement—well, Ryiah, you don't even have your robes but make no mistake, I will be suggesting the end of your apprenticeship as well."

Darren cleared his throat as Flint applied a new bandage to the wound on the back of his scalp. His interruption had the desired effect: our leader suddenly paled remembering his presence.

"That said," Mira amended, "we are all very pleased to have recovered you, your highness. It was not my intention to leave you behind, but you were well aware of our orders..."

Darren gave a false smile. "Just the same, I'm sure my father will be very pleased to hear how successful this assignment was. I would be the first to recommend you for promotion—perhaps a post in the Crown's Army? My father has been looking to the Council for recommendations, but I am sure I could put in a good word... assured the others are spared any mention in your report, of course. Surely you can see how their actions were only for the welfare of their prince, and who can fault such loyalty to the Crown?"

Mira's face fell. I watched the woman, waiting for her response. After what seemed like forever, she nodded sullenly, and then declared that she was going to check our course and make sure the winds still had us headed in the correct direction.

Darren's smile turned genuine as his gaze fell on the others. Andy and Cethan had done the impossible. Without them we would never have made it out of Caltoth. When the first soldier had appeared and Andy had shot out her lightning, instead of retreat both she and the large man had remained on the beach, fighting off as many Caltothians as they could in an effort to buy us time.

There had only been a handful of men—and by the time Darren and I had burst through the clearing they had just finished combat with the final one. Of course in Mira's eyes, Andy and Cethan's actions were a direct violation of her orders. According to Mira, they should have retreated to the ship the second they caught sight of the enemy.

"Thanks for that." Andy gripped the prince's shoulder in passing. Cethan just grunted with a nod in the young man's direction, following his friend to the front of the deck.

Then it was just the two of us. For the first time alone since we had boarded the ship the night before.

Darren stepped out to lean against the deck's railing. I followed him. A moment of awkward silence followed as we both stared out at the ocean.

"Have your feelings changed?" His voice was flat, distant. "Now that it's no longer a matter of life and death?"

He meant to let me down easy. *See Ryiah, I do care for you—but what I said back there on the beach? I can't. Princes can't call of engagements because they fancy a lowborn girl, even one so charming as you.* I glared at the icy cold waters below. "Just say it already."

"Say what?"

I turned to face him, hands on my hips. "Tell me you didn't mean what you said before."

Darren continued to stare at the water. He was quiet for a moment, then: "I still mean it. Every word I said. " He turned to face me. "Do you, Ryiah?"

My cheeks warmed. "Of course. I—"

I never got to finish the rest of my explanation—his lips were already on mine, burning, tingling, scorching. Every part of me was ablaze. I forgot where I was. Everything was a mist of red. Sparks of brilliant light darted across my vision as I met his kiss with my own. The only things I was aware of were his hands on my waist and the heat of his mouth on mine. He tasted like cinnamon.

Someone coughed behind us, loudly. I started to break free but Darren held me firmly in place.

The prince didn't look away from me as he said, "Andy, you are dismissed—I have been waiting a *very* long time to kiss this girl."

I started to laugh but then I caught sight of his expression. Dark, smoldering garnet held me in place, stealing my breath.

"You think I'm not serious?" Darren pulled me closer and then bent low so that his lips brushed my own. "Perhaps I need to show you then."

This time he didn't bother to hold back. Hunger took over my senses. Unrelenting and burning so hot that every part of me seemed to buckle and collapse... until he was left holding me against the rail, kissing me until I could no longer breathe.

Until every part of me was a slow, steady burn.

"Still think I was joking, Ryiah?"

I bit my lip, smiling. "I think you can do better than that."

"Oh really?" Darren chuckled. "Well, far be it to me to decline a lady's challenge."

"What are you going to say to him?" Darren's fingers were tracing a path up and down my wrist.

"Hmmm." I couldn't concentrate. Not while he was touching me, not with a surge of fluttering sparks racing up and down my arm, spreading across every inch of my skin like wildfire. It had been like this for the past ten days—apprentice duties during the day and then fire the second the rest of the crew retreated below deck. Every second I spent in his company was bringing me higher and higher until my body lit up whenever Darren was near.

It was getting harder and harder to pull away. To remind myself that when we returned to Langli it would have to end. At least for a time.

I didn't want to think about the future. I just wanted time to stop.

"Ryiah." The non-heir dropped my hand to lean in close. "You know it's not going to be easy—for either of us… Not at first."

I swallowed as I read the truth in his eyes. He was nervous.

Darren was *never* nervous. The realization hit me like a thick sheet of ice, my throat constricting against its numbing cold. This was real. There was no going back.

Tomorrow we would arrive in Port Langli and everything would change.

"We've planned it as best we could… We just have to make sure we don't make any mistakes." I wasn't really speaking to him. Darren was a master at keeping his emotions in check. *He* would have no problem continuing the charade until we reached the palace. "I—I will try my best to follow it."

Darren brushed a strand of hair from my eyes. "I know you will, Ry." He sighed. "I just wish there was an easier way for both of us." Then he pulled me back to him and held on tightly. "No matter what happens, Ryiah, I'm not going to give up. *No matter how hard it gets.*"

When we arrived at the port the sun had already set and we were greeted by a wave of fog that had just begun to settle on the beach. Above us I could see forks of lightning coming from the bluffs, and though we were still too far away to see them I knew somewhere up there was Master Byron and the rest of our faction.

Darren's grip on my hand tightened in one final reassurance and then he released it. The two of us had a long road ahead of us and it started with Ian.

After I had finished putting away my pack and taken a long, hot bath to scrub away a month's grime of sea and sweat I heard the rest of the girls enter the barracks. I had just finished pulling my shift over my head when Ella found me, shrieking and screaming that I was back and that I had better tell her every last detail of my trip.

Chuckling, I told her that I couldn't. Mira had made it very clear to Darren and me that our mission was never, *ever* to be discussed with anyone unless we had permission from the king himself. Not even Commander Chen knew exactly what our assignment had been. Our hostage and her daughter had already been transported out of the city. Mira and the rest of the crew were riding to Devon as we spoke.

"Has Ian seen you yet? Of course not, what am I thinking, he's going to be so excited…" Ella trailed off as she noticed my expression. Her face fell and then hardened. "You changed your mind." It wasn't a question.

"Shh!" I pulled Ella to the side. I didn't want anyone else to hear, especially Priscilla. I took a quick scan of the barracks and sighed, realizing there was no sign of the dark-haired beauty. Then I cringed as I realized she was probably looking for Darren.

Ella studied my expression. "I hope you aren't making a mistake." Her eyes spoke her thoughts, but she was too much of a friend to say them aloud.

I raced off in the direction of the men's barracks, wondering what excuse I would give to find Ian inside, when I noticed the curly-haired fourth-year outside talking to Loren. The second he spotted me Ian excused himself and ran over, a huge smile on his face.

My mouth was instantly dry. There was no question Ian cared, *loved* me even—and here I was, about to tell him I'd made a mistake.

"Ryiah!" Ian pulled me in a tight embrace and bent low to kiss me. I pulled back, shame filling my cheeks with color as his baffled eyes sought my own. Pain, hurt, and anger took over golden green so that all I saw was a mix of emotions and then the impact of my decision.

Ian didn't know that Darren had almost died, that it had taken losing the prince for me to finally acknowledge the depth of my feelings. All Ian knew was that I had chosen him, told him I loved him, and then tossed him aside the moment I was alone with Darren. After telling Ian multiples times that I didn't care for Darren, after assuring him that I was his. That I would never choose the prince.

My words to Ella during our first year of the apprenticeship came back to me: *I would never hurt Ian.*

I was a liar. "I'm sorry," I whispered, hating the look in his eyes as he took a faltering step back.

"I thought you were better than this."

I cringed—Ian's quiet anger was worse than shouting. I was unable to do anything besides blurt out, "I'm sorry!" again. He didn't need an explanation. There was nothing that I could say to change the way he was feeling.

"Did he say he's going to leave her?"

I nodded. "When we get to the palace."

"It won't last." Ian drew in a deep frustrated breath and stared at me. "He's only going to break your heart, Ryiah.

He's a prince—he's never going to choose you! You are lowborn!"

I opened my mouth and then shut it instead.

"You will never, *ever* be good enough. Not for Darren." There was so much fury in his eyes—and now there was anger building in me as well.

"*You don't know him!*" The words came out harsher than I intended.

Ian ignored me, continuing bitterly: "Whatever lies he told you, I hope the fleeting moments are worth it, Ryiah." Then he straightened. "When he betrays you—because he will—I hope you remember that."

I watched the fourth-year retreat angrily into the barracks, shoving past the prince as he exited the building. The two of them locked eyes for a single moment, and then Ian was gone and Darren was left standing outside, watching me.

I shook my head slightly. The prince watched me for another moment, and then sighed and disappeared back through the barrack doors.

I felt silent tears build up in frustration. I blinked them away. Now more than ever I needed to remain strong. Alone.

Everything depended on these next few months.

"Langli may be a beautiful city," Ella said as her horse dipped its head attempting to steal a cluster of tall, high grass, "but I am happy we are moving on now."

*It's almost over!*

I smiled to myself and let my gaze slip over to Darren, riding a couple spots in front of the faction. He was in the middle of a debate with Eve and Ray and a couple of the fifth-years they were friends with. After a couple seconds he looked back, sensing my stare, and he didn't look away.

My pulse stopped. I ached to cross the distance between us and touch his face, his lips, anything besides empty air.

The sensation became more desperate when I noticed the expression in Darren's eyes mirrored my own. It was like this every time one of us caught the other staring. Neither of us was capable of looking away—as if there were some invisible cord holding us in place, trapping us in a daze we couldn't break… until Eve tapped the prince's shoulder and Darren, jumping, returned to his dialogue with the others and his back to me.

I continued watching him, memorizing the confident way he spoke and the way he drummed the saddle with his long, lean fingers until Ella reached over to wave a hand in front of my face.

"Hey," she chided, "enough of that! We've still got a week to go before we reach Devon and I'd like to think I'll get some conversation out of you on the way there!"

I bit my lip. "Sorry Ella."

"You are worse than your brother and I."

I raised a brow. "You two only think you are sneaky. I know your aim hasn't gotten any better since you started those 'late night practice sessions.'"

"Well it's not as if I am being courted by Byron's favorite apprentice." She snorted and added quietly, "Darren could stare at you all day and the master would deny the entire thing. Meanwhile Master Joan catches one whiff of Alex and me and she sends us on latrine duty for a month!"

I lowered my voice, "Darren doesn't do that." Then I gave Ella a meaningful look. Priscilla might be out of earshot but there was still a chance someone could overhear us. No one could know about Darren and me. Well, Alex and Ella and Ian knew—but the first two would never tell, and Ian was too busy avoiding me.

Darren and I had to be very discreet. Right now the others could only speculate. They knew that something had happened while Darren and I were on the mission—it was obvious since I had ended things with Ian. But what they didn't know was what. Darren was still with Priscilla, and as far as they could tell Darren and I had never shared so much as a word in passing since we arrived.

Except for the staring.

On our last day on the ship we had both agreed that the best thing to do was wait until we reached the palace. If Darren were to publicly denounce his betrothal before that, chaos would ensue. Priscilla's father had too much influence, too much wealth. The king would be upset beyond measure if he found out from an angry lord first. An exchange of letters would never suffice. Darren needed to seek out his father in person and in private, *before* the news breached. He needed to give his father a chance to accept his decision before it was announced publicly. Otherwise… I didn't want to think what it would mean if the king refused.

It was our best chance.

Glancing back up front I saw Priscilla had joined Darren's party. My heart sped up, angry blood coursing across my veins as the dark-haired beauty took her place beside him.

The prince took her hand. My stomach twisted and I willed myself to ignore it. *He's just playing his part.* He raised her hand to his lips. One, two, three seconds passed. *Would the kiss never end?* My face was on fire.

Darren released Priscilla's hand, finally. The girl tilted her head slightly to find me watching. She smiled prettily. It took everything in me to stop myself from tearing across the crowd and ripping the smug expression off her face.

Ella noticed my reaction. "One more week, Ry."

I took a deep breath. She was right, of course. One more week and then I would never, *ever* have to see Darren's lips on Priscilla's hand—or worse, her lips.

He had warned me things wouldn't be easy, that he would have to continue his part to keep her suspicions at bay… But it had been one thing to hear him say those words. It was another to see him act on them. It was hard to remember that he wanted me—that he loved *me*—when he and I had never been able to do so much as hold hands since we arrived back in Langli.

*Everything will change once we reach Devon,* I reminded myself. Then it would be me, not her. I just needed to be patient for a little while longer.

"You know Alex is worried." Ella interrupted my thoughts. "He says you shouldn't get your hopes too high."

I frowned. "I know exactly what I am setting my hopes for."

"He's just trying to protect you. We both are."

"Well, tell Alex if he really cares he will keep his opinions to himself. This isn't a mistake. I don't tell my brother how to go about his relationships—gods only know he's made far more mistakes than me." I immediately regretted the choice of words when I saw the flush on Ella's face. "I didn't mean you!" I amended quickly. "You are the one good decision he's made!"

Ella pulled away, putting more space between our horses. "If anything, Alex's mistakes should tell you he has a point. He knows how a man thinks, he knows how they act, he—"

"Alex isn't Darren," I interrupted. "Alex doesn't have any idea what it is like to be a prince!"

Ella stared at me, hard. "Do you?"

I swallowed and felt my cheeks go red. "More than him!"

Ella sighed. "I wish you would hear your brother out, Ry. I've done my best this whole time to keep my opinions to a minimum but you should at least consider Alex's. He's your brother."

"When he apologizes I will talk to him."

Ella groaned. Alex and I had been feuding for weeks—ever since he blew up in a rare moment of anger and told me I was a fool for leaving Ian and that I was even more so if I thought Darren would ever leave Priscilla. "You've got some fancy notion in that big head of yours," he'd said, "and I'm here to set you straight. You can't have everything, Ry, and this one is out of your reach."

"I'll try and talk him around," Ella said finally. "He wasn't right to say those things to you." She attempted a smile. "You know Alex just wants the best for you, even if he is making a mistake in the way that he goes about it. I think he remembers what I told him about Blayne, and then that time when Darren hazed you during your first year… it's hard for him to forget that. He's your brother, and your twin, and I know more than anything he just wants to protect you."

I glanced to the right of our procession where the Restoration apprentices rode. I recognized Alex's telltale sandy brown hair and broad shoulders near the back. I straightened in my saddle and glared straight ahead. *I'm nobody's fool. You'll see, just give it a week. This one isn't out of my reach.*

I had just handed off my reigns to the palace hostler when I felt something soft pressed into my hand. I glanced down at my palm and was startled to find a piece of paper folded neatly on top. I closed my fingers over the note and looked for the shaggy-haired stableman but he had already disappeared while the rest of his men continued to collect the horses from the remaining apprentices.

Curious to see what the paper said, I hurried to my assigned chambers, locked my door, and then read the note:

*R,*

*Meet me at the palace gardens in one hour. Wait near the statue of Morteus. Look for an old hag with a long, gray braid.*

*-D*

I snorted at that last bit. What in the name of the gods was Darren up to? I hadn't expected to see him until he talked to his father, and an hour was hardly enough time to have such a serious conversation. We couldn't be seen together beforehand, so what was he planning?

I made a quick attempt to wash from the morning travel (the palace servants wouldn't see to the apprentices chambers until much later that day) and then fumbled around my luggage for the right thing to wear. I held out the dress I had worn to the solstice ball, but it was far too nice and I had no idea what Darren had planned. Would I even see him at all?

He wanted me to find an old woman so there was no point in dressing up for him. Ultimately I decided on a simple blue cotton dress that wouldn't draw attention. I pinned my hair back in a makeshift up-do and then left to find the gardens.

When I arrived at the statue there was a hunched figure in a red cape with a long, gray braid sticking out the side of her hood. I approached her nervously. "Ma'am?"

The figure spun around and I gasped when the person withdrew his hood, chuckling. It was Darren wearing a wig, pressing one finger to his lips as he beckoned me forward.

"Darren?" I croaked.

"Gran," he corrected with a grin. He pulled the hood back low over his face and grinned at me. "Are you ready for a real tour of the palace?"

I scanned the gardens anxiously. "What if someone recognizes you?"

"The only servants who know this disguise are loyal. The rest?" He snorted. "They are too blind to see who is right there in front of them."

"What about your father? Don't you need to talk to him?"

Darren shook his head, still smiling. "The king can wait." He drew a deep breath. "The second I tell him my intentions I will be yelled at from dawn until dusk." Darren took a step closer and took my hand in his. "Before I subject myself to that I'd like to spend time with the girl who convinced me she was worth it in the first place."

My cheeks burned. I still wasn't used to Darren talking to me like… like I was special to him. Like he was in love with me.

"Ah," he said, "there's that charming blush I was hoping for. I was beginning to think you didn't care at all."

I raised a brow. "Priscilla paraded you around in front of me for three months, what did you expect me to do?"

He grinned. "So you *were* jealous."

I glowered as he led me forward. "Of course I was, and don't think I didn't see you kiss her back! Was it really necessary to—"

Darren ducked under a nearby willow and dragged me behind him.

"Darren—what are you doing?"

Darren put a finger to my lips, eyes dancing wickedly. "But did I kiss Priscilla like this?"

When he had finished I was light-headed and the two of us were breathing quite heavily.

Darren released me, staggering backward with a groan. "By the gods, I forgot what that was like."

I just stared at him, unable to speak. How was it that I could have ever thought I'd be happy with Ian? Never once had I felt like *that* with the fourth-year.

"I guess I should take you on this tour before someone spots us." Darren's eyes fell back to my mouth and a wicked smile played across his lips. "If we stay here any longer, I'm afraid I won't make a very convincing grandmother."

My whole body was a quivering mess. I didn't want to do anything but grab Darren and let him make good on that threat. I didn't care if we were caught. I didn't want to stop this time. I wanted to... *What* was I thinking? Was I mad? *Focus Ryiah!*

I swallowed quickly. "Right, let's take that tour shall we... Gran?"

Darren noticed my hesitation and grinned. "Are you sure?"

"I'm sure!" The words came out much higher than I had intended.

Darren chuckled. "Alright then, let's start with the kennels—there's someone I want you to meet."

"So you are the girl who's put that dopey smile on his face." A large man with a gruff voice missing three front teeth beamed down at me. "'Course I shuda known that it could never be that other one. His highness has never once taken *her* to meet Wolf."

Darren rolled his eyes. "Just because I smile, Heath, doesn't make Ryiah special."

I elbowed the prince in his stomach and he grinned. "Well, maybe a little."

"So who is 'Wolf?'" I pressed. I hardly knew anything about Darren's life in the palace, and I was curious to find out who this person was.

The man chortled. "Not who. What." He led Darren and me through the building's doors to a large enclosure where twenty hounds relaxed on comfortable oak panels. A second set of steps led up to a second platform where even more of them slept. Against the wall were large metal bins for food and water, and another large door led to a grassy pasture where the dogs could roam during certain hours while the servants supervised. The falconry house was just a bit beyond and I could hear the angry bird cries across the room.

"Is Wolf a hound?" I asked nervously. A hole had formed in the pit of my stomach. I forced myself to ignore it.

At the mention of his name a thin, shaggy coated mutt lifted its head from the middle of the pack. Unlike the sleek, muscled palace hounds, this animal was clearly not used for the hunt. It was scrawny with gray matted fur and timid brown eyes peeking out of the long gray hairs that practically covered its face. It didn't look dangerous, but then old man Crawley's dog hadn't either.

"Come here, boy."

I turned quickly to look at Darren—the tone he had used to call Wolf forward was so different from what he usually used that I almost couldn't believe it had come from him.

Darren didn't notice; he had already hopped the enclosure and was busy embracing the mutt who had suddenly sprung to life and launched himself into his master's arms. The dog was yipping and thumping its tail so loudly that fur was coating the air beside him.

A sense of foreboding filled my chest. I knew what was coming next.

Darren glanced back at me. "Are you coming, Ryiah?"

I hesitated for a moment. Maybe. Maybe I could do this. I took a step forward and gripped the gate's handle, my knuckles white with trepidation. One of the hounds trotted forward to sniff at my fingers and I jumped back, retreating to where Heath stood a couple feet away from the gates. My hands were slick with sweat and I wiped them nervously against the skirt of my dress.

"I—I can't." My throat was dry and the words came out scratchy and odd—like I was choking on sand.

Darren frowned. "What do you mean you can't?"

"I mean…" I clenched and unclenched my fists anxiously. "I just can't, Darren."

"Ryiah." Something about the prince's voice made me look up. "Are you afraid of dogs?"

I forced myself to hold his gaze. "When Derrick was five, one of them attacked him. I was only eight. We'd both grown up playing with our neighbor's dog Bo and then one day it just turned." My breath hitched and I made myself breathe out more slowly. "It was terrible. Crawley had to—he couldn't call Bo off—he had to… And then Derrick had to spend two weeks being treated—we, um, we couldn't afford a healer so it was up to my parents to tend to his leg… It's fine, now, but I—ever since that I just..."

Darren hadn't once taken his eyes off me the whole time I was talking. Now he straightened and approached the gate's entrance with Wolf trailing behind. When he reached the edge of the enclosure, he rested his arm on the top of the barrier's railing. "Ryiah, I want you to come here."

I stared at him, wide-eyed. "You are mad if you think that I'm going inside."

"Ryiah," he said patiently. "You want to be a warrior mage. Facing your fears is part of that."

"Darren, I can't!" I was ashamed when my voice cracked.

"You can," he said patiently. His eyes held pity. "Ryiah, Bo was sick. It happens with the hounds occasionally when they are bitten by an infected animal—or even one of the strays. There's no known cure when it happens… there was nothing you could have done differently." He patted Wolf's head. "Heath and the rest of the kennel's staff know the signs. You are safe. Now come meet Wolf." His smile brightened as he looked down at the shaggy-haired mutt. "He's the only family member I can promise will give you a warm reception."

I forced myself to take a step forward, and then another, until I was in front of the gate. Darren nodded encouragingly as I unbolted the latch and timidly stepped through its entry, every inch of me on alert.

Darren held out his hand and I took it, hoping he wouldn't notice how clammy my fingers had become. I let him gently pull me closer to Wolf, and then held myself rigid as the mutt eagerly sniffed at my boots. The other hounds remained at a distance, seeming aware of my obvious discomfort. Wolf yelped and I dropped Darren's hand, heart slamming into my ribs. For a second all I could see was the cold, hard axe and Bo whimpering in a pool of his own blood.

"It's okay, Ryiah." Darren's voice broke through the haze as his hand found mine again. "Wolf just wants you to pet him."

The hammering in my ears shifted and I forced myself to look away from the prince and down to the panting gray dog at my feet. The dog looked up at me and thumped its tail, then made another whining noise.

"He's a bit needy, I'm afraid I've spoiled him."

I took a deep breath and reached out to touch him. Wolf yipped and jumped up to meet my hand. I stumbled, unable to stop myself from pulling back in fear, and landed on the ground with Wolf bounding up right on top of me. Wolf lodged his head at my throat and I shrieked, arms held up against my face only to feel his warm, wet tongue licking my wrists and hands enthusiastically. I lowered my arms, embarrassed, and the dog darted in to lick my face much to my chagrin.

Meanwhile, standing above me was Darren, shaking with laughter.

I timidly began to pet the dog, still keeping one eye on him while I shot Darren a half-hearted glare. "Thanks for that! I could have been mauled!"

"By what? Being licked to death?" Darren snickered and then crouched down beside me to rub Wolf's head. "Naw, this one is a coward. The palace cats tease him about it all the time. The hounds chase them and then they take their frustration out on poor ol' Wolf because he's not fast like the rest of them. He's only a stray."

I couldn't help smiling a little as I shifted to a crouch, still petting Wolf. *This isn't so bad—Bo was like this too, before it happened.* "A stray?"

Darren nuzzled his dog's neck, seemingly unconcerned that he was getting white and gray fur all over his dress. "Yes," he said absentmindedly, "when Wolf was just a pup Heath found him wandering the palace grounds… I'm not sure exactly how he got through the gates, but it was raining and he was nothing more than a pile of bones. At the time Father was pressuring me to get a hound of my own for the yearly hunt—I was ten. I was a bit defiant, as you know, so I chose the most pathetic animal I could find and that was Wolf." He grinned. "The look on Father's face was priceless when I showed up to my first hunt with a stray."

"So what happened?"

Darren's hand faltered on Wolf's neck. "Nothing I wasn't expecting." He glanced at his dog and the smile returned. "During the hunt one of the men broke his legs falling down a ravine and his horse didn't survive the drop. We separated in search parties to try and find him—I, well, Wolf found the man attempting to fend off a pack of feral wolves by himself… Usually they don't attack humans but that winter was particularly cold and I don't think they had had much luck with game of their own…

"The soldier and I managed to kill three—but Wolf did two all on his own. He couldn't have been more than six months at that time. It's how he got his name. After that, Wolf was a hero of his own right so my father let the kennel master keep him on."

"Yet the palace cats tease him?" I raised a brow.

Darren chuckled. "Well, those cats are smarter than most humans. You should see how the cook rants whenever one of his prized chickens goes missing. And it must happen at least once a week. They are merciless."

I rubbed Wolf's belly, pleased to note the anxiety I'd been feeling had all but disappeared. Wolf was making excited yips and rubbing his back against the ground so that Darren and I had no choice but to continue patting his stomach. "This one seems pretty smart on his own accord."

Darren grinned. "Wolf has had me wrapped around his finger since the day we met. There hasn't been a day gone by that I've been in the palace and not visited this kennel. Before I joined the Academy he used to roam the training grounds during the day and watch me drill. All of the servants, even my training master, loves him, and Wolf always knew better than to go near the gardens where the courtiers were likely to complain—"

"*He better not be with that filthy animal of his!*"

Darren and I glanced at each other: both of us recognized Prince Blayne's angry voice coming from the entry to the kennels. He couldn't be more than two minutes away.

"*Why he thinks it's appropriate to come here before seeing to his family is—*"

"This way." Darren hastily stood and pulled me up, leading me to the back of the enclosure. He gave a nod to Heath and the man strode off in the direction of the heir with a smirk. A moment later I heard him and Blayne exchange words—Blayne demanding to see the inside of the kennels and Heath insisting he hadn't seen Darren all day.

"Let's go."

I turned sharply and saw a doorway I had never seen before, it had come from one of the panels in the wall. "Where did—"

Darren yanked me through the door and slammed it shut just as Blayne's voice reached the hounds' enclosure.

"You see, your highness? Darren never—" I didn't get to hear the rest of their conversation, Darren was already dragging me behind him through a musty corridor that was hard-packed stone and completely dark except for the light Darren had cast in his palm.

I crinkled my nose—the entire passage smelled like mold and cold, dank earth. "Where *are* we?"

"The servant's use this tunnel to feed the animals. It's the shortest route directly through the kitchens. Cook gives them the leftover scraps—it helps the hounds keep up their stamina. Blayne doesn't know about it because he had never stopped to bother himself with…" Darren cut himself off, and I just knew he had been about to say something very derogatory about the crown prince.

"Blayne would see through your disguise?" I teased.

"Unfortunately, my brother is suspicious of everyone." Darren's tone wasn't particularly enthusiastic. "And with you there in a place you would never have been otherwise, he would have almost certainly guessed it was me… Ah, here's the door." Darren did something to the wall and a door swung open to a very hot room teeming with steam and the tempting aroma of fresh roast and stewed vegetables.

"What's this—why is a beggar woman in my…? Oh, please excuse me, your highness, I haven't seen you in that costume for quite some time." A hefty man in cook's robes flushed, cheeks red as cherries.

Darren patted the man's arm cheerfully. "It's okay, Benny, just tell me if Blayne has already been down here." He strode forward and snaked two peeled oranges from a large bowl on the counter.

"You put them back—those are for my marmalade!" The cook strode forward and snatched the fruit back with a huff. I smiled to myself. The man might be a servant but he was particular about his craft, even around the prince. "And, yes, your insufferable brother has already been down here twice asking if any of us have seen you. He's in quite a tiff, that one, raging about my kitchens and putting everyone in distress even though we have double the food to cook now that the apprentices are here. I told him you were probably with that mutt, he didn't seem too happy about it—and I can see from where you've just come that I was indeed correct."

Darren grinned. "We just missed him."

"Well, he's set to check the training grounds next so you've bought yourself a half hour before he returns."

"Thanks, Benny."

"Thank me by telling me who this young lady is. I must say I like her looks a lot better than that Priscilla who is always insulting my scones."

"This is Ryiah." Darren held my hand tight. "She is—well, let's just say there will be some big changes before I leave."

The man clapped his hands excitedly. "Does this mean…?"

"Don't say anything to the others, don't even *think* it," Darren warned. "I need to speak with Father first. If he hears a rumor, it will destroy any chance I have of convincing him and you will be stuck with Priscilla forever."

The man drew two fingers across his lips, indicating he would keep silent. "The day that horror can't dictate my scones will be the day I take a wife."

Darren snorted in disbelief. "Well, Ryiah and I had better be off so we don't catch Blayne in one of his moods."

"When is he not? It was nice to meet you, Lady Ryiah. I can tell you that anyone who takes Miss No-More-Raisins-In-My-Scones' place is a welcome addition to my kitchen. Especially such a pretty red-headed one as yourself."

I looked away shyly and Darren elbowed Benedict. "Enough flirting with the lady."

The cook winked at me. "Ohhh, I think he's jealous. Good, you'll need to keep this one on his toes—he gets too sure of himself if there is no one to challenge him."

Darren's gaze slid to me and he grinned. "Oh, she challenges me all right. Since the day we met."

I felt myself blushing from head to toe.

"Until we meet next time, Benny?"

The cook nodded and Darren led me through the back of the servants' hall to the fourth floor of the palace.

"Ryiah?" Darren had just asked me a question.

I startled. "Huh?"

"I said, did you want to see the Council's chamber? Usually it's off limits but I know they are in the war chambers with the commanders and my father right now—"

"Of course I do!" I squealed.

Darren raised both brows, trying to hide a grin. "If I knew I could get that response, I would have done this a lot sooner." He led me down a narrow corridor to the right, and up another flight of stairs past stained windows and powerful tapestries of previous kings. We must have walked another ten minutes before we finally found ourselves in front of an elaborate set of doors, stained black with metal engravings that stated, "Council of Magic: Official Chambers" and then in smaller writing, "Do not interrupt—meetings are by appointment only, please see Artemis to schedule."

"Who's Artemis?"

"One of the palace scribes. She's not a particularly cheerful woman. I wouldn't recommend sitting next to her at any of the dinners if you can help it." He grinned, opening the door slowly to tease me. "Are you ready for—"

"*You have no right to enter this chamber! What are your names? Explain yourself at once!*"

Darren's hand froze on the door. His face lost all of its color. I peeked over his shoulder and spotted the Three Colored Robes and King Lucius, along with a group of what look liked the king's advisors standing around a map of Jerar and its surrounding territories. Two guards strode forward and Darren swore under his breath. "Run."

The two of us took off, racing down the hall, ducking into random passages as Darren led us on in a mad dash to avoid the two men chasing us. Darren kept changing stairwells and halls so quickly I lost track of where we were.

"Almost—just a little bit further!" Darren turned down a wider hall than the rest. Gold, real gold sconces lit the passage and there was a lush rug padding our steps. I followed, clutching my ribs—I had forgotten how much faster Darren could run; my heart felt like it was about to explode from my racing pulse…

"In here!" The prince turned a key and then yanked me into the room behind him. He threw off his cloak and the wig and tossed them into a trunk at the foot of the bed. At that same moment there was a loud knock on the door. The guards had arrived.

I ducked behind the doorframe and Darren swung open the handle with a bored expression.

"Your highness."

"What is it?"

"I'm so sorry to disturb you, your highness, but we think an elderly lady and a young woman might have passed by here—we just want to make sure that you didn't see them."

"An old woman and her granddaughter?" Darren spoke a little too loudly. "You must have been nipping at Cook's wine, Torrance, no one has been anywhere near this hall but me."

"My apologies, your highness, we were on orders to check all the rooms."

"The only one with a key to this chamber is myself—and, of course, Father."

One of the guards muttered something unintelligible and then cleared his throat. "Of course, your highness, please excuse me for the error. You said you never saw them?"

"I didn't. But if I do I will be sure to send word."

"Yes, if you do please let us know…"

Darren leaned against the doorway and folded his arms. "Tell me, Torrance, what did you think?"

"The old woman? It's hard to say who she was."

"Didn't you say there were two of them? What was the younger one like?" I couldn't see Darren's expression, but I could tell from his tone that he was grinning. If I had been standing closer I would have kicked him. *What was he thinking?*

"I'm sorry, your highness, I—"

"I'll bet she was pretty." I could practically *hear* his laughter. "Did you think she was pretty, Torrance?"

"I'm not sure, I barely caught a glimpse, your highness."

Darren sighed. "That is all, you may go. And you too, Cyrus."

As soon as Darren had shut the door I glared at him, arms crossed. "Are you mad?"

His eyes danced. "I'm allowed to have a *little* fun at your expense, Ryiah."

"If they find out it was me—"

"They won't." The prince took a step forward, still smiling.

"But…" I never got to finish my thought. Darren's mouth was on mine and all protests were lost in the blink of an eye.

And then we were on fire.

I broke for air, gasping. My heart was racing and my legs were shaking and my head was spinning and I couldn't think, I couldn't-

Darren's hand grazed my waist as he pulled me back to him. "Ryiah," he said.

The two of us stumbled across his chambers. Behind me I heard the thud of something loud. Books falling to the floor. Darren pressed me against his bedside table and kissed me again, slowly, one hand cradling the back of my neck as he laid me down. Unable to stop I slid my hand under his shirt and felt him swallow. His chest was hard with smooth ridges and curves against the lean muscle. My hand trembled. I wanted to run my fingers across every inch of him and it scared me how badly I wanted to do it *now*.

Darren's hand ran down my ribs, my waist, my thigh, and then hooked up under my knee. I had to bite my lip as he pulled me even closer, not caring that the hem of my dress was riding dangerously high. Every part of me was burning higher and higher and higher and I knew we should stop but I couldn't bring myself to move even if I wanted to because, gods, Darren's hands were on my skin and in my hair and my entire body was a quivering mess.

Darren's breathing wasn't so steady either. His mouth fell to my shoulder and a whimper escaped my lips. *Was that really me?* I started to pull away, embarrassed, but Darren took my chin and kissed me hard, biting the bottom of my lip until I gasped.

My nails dug into his shoulders and I kissed him back, melting and burning and unable to keep my hands to myself. Gods, I was losing myself in what it felt like to be near him. Darren was dangerous, driving me to forget everything and everyone but this moment and I didn't ever want it to end.

Any semblance of control was broken. The non-heir choked my name, picking me up and throwing me onto his bed. Soft pillows feathered my fall. Darren's face was flushed and his eyes were wild as he pushed my wrists up against the frame.

I held my breath, my eyes locked on the two dark smoldering stars bearing down on me.

"You have no idea what it is I want to do to you," he whispered.

The only sound in the entire room was the frantic beating of my heart, slamming against my chest until I was sure it would break.

And then there was a loud knock on the door.

"Open up, brother, I know you are in there. The guards saw you."

The two of us jumped. Darren practically fell from his bed as I darted to a corner of the room, the two of us in a mad panic.

Darren motioned for me to hide behind one of the heavy brocade curtains hanging at the opposite end of the room. Then he cleared his throat loudly and made his way to the door, cracking it open it only a smidge to glare at his brother on the other side.

"What do you want, Blayne?"

"I have been looking all over for you. Father expected you to report to him as soon as you arrived."

"I was busy."

"Busy?" Blayne's tone was instantly suspicious. "Doing what? Avoiding your duties to the Crown? Priscilla said she hasn't seen you all day either. This better not be about that lowborn, brother. I have no more patience for whatever silly infatuation you've got parading around in that thick skull of yours."

The non-heir stiffened. "Ryiah is not lowborn anymore, and even if she were—"

Blayne ignored him and rattled on: "What you need is a good lay, Darren. I've seen how that redhead looks at you. Tell her whatever she needs to hear and the rest will take care of itself. Then you can get back to what's important. Like your role in this kingdom—or have you been training so long as a mage that you forgot you were also a prince?"

Darren's knuckles on the door's handle whitened. "I know my role," he said shortly, "and where my duties lie. I will report to father within the hour."

"Well, see to it that you do," Blayne snapped. "I can't be the only one who takes my role seriously. What Father sees in you I will never know."

A moment later Darren shut the door, as soon as he was sure Blayne had left the hall.

"I'm sorry you had to hear that."

I stepped out of the curtain, sick to my stomach. Even without the knowledge I'd been present Blayne had still managed to make me feel worthless. "*Tell her whatever she needs to hear and the rest will take care of itself.*" His words made me realize how close Darren and I had come to fulfilling his twisted prophecy.

This time when the non-heir took a step toward me, I flinched. Darren's shrewd gaze missed nothing.

"You are upset."

"I-I'm not upset," I stammered. "I j-just didn't think things would h-happen s-so fast."

Fury darkened the prince's face. "I would never ask you to do anything you didn't want to, Ryiah. I'm not my brother. I would never try what he and Ella—"

"I-it's not that." I was stuttering and I knew my cheeks were now as red as my scarlet red locks. "But..."

"But you can't stop thinking about what my brother said."

I couldn't look at him.

A hand entered my vision and tipped my face. Darren's eyes met mine and there was a grim smile. "Blayne's wrong," he promised quietly. "I'm in love with you, Ryiah. Nothing is ever going to change that."

# Chapter Thirteen

With my best impression of nonchalance, I exited the castle's formal ascension chambers and followed the remaining throng of apprentices into the grand ballroom. Everyone was chattering on in excited voices and even the ornate torches seemed to reflect the evening's enthusiasm, flickering wildly along the hall and dancing off the many-colored windowpanes surrounding it. The orchestra was already playing an upbeat march and the heralds were having particular fun announcing the newly graduated mages to the awaiting crowd of nobility.

As we poured into the brightly lit room I found myself scanning the mass for the one apprentice who had been noticeably absent throughout the entire ceremony. For the past week I had barely slept, tossing and turning, dreaming of that moment Darren finally appeared and put all my fears to rest. Five days had never passed as slowly as they had the past week. I was convinced that mountains moved faster than the sun, which appeared almost stagnant and solely there to test my will.

"Ryiah, don't you want to grab something to drink?"

I started, drawn out of my thoughts by the suddenness of my friend's voice.

"Ella," my twin's voice was filled with irony, "can't you see? She's waiting for *him*."

I glared at Alex. "You don't need to be so cruel."

My brother made a frustrated noise. "You don't need to be so naïve either, Ryiah."

"Like all those girls you courted before Ella?" I stood my ground. I would not let his doubt get to me. Not tonight. "Darren's not a hopeless flirt like you!"

"Ry—Alex, stop it!" Ella shoved herself between us to glower at my brother. "Alex, your sister is old enough to make decisions for herself. The least you can do is support her."

My brother stared at her incredulously. "Don't pretend to agree with her, El. You told me last night—"

"It don't matter what we think," she interrupted hastily, "this is about Ryiah and Darren. No one else matters."

I never got to catch my brother's reply. At that very moment the royal herald chose to announce the Crown. My heart instantly caught in my throat and my gaze instantly swerved to the room's entrance.

"King Lucius and his royal highness, Prince Blayne."

The king and his eldest son entered, their icy blue eyes casting out a silent chill as they made their way to the front of the room. They bore matching blood red cloaks and tight-fitted brocade that highlighted their health and the golden thread and gems that lined their heavy, chained fastenings. The room had gone silent the moment they made their approach—although it hardly seemed possible from the heavy pounding in my ears.

I watched as they settled into their chairs, and then I waited.

There was an odd moment where everything was still, and then the herald continued:

"Prince Darren, second-in-line to the throne."

I started to push my way to the front, eager to catch a better glimpse-

"And his betrothed, Lady Priscilla of Langli."

The loud clang of metal brought the eyes of everyone—including *him*—to me. I stood frozen in place, pale and unmoving as ice, while a red-faced servant bent to pick up his serving platter from the hard marble floor. It had been unceremoniously knocked from his arms just moments before.

I didn't hear the loud gasps coming from the crowd around me. I barely noticed the red stains that now covered the hem of my blossoming skirts. My eyes were glued to the indifferent prince staring back at me.

Two pairs of hands took hold of my arms and gently led me to the back of the room, out of the attention of others, while I watched the dark-haired stranger and his lady resume their procession.

"Ryiah?"

I watched as the young man took his seat beside the king and his heir, with the dark-haired beauty standing close by and casting a simpering smile while he talked. Not once did the stranger's gaze stray from her face, nor did he hesitate to kiss her hand and laugh easily at something a nearby courtier said in response to the lady's question.

"Ry, if you want to retire early I'd be happy to join you." Ella's voice was strangely muted—like she was speaking through glass. Her voice was distorted and muffled, more like one long humming stance than a question.

*What was happening?* Why was he smiling at *her* like that? I kept staring, waiting for a break in the façade. Just the barest hint that he wasn't enjoying himself, that he felt something—anything—other than the nonchalance that was plastered all over his face.

"You should just take her now." My brother's hushed whisper seemed even further away. "Before she does something rash."

*I know they forced you into this.* My breathing became calm, steady. That was it, of course. Darren needed more time to talk the king around. It wasn't something either of us had prepared for, but we would find a way.

Warmth returned to my limbs and I found that the numbness in my legs and arms had receded. I hugged my arms to my chest. He loved me. So I would wait. I had already waited three years, what would a little more time be?

"Please excuse me." My voice caught. I didn't bother to look to my brother or friend as I pushed my way through to the hall. Faces passed by in a blur, though it was only as I entered my chambers that I realized why.

Tears.

I might be willing to wait, but I could not very well stand by while Priscilla paraded the boy I loved in front of me.

I waited, counting out the opening and shutting of chamber doors until I was certain the last apprentice had returned from the palace's late night festivities. I waited for an additional toll from the great bell tower and then stealthily exited my chambers, careful not to slam the door and draw the attention of any loitering servants or guards posted nearby. Most were too busy cleaning up after the feast to notice, but one could never be too careful.

I drew my cloak close and passed the women's hall, continuing on past the men's and then finally up the many flights of stairs and twisting corridors—retracing my steps once or twice—in an effort to locate Darren's chambers.

"Excuse me, miss, no one can pass this point without an official summons." Just as I reached the final hall I found two guards blocking its entrance. The one who had spoken was eyeing me with a skeptical expression and the other was tapping his scabbard. Tick. Tick. Tick. Neither looked particularly willing to let me pass.

I had been expecting as much. I let the hood fall from my face so that they would recognize me as one of the apprentices. "Please, if you could tell Prince Darren it's Ryiah, I am sure he will make an exception."

The first guard yawned loudly. "Lady Ryiah, if we interrupted the Crown for every person seeking audience we would be out of a job."

"Yes, but I'm not—"

"Let her in, gentleman, I can vouch for this one *personally*."

Every hair on my neck stood on end. I knew that slick voice like the back of my hand. Blayne. Bells of alarm rang out loudly in my ears but I tried not to let the panic show in my face. Why was *he* coming to my aid? He hated me.

Something was wrong.

The guards lowered their weapons and stepped to the side as the heir to Jerar escorted me forward. I tried not to flinch as he tugged me along, a deep sense of foreboding as we reached Darren's chamber. The last time the two of us had crossed paths, Blayne had made it perfectly clear what he thought of the lowborn girl who shared a friendship with his brother. And then I had attacked him. Even if Darren had informed his brother of his intentions, I highly doubted Blayne had forgiven me for *that*.

I hesitated at the door, wondering if Blayne planned to witness my confrontation with his brother.

"Go on. Knock." The words came out silky and dangerous, with a hint of disgust that was fully evident now that we were past the guard's hearing. I chanced a glance at Blayne's expression and saw the malignant curve of his lips.

Rapping twice against the dark wood I waited, my stomach in knots. I heard the soft pad of boots against carpet, and then the door swung open to reveal Darren, half-dressed in dark breeches and a loose cotton shirt. Dark bangs fell to the side of his face—but it wasn't enough to shield the guilt that flared in his eyes for just a moment before quickly melding into cool indifference.

Darren's mouth hardened into a small, thin line. "What are you doing here, Ryiah?"

My whole body went cold, and for a moment I couldn't believe it was Darren standing in front of me. There hadn't been a single hint of emotion in his address.

"I need to talk to you." I was trying my best to sound calm. "Alone."

The non-heir's gaze slid to his brother, and then back to me. His expression didn't waver. "There is nothing to discuss."

"Darren." My voice cracked. "*Please.*"

Blayne—who up until now had been a smug spectator, leaning against the frame of Darren's door lazily—snorted rudely. "My dear," he drawled, "my brother has given you his answer. Pick up your lowborn pride and leave before this gets worse. I only brought you so you wouldn't assault those poor guards trying to get over here in the first place. I am well aware of your *temper*." He pronounced the last word distinctly.

I ignored Blayne and kept my eyes locked on the one person that mattered. "What did they say to you, Darren?" My pulse was racing. I could feel my heartbeat in my throat. I swallowed and forced myself to continue. "I'll wait... If you tell me you need more time to talk your father around—"

Blayne let out a high-pitched laugh.

"Ryiah." Garnet flames stopped me mid-speech. "I don't want you to wait."

It was as if someone had just plunged me into a bath of ice. "What do you mean?"

Darren was silent.

I felt hysteria rising. "Darren." I took a step forward—ignoring his brother's sharp intake of breath—and took the non-heir's hand. "Don't do this. I—" My voice caught. "-I love you."

The prince frowned and looked pointedly to his brother. "Might we have a moment alone?"

Blayne's blue eyes narrowed in suspicion, but he stepped back with a curt glance at me. "Remember," he snarled, "if you try anything I will have the guards over here at a moment's notice."

I glared back at him. "I believe your brother asked for some privacy."

Anger shot across the heir's features—but before he could say anything in reply Darren had pulled me into his chamber and shut the door. Then it was just the two of us facing one another, no noise except for the quiet beating of our chests and Blayne's pacing outside the room.

"*What are you doing?*"

"I am making the best of a bad situation." Darren dropped my hand as he added, "It will be best if you don't make a scene."

"A scene?" My voice was shrill. "Darren, you told me you were leaving her! Why are you still betrothed to Priscilla?"

"You know why."

"I thought you were tired of following rules!" I shouted, furious. "You told me—you *promised* that day on the ship—even if things became hard you wouldn't give up on us!"

The prince didn't respond. I closed the distance between us and grabbed both of his shoulders, shaking him. "Darren, look at me!"

Darren shoved me away angrily. "What do you want me to say, Ryiah? I made a mistake."

For a moment there was only silence.

"We aren't a mistake." Tears were burning my eyes.

"You had to know we would never be able to marry." His eyes were fathomless. "Even if I had somehow convinced Father to break off my engagement to Priscilla and court you, it never would have lasted long."

I couldn't breathe. For a moment all I could hear was the angry pulsing of blood.

And then:

"YOU COWARD!" I picked up the nearest object I could find—a large glass globe—and lobbed it at his head. "YOU AREN'T EVEN TRYING TO FIGHT FOR US!"

Darren dodged the globe easily and there was a loud shattering as millions of tiny shards misted the air between us.

"You shouldn't have done that, Ryiah," he said.

The chamber door swung open as Blayne and the two guards from earlier strode in, weapons raised.

I dropped my hands and let the two men bind my wrists, two sets of rough hands dragging me away from the prince. "All this time I respected you for trying to prove you were more than a prince, more than some privileged highborn!" I spat at him. "It's a shame to find out you are no more than your father's whipping boy!"

Darren's stopped looking indifferent—now the expression he wore was livid. "You want to know the truth?" He shouldered his way past the guards so that he was inches from my face. Blayne watched the both of us with keen interest.

"I never loved you."

"LIAR!" I wrestled with my restraints, but the guards were too strong.

"I never loved you." Darren's laugh was cold and unfeeling. "Did I want you? Of course, I would've been a fool not to... But love? Well, that's just something one claims to win certain privileges."

"*You are lying!*" I couldn't believe him. I wouldn't. He was only trying to hurt me to make this easier. It was like our first year at the Academy: he was protecting me, I knew it. *He had to-*

"Ryiah, Ryiah." Blayne's tone was scornful. "Surely you know better than that. Think about it. When has prince of Jerar ever married a commoner? Darren didn't want to court you—he wanted to bed you." He snickered. "Why do you think he was so quick to end things after you turned him away?"

"No." My whole body was shaking. "*No!*"

"I'm sorry it had to come to this."

I couldn't speak—not without bursting into angry sobs, and I would *not* let him see me cry.

"You should leave now, Ryiah." Darren's voice was void of emotion.

My hands trembled violently and I couldn't stop gasping for air. *What was wrong with me?* I felt like my chest was being ripped apart at its seams.

"Guards, take her away." Blayne had stopped looking entertained. "This has gone on long enough."

*You do not control me.* Before the guards could drag me away I slammed a heel into each of their boots and then bit down on my tongue until it bled, letting the momentary pain send enough magic for my bonds to break.

Then before the men could stop me I gathered my skirts and gave a mock bow to my audience. "Your highnesses."

I didn't bother to wait for a reply—I ran down the hall half-aware of Blayne's shouting and Darren's mumbled response. I kept waiting for the sound of angry footfall behind me, but it never came. Darren must have convinced the guards to let me go.

*"I never loved you."* I threw open the door to my chambers and slammed it shut behind me. *"Love?"* I threw myself onto the bed. *"That's just something one claims to win certain privileges."*

Darren was the world's greatest liar. Or I was the worst kind of fool.

Either way there was no victory to be held. Everything had played out exactly the way the others had warned me it would. I had chosen to fly—was it really any wonder the fall would be so steep? My breathing hitched and an unbidden sob tore its way across my chest.

Then the tears came...

I wasn't sure they'd ever stop.

They did, eventually.

But that only made it worse. I was still crying, screaming, dying inside.

I didn't remember falling asleep.

# CHAPTER FOURTEEN

"Alright, listen up, apprentices, I don't want you parading around like a bunch of girls at a convent because you have an audience during today's drills. This morning's exercise was particularly shameful."

"Is the entire court going to be watching all year?" The words burst from my lips before I could stop them. I couldn't help it—for the first half of our day the palace nobles had been everywhere. Watching the morning run and warm ups around the practice yard, commenting during the non-magicked weapons drills, placing bets on our prowess and rooting for favorites... it was like our first-year trials all over again.

The highborns had returned to the palace grounds for lunch, but there was always the threat they could return.

Master Byron scowled as the rest of the class turned to watch his reply. "Yes. This is one of the court's favorite activities when the apprenticing mages and squires are stationed in Devon. The king himself commissions it. Do you have a problem with spectators, apprentice?"

I bit my lip. There was no point arguing with our training master, hadn't I learned that by now? "No."

Byron's stern gaze slide to the rest of his audience. "Anyone else?"

Silence.

"Good. Now that Apprentice Ryiah has withdrawn her complaint, let's resume what matters, shall we?" The man made a face. "This year's castings will be particularly poignant. Mentors, you will be casting on command. Mentees, I leave it up to you to form the appropriate deflection."

"How do we know which casting to defend ourselves with?"

I cringed as I watched the Master of Combat turn on the second-year who had spoken, an anxious-looking girl named Tully. His face was a mottled shade of red.

"Common sense. And practice. Lots of it. Do not interrupt me again, apprentice." The training master glowered at the rest of the class. "*As I keep attempting to say*, these drills will build up your reserve to a multitude of attacks… Given a couple of weeks I am sure most of the fourth— and fifth-years will be ready to advance to un-dictated exchanges, but for this first month I would like the entire faction to train together. Now, everyone take your positions."

The class quickly dispersed and I found myself trailing after Ella and her new mentor Bryce to the end of two parallel lines. Both apprentices avoided looking directly at one another as they waited for the drills to begin. I cringed inwardly. Ella's pairing was almost as painful as mine. Bryce was one of Priscilla's friends and shared many of her condescending views. This morning he'd made the mistake of telling his mentee she was a fool for consorting with lowborns. Before my brother and I had even risen Ella had already thrown the entire contents of her porridge into the highborn's face.

Now she had latrine duty for a week.

Needless to say the two were at an uncomfortable impasse.

Still, I had to think animosity was better than guilt. Ella could at least channel her frustration into her castings. With my fifth-year mentor I had already made a fool of myself holding back in a misguided attempt to spare him. Two times during the morning's non-magic sparring I had received a stiff reprimand from Byron and an unpleasant bruise where my new partner's blows had landed.

I vowed not to let pity affect my actions for the rest of the afternoon. The last thing I needed was for the Master of Combat to assume I'd gone soft.

Taking a deep breath, I took my place beside Ella, shifting my feet into a comfortable stance as I faced off against the sandy-haired fifth-year fifteen feet across from me.

Ian met my eyes without expression. He hadn't said a word to me since our unfortunate pairing. Not that I could blame him. The last time we'd exchanged a full sentence I had broken his heart and subsequently ended our friendship.

*Not unlike what Darren did to me.*

I shoved the thought away as soon as it came. I wouldn't, *couldn't* think about the non-heir now. Not unless I wanted to spend the rest of the day fighting back tears. And I was done crying. I'd had three weeks of that during our travel from the palace to the Academy and then back again. If anything, that experience taught me exactly how heartless I had been to Ian.

I deserved the fifth-year's silence.

But it made things extremely awkward. Mentors and mentees were supposed to trade advice and feedback. Suggestions. It wasn't exactly possible if you weren't speaking to one another.

"And begin. Mentors: *ice*!"

I barely had time to throw up my defense. In the blink of an eye Ian had cast out an onslaught of icicles. Sharp, spinning torrents of water tore into the metal shield I had cast. An unfortunate choice. Within seconds the casting had frozen the metal and sent a chilling burn down my arm.

Ian released his casting just as I dropped my shield to the floor. My whole arm stung. Stupid, stupid, *stupid*. I knew better than to cast iron against ice. My guilt was going to ruin my training if I kept forgetting to *think*. Ian could handle himself—any feelings of ill will were buried behind a stone wall of silence.

It was me that needed to focus.

Massaging my arm I forced myself to straighten back up and take in the rest of the class around me. I was relieved to see I wasn't the only one who had cast metal… but then it came to my attention that the only mentees foolish enough were second-years. The rest of my year had used fire.

I nodded to Ian for him to start again and then cast out a barrier of flames. At that exact moment Byron called out "Wind!"

I barely had time to fall back before a huge gust of fire came sweeping toward me. Ian ceased his attack immediately but it was too late for my pride. I could hear Priscilla's tittering laughter a couple spots down.

I turned my head to glare at the girl and immediately regretted it when I noticed the non-heir watching me.

My pulse stopped.

I couldn't breath.

I couldn't think.

I couldn't *move.*

"Keep drilling, apprentices, I didn't tell you to gawk!"

*What was wrong with me?* I swallowed the bitter taste in my mouth and made myself block out everything but the green-eyed fifth-year directly across from me. My mentor's blank expression gave no hint to his feelings. If he was secretly pleased I was making a fool of myself in today's lessons, he gave no sign of it.

"Fire!"

At least this time I was ready. Before the flames had even traveled half the distance between us I had a spiraling tunnel of sand chasing across the field to squelch them. There was the sizzling hiss as sand collided with fire and then a loud clap as the flames died.

The remains of sand sprayed across Ian and the mentors closest.

Several of them—including Bryce—shouted insults. They stopped their own castings to brush sand off their clothes and skin, glowering. Master Byron issued the command to stop and then came barreling down the field to rest directly in front of me.

"*Have you lost all common sense, apprentice*? I told you to defend yourself—not show off in front of the entire faction! You are supposed to conserve your castings! *Conserve*!" He took a deep, exaggerated huff. "Your little display just cost you an unnecessary amount of magic. Flashy casting doesn't win a war—the mages fool enough to use it will be long dead while the rest of the enemy mages are left standing!"

*Why me?* If I had been anyone else Byron would have seen fit to offer a short rebuke and move on. But never with me.

"Yes, sir."

"If you can't control your castings then you don't belong in Combat."

I stayed silent.

With a satisfied grunt the master retired to his post near the second-years and called out his next command. Byron remained there for the rest of the exercise. Not once did his hawk eyes leave my face.

By the time our drills had ended I was ready to collapse. As soon as we were dismissed Ian brushed past me in a hurry to spend as little time together as possible. Ella joined me in my slow march to the commons. My friend knew better than to say anything. Instead, she linked elbows and sighed loudly.

Students hurried past us, eager to beat the others to the evening meal. Ella and I took our time. This year was different and neither of us had been prepared for how much.

When Byron had first announced our new city was Devon I had thought it a joke. A very cruel, very pointed joke.

And then, after we returned from picking up the second-years, I'd found out he was serious.

We really *were* in Devon.

The capital was different. Ishir Outpost and Port Langli were important, but neither of them could compare to a regiment ten times their size. The Crown's Army trained, if it was at all possible, harder than anyone else.

The army was so large the capital had built four training arenas—a small one inside the palace walls for the King's Regiment, and three much bigger grounds outside the township where the army's soldiers, knights, and mages spent their days endlessly drilling until they were called upon for service. It was a good ten-mile ride east of the palace. The site housed an enormous armory, an equally large stable, two bathhouses, two outhouses, a giant cook's camp, and an impressive expanse of tented housing just south of its arenas.

It was the city regiment we had the highest chance of being placed in after our ascension. That was the first thing Byron had told us when we arrived the night before. It was for that reason alone I had dried my eyes, taken a deep breath, and told myself to forget the past three weeks.

I needed to toughen up quick, or risk becoming the laughingstock of not just my faction but the Crown's Army.

That, and I was done with my body's traitorous reaction any time the prince looked at me. I couldn't survive two more years of this apprenticeship if I let myself feel. I was done with misery. I would *not* let my learning be squandered by a broken heart.

"Ry! Ella! What took you two so long?"

I made a face at my twin. "It's been a long day." Alex was already seated on one of the outdoor tables with a mountain of noodles piled high on his plate. Beside him sat a couple of his factionmates and Loren and Ray—none of which had half the servings my brother did.

Ella's mouth hung open in shock. "You know the cook has to feed the whole camp, right?"

Alex grinned. "Only the ones that arrive on time. After that it's fair game."

I snatched a roll off his plate before he could stop me. "After that we'll just take it from you."

My twin rolled his eyes and then changed the subject. "How was casting? Loren was just telling me Byron yelled at you in front of the entire faction."

"How is that different from any other day?"

Alex didn't let it go. "What did you do?" He lowered his voice. "Please tell me you finally gave the prince the thrashing he deserves—" My brother didn't get to finish. Ella had elbowed him, hard, in the chest.

I stared at the sky in frustration. I wanted to move on. I did. But no matter how hard I tried there was always something or someone there to remind me. Alex knew this, of course. Since the ascension ceremony he had tried to keep his outrage to a minimum, but it still slipped out whenever he wasn't careful.

Alex swallowed guiltily. "Sorry, Ry."

I stood up, ready to fill up a plate of my own and leave the uncomfortable exchange behind. "Don't be. If I couldn't be imprisoned for attacking a king's son I probably would have done just that." I left the table without waiting for a response.

A flurry of days, and then weeks, swept past before I even had a chance to catch my breath. I quickly got used to the stifling conditions of Devon's giant training camp and the constant presence of the king's court in our early morning practices. I even got used to interpreting the stony silence of my mentor.

I avoided the prince at all costs.

Before noon every day Byron had us wielding axes. They were the weapon of choice for the Crown's Army, which meant they were what we spent the majority of time training with.

Out of all the battleaxes, we drilled with the poleaxe and halberd most. The training master was quick to point out how easily they could break enemy lines. We spent most of our days nursing wounds from slashed mail or dented armor.

When we weren't drilling on the ground we did it as cavalry. Against one partner or a cluster of them. The axes made a formidable opponent against crowds. In other words, Bryon was quick to note, their haft was ideal for mass attacks on horseback.

We learned when it was better to bludgeon and slash, when to thrust with the spike's head, and how to disarm an enemy in a slight of hand.

It was an endless cycle of drilling, but by the end of the second week I had no reservations going up against Ian. He was a formidable opponent—being the son of a blacksmith brought many advantages—and any time I had caught myself holding back I quickly received a painful reminder why that was a mistake.

Ian still wasn't talking to me. But he treated me like an equal. If he had really wanted to hurt me he could have held back in his attacks. There was nothing worse for a warrior's training than an easy teacher, and for that I was grateful.

Our mid-day lessons were spent in one of the camp's largest tents. Crown's Army meetings were held inside the palace walls but for our training purposes the tents would do. Local command—including Eve's father, Commander Audric—and even the Colored Robes made an appearance from time to time to assist with lecture. Most of the military's special strategies were released on a need-to-know basis (especially given the recent rebel activity) but the officials did give us plenty of other things to consider.

The majority of the time the men and women of the Crown's Army stayed on base training, enforcing Crown Law, and assisting Devon's local farmers. Only a small grouping (in comparison to their actual number; I hardly considered one thousand men—the size of Port Langli's local regiment—"small") regularly patrolled the countryside. The army was too expensive to house in the capital so the camp was at the city's outskirts.

The soldiers who resided in camp took care of its upkeep and any services that needed rendering. Units took turns cooking and cleaning, hunting and building to keep the costs to a minimum. Still, the commander made it clear the army's salaries alone ate away at the Crown's coffers. Housing a large army was an incredibly expensive feat, and it was easy to see why the king considered Caltoth's frugality suspicious.

While we didn't get to learn as many specifics as I had hoped, the leaders did spend a lot of time addressing each mage's role in the event of a siege. Devon was the most important city of Jerar, and as such there were certain tasks that needed to be seen to first.

I was so distracted with all of our learning that I almost forgot about what was coming.

Ella was quick to remind me. "The mock battle, Ry, it's tomorrow." Three months had passed in the blink of an eye. I was so stupefied I almost fell out of my chair.

To calm my frazzled nerves my friend suggested we spend an evening outside of the barracks… Which was exactly how Ella, Alex, and I found ourselves in one of Devon's local taverns the night before the big match.

Interestingly enough we weren't alone. Half the factions' apprentices and some of the Crown's Army were already crowding the tables by the time we arrived. "The Lusty Wench" was, apparently, a local favorite.

Waiting for the others to get back with the drinks I pulled out Derrick's most recent letter and read:

*Dearest sister (and Alex who never writes back—for shame!),*

*I'm a soldier! I know, I know, you never had any doubt but it is still such a relief to be out of Demsh'aa for good! I love our parents dearly but I believe the three of us have all seen enough herbs to last a lifetime, eh?*

*They already have us stationed along the northern border… I've only been here two months but it is has quickly become evident the instructors weren't exaggerating. There's already been two raids since we arrived! Both times I was asleep, and by the time my section of the barracks was awoken the enemy was gone.*

*I know it is not good thinking but I really hope I get to serve during the next one. Some of the other boys are already bragging that they've made their first kill. I don't want to kill anyone—I know I will have to, it's only a matter of time—but I would like to serve Jerar and keep those nasty Caltothians out.*

*I hope your apprenticeship is going well. You and Alex are fourth-years now—just one more year after this and you'll be mages! MAGES! Just in time for the Candidacy, too!*

*Write back and say hello to your pretty friend Ella—tell her if Alex messes this one up I'd be happy to prove not all men in our family are halfwits!*

*- Derrick*

I set my brother's letter down with a chuckle. It might be my most challenging year yet, but at least Derrick was having a good time. Someone should be.

Alex snorted loudly, having finishing the letter over my shoulder just moments after. "That little pest is full of himself now that he's got himself a soldier's blade."

Ella smiled widely. "I don't know, Alex, Derrick *is* pretty handsome."

My twin choked. "He's three years younger!"

I let them continue their banter. I couldn't wait to be stationed up north with Derrick next summer. Everyone knew Ferren's Keep was one of the four cities the apprentices trained in and it was only a half a day's ride to the border from there. I had missed many things since Alex and I had first set out for the Academy three years ago, and my family—especially Derrick—I missed the most. Already my younger brother had matured from a feisty twelve-year-old into a young man. Cavalry didn't have a four-year apprenticeship period like the other war schools but I still couldn't believe Derrick was a soldier. I had missed that period of growth from child to adult and it was alarming how quickly it had happened.

Next year couldn't come soon enough.

"Do you think we will lose again this time?"

I glanced up over my plate of roast boar to frown at Ella. She was talking about the mock battle. "You think we will?"

"We are mentees. The odds aren't exactly in our favor."

Alex put his arm around the girl's waist. "We won our first year—and we were the underdogs then too."

"Yes, but we won because Ry was able to bat her eyelashes at Ian instead of fighting him. Somehow I don't think that tactic would work quite as well this year."

"Hey!" I huffed indignantly. "I can fight him."

"Sorry, hun, but he *is* your mentor. I've seen the two of you in practice." My friend looked sympathetic.

I cringed. She was right, of course. Ian *did* beat me most of the time. The last two months Byron had let the fourth— and fifth-years cast on their own. Without the master's split-second commands to prepare me for my defense I had struggled to keep up with the random assault of attacks. Still, I liked to think I had done better than most of the other fourth-years.

That, and I was still better than Ian at pain casting. Darren and I were better than *all* of the fifth-years who could pain cast… but that didn't really matter when the third-years were still much better than our second-year mentees.

Overall the mentors still outperformed us in casting *and* physical prowess.

"If you think about it, since we started the apprenticeship the mentees have won every year." Ray joined us at our table, eager to be included in the night's debate.

"That's true." Ella stirred her cider with her finger. "And it's uncommon enough as is. Perhaps the streak will continue."

The tavern was noisy—but not so much so that I couldn't hear the door swing open for its newest customers. Especially when the whole room went silent. I turned just in time to see Priscilla, Darren, and Blayne appear in its entry all laughing loudly at something their unknown companion had said.

My blood turned to ice. I was all too conscious of *his* presence. I fought myself to keep from staring.

To redirect my thoughts I studied the stranger instead.

The girl was of islander descent like Lynn, with the same straight black hair and almond eyes. Unlike the apprentice, however, she dressed much more elaborately. The material that made up the stranger's gown and cloak was something I had only seen once before, in one of the merchant stalls in Langli. Borean silk.

What really caught my interest was how the girl held herself. When she spoke to the crown prince and his brother there was no hint of awe, no fear, none of the usual trademarks of someone addressing their better. Either the stranger knew Blayne and Darren very well, or she was royalty.

"Is that…?"

"*Princess Shinako!*" Lynn squealed. I watched as the fifth-year ran up to greet the girl in fine dress.

Shinako instantly broke off her conversation to embrace her old friend. The two started to exchange excited greetings, but Blayne interrupted with a curt, "Shina!" The princess rolled her eyes and then Blayne grabbed her arm, whispering something that made her redden instantly.

The princess murmured an apology to her friend and then shoved her way past Blayne to strike up a conversation with his brother instead.

"What do you think he said to her?" Ray wondered.

"It's Blayne," Ella's gaze followed the princess, sympathetically, "so probably something horrible."

Alex darkened. "If I ever catch him *or* his brother in an alley alone…"

"You won't do anything." Ella gave my brother a sharp look, but her voice softened as she added, "Because if you do, you'll be thrown in prison and what life would that leave *us*?"

Alex gripped my friend's fingers tightly.

Neither of them said anything more. They didn't need to.

I turned to Ray, feeling uncomfortable with the exchange. I was happy for Alex and Ella, I was, but every time I saw how easy it was for them a dark, gnawing jealousy began to eat away at my stomach.

"Romance only slows you down."

I tried a smile and found it came a bit easier than it would have three months back. "Thanks."

"What are you thinking for tomorrow's strategy?"

The tavern door swung open again and I found my eyes unwillingly tearing toward it. A second later I regretted the action when I realized who it was.

It took Ian even less time to spot me. The moment he did irritation crossed his features.

A second later the fifth-year turned heel and strode back through the exit.

Ian would be not partaking in the festivities tonight, not as long as I was part of them. The door slammed shut and I heard Ray's low whistle.

"Guess it slows others down too."

# Chapter Fifteen

"Why should *he* lead?"

The entire grouping of second—and fourth-year mentees swerved their heads to look at me. Even Ella and Alex looked surprised.

I held my ground and repeated myself. "We didn't even vote. Darren shouldn't get the role of command just because he is a prince. There are other fourth-years who would like the opportunity to try."

"Like you?"

I swallowed as Darren's garnet fell to me. For a moment he almost looked hurt, but any residual surprise quickly morphed into indignation.

"I have led us for two years."

"And only once to victory—which you wouldn't even have been able to do without me." It felt good, I realized, to speak out.

"Last year we failed because of your and Ella's flagrant disregard for orders!"

"Your orders were wrong!"

"I was the leader, even if my orders were wrong you should have listened to me!"

"So I should just blindly follow an idiot?"

"*Enough!*"

Both us stopped arguing as Eve stepped in between us. The girl, usually soft spoken, was unusually loud.

"I don't want to hear about any more of our past battles. We won one, we lost one. For everyone's sake I am going to offer myself as commander. I don't agree with Ryiah's assertion that Darren was chosen for his bloodline—I happen to think he is very good at leading—but I do think it would be a nice change to let someone else take the reins for a day. And, no, Ryiah, I don't think it should be you. You and Darren are too much alike. Both of you are risk takers. It's time we had someone who approached things more cautiously."

I bristled at that last insinuation. That Darren and I were the same in anything irked me to no avail. I was *not* reckless. Darren didn't look too happy either.

"I second Eve." Ray stepped forward shooting me an apologetic smile. I remembered our first-year trials and the stunt I had pulled during our duel. *Maybe I was a little reckless.*

"I, as well."

"Me too."

Within seconds the mentees had all agreed to a change of leadership. Even Ella and Alex. The only person who did not was Priscilla but she was outvoted.

"Sorry, Ry," Ella murmured as Eve launched into strategy talk. "I'm sure you would have done well but I think everyone knows Darren would not be very cooperative if it was you, and we need all of us working together to win this."

I sighed. Once again the non-heir had found a way to make my life difficult. No one wanted me as a leader if it meant our most powerful fourth-year was against it.

*How could I have ever fallen for someone like him?*

We spent the next hour following Eve's directives. I had to admit she knew what she was doing. Having a father in charge of the Crown's Army had made her the ideal commander for a mock battle in Devon. She had the Alchemy apprentices busy mixing magicked oils to strengthen the weak armor our team was supplied. Restoration was already scouting the southern district, looking for possible safe houses to mark with our agreed upon sign.

Combat, of course, was busy planning the attack. Eve led the discussion, citing the best and worst locations for an ambush.

The entire township of Devon had been evacuated for our mock battle. All around the edges of its agreed upon border were families of merchants, farmers, nobility, and any of the King's Regiment and Crown's Army who had received the day off. They were all watching alongside our factions' masters and Commander Audric.

It was intimidating.

For the day's event each team had been allotted five horses, six breast plates, five chain mail shirts, a handful of wooden shields, six poleaxes, five halberds, a rucksack of woolen bandages and salve, and a small barrel filled with the ingredients Alchemy needed to cast their potions.

We quickly divvied up the components and gave the second-year mentees the spelled plate armor, halberds, and horses. They would need the most advantage and plate armor was too heavy for quick movement on foot.

Eventually, it was time to begin.

I fell hard, my palms slapping the ground and the rustle of small metal ringlets ringing in my ears. Moments later a spiraling torrent of ice slammed into the wall behind me, just inches from where my head had been. I barely had time to choke out a small gasp of relief and then I was on my feet, sprinting as fast as my legs could carry me.

I threw up a barrier behind me and prayed it would hold. It was a costly casting—something I usually didn't like to invoke since the sphere tended to drain my magic's stamina much faster than a shield. It was a combination of phantom currents: steel, wind, and crackling power all thrust into a giant purple globe. But I didn't have time to predict my pursuers' next casting—not while I was out in the open.

My feet pounded along cobblestone as I searched for a safe house, wishing desperately I had remembered Eve's instruction from earlier that morning. The mock battle had been going on for three hours and I already seemed to have forgotten most of our strategy.

"*You can't run forever, Ryiah!*" Laughter echoed down the street. I kept running.

Alex and the rest of his Restoration mates had spent twenty minutes going over the safe houses. Our signal was supposed to be a small splatter of mud at the bottom right corner of the doorway, inconspicuous to all except one who knew exactly what to seek… but try as I might I could not spot any in the buildings I passed.

I must have heard wrong.

I knew a safe house had to be somewhere close—just two shops further and I would be crossing into the northern half of the city where the mentors patrolled. At the start of our prebattle planning the masters had assigned us the southern section. Which meant if I didn't pass a safe house soon I would be forced to turn back and face my two attackers alone. It was reckless to go into mentor territory, and there would be no help there.

If I found a safe house nearby I could get another Combat apprentice to help me take on my two followers. The houses here weren't just a haven for Restoration and mentees in need of healing, they were also where Alchemy and Combat mages could confer until they were ready to come back out of hiding. If I fought the mentors pursuing me now I would win—but it would cost almost all of my magic to do so. And who knew how much attention the attacks would draw. If more mentors spotted me I'd be forced to surrender in a second.

I needed help.

This was exactly what Eve had warned against. It was the reason she had asked us to patrol and scout in pairs. Our team was counting on the fourth-years mentees to secure victory—all but one of our Combat second-years had already surrendered during the first two hours of battle. More than ever we needed my magic.

The original plan had been for the Combat mentees to travel in packs of two: one fourth-year and one second-year each, with Eve, Darren and their second-year mentee as our sole grouping of three. We'd been instructed to carefully scout the city limits and take out any solo Combat mentors that might be foolish enough to enter the southern territory alone.

Unfortunately for us, the mentors had also traveled in packs. Which was how, when we did cross paths, Priscilla, Ella, Ray, and I lost our mentee partners as well as their horses in a lightning-quick skirmish.

Now we were all separated, scattered across the city, seeking the others we had lost track of before. I thought I'd seen Ella take off east—the direction I'd been heading in—but everything had happened so fast and I wasn't sure of anything anymore. I'd been cut off from the others when the third-years had caught up to me twenty minutes back. Theo and Merrick had refused to give up chase and I'd spent most of my energy ducking and dodging since.

*There.* I sprinted toward the doorway with the telltale sign. The casting I'd been holding onto was starting to give me a headache—I needed to end it now before I wasted any more of my magic. I dropped my casting just as I tore open the door to find Priscilla, two of Alex's Restoration mates, and Ruth staring wide-eyed at the street behind me.

"You idiot!" Priscilla screeched. "You led them right to us!" But before I could argue she had shoved her way past me and cast out a large assault of flying daggers. One of the mentor's own blade's caught her shoulder and the highborn swore loudly.

I stumbled back after her, panting heavily, and helped Priscilla's casting. One of the blades hit Theo's horse and it reared, throwing off its rider.

Merrick tried to take on his cousin directly but a large torrent of power knocked him off his feet before he had the chance. Priscilla and I raced forward with our halberds and got the two mentors to surrender before they could cast out anything else.

As soon as the mentors had said the words, Priscilla and I went back into the safe house while a Restoration mage came forward to escort the two out of the city. The woman bore a red silk robe that proved she wasn't a part of battle in case any of the others came across her while she escorted the surrendered apprentices to the palace infirmary.

"Erik, do you have any more of that healing balm? It looks like Ry needs some for her leg and I need you to see to my shoulder."

My head swiveled to Priscilla. I couldn't keep the surprise from showing on my face. Now that we were out of danger she was still helping me.

"Don't look so surprised, lowborn, I'm not about to let my disgust for you as a person keep me from trying to secure a victory." Priscilla's tone was anything but kind.

Well, *that* at least made sense. She wanted to win, *even* if it meant playing nice.

I took a steadying breath as the Restoration apprentice treated the deep gash on my leg. It had happened when I'd tried to save Phillipe, my second-year partner. *Much good it had done me.* "How long have you been hiding out here? Have you seen any of the others?"

Priscilla sniffed. "I got here a half hour before you did. And no, I haven't been reckless enough to risk my neck without backup. I have no idea where the others are."

"I think we should go find them." I helped the apprentice finish wrapping my leg.

"Are you mad? You only just got here!"

"But what about Ray and Ella? What if they didn't find each other like we did? We can't let the mentors pick us off one by one! Like Eve said, we only have strength in numbers when we are going up against the mentors!"

"We should wait for them to find us. How do you know they aren't already together? Maybe they are with Darren and Eve."

"Priscilla, don't be a coward."

"I helped *you*, didn't I?"

"Well, help me again. Help our whole team."

"I am helping the team. I'm helping the ones in here right now."

Ruth interrupted Priscilla. "You know Ry is right. You two have to find the others. Eve's plan stated you were only to use the safe houses if you were injured or alone. Once you have help you need to go back out there and fight."

Priscilla kicked a pebble across the street, sulking, as she studied the houses behind us. We were back-to-back scouting as we made our way through the southern streets of Devon. Both of us were looking for any of our teammates, another safe house, or potential enemy mentors.

"I hope you know what you are doing."

I didn't respond. All of my senses were focused on the path in front of me. If we came across a pack of mentors we needed to spot them before they us. We could not afford to get caught off-guard. Again.

"Don't think that I didn't know you were trying to steal Darren away from me in Port Langli."

*That* caught my attention. It took all my effort not to divert focus as I said quickly, "Priscilla, now is not the time."

"But it's the only time I don't have to worry about running into you with your pack of friends. So, yes, now *is* the time."

I felt my face start to heat up. My blood was racing and I knew it had nothing to do with the stagnant landscape in front of me. I forced myself to swallow. "It was a mistake—I thought he loved me." It hurt to say the words aloud. Especially because if I said much more I knew the pain would come flooding back, and I'd be powerless to stop it. No matter what I said or how I acted, I still loved him. It was a disease I was fighting to cure.

"Let me let you in on a little secret, lowborn: he doesn't love me either."

I stumbled and barely had time to catch myself.

"He never has. Probably never will. But that's the way of the Crown and you of all people should know better than to try and change him. If you want proof, just look to Shina—excuse me, *Princess Shinako*—the next time the two of them are together." Priscilla sounded bitter.

"What are you talking about?"

"People like Darren place power—and wealth—above all else. If Blayne hadn't secured that princess Darren would have done so himself. It doesn't take a fool to see what *he*'s after."

"You don't love him?"

Priscilla laughed. "Love Darren? Of course not. Love is for fools not smart enough to see the path in front of them. That's the difference between you and I, Ryiah. I see the truth and accept Darren for what he is. You just see what you want to see. It's why I will wear the crown and bear his children while you are left wondering why you were never good enough."

I wanted to turn around and tackle her to the ground. She was deliberately using this mock battle to bait me. The highborn knew I wouldn't dare attack her while we were being observed by an audience. "I don't believe you. You wouldn't be jealous of Shina—you wouldn't have spent every moment you could tormenting me—unless you saw something you were afraid of."

Priscilla laughed scornfully. "Even if I was doubtful for a second or two, it's obvious the prince has moved on from whatever tryst the two of you shared on that mission. Why else would he have moved up our wedding date?"

I felt as if the ground had slipped right out from under me. "W-what?"

"That's right. The night of the ascension ceremony—right after you made that whole scene with the platter—the king announced the new date. You had already left the ballroom by then, of course, but then again it is your nature to rise to dramatics anytime something is not going your way. Like the pig's blood. Really, Ryiah, it was a harmless hazing and you—"

"*Stop talking, Priscilla!*"

"What are you—"

I turned around and slammed my palm over Priscilla's mouth and dragged her to the side of the closest building to our left. Not one moment later a cluster of mentors appeared, one of them wearing a black armband. It was Ian.

Priscilla stopped trying to claw my hand and let out a low gasp, pointing at the green-eyed fifth-year. I nodded. Now we knew who was commanding the mentor's team.

We stayed in hiding until the patrol had passed and then we looked to one another.

"We should follow them," I said before she could speak. "We should try to pick them off one at a time."

"We can't be heroes—we need to find the others first."

The two of us stared at each other stubbornly.

"Fine. How about we continue to follow them and look for the others at the same time? It's possible they know where the rest of our team is and are heading in that direction anyway."

She sighed, "Fine. But don't do anything reckless, Ryiah; we all know you have a reputation."

I glared at her. "Let's go. If you waste any more time insulting me we will lose sight of them!"

The two of us took off in the same direction as Ian and his two accomplices. We trailed stealthily behind, using the tracking skills the Ishir regiment had taught us during our desert stay.

We had gone on for about twenty minutes when we caught sight of another safe house.

Priscilla raced ahead to see who was inside while I kept a lookout nearby, hidden behind some brush. A minute later she emerged with Ella. I breathed a sigh of relief: Ella was still okay and I could see Alex and another Alchemy mentee inside.

Ella followed Priscilla to my hiding spot. She wore a funny expression. Probably at the idea of Priscilla and me as partners.

The three of us continued tracking the mentors to an armory on the northern side of the city. We had just set up watch a quarter of a mile away when a loud crash sounded behind us.

Before I even had the chance to cast up any sort of defense, Ella and Priscilla were sent sprawling into the wall behind me. I whirled around to see Bryce and Loren smiling.

"Surrender?"

Ella and Priscilla attempted to stand. Bryce cast out two swords at their throat and Loren pressed his poleaxe against mine. "Don't try anything," Loren warned, "I don't want to hurt you if I don't have to."

"Bryce," Priscilla's voice was sickly sweet. Ella made a gagging sound but our teammate continued. "Please, let us go, or, at least, me. You can trust me. You *know* me."

The mentor laughed shortly, not swayed by the friendly tone of his highborn friend. "You are such a liar, Priscilla. The second I let you go you'll free these two lowborns to impress your betrothed." He cleared his throat. "Surrender now. Say the words, or this will get a whole lot worse."

Ella's eyes shot to me and I swallowed. I could see her question: *would I pain cast to try and set us free?* Loren's blade was close. If I could press into it…

"Don't even think about it, Ryiah. We've been following you three since that safe house you pulled Ella out of," Loren said quickly. "If you do, our first order of business after we take out the three of you will be to get your brother and his friends. We won't give them an option, we'll just let them burn. Wonder how long it'll take the Restoration mages to treat Alex in the infirmary afterward?"

My stomach clenched. I knew Loren was a friend but in that moment I hated him for playing my twin against me. I opened my lips to speak.

A huge flare of light and a loud boom. The ground shook.

A rush of thick gas flooded the air around me.

I couldn't see anything as I choked back my breath. I could hear crying and someone shouting but everything was hazy. A second later I lost control of my balance.

As I fell, I wondered absentmindedly which Combat apprentice—mentee or mentor—had cast enough magic to make the rest of us weak enough to lose track of our limbs.

Two sets of arms gripped mine and pulled me up, running and dragging me out of the fog. I followed as best I could but I wasn't much help. At some point I must have lost track of consciousness because the next thing I knew, cold water was being splashed into my face.

I spit out a mouth full of water, sputtering.

My vision cleared and I saw Darren and Ray clutching a bucket with Eve leaning against a bed frame shortly behind them. We were in another safe house—only this one didn't have a Restoration or Alchemy apprentice in sight. Ray saw the question in my eyes and said, "They were caught," by way of explanation.

"Where are we?"

"Just south of Ian's hideout."

"Why did you only rescue me?" Because that's what this was, I realized, a rescue.

"Because you are the most powerful one and we only had time to save one of you." Darren didn't look at me as he said it.

"I would have helped if I could but we were too afraid of being ambushed. I had to stay here," Eve told me. "The mentors have been systematically combing the south. We've had to change hideouts three times and there are always more nearby. It was too risky to reveal my location."

I was lying awkwardly on a bed. I forced myself to try and sit up. It was surprisingly easy.

Eve noticed my expression.

"We gave you one of the Alchemy mentees' special drafts." She pointed to the empty vial beside me. "I had the girl make two in case we needed to get away in a hurry by using that gas. Hopefully we don't have to use the other."

"What's our plan?"

"You are going to distract Ian's guards while the rest of us ambush his hideout." She said the words matter-of-factly. Like it wasn't a big deal that our entire plan hinged on my performance.

I stared at her. "But the guards are Lynn and Morgan! They are both fifth-years, Eve. If they only see me, they are going to suspect a trap. They will know I'd never be foolish enough to attack them alone."

"If you tell them you are pain casting they'll be wary. You and Darren are the most powerful in the class. The mentors will be too busy watching you to notice when Darren, Ray, and I come out from behind."

"You think so?"

"It's our best chance."

While the others waited in the shadows of a building to my right, I made my approach, coughing loudly in case my footsteps weren't enough to draw the notice of the two mentors guarding the armory Ian was in.

Lynn's face fell and Morgan didn't look too happy either. "*Great*," the girl muttered, "I thought she had already surrendered." I could hear the dislike in her tone. Lynn still hadn't forgiven me for stealing Ian that night in the desert.

"Are you really this foolish, Ryiah?" Morgan wanted to know.

I shrugged. "I can pain cast, or did you forget that? I can have the two of you gone like that." I snapped my finger and then tossed my chainmail to the ground so they could see my bare arm.

In my other hand I produced my weapon.

The door to the armory swung open to reveal Ian who had heard the commotion outside. He frowned when he saw me standing there alone. “It’s not just you, is it?”

“Ian, run!” Lynn screeched. “Morgan and I can hold her off—*go*!”

I slammed the halberd’s axe end into my left wrist, biting back a scream as I sent an eruption of power into the air around me. I was hardly conscious of the pain. Raw magic had taken over my thoughts.

I called upon every last ounce of magic I had and launched it at the three mentors as hard as I could. I heard their scattered cries, a series of clashing, and then, somewhere, Ian’s shouted surrender.

I started to release my magic and the ground gave way beneath me.

Instantaneous darkness. *Victory.*

# Chapter Sixteen

"Wow. That's very impressive—two wins and both of them as a mentee." The man laughed heartily. "Good for you, Ryiah, I always knew you and the rest of your lot had enough fight to do well in an apprenticeship. Who's your mentor this year?"

I grimaced and Sir Piers caught the motion.

"Bryce?" he guessed. "That one always was too big for his britches when I had him in my class."

"No." I shifted from one foot to the other. "It's Ian."

"Ian?" The man's brow furrowed. "He's a bit of a rogue but the boy's harmless. Besides... aren't the two of you friends? I thought I saw the two of you dancing during the solstice last year."

"We used to be."

Recognizing my discomfort, Sir Piers changed the subject to my conditioning, eager to see if I still kept up the same rigorous routine as my first year at the Academy.

I answered his questions easily. But the entire time I was still thinking about Ian.

If anything, our mentorship had only become more strained since the mock battle. The worst part of my day was during Byron's lessons in the apprentice study upstairs. Going over potential battle strategy with someone who barely talked to you was tedious. It was like prying teeth from a rabid animal: you were always afraid of the bite. I could tell Ian was still trying very hard to be polite—painfully so—but every once in awhile his efforts would break and there'd be a flash of anger in his eyes or a snappy retort that reminded me just what he really thought of me.

It had only been made worse by Byron's evaluations. The master had delighted in tearing apart every solution Ian and I came up with. No matter what strategy we suggested it was never, *ever* good enough. We were the two troublemakers the master despised, and so his lessons were just one more way to repay our years of insolence.

Which is what had led me to the practice yard this evening, in an effort to clear the frustration that had been building since the day we arrived two months back. It was also, coincidentally, how I had bumped into Sir Piers, who had been participating in an evening regimen of his own.

"Things will get better," the big man said, gripping me hard on the shoulder. "I know you and you are a fighter, apprentice. Do not let anyone or anything tell you differently."

Easier said than done. I smiled weakly. "I appreciate your confidence."

The former commander nodded and then pointed to a hill in the distance. "Time to get back to my run."

I watched as Sir Piers disappeared into the night. He was right. I shouldn't let Ian's resistance dampen my drive. There was too much at stake.

I had barely turned around when I caught sight of Darren exiting the Academy with a training sword in hand. As soon as he saw me his expression darkened. "Coming or going?"

His words were so distant, it was like we were strangers. And it hurt. "Why?" I snapped. "So you can make sure you are not stuck in the same place as me for more than a second?"

"I am trying to keep things civil between us, Ryiah. Forgive me for saying so but you have never been known for your easy temper."

"Well, my temper goes hand in hand with your benevolence. And it is abundantly clear now that you have none."

Darren's hand on his blade tightened. "You don't know anything about me."

"I know *exactly* who you are." I took a step forward, and another, until I was standing right in front of him. Then my words turned to ice. "You are the selfish, spineless son of a king who is too afraid to be his own man. You would rather hide behind your status than fight for something that could actually mean something." There, that felt *good*. "And it's a shame, really it is, because, according to you, I was the one true friend you had."

Something flared in the non-heir's eyes. But it was quickly replaced by a malicious smile. "That's where you are wrong. We were never friends, Ryiah. I was only telling you what I thought you needed to hear."

I shoved at Darren, but he was ready and caught me by the wrists, holding them high above my head. He leaned in so that I was forced to stumble back.

"Do you remember our first year at the Academy? I said something to you once, in the library." His breath was hot on my face and my cheeks flushed—from anger or unwilling attraction, I wasn't sure.

"I remember you saying a lot of mean things," I spat.

"I told you not to trust a wolf," he continued. His words dripped like honeyed venom. "Because it would only ever want to break you." Darren let out a small, harsh laugh. "Haven't you figured it out yet? I'm the wolf, Ryiah. I guess what I really should have told you was to never trust a prince, but that's not quite as memorable."

I broke free of his grip with an angry jerk of my hands. Then, before he realized what I was doing, I slapped the prince across his face. Hard.

He said nothing. Which only infuriated me more. *Say something, you coward!*

Tears were spilling down my face. "I hate you," I whispered.

Darren nodded once, and then turned and walked away. Leaving me there. Alone.

Again.

*I hate you.*

By the time we returned to Devon after the winter's solstice, I was more than ready to face a cold season at camp. The frost in the Crown's Army training grounds was a welcome distraction. With a hatred for the bitter cold I was able to forget my unpleasant mentorship and the breaking I felt around Darren. In a way the frozen earth was exactly what I needed.

Almost as soon as we arrived we were deployed to assist the Crown's Army with King's Road patrols up and down the central plains of Jerar. In truth we were probably only stationed in the capital two or three weeks total, the rest of our time in active duty. Since they were regular patrols, we didn't see much battle. Most of our days were spent hunting down bandits or helping out local regiments with their training.

I didn't get to see Derrick. We only traveled as far north as the base of the Iron Mountains and as far south as the Red Desert Gate. Every morning we drilled and trained alongside the Crown's Army mages and it was during that time we really got to learn what service would be like in Jerar's largest regiment. None of the men or women were quite as fun as Andy from Port Langli, but they were still very helpful in their opinions of which territories to serve and what commanders to stay away from.

"If you want action, it's best to take a position north," Hannah stated. She was one of the few female Combat mages traveling in the same unit as me. "It's messy, what with all the rebel activity and border disagreements, but it's the best place to be if you really want to make something of yourself. Most of the mages who enter the Candidacy have served in Ferren's Keep or one of its nearby townships at one point or another. And if you have any mind to become a candidate I'd suggest you do the same."

"It's also the territory with the highest death count," Brennan, another Combat mage, supplied. "So keep that in mind. You might be brave and you might be strong but it means nothing when you come across a lot of Caltothian mages and you are without backup. My best mate died in his second year of service because he thought he could take on five of them on his own during a routine raid. We lose a surprising number of Combat mages up north because of our faction's heroic tendencies. Now, it's not to say you won't find glory—they memorialize every one of our deaths and the Crown supports the deceased's family heavily—but every bit of fame has its price."

Ella stared at the man curiously. "So you are not one for fame?"

Brennan snorted. "Of course I am. I spent my first ten years in Ferren's Keep building up a fancy reputation."

"Why did you leave then?"

"The north is no place to start a family. If you have half a mind to fall in love, don't do it there."

In no time at all we had finished our final patrol and it was time to return to the palace for the fifth-year's ascension ceremony.

I swallowed as I unpacked my belongings. In one year's time it would be *my* turn.

*Assuming I don't ruin my chances by stabbing a prince or two.*

I had only seen Darren and his brother once since we arrived. I preferred to keep it that way. The little time I had spent in their company already had been far from pleasant.

Blayne had gone out of his way to insult me, and all the while Darren had looked at me like I was a cockroach in need of smashing.

Yes, I was going to stay far, far away from the non-heir and his entourage, as much as humanly possible.

Well, that's what I told myself, in any case. And I really was doing well—until I ran into Priscilla on the third night. The girl made a face as soon as she spotted me.

"Why aren't you at that musty old tavern with the rest of your lowborn friends?"

I stared at her. Even for her that was unusually curt. "I don't need to explain my actions to you." To be honest, I was pretty sure Alex and Ella had wanted some time alone without me tagging along. But I wasn't about to tell her that.

"You stayed behind looking for *him*, didn't you?" Priscilla laughed brazenly and it was then that I realized the wine goblet in her hand.

"Are you drunk?"

"No." She hiccupped. "Because if I was, I'd be sure to throw this in that harlot's face."

For the first time it wasn't me Priscilla was referring to. I smiled to myself and then prodded her, curious by the sudden change in demeanor. "Who is bothering the great Priscilla of Langli?"

"Don't mock me, lowborn, it makes you look graceless." She covered her mouth and belched. "Like *her*. Why don't you take a nice long stroll to the library and see exactly why you should never fall for a man with a crown."

My pleasure instantly dissipated. There was only one reason Priscilla would send me to see Darren and that meant it would hurt me. *She* was upset and drinking wine at the prospect of lost status. *I* would be broken.

I shook my head. "I have no care to see Darren's newest conquest."

"Well Blayne sure will when I tell him how much time Darren has spent romancing that future wife of his. Why, the two of them have been inseparable since we got back!" She sneered, "It's like when we were kids, only now they spend late nights in his chambers... and no, I am not lying, Ryiah, his servants confirmed that to me just last evening. They even took me by so I could hear them myself." She dropped the goblet and let it clatter to the ground.

Taking a wobbly step forward the girl grabbed me by the shoulders and whispered loudly. "They were talking about marriage. I heard them." She laughed haughtily. "Though why a princess would choose the non-heir over a crown prince is beyond me."

"I'm sure you heard wrong." The words were thick on my tongue.

Priscilla pursed her lips and released me. "I won't lose my chance at the throne to you *or* a Borea Isle princess. The Crown needs my family's wealth *and* Shina's. Blayne will put a stop to this. I know he doesn't want to waste another year trying to secure another engagement. Blayne *has* to marry above his brother. The only two higher than Shina are the princesses in Caltoth and Pythus, and believe me when I say neither of those countries—or their ambassadors—like Jerar enough to support a marriage. I know what Darren is trying to do and it won't work. The king will never make him his heir."

*Is that what this is about? Is Darren trying to convince his father to make him crown prince?* Suddenly it all made sense. It explained why he was suddenly pursuing Princess Shinako. He was trying to steal Blayne's betrothed right out from under him. The non-heir was more ruthless than I had ever given him credit for.

I had heard of families feuding in the old scrolls, but there hadn't been a fight over the crown in ages. Strife between the royal family was bad for politics, and it was even more foolhardy while Darren was pursing magehood.

*Would the Council of Magic force him to give up his robe?* Council Law stated an heir could not be a mage. But maybe they would change that. They'd already bent the rules to let a member of the royal family participate.

*Was everything Darren ever did a play for power?*

My head was spinning from the possibility and Priscilla's words were ringing in my ears. Maybe I really didn't know him. *Love must really be blind.* Four years of knowing Darren and it had taken me until now to see him for who he really was. A wolf; a power-hungry, ruthless wolf who had tricked everyone, including his own flesh and blood. And I'd had to hear it from the girl I had spent four years believing my enemy.

The irony was that my real enemy had been there all along right in front of me. Smiling crookedly and convincing me we were friends. Trying to seduce me for the thrill of the chase. Chastising me for not trusting him that first year in the tower stairs at the Academy… Telling me he loved me.

And then tossing me aside the second I jeopardized his dreams. I wasn't what he had wanted all these years. I'd merely been a diversion in his pursuit of the crown.

I never should have trusted a prince.

During the night of the ascension ceremony a huge fight erupted in the great hall. I wasn't there to see but I heard about it when Loren and Ray joined us in the tavern for a nice dinner to celebrate our new status as fifth-years.

"You should have seen it!" Loren was laughing. "Blayne may be fit but he doesn't have a chance when his brother uses his magic!"

"Yes, but Blayne gave Darren a good shiner at the beginning!"

"And then Blayne was out cold. The king couldn't stop laughing! You would think he'd be angry but he actually enjoyed his sons' brawl…"

I concentrated on my stew and tried not to listen closely as Alex and Ella quizzed Loren and Ray on the action. I didn't want to know. It just made Priscilla's words that much more true.

I had just braved another large sip of the steaming hot liquid when Ian swung open the tavern door. He looked handsome in his black mage's robe—such a change from the training breeches and linen shirts apprentices wore. He pushed back some unruly curls and then spotted me at one of the far tables directly across from him.

I had been so busy in the past couple of months, training and training and not letting myself think about anything except the apprenticeship, so it was a sudden jolt to the system when he nodded in my direction and pointed to a small table in the corner.

Ella and the rest of my friends were too absorbed in conversation to notice. I didn't bother to excuse myself before making my way over to the newly ascended mage.

I didn't know what Ian wanted but I thought it was safe to congratulate him on his new status.

"Thanks." Ian cleared his throat, gold-flecked green eyes bright. "Care to join me?"

I sat. And then waited, drumming my fingers against the rough table's wood, waiting for him to say whatever it was he had planned. I owed him that much.

*Maybe he will finally tell me what he really thinks of me.*

Ian drew a long breath. "I'm sorry I was so cold… I wish I could have said it sooner but I needed time."

"I'm sorry I hurt you." I forced myself to speak. "You deserved much better than me, in any case."

"For what it's worth, I really thought the prince cared. I know what I said, but at the time I was just trying to hurt you."

"Well, it looks like we were both wrong." I wonder, I thought, what it means that I chose someone as cold as Darren over someone as kind as you?

The Combat mage held up his drink. "A toast to better love in our futures."

I joined him. "May the ones we love, love us much better."

Silence.

Then: "Have you received any offers?"

"A personal request from Commander Chen in Langli. Apparently my performance in the port's mock battle impressed him."

"Are you going to take the position?"

"I already have. He was at the feast earlier when I accepted."

"You'll have good company." I smiled. "There's a mage who goes by Andy in their regiment. She's got the same humor and reckless disregard for authority you and I share. And you'll like Cethan, too. I served with him during that mission. He's a quiet brute, but he's steady."

Ian took another sip of his drink thoughtfully. "Where do you think you'll end up?"

"Wherever they'll have me."

Ian gave me a strange look. "Ryiah, you and Darren are the top of your year. You'll have commanders lining up to beg you. Don't forget it was *your* pain casting that won two mock battles, and you've still got another year to add another victory to your belt."

"I won't get any good offers when Byron gives me my ranking. Even if I am second only to Darren—which I'm not sure that I am—it doesn't mean much if I am at the bottom of the list during the ceremony. Byron despises you but he still gave Lynn the worst rank because she's a girl. Everyone knows the two of you should have placed first and second. Me? I'm a girl *and* he hates me—I'll be dead last in a procession of six."

Ian shrugged. "It won't matter. It didn't for me. Chen didn't choose me because I placed fourth, he chose from what he saw when I trained in Langli."

I sighed. "Well then, I definitely won't be stationed near you. We lost the mock battle that year—and Ella and I were the ones to cause it."

Ian gave me a crooked smile. "I guess not. But I'm certain tonight won't be the last time we cross paths. The Candidacy is only two years away. Maybe we'll finally get to have our duel? I know you've been dying to test your prowess in an arena. We are each one of the best in our years, after all. Who knows which one of us would win?"

I lifted my mug. "To our future match."

Ian winked. "To my beating you."

# Chapter Seventeen

In the four years since I had walked through the Academy's doors, I had come a long way from the girl who had struggled to cast a tree limb on fire. Unfortunately, my first day in Ferren's Keep did not attest to that… I was too busy counting down the hours until I could see a certain young man with dancing blue eyes and blonde curls that was three years my junior.

"Apprentice Ryiah, if you fancy my lessons pleasant enough to daydream in, then clearly I have been too soft on you. This is the third time today your head has been in the clouds. One week polishing the regiment's armory starting tomorrow—and if I catch you at it again I will not hesitate to triple your time!"

*Of course he wouldn't, the old crow.*

Ella elbowed me lightly in the stomach and I gave her a helpless shrug as soon as Master Byron's back was turned.

"Pay attention!" she hissed. "You really don't want to spend the next year scrubbing mail, do you?"

Another voice chimed in. "Yes, and *I* will never forgive you for jeopardizing my training, Ryiah!"

I glared at the sour-faced boy in front of me. Another of Priscilla's bratty cousin Merrick's fourth-year friends. Not once had I been bestowed with a sweet-faced mentee to train.

Byron had undoubtedly chosen this one on purpose.

I made a face. "Your training was already jeopardized long before you met me, Radley."

The rest of the day's lessons finished with much difficulty on my end. My overconfident mentee had a flagrant disregard for all of Byron's cautionary measures and I spent a good amount of time nursing injuries when he went too far in his castings. Especially during the final drill.

Radley still seemed to think the only thing that mattered in pain casting was power. Which meant that he didn't bother to practice any semblance of control.

I had to remind myself that revenge was less important than performance. I needed to spend my final year carefully crafting my own pain castings. I had improved greatly over the last four, but so had Darren and Eve—and I so desperately wanted to excel in something.

I was tired of being third in everything, and I would have been lying if I didn't admit it would be nice to watch the look on the prince's face when he lost. Someone needed to knock Darren off that pedestal—he'd been enjoying its light for far too long. It was time for someone else to shine and I wanted it to be me.

I could have sent my ungrateful mentee flying into the tall pines behind us, but I chose to focus my energies on a carefully exerted force. Stop and start, change direction, send my crackling lightning flying to the side only just in time—all from a small blade's pressure on my forearm.

I glanced to watch Darren with Merrick. He and Ray were sharing the same mentee this year. Another stark clash of light and the familiar smell of burning wood where his bolt landed just inches from mine. *Was that deliberate?* I stared at the prince and saw a small upturn at the corner of his mouth. He was trying hard not to smirk, but I knew, I just knew, that he had done that last casting on purpose.

I straightened and prepared for a cut that would show that smug non-heir exactly who he was going up against… and then stopped myself. *What am I doing?* I didn't let Radley's castings get to me so I certainly wasn't going to let Darren's.

*Me. This year is about me.* I took a deep breath and focused on imitating my last casting, flexing my magic as I pulled back a second sooner. Perfect. Now just ten more minutes and we would be dismissed.

And then I could finally seek out the one person I had been looking forward to.

"Is this what my no good brother has become? A soldier who falls asleep at pubs?"

Derrick's head shot up with a start and I laughed as the drink he had been resting beside spilled all over his table. "Ry!" He was out of his stool in a second.

Laughing, I embraced my younger brother, who had grown even taller in my absence. And bigger. He now carried twice as much muscle and my head only went up to his chin. When he released me I stepped back in shock.

"You're huge!"

One of the soldiers who had been sitting next to Derrick choked on his roast. "They feed us well. And this one has an appetite. He won a contest against everyone else in our station."

*Just like Alex,* I thought wryly. *Some things never change.*

"Did you just arrive today?" Derrick dragged me over to an empty chair.

"We did." I grinned. "I rode all night to get here."

"By the gods, Ry, Ferren's Keep is a good three hours from Tijan! You are mad! Weren't you riding two straight weeks before this?"

I waved his shock away. "It was worth it to see my favorite brother."

Derrick grinned, dimples forming at the corner of his cheeks. "You are such a bad liar, Ry. You only say that now because Alex is nowhere in sight… Where is that lug anyway? Why isn't he here visiting me with you?"

"He's coming tomorrow. He told me to tell you there was no way he was going to spend another night in the saddle." I snorted. "He had really bad sores from this last ride in the mountains and unlike us, he's not exactly warrior bred."

Derrick snickered. "Trust Alex to become a healer. That's about as dandy as it gets."

I yawned. "We shouldn't mock our poor brother just because he likes to be comfortable. I don't know about you, but there are certainly days I dream of leaving Combat behind and taking up something easier instead."

"But you never would."

"No. But it's a nice fantasy. Especially when Byron spends all his time ripping me apart."

"Is he worse than Sir Piers?"

"You have no idea." I took a bite of my brother's dinner, or what was left of it. "Besides, Piers always believed in me. Byron is just looking for ways to make me quit."

"Our commander out here is like that. But I think it's because he cares and doesn't want to see us unprepared."

"Byron doesn't care if I'm prepared or not, he just wants me gone."

"Surely he's like that with everyone?" That question came from one of Derrick's female comrades.

I smiled weakly. "Only the women. And one of my friends when he was with us. But, no, it's mostly me. The master *loathes* me."

Derrick looked amused. "Because you are stubborn."

I sighed. "Because I am everything he hates—but enough about my miserable existence, let's hear what life is like for a soldier in Tijan. How has the action been up north?"

I must have asked the right question because the next thing I knew, every single soldier in the place was bellowing over the other to tell me their wildest stories since coming into service. My brother and his cohorts had had quite the adventure in the year since they started and some of the older men had tales as far back as twenty.

I spent the rest of the evening listening to tales about Caltothian skirmishes and the pranks the soldiers liked to play against one another in their down time. It was nice to see how happy Derrick was with his new friends. While a soldier's life was certainly challenging, they clearly knew how to smile at the end of a long day.

Much glory was given to the mages, but it was the soldiers who were always the first line of defense. It was a fact I had tried not to ponder too heavily when I thought about Derrick. Especially when I remembered that he was stationed along the border where most of the fighting took place. Neither he nor his comrades seemed too concerned, or if they were afraid, they hid it well. But I worried. Because that was the only thing a big sister could do.

Still, it was meant to be an evening of festivity, not solace. My brother was one of the best in his year, and he was not a fool. He would be smart about any action he took and I knew he trusted me to do the same. I forced myself to smile and enjoy the rest of the night.

By the time I finally said my goodbyes and saddled my horse, it was easily two hours past midnight. I was fighting sleep and not looking forward to the three-hour trek back to Ferren's Keep. But if I missed the morning warm ups with the regiment, Byron would notice, and then I would be stuck cleaning the armory for the rest of my apprenticeship. So it was one night without rest, or ten months of polishing armor. I chose the former.

I just hoped the next day would carry on much faster than the first.

"You feeling alright, Ryiah?"

I just shook my head and then laid it back on the table while the others continued their morning meal.

"She didn't get any sleep." Ella patted my back sympathetically. "I don't think it agreed with her."

"Derrick and his friends kept her that late? That oaf should have sent her on her way after an hour," Alex declared.

"I wanted to see him," I mumbled without raising my head. If I did, the room would start to spin and then I'd be right back where I started.

"A lot of good that did you."

"I only have to get through the rest of practice and then I'll get to sleep."

"You forgot the armory," Ella reminded me.

I groaned. *Why did Byron have to hate me so much?*

After the second bell I followed Ella out of the dining commons to Combat's training grounds with a quick departing wave to my twin. Ferren's Keep, like the other three cities we had trained in, was as different as could be. Which meant, of course, that our training was different as well—though just *how* different, I hadn't expected.

First things first, the keep was actually *inside* a giant fortress built into one of the Iron Mountains. Like Ishir Outpost, the rock city provided a safe refuge for its inhabitants, but it had the added bonus of a dense forest and raging river just south of it.

The fortress was as large as the king's palace in Devon with a similar wall guarding its face. The fortress hosted row after row of sentry posts and a high tower to its north. Add to that an endless supply of lookouts and a guard at every possible entrance to monitor the people's coming and goings and it was easy to see why our training focused on defense instead of what we were used to, the attack.

"The balance of power favors the defender." That was the first thing Commander Nyx said when we arrived. "This keep is impenetrable so long as our regiment continues to make it so."

During our non-magic drills, we spent a good deal of time running back and forth along the narrow sentry wall, taking turns with our partner as one attempted to scale it while the other employed various techniques to hold them off.

Those "techniques" had included longbows and cross-bows—the two favorite weapons of the keep's regiment, whose main role was servicing the wall as a sentry.

We also trained with knives since they were easy to carry during a climb.

Then we practiced loading and unloading the heavy catapults, and then took turns aiming heavy piles of rock at landmarks below.

The last exercise was the worst, I was quick to discover. I was already so tired from a lack of sleep and the morning warm-up. By the time we had started the catapults, my arms were shaking so badly I dropped two large stones I was carrying. The second time, one landed on my right foot. I spent the rest of practice limping through my drills. Byron, of course, had deemed my injury "not serious enough" to warrant a trip to the infirmary.

At the end of practice I chanced a peek under my boot to see how "serious" my foot really was and shuddered at the spotted purple and red bruise in its place.

"Where did you get that little nasty from?"

I turned my head and realized a woman with short-cropped blonde hair was staring at me and the foot cradled in my hands. I immediately dropped it. She had steel gray eyes and a permanent frown. Which meant only one person: Commander Nyx.

I instantly felt myself go red with embarrassment. The last thing I wanted was the leader of Ferren's Keep's regiment to consider me soft.

Especially if I wanted a chance of being offered a post next year.

The commander stepped forward, still squinting at me. "It was the catapults, wasn't it?"

I nodded mutely.

"If you have time to swing by my chambers during lunch, I've got some bruise balm for it. I tend to keep some on hand whenever the squires or apprentice mages are stationed here. Someone always manages to drop those rocks at least once a day for the first week or two."

*Was she really this nice, or was it a test to see if I was weak-willed enough to accept her help? I'd heard rumors about how Nyx got her post… You had to be a very tough sort of woman to beat out hundreds of other knights for Jerar's highest position up north.*

I decided I didn't want her aid either way. Alex had helped me that second year back in Ishir, but that had been for a broken arm—not a bruise. What was Byron always saying? "Pain is how we build strength." Well, I could certainly use some after today.

"I'll be just fine, but thank you for the kind offer."

The woman cracked a toothy smile. "Wise choice. I've offered it to two others so far and you are the first to turn me down. I can't respect anyone who coddles themselves."

A wave of relief washed over me. I would not be one of those people she marked off her list for potential service, at least not yet. "Who were the other two?"

She chuckled. "Check the dining commons. Byron and I have a little game we play every time he brings his apprentices to my keep. I give him the name of any apprentices foolish enough to accept the help I offer and then he orders them a week without rations to help them build their resistance to pain. It saves my cook's stores as well, so it's win-win."

I was doubly glad I had refused her offer. One night without sleep and a throbbing foot was bad enough; I did not need to withstand a week of starvation as well.

"Be sure to tell Byron I refused your offer, he doesn't like me much," I told her. It was reckless, but I felt a lit bit braver now that I hadn't fallen for her hoax.

Commander Nyx's eyes crinkled. "He doesn't like me much either, but his methods work. Have no fear, apprentice, I'll make sure to put in a good word… What is your name?"

"Ryiah."

"Well, Ryiah, welcome to Ferren's Keep."

In the next couple of days, three more Combat apprentices went a week without meals as our training got more intense and they caved to Nyx and Byron's scheme. I had been delighted, at first, to find out Radley was one of them. But then he became more nasty than usual and it was even harder to resist casting him off the steep forest backdrop behind us. I became so consumed with fighting off my growing dislike for my mentee that I almost forgot about Darren.

*Until* the afternoon I ran into him and Priscilla arguing quietly outside the men's barracks. The girl was clutching a letter in one hand and brandishing her fist with the other. I heard her shout "Shina" before I turned heel and left. I didn't want to hear anything else. I didn't need to.

When I ran into Darren later that day I avoided his gaze. I was sad and upset, and I wasn't sure which one was worse. Depressed that I still wasn't over him? *Or angry that I really hadn't known him at all?*

For a while last year, I had entertained the notion that maybe the prince did care. I'd told myself his father forbade him. Threatened his life even. Poor Darren, he'd had no choice in the matter. He loved me, but he'd been powerless to stop his family.

But that dream had not reconciled with his words at the Academy and the fight on the night of Ian's ascension ceremony. Darren hadn't been afraid to disobey the king then. No, he had openly fought for the princess he wanted and tried to make himself his father's heir. That Darren was fearless, and not the least influenced by what his vile family said.

Seeing Darren's letter from Princess Shinako only made the truth that much worse.

Between drills, weekly visits to see Derrick, the occasional armory chore, and all the extra arm-strengthening lessons I could manage, I quickly lost all track of time. I didn't really lose track of Darren, but then again that had never been an option.

As much as I might wish it were.

# Chapter Eighteen

"I second Eve."

"Darren."

"I also vote for Eve, she did a great job in Devon."

"Eve for me."

"I nominate Ryiah."

At that I gave Ella a grateful smile. I knew our fifth year was critical, I knew what it would say if we lost, but I really, *really* wanted a chance to try. And this was my last year to do it.

"I second Ryiah." Ray gave me a rueful smile, perhaps to make up for voting for Eve the year before.

"Well, I vote for Darren," Priscilla said shrilly. "I will not follow a lowborn."

"We vote with Priscilla. We want the prince." Merrick and Radley made no attempt to sound partial.

"Ryiah," Alex and all four of his comrades spoke at once. I grinned. Restoration's pride wasn't at stake the way it was for Combat so the fifth-years in his faction were more open to change.

"Ryiah. Give the poor girl a chance. If she wants to risk commanding this year, it will be her fate on the line if we lose.

All of us know Byron will blame her anyway." Ruth winked at me from her circle of Alchemy mentors.

The rest of the class spoke out. Eve made a bold move and took herself out, voting for me in a pleasant twist of fate. Darren and I were tied… it came down to a third-year boy in Alchemy.

I stood tall. "You should vote for me because everyone deserves a chance. That's how we all became apprentices, isn't it? We were allowed to try… So you should let me try." I smiled sweetly and the boy blushed. *Beat that, Darren!*

Darren stepped forward and said loudly, "You shouldn't pick Ryiah because she's lowborn and reckless—"

I made a choking sound.

"-And did you hear why the Academy's armory had to be rebuilt the year before you started? That was because *Ryiah* made a rash decision that brought the whole thing down and almost killed herself *and* Ray here. The only reason she didn't lose was because *he* was able to save them. If she does that this time, who knows what will happen?"

I broke free of Ella's hold. I didn't even care that all of the mentors' eyes were upon me. I was done trying to ignore the prince.

I would not let Darren sabotage another part of my life.

"You and me," I growled, "duel. Pain casting. Now. Let's see which one of us has more control *then*."

"You know I would win," Darren shot back, "and at least *I* didn't resort to petty flirtation to sway someone's vote!"

"Flirtation is hardly the same as insult!"

"It's not an insult if it's true."

"You called me lowborn and reckless!" I put my hands on my hips.

Darren raised a brow. "Well, you *were* born in Demsh'aa and that decision *was* reckless."

"You know exactly what you were implying, Darren, don't you dare try to—"

"I want Eve."

Both of us turned our heads to face the boy we had been fighting over. We had forgotten about him.

"I want Eve too," another girl from Alchemy spoke up. "I want to change my vote."

"Both of you are wasting our time. I vote for Eve as well."

Before my eyes, I watched as the rest of the mentors turned against Darren and me with the exception of Priscilla, Ella, Ray, and Alex, who loyally kept their votes. When it was all said and done, Eve beat out Darren and me for the second year in a row.

Eve walked over to the both of us. "I don't want the two of you distracting everyone else from what needs to be done. Both of you can scout the grounds below the wall. When you are done, I want you both to report to me and we will station two of our third-years as sentries in whatever location you deem best. This way we'll be warned before the mentees arrive and I won't have the two of you hindering the rest of our planning."

My face fell. "How will we know what to do during the battle if we spend the whole time before it scouting?"

"Yes, Eve, how will I know my role if I'm out counting trees?" Darren's tone was incredulous. "I'm one of the most valuable people you have!"

"You should have thought about that before you decided to stage a fight during the middle of our vote." Eve frowned. "You two will be stationed next to me during the actual battle. But until then you scout. Understand?"

"Have you heard anything yet?"

I glared at Darren. "I thought you were keeping track of the bell tower."

"I *was*," he snapped, "but you kept bringing us further into the forest and I can't see it anymore… I was hoping we'd be able to hear it but—"

I threw down the charcoal I had been using to map our location. "But what?"

"I think we are too far out."

"You couldn't have mentioned this sooner? How many tolls do we have left?"

"Just the ten minute warning bell before it begins."

I stood up with a start. "Darren, we are *twenty* minutes away from the wall!"

"That was when we didn't know where we were going." Darren's tone was anything but helpful. "Now we do. If we run we should be fine."

A bloodcurdling scream shot out, echoing across the clearing. I whirled around to stare into the woods behind us. "What was that?" I kept my voice low. "Did the battle already start?" *Leave it to Darren to lose track of our time!*

"I'm not sure." Darren was staring in the same direction as me. He seemed puzzled. "Only it doesn't make sense. All of the other mentors are at the keep, so why would a mentee attack one of their own?"

"Maybe they know we are out here? It could be a trick."

Darren rolled his eyes. "But why would they think we would help?"

There was a loud boom and the ground beneath us shook violently. That same second, a chorus of men's shouting rang out just north of us.

"I don't think it's the mentees trying to trick us." I reached for my scabbard at the same time that Darren cast out three bolts of lightning into the sky, one by one. They flashed directly above us.

My lips parted in surprise. "What was *that* for?"

Darren grabbed my arm and started to run, dragging me behind him. "A distress call."

I stumbled along behind him, trying to keep up. "Caltothians?"

Darren released me and pointed to the same path we had taken from the keep. It was at least fifteen minutes from the fortress.

I started to walk toward it and then froze. Darren wasn't following. "Darren," I whispered loudly, "what are you doing?"

"I'm going to find out what is happening."

I stared at him. "Are you mad? What am I saying, of course you are! Darren, you can't—who knows how many of them there are!"

"Ryiah, this is not a request. I am *ordering* you back to the keep. Warn the others!" His garnet eyes flashed. "I am a prince; you are my subject. Now is not the time to question me!"

I ignored him. "Darren, you can't do this on your own! You need me."

"I need you to do what I..." He gave up when he caught my expression. "Fine," the boy snapped, "but Ryiah, no heroics. I will *not* have your blood on my hands."

"So kind of you to care." I couldn't keep the sarcasm from my words.

"I mean it, Ryiah."

"Are we going or not?"

I followed Darren, darting from one tree trunk to the next and peering out into the dark forest beyond. It was hard to see—the sun was almost completely blocked out by the towering pines crowding the sky... but what I did see through narrow shafts of light was alarming.

Five knights, four men and one woman, were tied and bound in a circle on the ground. Scattered nearby were three bodies with blood pooled around their necks. With a sickening realization I noticed their heads were severed, with just a small patch of skin connecting the neck to the body. I recognized one of them as a soldier from the keep's regular patrol. The young man had escorted me on my weekly visits with Derrick.

My chest tightened. *Hensley.* He was my age. He had told me he missed his old comrades in Tijan… Now he would never see them again.

The sun's next ray revealed a large gathering of men and women in dress I did not recognize. Caltothians. Their clothing blended in with the surroundings—dark brown breeches and long green tunics, covered in a thick brown cloak that hooded their faces.

One of the first things I noticed was that there was no chainmail or plate armor anywhere on them. *That must have helped them catch the keep's regiment by surprise.* Without the rustle of metal rings, the enemy had managed to blend right in with the rest of the forest… until a passing patrol had come across their place of hiding.

Who knew how many more would have been captured had it not been the day of our mock battle? Most of the keep's regiment had been dismissed to view the affair from the keep's towers; only a few had been assigned to patrols.

"I count fifteen, but there might be more out back." Darren's voice was barely a whisper.

The Caltothians seemed to be arguing over what to do with the remaining hostages, although it was hard to know for sure as they were all speaking at once. Only short fragments of speech carried over to where Darren and I hid crouching.

At one point, one of the Caltothians strode forward and grabbed a prisoner by the back of his braid. She brandished a jagged-looking blade against the base of his throat and shouted something to the others. Another Caltothian rushed forward to pull her back but it was too late. The woman dropped her grip and a thick spray of blood spewed from the man's neck.

One of the hostages let out a muffled cry.

My fingernails dug into Darren's arm so deep he bled. I dropped it immediately. Three soldiers—and now one knight—were dead. I glanced at the non-heir and saw fury.

"We've got to do something," he growled. "I can't just watch them slaughter my own people."

My throat burned and I forced myself to speak softly. "I can light a fire." I could see it now. "I could cast one large enough to get the Caltothian to investigate… I know they probably won't send all of their men, but they might be confident enough to leave only two or three guarding the prisoners since they are already bound."

Darren's jaw clenched, and for a moment he looked like he was fighting himself. Finally he said, "You need to go far enough that it takes them a while to return. I can handle the ones that stay behind, but I need to know you'll hide as soon as you've got their attention." He ran a fist through his hair. "I'll help the hostages back to the keep, but you need to promise me you'll stay safe until I can send help."

I squinted into the trees. The woman was already pointing to another one of our knights. I needed to go. *Now.* Before the others found the same fate as the man with the braid. I stood and Darren grabbed my arm.

"Don't you dare get caught." His voice was oddly strained.

"Why?" The words fell from my lips before I could stop them. "Why would you care?"

Darren looked away from me. "Just don't, okay?"

"Okay."

He looked at me then. For a moment he said nothing. When he finally spoke his expression was dark. "Run, Ryiah. Run fast."

And with that, our plan was set in motion.

I sprinted through the trees, leaping over jagged granite and forcing my way through thick brush as I made my way across the dense forest. I needed to get as far away from the Caltothians—and the Keep—as possible. It was hard to keep track of time as I ran. I needed to put at least ten minutes between us. I wanted to do more but I was afraid if I spent any more time running, another knight would die.

I came to a stop in front of a towering pine. Just behind it was a thundering white stream. The river would keep the fire from spreading west, which was where I would seek shelter. The pine's thick smoke would draw the Caltothians out and there was no chance the Ferren's Keep regiment would miss it.

I placed my palms on the trunk of the tree and set to work projecting my casting. The pine was close to three hundred feet—at least fifty taller than the rest of its surroundings. It would take much more power than normal to exert a casting of its range, but I had not used my magic once that morning. I had a full reserve to draw from. And pine burned fast.

In five minutes I had the highest branches roaring in red. A thick gray cloud straddled the sky. The top quarter of the pine was engulfed in flames.

I released my casting and stumbled back, slightly dizzy. The distance had been a greater effort than I expected. Still, the fire was burning high and there was no missing its smoke. Darren would see it any second.

I raced over to the stream and then, standing in the shallow shore, cast a cursory brush of wind to displace any dirt I had marked with my steps. The rest of the river was too powerful and too fast to swim. I could feel its undercurrent dragging at my feet.

Summoning another casting, I transported myself to the other side. It took a great effort to carry my weight across. Self-levitation was always costly, but I didn't trust myself to balance on a log. The river was too dangerous.

When I reached the other side I immediately dropped my magic and sprinted into the thick forest beyond. My heart was racing and every breath sounded louder than before. I clawed at blackberry brambles and forced myself to keep on running anywhere with brush so that it would be much harder to track the path I had taken.

I wasn't sure how much time had passed. I was crouched behind a tree, watching, waiting. I had heard shouts for a while now, but none of them had come close to where I knelt hidden. I couldn't see anything except for a few feet in front of me, but I was confident I wouldn't be caught off-guard. After finding my spot, the first thing I had done was cast a thick mess of dead leaves in a large radius surrounding me.

I would hear my attackers before they found me.

When the shouting got closer, I was able to count eight or nine voices. Relief flooded my chest. I had been afraid most of the Caltothians would stay behind. My plan had worked.

*Darren is freeing the hostages right now.*

I took a deep breath and then choked as I breathed in a new scent. Either the Caltothians had Alchemy potions on hand, or they had a Combat mage in their midst. I recognized that foul stench from the mock battle in Devon—it had come with the mentors' fog. The same poisonous vapor that had made me lose control of my body.

I had to move. The thick silver fog was spreading fast, any moment it would reach my tree line-

I made a split second decision to rip off my tunic. Then I wrapped it around my face so that my ears and mouth were covered. Then I ran, fast as my legs could carry me, ringlets of chainmail clanging against my skin now that the tunic was not there to muffle them.

"*There*! You see her?"

Shouting sprang up behind me but I didn't dare look. I cast out a giant sphere at my back and sprinted deeper into the forest.

To my right a tree exploded in flame.

I ducked right and started to zigzag among the trees and rock, hoping to lose the party tracking me. But I had no such luck. The shouting kept getting closer.

And the castings were multiplying.

They most definitely had a mage. And from the number of castings so far, they had at least three, if not more. A well-trained war mage couldn't cast as many attacks as the ones I was avoiding now. Not at once.

At some point I came across the same river from earlier. The burning tree was just beyond it, now a towering spiral of flame.

My stomach fell. I had to cross. Every other direction I was surrounded. My pulse was racing and I could barely breathe. My vision swam in front of my eyes. I could not maintain the defensive sphere and levitate at the same time.

My magic was depleting fast.

I sent a swift plea to the gods and dropped my defense, casting myself into the air. It would only take me twenty seconds to cross…

But a biting pain tore into my side before I had even completed ten. The sudden shock shattered my concentration and my casting fell away.

And then I fell. Into the raging stream below I lost control of my magic. It was too late to attempt another casting—it was impossible to focus. White water swarmed me and I was thrust under its surface. I choked liquid as I fought to get air, only to be tossed again, rock after rock in the stream's rapid course.

The river was ice cold and the sharp pain in my thigh became more intense. Red blood and white waters threw me against the current, beating my body with every river rock along the way. I fought to the surface each time, only to get sucked under and then out. My fingers rubbed raw from scraping against rock.

I couldn't cast. Not with the collision of pain and water choking my lungs. My legs were numb and it was becoming harder and harder to swim. I couldn't see anymore. Darkness was grabbing me, pulling me under.

My arms held on the longest, but eventually those two slowly slipped away…

All at once I was conscious of gold. Sunlight streamed down from above, blinding me. I was at the surface. I could breathe.

There was shouting in the distance. My ears were pounding too heavily to notice.

My entire body ached, my skin felt like ice.

I opened my eyes and saw that the raging river had fettered out into a shallow stream. I had washed ashore. There was a deep gash in my left leg. An arrow had struck it. Part of the shaft was still in it.

But I was still alive.

All at once the shouting drew closer and my heartbeat could no longer block out the words.

"We found the mage girl!"

"Get her bound and gagged—she might be able to pain cast!"

I tried to move, stand, anything, but my limbs were still catching up from the cold.

I tried to cast but my vision just spun and spun and a sharp pain probed at my head until I was forced to vomit the contents of my breakfast onto the sand beside me.

I couldn't escape: I needed to do exactly what the Caltothians feared. I needed to create more pain. I blinked at the shaft in my leg. *If I could just roll myself onto my side.*

I shifted just slightly and pain tore into my thigh. I screamed. Magic came rushing out and I thrust as much of it as I could muster into the band of enemies racing toward me.

But I missed. My lightning missed its mark.

And now I didn't even have pain magic. Not unless I wanted to kill myself summoning more.

Two sets of hands pinned my arms and legs to the ground. My hands and feet were bound in a matter of seconds and then an oily cloth was shoved into my mouth as another wrapped it in place.

A face entered my vision and I saw the same woman who had killed the knight squinting down at me. Her lip was curled in disgust.

"Who else is with you?" she demanded. A large wad of saliva landed on the side of my cheek. "Hold up your fingers for the count of your men."

I trembled. I would not tell her anything. From Derrick's past accounts I knew I was going to die no matter what. Calto-thians never kept prisoners. But at least I would not die a trai-tor.

The woman slapped me hard across the face. My lip split open from the sting of her impact.

"Tell me and I will let you live."

*Never*. I shook my head and tried to ignore its unwelcome spinning.

"Kinsey, shouldn't we keep this one?" one of the men probed. "She put up a good fight. If we break her, I bet it would be worth our time. We could use another mage—"

"You know the orders as well as I do, Wade, no survi-vors."

"Not if we don't tell them."

"Do you really want to take that chance?" Kinsey drawled. "Two times a traitor would only bring a slow and painful death."

The woman pulled out a curved dagger. It was the same blade she had used to slit the knight's throat. She cradled it against the side of my face. "One more chance before I gut you like a fish," she crooned. Her blade carved a shallow cut across my neck.

*Be brave, Ryiah.* I shut my eyes. I would spend my last moments of life envisioning something more pleasant than the ugly face of my enemy.

*What would I see in my last breath*, I wondered, *Derrick's laugh, Alex's crooked grin, or my parents' kind smiles?*

Kinsey cackled. "Enjoy the Realm of the Dead."

*Darren.*

In my last moments I saw *Darren.*

A sharp sting was followed by the withdrawal of pain and the shrill sound of a woman's scream. I opened my eyes and realized that I was not, in fact, dead. I touched my throat and realized the blade had only nicked it.

I was very much alive.

The woman who had been brandishing the knife was not so fortunate. Kinsey lay face down in the sand next to me, dead. A javelin was in her back.

All around me was panicked yelling.

Sensation returned to my limbs. I propped myself up with my elbows so that I could take in the scene around me. *Was it too much to hope? Had someone seen my casting?*

All around me were great flashes of light and smoke. The heat from the forest fire was growing: the air was sweltering. Any residual cold from my icy bath had faded quickly in its presence.

The Caltothians guarding me were busy, engaged in a battle of sorts with two others in the clearing ahead. It was hard to make out my rescuers' faces but I could tell from the way they fought that they were winning.

Only three of the Caltothians were mages and one of them—the woman who had threatened me—was already dead. The enemy soldiers were hiding behind their mages—only one of them was an archer, the rest carried swords.

There was another great blast of magic and a storm of knives rained down from the sky. The enemy shrieked and scattered. The only two still standing were the Caltothian mages.

Another great blast of magic and the mages were forced to flee—leaving me behind as they relocated to the opposite side of the forest. As they traded sides my rescuers drew forward, one leading the way while the other guarded his back.

I choked back a cry of relief. It was Darren and Eve.

He had come back for me.

The prince set to work on my bonds. "Just couldn't stay out of trouble, could you, Ryiah?"

"Mmmph." The gag was still in my mouth. When it finally came free I turned to Eve. "How did you find me?"

"I went looking for the two of you when you never returned. Then I saw the fire and decided to investigate." Eve shot out another barrage of weaponry at the enemy mages and checked Darren's progress. "How are those ropes coming?"

"Not fast enough," he said through gritted teeth. "Whoever bound them wanted to make sure she stayed that way."

"Well, make it faster." Eve's skin—already so pale—was even more so. There were beads of sweat trailing down from her brow to her chin. Her violet eyes were bloodshot and I could tell from her stance it was costing her a great deal to continue to hold the two mages off.

"Got it!" Darren hacked off the last bit of leather rope proudly and held it up for Eve to see. Just as he did, his eyes caught sight of something behind her. He cursed.

Eve and I followed his gaze.

"There's more."

"It's the ones from before." Darren's voice had lost its edge. "They must have seen Ryiah's lightning."

My stomach fell. *More* Caltothian mages. The barrier Darren and Eve had cast was already faltering. The two mages Eve was holding off were growing confident. A couple more castings would shatter it.

"I can't pain cast." My panic had returned in light of our newest discovery. "I've already reached my limit." Not unless I wanted to kill the others—and myself—in the process.

"There are three of them." Eve's voice was labored from her continuous casting. "Plus the two we've already been fighting. We might have been able to take on two but—"

"-But we don't have enough magic left to take on all five." Darren's statement was void of emotion. "The new three haven't even touched their magic. They'll have full reserves."

My voice quavered. "Then we don't fight."

Silence, then:

"Yes." Darren nodded. "Ryiah is right. We need to run."

"On my count," Eve said, "we drop our casting and head east."

I glanced to Darren and saw him pocket the blade Kinsey had dropped.

"One."

*What was he doing?*

"Two."

He was facing the wrong direction.

"Three."

There was a loud whoosh as the non-heir and Eve released their magic. I hardly noticed it—I was too busy tackling Darren to the ground. A heavy mist of sand rose up around us as I wrestled the knife out of the prince's grasp.

"Ryiah!" Darren spat through a mouthful of dirt. "Let me go!"

"You are not going to be a hero today, Darren!"

"That is not your decision to make!" He struggled to break free of my hold. When he found the effort harder than he expected, he glared at me. "Let me go or I'll cast you off."

"You can try but I'll still—"

All at once, an ear-splitting screech rang out across the forest floor and I was sent flying back into the shallow stream behind us. A second later, Darren landed to my right. There was a loud slap as his body hit the water. We barely had time to catch our breath before the trees began to tremble and groan.

The two of us scrambled to stand just as the first pine fell. One by one they all broke free of their giant roots. Great towers of flame were crashing down all around us.

"What's happening?" I squinted, trying to see through the thick cloud of smoke. I could hear screaming. "Is it the regiment?" *Had help arrived?*

"I don't—I can't see any..." Darren abruptly stopped talking and he started to sway. I was close enough to steady him just before his knees buckled and collapsed.

"Darren?"

"Eve." His entire body was a series of tremors. "She..." He pointed. "She had the same idea as..." He couldn't finish, choking on his words.

My heart stopped. I had been so focused on stopping Darren that I hadn't bothered to consider what Eve might do.

Somewhere in the burning forest to our right was a pale girl with ash blonde hair and violet eyes that had just closed for the last time.

Darren was having trouble breathing next to me. I could hear his ragged breaths, in and out, his shoulders shaking. I hated him, or I wanted to, but my hand still fell to his arm.

Eve had never intended to run. Neither had the prince. *I* had been the only one foolish enough to think we would—Darren and Eve had been too busy plotting how to let me and the other one survive. Because there was only one way any of us could evoke enough magic to take on five mages in our weakened state.

*Pain casting. By death.*

Eve had given her life to save us.

And that's when I saw it—a dark silhouette making its way along the flickering river of flame. I strained to see through the smoke. *Was it Eve? Had Darren been wrong—was she alive?*

The limping figure was much too tall.

"Darren." I shook the prince's shoulders and said in a loud whisper, "Darren!"

He didn't hear me.

"*Darren, we've got to get out of here!*"

I could see more clearly now. It was a man. One of the mages from before. He was making his way among the trees, one palm in front of his face as he parted the flames in his path.

I drew a sharp intake of breath. The mage still had magic.

Angry eyes met mine as he spotted me from across the clearing.

I was done waiting. I shoved Darren back behind me and pulled out the blade I had stolen earlier. I wasn't going to let Eve's sacrifice be in vain. I lifted it to my wrist-

Darren's hand clamped down on my arm while the other sent my knife skittering into the stream behind us. He had recovered fast. "Don't you even think of it!" he snarled.

"Darren, you are a prince of Jerar!" The man was almost out of the fire. "I can't let Eve's death be for nothing."

His eyes were hard. "I couldn't stop Caine or Eve—but by the gods, if I must die, I want to die knowing it is not because everyone is proffering themselves up as sacrificial lambs every time my bloodline is in danger!" He released my wrist and handed me my cut bonds from earlier. "You are not going to die today, Ryiah. Now take these. That mage must have used up quite a bit of magic to hold off Eve's casting. I still have some of mine, and you have this rope. If you want to fight then *fight*, but don't you *dare* sacrifice yourself for someone like me."

My lips parted in surprise. "*Don't you dare sacrifice yourself for someone like me?*" That didn't sound like Darren the Wolf at all. It sounded like the boy I had fallen in love with.

*Now is not the time to question things.* I studied the landscape, knotting and unknotting the leather cord in my hands. The mage had finished crossing the flames and was now running toward us. He still had quite a distance to cross, but he would reach us soon enough. "*A mage employs every resource he has. We don't spend years training you in both types of combat just so you can shirk your duties the second you've used up your magic.*" I bit my lip. *You are still a warrior, so think like one.*

I pointed to a thicket a quarter mile away half-covered in ash. "There's a steep ravine just east of that brush. When I was looking for a place to start the fire I almost missed it."

Darren drew a sharp intake of breath. "So the mage wouldn't be able to flee east. We could cut him off if we can lead him to it."

The two of us both took off at a sprint. It only took me a second to realize my mistake. There was no way I could cross the distance in time. The searing pain in my thigh was a quick reminder why. I hobbled after Darren, my pace no faster than a walk. I was skipping, half-dragging my leg behind me as the mage drew closer. The man still hadn't cast—it was a good sign that he was conserving his magic—but he would be upon me in less than a minute.

Darren looked back to see where I was and stopped running.

The dark-haired prince was racing toward me just as the mage raised his hands.

I ducked and a series of sparks shot out across the distance between us. The mage's magic collided against a barrier not two feet in front of me. There was a loud crack and then Darren's casting shattered, shards of glass splintering the air around me before subsequently vanishing with Darren's magic.

"Get behind me," the non-heir gasped. The mage was already calling upon his next casting. I shook my head and took a stand stubbornly beside him.

There was less than fifteen feet spanning the distance between us and the Caltothian. We could not outrun him if we tried. And judging from Darren's last casting, we wouldn't be able to out-magic him either.

"If we are going to die today," I told Darren, "let's make it the best fight of our lives."

Before he could stop me, I had thrown myself forward with the leather strap high above my head. I paid no attention to the agony in my leg. I cut the distance in half, springing into the air with the balls of my feet. The thick rope shot straight up and then I let my elbow bend and snap.

There was the satisfying crack as the leather met the mage's shoulder and then I fell to the ground, doubled over in a pain so terrible I couldn't think. I heard Darren roar and shut my eyes against a huge flare of light. Two men's screams were followed by a loud thud.

I opened my eyes. My surroundings flickered and spun, over and over. My stomach ate at me from the inside. Something was piercing my abdomen. Black and red swarmed my gaze and I could barely make out the dark heap in the grass next to me.

Then I heard the short, sputtering coughs as the person struggled to breath. There was a hoarse gasp and then a terrible moan.

Darren.

I reached across the distance and tried to find the prince's hand. My fingers caught his and I held on tight. I knew it was wrong but I didn't care. I couldn't speak, my pain was building and building and all I could do was shut my eyes and pray to the Shadow God that death would come swiftly for both of us.

"Ryiah," Darren whispered. "I'm sorry I made a mess of everything." He tried to laugh and then choked, sputtering for air.

Something broke in me.

Pain was deafening my senses but an unrequited anger rose when I heard Darren utter what he thought would be his last words. An apology. For everything. In his dying breath the non-heir wanted to tell me he was sorry.

And that's when I realized Priscilla was wrong. I was wrong.

*Whatever he had put me through, Darren was good.*

Darren could have waited for the keep's regiment but as soon as he'd freed the others, he had come back for me.

Like Eve, he'd never had an intention of fleeing when he told me to run.

That was two times Darren had chosen to save me instead of himself.

A prince of Jerar had decided a lowborn's life was more important than his own.

*No one that good deserved to die.*

I heard the crunching footfall of boots. I heard the mage's labored breathing as he drew close.

I let my hand fall limply to the side.

"Ryiah?" Darren's voice rose.

I didn't respond. I let my eyelids flutter shut.

"*Ryiah!*"

I held my breath.

"She's a pretty thing," the Caltothian declared. "I can see why you wanted to keep her alive."

*"Don't you look at her!"*

"You can't stop me, boy, you are dying yourself." The mage laughed raucously.

There was a sudden clatter and then Darren gave an ear-shattering scream. It took everything in me not to move.

"You shouldn't have tried to pain cast," the man addressed the prince, "not against me."

I exhaled and began to inch my hand slowly, closer and closer to my abdomen. As soon as my fingers closed around the dagger embedded in my stomach I took a deep breath and waited. One. *Two.*

The soft crunch of grass alerted me just as the man stepped on the ground near me. I kept my hand frozen in place. There was the rustle of movement and then I cracked open one lid, just in time to catch sight of the man hovering over the prince.

The mage held out his hand and a shimmering orb of fire appeared in his palm. "I would have made your death quick, like the girl's," he told him, "but since you tried to trick me I'm going to let you burn. *Slowly.* I want you to feel every second of it."

I didn't waste another moment. I wrenched the blade free and bent forward, slashing at the back of the mage's leg with all the strength I had. I caught the steel along the curve of his thigh and dragged down, deep, *deep* into his calf and fell back with a cry.

Then the pain took over.

My whole world reared up around me as blackness took hold of my sight.

# Chapter Nineteen

I couldn't see. Couldn't breathe. Couldn't feel.

All I could do was listen.

Harsh pounding. In and out. In. And out. The murmur of something faint. His voice.

One word. Over and over.

*Ryiah.*

# CHAPTER TWENTY

"I'm alive?" Though I had spoken the words aloud, they still seemed at odds with my memory. *Wasn't I supposed to be dead?* Dead with Darren and Eve in the northern forest of Jerar? Surrounded by burning pines as I bled to death from a fatal wound to my stomach?

Which brought me to my next question: "*How?*"

Derrick snorted. "That would be the first thing you ask us, wouldn't it?"

Alex, meanwhile, was glowering down at me with a concerned-looking Ella clutching his arm. "You must have a death wish," he bellowed. "This is the fifth—no, the *sixth*—time I have had to visit my sister in an infirmary because she thinks she can take on the world by herself!"

"Alex, that's not fair," Ella interrupted, "most of those were because of mock battles, you can't blame your sister for—"

"*I don't care what they were for!*"

"Alex!" Derrick looked annoyed. "Don't yell! The healers!"

"*I will yell if I want to!*" my twin shouted. "*The lot of you are fools for choosing Combat. Fools! And you, Derrick, choosing to be a soldier—did you not hear that four of your own were mur-*

*dered? Slaughtered like pigs for a butcher! What kind of idiot signs up for—"*

"Alright, Alex, that's quite enough." Ella pulled on my brother's arm with an apologetic look to me. "Later," she mouthed as she escorted my twin firmly out of the room.

"So," I said weakly to my last remaining visitor, "he's mad at me again."

Derrick guffawed. "Alex is always mad. Just because the rest of us live exciting lives is no reason for that grouch to bring you down." He paused. "Besides you and Prince Darren—"

"He's alive too?" I couldn't keep the relief from my tone.

"Of course he is, silly," Derrick chided. "You two are the talk of the north right now. All the local regiments heard about how the two of you risked your lives to save the keep's knights! I wouldn't be surprised if they made a song about it!"

I cringed. The last thing I wanted was to hear my "deeds" memorialized in song. Especially when the only thing I had done was almost die... "Eve," I asked suddenly, "did she—"

"She's dead, Ryiah." Derrick's voice has lost its humor. "It was quick, if that helps. Stabbed herself in the chest. I overheard Master Byron telling someone it was a 'mage's last stand,' whatever that means."

I swallowed. When someone willingly brought on his own death to exert an extreme pain casting, it was known as "the mage's last stand." "She was a hero," I said softly; "without her magic, Darren and I would have died."

"Probably why the prince is in Devon."

"Darren left the apprenticeship!" I sat up with a start and then regretted it immediately. My whole body roared in protest. "Why would he...?" *Why* wouldn't *he after what had happened?*

"Are you mad? Of course he didn't leave."

"But you said—"

"He's visiting that girl's father. Eve. He said it was something that couldn't be put in a letter." Derrick looked sideways at me. "The prince is nice, actually. I don't understand why Alex hates him so much."

"He was here?"

"He was here for the first four days. Granted, two of them he was recovering in the cot next to yours, but then he kept coming back. That girl you hate? Priscilla. She caused a huge scene when she saw him in here."

"How…" I cleared my throat and tried again. "How am I…?"

"Alive?" Derrick was amused. "Ryiah, you were never dead. No matter what our charming brother might claim, Restoration is not that good… The prince gave a full account to Commander Nyx. The two of you were fighting that last Caltothian when you pulled that dagger out of your stomach—madness, really—and caught the man off-guard by slashing at his leg." He grinned. "You lost consciousness right after but the prince was able to finish the job. He wasn't faring much better, but he still managed to carry you halfway back before the regiment arrived. They brought you two to the keep while the rest of the mages put out that fire you started. In case you are wondering, Ry, a quarter of the northern forest is now gone. It's going to take years to grow back..."

The whole time my brother was talking, I couldn't help but remember the one thing that had been bothering me since I awoke: the dreams I'd had. The ones where I kept hearing Darren's voice. He'd been saying my name. Over and over. Had that been real?

*What does it matter? Nothing has changed.*

"Ryiah? Are you still listening?" Derrick looked concerned. "You probably need rest," he surmised, "I should leave... All of the factions were delayed by the fire but now that you are better, I expect the masters will want to set out tomorrow."

Almost as soon as he spoke a wave of lethargy reared its head in rebuttal. I barely had time to say my goodbye before my head hit the pillow, overcome with sleep.

"Apprentice Ryiah?"

My eyes flew open and I found the commander of Ferren's Keep standing over me, her steel gray irises studying my face. My skin jumped and I found myself sitting up with a start. This time with much less pain than before. "C-commander Nyx?"

"I am sorry to wake you, apprentice, but I have a matter that cannot wait."

I waited for her to continue.

The woman pulled a chair to the side of my cot and leaned forward. "I have already spoken with the prince, but I need to know if you saw anything strange—anything at all that might merit questions—that day in the forest?"

The confusion must have shown on my face because she tried again.

"Anything odd, Ryiah. Anything that struck you as contrary?"

I shook my head. "I'm not sure I understand what you are asking."

The woman sighed and stood up, pressing the chair legs back with a loud squeak. "If you think of anything, no matter how silly or minute the detail might seem, please send for me."

I nodded and promised to do just that. The woman left the room with a wish for my speedy recovery and then I was left once again with an overwhelming fatigue. I drifted off quite quickly, but as I did one question pressed at my thoughts:

*What was that about?*

On the second week after we arrived at the Academy, Darren finally returned from his visit to Devon. I was at odds with his arrival. I couldn't hate him like before, not after what had happened. I didn't know what to think.

I spent the next couple of days lost in my own dance of drills and meals with my friends. At one point I turned around to ask Eve her opinion—and then caught myself. I had a sickening moment where that day in the forest came rushing back and I decided to retire early that night.

It was as I was turning the corridor to my room on the Academy's second floor that I finally came across the prince. He was not alone, however.

"Now is not the time to discuss our wedding!" I entered the hall just in time to see Darren slam a chamber door in Priscilla's face.

The girl let out a loud shriek and picked up a nearby vase and threw it against the wall. It shattered into a mass of tiny shards, wilted flowers and water flooding the floor. Then she turned around and caught me staring.

"He wasn't just visiting her father," she sniffed. "He was with *her*. My friends in the palace tell me everything."

I didn't know what to say. Once again my chest was being ripped at the seams. I felt torn between three states: pity for myself who loved such a capricious person, pity for Priscilla who spent her whole life fighting girls like Shinako and me to keep the prince and her position in court, and then frustration at Darren for saving my life and being so heartless and power-hungry in the same breath. Why couldn't a person just be good or evil? Why couldn't Darren pick a side? I was tired of trying to guess which one he was, and it was beyond aggravating when my heart was involved.

"The day I am crowned princess will be the best day of my life," Priscilla continued. "Believe me when I say you are lucky to be lowborn, Ryiah; a highborn's struggles are more tiresome than you could ever know."

*There*. That was the reason I didn't pity her. Not truly. "One. My status as apprentice means I am no longer 'lowborn,'" I snapped. "And two. My struggles are just as relevant as yours."

The girl rolled her eyes.

"I find great pleasure in knowing that it is one of your own that is stealing him away," I told her flatly.

"And here I was trying to be polite!"

"You are wasting your breath. You are just as cold-hearted as Darren. Any pity I feel at your situation vanishes every time you open your big mouth."

The girl stopped smirking. "You have grown vain in light of your magic, Ryiah. Were we friends, I might use my influence to have Byron give you a high rank at our ascension—but *let me assure you*, even if you were the best apprentice of our year, you will be ranked last without my help."

"I'd rather be last than align myself with you."

The girl glared at me. "You are making a mistake."

"Her only mistake is talking to you. Why don't you find some other hallway to haunt with your presence?"

I grinned as Ella appeared next to me on the stair. Priscilla spun off to find better company and I turned to Ella. "Thanks. That girl spends half her time trying to belittle me and the rest of it trying to convince me to join her little army of minions."

"She is afraid of you. Priscilla knows you have power and it scares her. Last thing she wants to do is make enemies with the future Black Mage."

I snorted. "I find that highly unlikely."

Ella looked thoughtful. "Maybe. And maybe not."

The rest of our time at the Academy seemed to pass by even faster. Suddenly the solstice had arrived and the castle grounds were covered in snow. Most of my time leading up to the ball was spent with Alex, who had calmed down since his temper tantrum in the keep's infirmary.

When it was time to dance, I left my friend to my twin and headed outside after a quick visit with Sir Piers. It was strange to be surrounded by so many eager-faced first-years and know that I had been one of them, enthusiastically sharing in drinks and laughs, just four years ago. I still had five more months at Ferren's Keep, but the ascension took place in Devon, not Sjeka. Tonight would be my final night within the Academy walls.

"Feeling nostalgic?" Darren appeared beside me, peering over the balcony rails at the white landscape beneath. I started. I hadn't even noticed him enter.

"I spent so much time dreaming about becoming a mage." My words were barely a whisper. "I don't think I'll know what to do with myself when it becomes real."

"I doubt that." The prince's expression was wry. "I think the second you are ranked, the commanders will all be scrambling to give you a spot in their regiment."

That was the second time someone had told me that. I still didn't believe it. "I hardly think that will be the case."

"I do."

An awkward silence followed and then Darren cleared his throat. "I never got a chance to ask," he said quietly, "how you were faring. After the battle."

"Are you asking me now?"

"I am."

"I'm fine." I couldn't think of what else to say. Anything else felt like a betrayal.

"I'm glad." I made the mistake of meeting his eyes and saw... I'm not sure what I saw. My emotions were running so wild I couldn't trust myself. Every inch of me was screaming at his proximity and my skin was fighting to make contact.

"Thank you..." I swallowed. "For coming back for me that day. I'm sorry about Eve... I know she meant a lot to you."

"She..." I could hear the break in his voice as he said it. "She didn't deserve to die. Not for me."

"I'm sorry."

"So am I." Now he sounded angry and his eyes were flaring crimson. "Her death will not go unpunished."

"What are you going to do?"

"When I returned to Devon, I met with my father. The Council and his advisors have been adverse to take action but this time it's different. The Caltothians have grown bold—sending that many men to attack our key northern post. Our men and women depend on that forest for lumber and now a quarter of it is burned to the ground. The daughter of the Crown's Army command is dead. Several of the regiment? Dead. You and I were almost killed." He clenched his fist. "I admit the nobles could look the other way while half of Jerar is destroyed—they are that opposed to war—but they can do little to ignore Father after he found out his own son was almost murdered."

I bit my lip. "So we are going to war?" The Great Compromise had been in place for almost a century. It seemed impossible.

Darren looked away. "As soon as my brother and I secure our marriage dowries to finance his army."

*Oh.* How could I have forgotten? It must have been because he was standing so close to me, eyes burning like fire. Robbing me of the last year and a half. Darren was still Darren. Just because he was kind did not mean he loved me, or that he wasn't a prince. It didn't matter how he looked at me. Nothing had changed.

That same night I arrived at my chambers and shut the door softly behind me. It was only after I heard the lock click into place that I let myself breathe. I felt myself slip to the floor, fingers tracing the wooden panels above as my heart pounded traitorously hard in my chest.

*Why did I do this to myself? Why did he have to be kind? Why couldn't he be cruel?* It wasn't fair. Darren had broken my heart. And he was continuing to shatter it every time he looked at me.

We couldn't be friends. We couldn't be enemies.

*So what were we?*

It was the worst winter I could remember. We could see every breath we took. Thick, dense white frost took over our sight. Ella and I were beyond miserable.

Then we were deployed in one of the keep's regular patrols.

"What do you mean, we have to camp in the snow?" my friend whispered, outraged. She was smart enough not to speak in Master Byron's presence, of course.

*"For this next week I want you to go completely without using your magic,"* the training master had said. *"Absolutely no casting. Unless we come across a raid, I want you to learn how to survive a harsh winter climate without using your powers. The soldiers and knights do it all of the time. This will help prepare you for a position in the northern regiment. Your magic will be needed for battle, not comfort, and as such I expect the next seven days to reflect this. Afterward, we will resume our regular lessons."*

"Madness," I told her, grinning, "absolute madness."

She elbowed me. "Don't mock me, Ry. By the second night you, too, will be wishing for summer."

"Not as much as my dear brother, I expect."

Ella blushed. "Yes," she admitted ruefully, "I suppose I'm not the only one."

"He wants to marry you, you know."

"I know." Her face was in flames. "I'd be a fool to say anything but yes. I love the both of you more than what is healthy, I am sure. My parents will undoubtedly consider me a traitor to my heritage."

"Commander Nyx!"

The woman paused. "Yes, apprentice?"

"You asked me to find you if I remembered anything strange?"

The commander's hurried expression quickly changed into one of keen interest. "Yes, Ryiah, I am so sorry. Please forgive me, my mind was elsewhere."

I shifted from one foot to the next. "I'm sure it is nothing of importance," I stammered, "but my friend said something…'" I was sure I looked foolish. I felt like a fool, that was for certain. But when Ella had called herself a traitor, I'd been plagued with nightmares of that battle. Every night for the next month I'd been unable to dream of anything else.

And then I'd remembered.

"She called herself a traitor. She didn't mean it, of course. But it reminded me of that day. One of the mages said something very similar. He was arguing with his leader whether or not to take me as a hostage, and she asked him if he really wanted to defy their orders. She said 'two times a traitor would only bring a slow and painful death.' I didn't think it then, but now it struck me as an odd thing to say… What did she mean? Why would a Caltothian be 'two times a traitor?'"

The commander smiled. She never smiled. It made every inch of my skin crawl. "Have you ever considered a position up north?" the woman wanted to know. "Ferren's Keep, perhaps?"

My ill ease was immediately forgotten. *Was she offering me a position? Before my ascension ceremony?* "I have thought about it." I tried to keep the excitement from my response.

"Well, if you decide that answer is yes, you would be guaranteed a place in my regiment."

I couldn't breathe. "Really? But you don't even know my rank yet, and Byron…"

"I judge a person by their merits, not hearsay," the woman interrupted. "And you, my dear, have impressed me far more than any of your factionmates. You passed an initial test half your year failed, and then you saved my regiment. If I were to go by hearsay then I must tell you the northerners are singing you nothing but praise. Either way, you will always have a place in my keep." She reached out to grasp my arm firmly. "We need more fighters like you, Ryiah."

"And Darren," I said weakly. "He helped save your regiment too."

The commander's gaze seemed far away. "Yes," she said, "I suppose he did." Then her focus cleared. "Nonetheless, I am sure he will be stationed close to the palace. Darren might be a mage, but he is still a prince. I believe the king has been generous in allowing him to spend so much time abroad."

I nodded, feeling silly I had forgotten. Of course he would not accept. The prince would serve a much higher rank close to home in the Crown's Army.

I didn't understand why I had felt it necessary to remind her of his prowess. The whole country knew. Was I so desperate to spend the rest of my life fighting alongside him? I should have been happy to finally free myself after spending so much time together. *Why in the name of the gods was I trying to keep him here?*

"If I wanted to be saddle sore," Alex griped, "I would have joined Combat. Not Restoration."

"Calm down, big brother," Derrick teased, "you'll have plenty of time to grow fat and old after your ascension."

I snickered as Alex glowered at Derrick over his meal. "You might think yourself wise because you've enjoyed two winters in this gods' forsaken place," he said brusquely, "but there is nothing wrong with choosing a comfortable life."

"A shame you fell in love with a Combat mage."

"A shame indeed." Alex looked wistful.

"You know Ella wants to be stationed up here, right? She hates the cold but she still wants the glory." Nothing was more fun than teasing my twin. Especially in the recent months. It was obvious to everyone except him how deep he had fallen. The poor sap didn't stand a chance.

Alex made a face. "I will make it my mission to talk her around."

"You only have a couple more weeks," I replied snidely, "and then we will be in the capital."

"You grow more insolent every day." Alex threw a piece of his toast in my direction. I dodged it easily. "Must be your inflated sense of pride. You and Derrick are one in the same. Nothing but a bunch of overfed peacocks."

Derrick winked at me. "That we are." He turned to Alex with a sly grin on his face. "Well, if your lady love declines to join you south, I would be happy to have her stay up north with Ryiah and I. Ella grows more lovely every time I set eyes on her." Derrick ducked just in time to avoid Alex's fist.

The innkeeper barked at Alex to stop riling his customers.

I shot my embarrassed twin an amused expression. "You know Derrick only teases you because you are so easy to rattle."

"Yes," Derrick declared, "that and I'm afraid I've grown restless. Eight months is far too long to go without fighting any Caltothians." He shrugged. "Those drills my commander puts us through are no use. I'm not accustomed to peace."

"It's not peace," I reminded him tersely, "it's the quiet before the storm." I glanced at Alex. "And you. Even if you two aren't stationed together, she'll wait for you. All you have to do is ask. I, for one, would love to have another girl in this family."

Alex turned a deep shade of red and busied himself with his stew. Derrick, meanwhile, picked up the conversation, steering me toward a much-needed debate on the merits of a two-handed axe. I became so engrossed in conversation I almost missed the tolling of the midnight hour. Alex and I groaned our apologies to Derrick and then retired to the stables for our final night's ride to the keep's barracks.

In a couple short hours we would be back on King's Road, headed for the palace… Only this time we would leave it as mages.

# Chapter Twenty-One

"I have never been more terrified in my life." Alex was writhing in his best clothes—a silk-lined tunic and fresh-pressed breeches. Ella reached out to straighten his hem and then pushed back his bangs, laughing.

"Master Joan is much less intimidating than Byron," she teased. "It'll be over before you know it. And just think, when it is, you'll emerge looking handsomer than before in a red Restoration robe."

I smirked. "And if not, at least your face will match the rest of you."

Alex paled and Ella gave him a quick kiss in the cheek, wagging her finger at me as she did. "Leave your poor brother alone," she chided. "If he gets any more nervous he'll sweat through his shirt. I hardly think we can find another in time for the ceremony."

I fingered my own outfit and vaguely wished I shared some of my twin's own discomfort. I felt exposed in the dress I was wearing—a soft lilac thing with a bodice that felt much too tight. It didn't seem right to wear something so feminine going into an ascension for Combat, but Ella had assured me that was exactly why I should. "*You are a woman,*" she'd insisted. "*We are already a minority in all of the war schools—not just our own faction as mages. It would do good to remind the audience that we can be both."*

And so now here I was, unable to breathe—which I must admit was becoming a common occurrence around Ella during important occasions in general—and dreading the rest of the evening. Master Byron's attitude toward me had only grown worse in the last couple of months, and I had no doubt what my standing would be at the end of the ceremony. Even though I had Commander Nyx's offer to hold onto, it did little to sway the deep sense of foreboding that was growing more prevalent by the second. In less than an hour I would have to face the world as a fifth-rank mage.

By the time Ella had finished adjusting my twin's new tunic it was time to go. I gathered the hem of my dress and followed my brother and friend into the palace's throne room. There was a red and gold-lined rug that trailed down the center of the great hall, folding several times on tall steps before finally resting under a large gold-adorned throne marked with plush red cushions and thick golden arms. The king studied the apprentices as we entered.

One by one, each one of us kneeled before him and then separated into three distinct rows: Restoration closest to the front and Combat at the rear.

Prince Blayne sat in a less ornate chair than his father, but he still looked very regal and cold in the same hematite and steel crown. He had a look of extreme boredom as each apprentice entered, with only the slightest expression of interest when his brother appeared.

Behind the throne, three massive stained glass windows cast rays of light across the hall and onto the side risers at either end where the nobility and our younger factionmates sat watching. Several members of the King's Regiment stood guard at the front and back of the room while the Council of Magic and Crown Advisors sat in a small stand to the left of the king to watch the proceedings from their own special box.

The three faction masters strode forward to begin our rite. Ella giggled into her hand and pointed. Master Byron looked beyond miserable standing between Master Joan and Master Perry. From his strained tone, it was obvious he would rather be anywhere else than close quarters with the two female mages.

"...To defend all those in need of rescuing."

We all answered in unison. "I solemnly pledge."

"To speak the truth to all questions asked. No matter the consequence."

"I solemnly pledge."

"To be loyal to your commander in trying times. To exercise caution before magic."

"I solemnly pledge."

"To be brave in times of danger. To obey Crown and Council Law in all matters of service."

"I solemnly pledge."

"To be kind in times of need. To only fight when it is necessary. "

"I solemnly pledge."

"To be a mage of honor and valiance. To always put the Crown before yourself."

"As a mage to the Crown and Jerar, I solemnly pledge."

Commander Joan took a step forward to call on her Restoration mages, one by one. When she called Alex, he was given the third rank. Though we were supposed to remain silent during the entire ceremony, it did not stop me from letting out a small shriek and Ella from clapping almost hysterically loud.

Master Perry went next with her Alchemy mages. Ruth was given first-rank. I should have known. She always was the best of her faction. I watched her, envious, as she returned back to her seat.

Then it was time for Combat.

Master Byron stood proudly as he called, "In the matter of first-rank ascension I would like to call forward our very own Prince Darren, second-in-line to the throne and now first-rank mage of Combat."

I watched as the non-heir left his position in line to kneel before his father, his brother, and then, finally, Master Byron.

When he arose, a servant handed him a silken black robe. Darren's face was expressionless as he slid the smooth mage's robe over his regular clothes, letting the hood rest on his forehead for just a moment before it slid back onto his shoulders.

There was a hushed silence as Darren turned back to face the crowd. I lost my breath. Blayne might wear the crown, but Darren was the one who looked like a king. I was jealous and proud. Whatever I might think of him, the non-heir had earned that robe.

Darren returned to his seat beside Priscilla and I waited with bated breath. Who would Byron name next? The only other male in our faction, or the future princess of Jerar? I was sure he wanted to name Ray, but the master would not be so quick as to snub someone of great influence.

Ella nudged me with her arm. "Ryiah!"

"Shhh." I nudged her back. "I'm trying to hear who they pick."

"*Byron just called your name!*"

"You are joking."

"No. I'm not." She jerked her chin to point in the direction of the throne.

All the blood rushed from my face as I realized she was telling the truth. The training master was glowering at me from his position beside the king. I hastily pulled myself off the cold marble floor and raced over to stand before the throne. I kneeled before the King Lucius, Prince Blayne, and Master Byron.

"Ryiah of Demsh'aa, I award you second rank for your..." The man paused uncomfortably. "Your outstanding apprenticeship. I'd be a fool to ignore power when I see it, even if you are a—" He coughed. "-A woman. Please stand and accept your new status as a second-rank mage of Combat."

I stood, hardly conscious that I was sobbing. I only realized it when the servant handing me my robe touched the side of my face and showed me my tears. "Not many mages cry," she told me kindly, "but I like to think it's the best of them that do." I nodded, wetness staining my cheeks, and then let her help me with my robe.

Then I turned back to face my audience. I could hardly see straight, tears were blocking most of my vision, and by the time I reached my seat my sight had cleared just enough for me to find my place beside Ella.

"You blubbering mess," she teased, "you are making a fool of yourself."

"I d-don't care." And it was true. I was smiling so hard my face hurt.

Master Byron called Ella next—much to her extreme shock. The girl almost screamed when he said it. And then it was time for Ray.

Priscilla was last. When the dark-haired beauty left the podium she was seething, anger piercing the gaze of any person foolish enough to lay eyes on her. I, for one, had trouble containing my glee.

Almost immediately the newly ascended mages were called from the throne room to take the ceremonial banquet in the king's dining hall. Having never before partaken in the meal (apprentices were always directed to the ballroom with the rest of the visiting mages and court) I was eager to see how it transpired. Only the Council of Magic and the king's family were allowed to dine with us.

I took my seat between Ella and Alex. Within seconds the room had filled with the rest of our year, chattering on in quiet but excited voices as they found their place along the table. At the very front of the table sat the three Colored Robes, King Lucius, and Prince Blayne.

I did a double take when I realized who was still missing.

Two seats down from me I heard Priscilla complaining to one of Ruth's factionmates. "I told him not to go anywhere but did he listen to me? Of course not. Well, when Blayne finds out he is off with that trollop again—"

The chamber door swung open to reveal a red-faced Darren and Princess Shinako clinging steadfastly to his arm. My pulse stopped. *Dear gods, no.* I was so close to being free of him.

Couldn't he just wait until tomorrow to proclaim his love for her? Even on my happiest day he had found a way to ruin it.

King Lucius looked up at his son and the crown princess of the Borea Isles, startled. Blayne was clutching his wine goblet, his face tight with rage.

Darren cleared his throat loudly. "Everyone, please stay where you are." The whole room fell silent. "Princess Shinako and I have an announcement to make and I want all of you to bear witness."

*No. No. No. Why was he doing this now?* My eyes sought Darren's but his attention was focused on the king.

"Father." Darren took a deep breath. "You promised if I secured a dowry equal to Priscilla of Langli I would be free to break off my current engagement in favor of that opportunity. You have said that Jerar is our utmost concern, and its strength triumphs all."

Priscilla's face went white as a sheet.

Prince Blayne pushed back his chair, spitting wine as he cried: "He did not give you permission to steal *my* future wife, you ungrateful, power-mad—"

Darren held up his hand. "I am not stealing her, *brother*."

Blayne sat down, eyes suspiciously fixed on the non-heir. "Then what is the meaning of this ridiculous speech?"

"Princess Shinako and her father have been kind enough to guarantee us the sum of her dowry and a pledge of support—equal to what the two of you would receive once wed—in exchange for the same pledge from us and a dissolution of your intended marriage. We received a signed letter from Emperor Liang just this morning."

"Father, this is madness!" Blayne turned to the king in horror. "Tell him to put an end to this!"

The king scowled at his oldest. "Let him speak, Blayne. I must admit even I am intrigued."

"Not only have I secured Jerar more wealth than any daughter of Langli, I have also given my dearest brother the opportunity to marry a princess from Pythus and amass an even greater dowry and support for this great country."

"The king of Pythus would never marry one of his daughters to me!" Blayne's face was as red as his venison.

"Perhaps you haven't tried hard enough to please him." Darren didn't look perturbed.

"Father!"

"Silence, Blayne!" the king snapped. "Your brother has done a great thing for us. Foolish, but great. I will not be so blind as to deny it would benefit us greatly, and you most of all." The man turned to Darren. "Very well, your previous engagement has been ceded in favor of this new proposal. Pending the signed pledge, of course."

The door slammed shut and I realized Priscilla of Langli had left the room. The king chuckled and indicated for Darren and Shinako to take a seat.

"That is not all, Father."

The king stopped laughing to stare at his son, his eyes narrowing. "Isn't it?" His tone held a warning.

"No. It's not."

My heart began to slam against my chest—so loud and so fast I was sure the whole room could hear it. *Ryi-ah. Ryi-ah. Ryi-ah.*

What if it hadn't been a dream?

Darren's eyes found mine.

My fork clattered to the floor.

"I wish to secure a new engagement with the dowry Princess Shinako has so generously bestowed."

"I gave you what you wanted." The king's eyes were furious. "You are free of that Langli girl. Anything more and you have overstepped your—"

"I wish to marry Mage Ryiah of Demsh'aa."

Several people exclaimed at once. My brother choked on his water. Ella grabbed my arm. The king clutched his knife so tightly his knuckles went white.

"*Absolutely not!*"

I just sat there, motionless. *This isn't real. It* can't *be real. It's a dream.* I watched Darren, standing there in front of his father with his back erect.

"I believe Master Byron just deemed Ryiah one of the most powerful mages in this room," Darren said slowly, "and if we all know Byron, he is nothing if not stingy in his praise where women are concerned..."

The training master's face went up in flames. Somehow I knew his praise was anything but voluntary.

"...In fact it was Shina, excuse me, Princess Shinako's only stipulation that the dowry she so generously bestows go to Mage Ryiah specifically, was it not?"

The princess nodded demurely, smiling. "Yes, it is the least I can do. Darren and I are good friends. Nothing would please me more than his happiness."

"So you see, Father, there is absolutely no one who would benefit me—or Jerar—more than Ryiah of Demsh'aa. As you said, strength triumphs all and Ryiah's dowry and status would certainly bring the Crown strength." Darren pulled out a scroll tucked into the sleeve of his robe. "Your advisors have already given this union their full blessing, here is a letter stating their support..."

"*This is ridiculous!*" Blayne shrieked. "*Father, do not let him marry that lowborn!*"

"Your Majesty." The Black Mage stood with the two Colored Robes at his side. "The Council of Magic would be in full support of this union. We think it a very wise proposal."

The king stood, fists clenched. When he finally spoke it was strained and full of unspoken rage. "Then it appears this is indeed Jerar's best interest." The man turned to his youngest. "Congratulations, my son, on your new wife."

King Lucius strode out of the room without another word.

The moment the king and his heir departed, the room became chaos. I flew out of my chair, slamming the door behind me as I tore into the hallway beyond. My heart was beating so fast I was afraid my ribs would explode. I could barely breathe; air was coming out of my lungs in quick, choking gasps.

I hunched over, leaning against the side of the wall while the room rose and fell all around me in a dizzying mess. I stayed there for a couple of minutes, breathing in and out, in and out, until the room began to seem a bit more static.

The door opened and closed behind me.

I turned and saw Darren standing there. "I was looking for you," he said.

When I didn't reply, he made himself speak.

"I know you are mad at me." Darren took a step forward and then stopped himself. His eyes found mine and he took a deep breath. "If you'll let me explain—"

"You lied to me."

"I did." His gaze didn't waver. "I lied, and I lied, and I lied to you. Over and over. I know what I did. I know what I said. I wanted to make you hate me."

"But why?"

"Why, Ryiah?" Darren made a frustrated sound. "Because what kind of prince would I be if I let my love for a silly lowborn blind me from the fate of my country?"

*A silly lowborn?* Tears stung my eyes and I turned away, biting back a sob.

Darren's hand clamped down on my arm, and he spun me around, eyes blazing. "I needed to do the right thing." His face was flushed. "Don't you see, Ryiah? I would have been exactly what you accused me of—a coward—if I had let my love for you blind me from what has been happening all around us! I know you despise me for what I did, but when I went to my father that day, he told me that we were going to war with Caltoth. That hundreds of our men were going to die, and if I chose to marry for love over wealth I would be ensuring millions more." He cursed. "The king was right. I couldn't marry you without a dowry, not unless I wanted people like Caine and Eve to die every day all so I can have a bit of selfishness."

I shoved him away. "But you never told me, Darren! You made me *hate* you, you told me—"

Darren caught my hand in his and I trembled. "I had to." His voice was hoarse.

"Ryiah, I was willing to jeopardize the fate of this country just for a chance to be near you. I needed you to hate me, because it was the only way *I* could do the right thing."

"I thought you were in love with Princess Shinako. Or that you were trying to impress your father so he'd make you his heir." I could barely get the words out.

"So did my brother. So did everyone." Darren's laugh was bitter.

My hand fell away and I took a step back, shaking. I had cried myself to sleep for the good part of two years. My heart had shattered every time he looked at her.

Darren said the next words so quietly I almost missed them. "I kept telling myself it was better than them assuming the alternative."

"What was the alternative?"

"That I had never gotten over you." Darren slammed his fist against the wall. "That I was still madly in love with a girl who hated me by sight. That Shina loathed my brother and cared for a young man in her home country. That we were both trapped in arranged marriages, wanting nothing more than to find a way out. That every time I fought with you I was really fighting myself, wanting nothing more than to grab you and kiss you and tell you that it was all a mistake. That I missed my best friend and the taste of your lips and every night that I dreamed it was only ever of your face."

My heart was slamming across my ribs and I couldn't seem to breathe.

His eyes found mine. "Ryiah…"

I forced myself to speak. "You and Shina planned this?"

"We grew up together. I knew she hated my brother, she always had. When she arrived for her engagement and told me she couldn't stand the thought of marrying Blayne, I told her about you. The two of us were miserable. At first we would just talk about how angry we were that we had to marry for duty, but then it occurred to me that maybe the gods had intervened on our behalf. The emperor wanted a new treaty with Jerar—he knows war is coming, but who was to say the treaty had to be from an arranged marriage? All my father ever cared about was a dowry. It took us a while to convince the princess's father, we had to be careful in our correspondence, but when I finally returned home after the battle in Ferren's Keep, Shina pulled me aside to tell me he had finally agreed. We still had to get my father's advisors to agree to his letter, but it wasn't that hard when any fool could see it would only bring Jerar more wealth than before."

Darren paused. "I knew we would have to wait for the ascension. We needed to have the Council present and until a few days ago they had been busy along the northern border, meeting with local commanders and their regiment to make sure our defenses were sound after the incident at Ferren's Keep."

"After you started talking to Shina," I said quietly, "why didn't you say anything?"

Darren looked away. "I wanted to tell you, Ryiah, but after everything I'd put you through, I couldn't bring myself to say it.... *Because what if it didn't work?*" He swallowed. "And then that day at the Academy, you told me you hated me. You wouldn't even *look* at me."

"I couldn't." The words were barely a whisper.

"I believed you." Darren's voice cracked. "I started to think you were better off if I left you alone. But then that day at Ferren's Keep—you saw what I was trying to do and you stopped me. You hated me, you had no reason to let me live, and you still wouldn't let me die—*even if it would save you.* I kept thinking about that when I left for Devon. I thought maybe I'd been wrong. That you didn't hate me."

I held my breath as Darren stepped right in front of me. "That maybe you still might love me." His hand found mine. It was shaking. We both were.

"Because I still love you," he whispered desperately.

"I..." I swallowed. "I never stopped. I wanted to." I was rambling now. "I hated myself that I couldn't... That I wasn't strong enough—that I—"

Darren pulled me to him and the rest of my words fell to the floor.

He kissed me.

...And as he did I smelled pine. Cloves.

I tasted cinnamon.

There was only one word to describe it. One word that came rushing back after all of this time.

*Home.*

How could I have forgotten?

Darren was *home.*

When we finally broke for air the non-heir was grinning.

"Who would have thought," he teased, "that the girl who tried to get me kicked out of the Academy—"

"That was Ella!" I shoved Darren and he caught my hands in his.

"It was both of you." His smile was wicked. "As I was saying, this girl who tried to get me kicked out of the Academy, this girl who tried to light me on fire, this lowborn girl I absolutely couldn't stand—"

I scoffed. "Please! You insulted me, mocked me, tricked me, lied to me—"

Darren's hand lightly clamped over my mouth so that the rest of my speech was muffled.

His eyes found mine. "Let me finish, love."

My heart skipped a beat.

"That somehow, this insufferable girl would become the one person I am forever, hopelessly, *madly* drawn to against my will and possibly even my better judgment."

I smiled faintly. "I don't think either of us had a choice in the matter."

"The higher powers are probably having a good laugh at our expense." Darren touched the side of my face, eyes gleaming. "Though perhaps they are right about this one."

I started to lean forward and paused. "Wait. Does this mean you were behind my ranking tonight?" My heart stopped. It was him. Of course it was Darren. *I should have known Byron would never give me second rank willingly.*

Darren's expression was amused. "I can assure you I had nothing to do with it. I was as surprised as you were. Not that you didn't deserve it, of course, but that Byron could move past his... er, difficulties where you are concerned." He paused and then a devious smile spread across his face as he caught sight of someone behind me. "But I bet I know who did."

"Who?" The only person I could think of was Commander Nyx and she detested the training master almost as much as myself. There was also considerable doubt that a woman would ever be able to influence a man whose reputation was built on a hatred of their gender.

"Why don't you see for yourself?"

I spun around and found myself face-to-face with none other than the Black Mage himself, Marius.

"Hello, Mage Ryiah," the man said smoothly. "Did I not tell you we would talk again? Congratulations on your engagement, if I might add."

"It was you," I stammered. "You convinced Byron to rank me second?"

"I merely reminded your headstrong master what a fool he would look should a woman win the next Candidacy... I must say I'm sorry I hadn't corrected his egregious bias sooner, but as it is with most politics I am slow to catch on." The gold hoop of his ear glimmered, dancing off the windowpanes behind us. "As to second rank, well, my dear, he did that all on his own. I suspect the Ferren's Keep commander would have made his life difficult if he had shunned a northern hero."

I blushed. "I'm not a hero."

"My dear, each one of us is a hero. The irony, of course, is that most will never receive the title. Bask in the recognition, for I suspect it shall not last as long as one might hope, especially with the rumors of Caltoth…" He cleared his throat. "But enough of that. Drink. Dance. Be merry. You are a mage of Combat and betrothed to a prince of the realm. What more could you desire?"

Nothing.

But then a thought occurred. "A black robe would be nice."

Darren gave me a sideways glance. "What are you talking about? You are already wearing one."

My eyes were dancing. "Maybe like the one Marius is wearing."

"With the gold lining? Ryiah, only the Black Mage…" Darren stopped talking as he realized what I was implying.

Marius smiled. "Yes," he surmised, "I believe I was right to bet on you that day at the Academy. Your future, dear Ryiah, has just begun."

# About the Author

**Rachel E. Carter** is a young adult author who hoards coffee and books. She has a weakness for villain and bad boy love interests. When not writing, she is usually reading, and when not reading she is usually asleep. To her, the real world is Hogwarts and everything else is a lie.

*The Black Mage* is Rachel's first YA fantasy series, with many more to come. She loves to interact with fellow readers & aspiring writers, and here is a list of places you can find her online:

**Official Site:** www.rachelecarter.com
**Facebook:** www.facebook.com/theblackmageauthor
**Instagram:** https://instagram.com/rachelcarterauthor
**Twitter:** https://twitter.com/recarterauthor
**Pinterest:**www.pinterest.com/recarterauthor
**Tumblr:** http://rachelcarterauthor.tumblr.com
**Goodreads:** www.goodreads.com/rachelcarterauthor
**Email:** rachelcarterauthor@gmail.com

Clean Reads
ALL STORY. NO GUILT.